PRAISE FOR]

"In *Goodnight from Paris*, Jane Healey reels readers in to the inspiring tale of real-life Hollywood actress Drue Leyton Tartière, when she leaves acting for a Frenchman and becomes part of the Resistance in Nazi-occupied France. Drue's courageous actions—engaging in dangerous work broadcasting radio programs designed to prompt America to action and then assisting in the escape of over a hundred Allied pilots—are riveting, and through the pages of this novel, they will finally be better known."

—Marie Benedict, *New York Times* bestselling author of
The Other Einstein, The Only Woman in the Room,
and *Her Hidden Genius*

"In *Goodnight from Paris*, Jane Healey illuminates the fascinating story of Drue Leyton, the Hollywood starlet turned Resistance heroine. Combining romance, adventure, friendship, betrayal, and redemption, Healey weaves a heady, larger-than-life tale against the vivid backdrop of France during the Second World War."

—Pam Jenoff, *New York Times* bestselling author of
Code Name Sapphire

"Jane Healey excels at showing ordinary women rising to the occasion in extraordinary circumstances. You'll be cheering for this forgotten real-life heroine, American movie star Drue Leyton Tartière, as she turns down the chance to leave embattled France for Hollywood and, instead, defies the Nazi occupiers, risking her life again and again in the cause of freedom. A riveting story of true heroism."

—Lauren Willig, *New York Times* bestselling author of
Two Wars and a Wedding

GOOD NIGHT FROM PARIS

ALSO BY JANE HEALEY

The Secret Stealers
The Beantown Girls
The Saturday Evening Girls Club

GOOD NIGHT FROM PARIS

A NOVEL

JANE HEALEY

LAKE UNION
PUBLISHING

Published by Lake Union Publishing, Seattle

www.apub.com

Amazon, the Amazon logo, and Lake Union Publishing are trademarks of Amazon.com, Inc., or its affiliates.

ISBN-13: 9781662505294 (paperback)
ISBN-13: 9781662505300 (digital)

Cover design by Faceout Studio, Amanda Hudson

Cover image: ©Joanna Czogala / ArcAngel; ©David Paire / ArcAngel; ©Piyaset / Shutterstock; ©Charday Penn / Getty

Printed in the United States of America

For Charlie

Only when we are no longer afraid do we begin to live.

—*Dorothy Thompson, American journalist*

Part One

Chapter One

October 30, 1939
Paris, France

When I walked out of my apartment building on Rue Saint-Dominique, I nearly collided with my neighbor, the elderly Madame Vachon. She was returning from a walk with her two enthusiastic black-and-white papillons, Oscar and Titou, so I held the door for her, almost getting tangled in the little dogs' leather leashes. It was a crisp October afternoon, and I had decided to bike to Les Deux Magots to meet Elise, my agent in France. With my hair tucked under a navy-blue beret and my windbreaker over my dress to protect me from the autumn breeze, I rode through my adopted city, reminded at every turn why it had captivated Americans like me for centuries—from the picturesque bridges crossing the Seine to the cream-colored apartment buildings with their matching balconies and mansard roofs to the ornate street signs. And then there was my favorite part of Paris—the cafés on almost every block, their terraces crammed with Parisians sitting together around tiny wrought iron tables sharing drinks and cigarettes.

Though just beneath the gorgeous facade lurked the palpable tension of a city whose citizens were on edge, clutching their gas masks everywhere they went. You could see it in the expressions of many of the patrons sitting at the cafés—the worry in their eyes, the serious conversations about a brother or son who had gone to war or about the recent air raids and blackouts. And the topic that was on every Parisian's mind—whether to leave the city for the coast or someplace of relative safety or stay in the capital.

And since my husband, Jacques, had left, I too had been dealing with this question, as well as my own feelings of heartache and anxious worry. The brilliant, handsome Frenchman Jacques Tartière had been my adoring husband since the previous summer. Paris had been our home together for just over a year. But in mid-September, after being turned down by the French army due to his weak lungs, Jacques had accepted a role as a liaison for the British troops arriving in Brittany. And now that he was gone, I felt like a foreigner again—alone and adrift, an unemployed expatriate who spoke heavily accented French. Jacques had been my anchor to this city and this new life. I desperately needed something else to ground me here while he was away. Today I hoped Elise might have the answer.

The café Les Deux Magots was in the charming Saint-Germain-des-Prés district. Opened in 1885, it was one of Paris's oldest cafés and, since 1933, had become a bastion of cultural life in Paris and a favorite spot for both famous and unknown artists and writers. Jacques had taken me to Deux Magots on one of our first warm summer evenings together. Sitting at an outside table at dusk, we had lingered for hours enjoying Clacquesin, a popular aperitif, watching the people passing by and basking in our newlywed glow.

"Do you recognize that man over there? The one with the pale-blue shirt?" Jacques whispered in my ear, nodding to a crowded table of people on the opposite side of the café. They were all smoking cigarettes and had gone through several bottles of red wine. The man he was referring to was small and compact, with a receding hairline and large, intense eyes.

"I do . . . but I can't place him . . . ," I said. "Who is he?"

"Pablo Picasso," Jacques said, running his fingers down my arm in a way that made me shiver.

"Oh, yes, of course," I said. "Fascinating. And he's just sitting there holding court, enjoying his friends."

"Would you like to meet him?" he asked. Jacques was acquainted with many in the artist community in Paris. "I am sure he would love to meet you. He loves to meet beautiful women."

"Maybe another time," I said, grabbing his hand, putting my other hand on his cheek. "I'm quite content with just you tonight, my darling."

"Ah, good answer," he said; a thrill ran up my spine when he leaned over and kissed me. "I just want to introduce everyone to my incredible new wife."

Nostalgia and longing washed over me now as I pulled up to the café and saw the table where we had sat that evening. It seemed like both yesterday and a lifetime ago, and I wondered when we would have a night like that again.

Elise had not arrived yet, so I requested a table outside in a quiet corner, away from the street, right in front of the restaurant windows. I took off my beret and shook out my blonde curls, and as a portly gray-haired waiter who knew me from my many visits with Jacques led me through the maze of tables, a few patrons glanced up at me and did a double take. A couple sitting at a table in the heart of the maze openly stared at me, and I knew at least one of them must be American. My suspicions were confirmed when I walked by them and heard the man speaking English with a distinct American accent, his eyes on me the whole time.

I was curious every time I heard an American accent on the streets now because there were fewer of us in the city every day. I wanted to ask why he was here, what his Paris story was, why he stayed in this foreign country now at war. But he had recognized my face, and today, I didn't feel like putting on my "movie-star smile," as Jacques had called it.

At this point in my career, I was accustomed to stolen glances, and I'd become skilled at pretending not to notice. I avoided the man's gaze, ordered a coffee, and waited for Elise, trying to guess what kind of opportunity she had in mind for me.

"Drue! There you are, *chère amie*," Elise Cremieu said as she hurried over, and we greeted each other with kisses on each cheek. She was dressed in a fine-looking pinstriped crimson suit that flattered her thin frame and olive skin. Her thick, dark hair was pinned up in a low bun underneath a jaunty black straw hat. I had met Elise through Jacques upon moving to Paris. They had been friends since their days at the Sorbonne, and I had liked her immediately for her honest, no-nonsense demeanor. She now represented me for any theater or motion-picture projects in Europe.

We exchanged pleasantries, and as she sat down and ordered a coffee from our waiter, the American and his companion walked up to our table.

"So sorry to disturb you," the man said, in an overly polite, hesitant tone. He had strawberry-blond hair and a round Irish face, and I guessed him to be in his early thirties. "It's just that . . . you're Drue Leyton, the film star, right? From the *Charlie Chan* movies?"

"Yes, you are correct," I said, giving him a warm smile. "Though my name is Drue Leyton Tartière now. I got married last year; my husband is French."

His companion appeared perturbed to be standing there. She looked me up and down in judgment, to see what kind of woman had interrupted their romantic tryst. Like stolen glances, jealous looks from other women were not new to me.

"I heard you were living here," the man said. He pulled a pen out of his coat pocket and withdrew the Deux Magots menu that had been tucked under his arm. "Miss Leyton, if it's not too much of an imposition, my father is a huge fan of yours. He's back in New York and hasn't been well. Would you mind signing this menu for him? I want to send it to him as part of a birthday package."

"Um . . . I'm happy to," I said, taking the menu and pen from him, wondering if Les Deux Magots minded him stealing a menu for such a purpose. "What's his name?"

"Richard. Richard O'Brien," he said, his round cheeks turning pink. "I'm Richard Jr., and this is my . . . my friend Claudia."

Claudia just nodded and muttered a greeting in French, making it clear she was unimpressed with me. I handed the autographed menu to him, and he stood there as if he was trying to think of something else to say.

"What do you do here, Richard?"

"I work at the American embassy," he said.

"I'm surprised I haven't seen you there before," I said. "Bill, Ambassador Bullitt, is a friend."

"There's been quite a bit of turnover since August, as you can imagine," he said. "I've only been there a few weeks. Please come say hello next time you're there."

"I will," I said, smiling. We said our goodbyes as his companion pulled him by the hand out of the café.

"It is no wonder you moved to France," Elise said, amused, as we watched them walk away. "Did that happen to you all the time in the States?"

"Since the *Charlie Chan* films, yes. And it's very flattering. I'm grateful that anyone watches my movies. But . . . it can get a little intrusive."

"Indeed."

Our drinks arrived, and, as usual, Elise got right down to business.

"I have two job opportunities I would like to discuss with you, as well as a charity event that just came up," she said. "But first, how are you? I haven't seen you since he left."

"Did Jacques tell you to check in on me?" I asked.

"You know he did," she said with a smile. "You look as beautiful as ever, just a little . . . sad around the eyes. Are you holding up well?"

"I am," I said with a sigh. "I did get to see him at the end of September for a weekend, so that helped. I miss him terribly, and I'm sick with worry about what might happen to him. With his weak lungs and the weather turning colder I pray he doesn't come down with pneumonia. But I am . . . adjusting. Because what else can I do, really?"

"Good," Elise said. "You're absolutely right; you will adapt, as everyone has to in wartime. I've gotten used to it. In the beginning I didn't think I ever would."

I nodded in agreement. Elise's husband, Philippe, was also serving in the military, somewhere near the Maginot Line. But the fact that we were now "in wartime" was something I still hadn't fully absorbed.

"So, please, tell me about these possible jobs . . ."

"I will, but first, you've received an interesting invitation to perform the lead role of Célimène in Molière's play *The Misanthrope* at the Comédie-Française. It's the first time a foreign actress has ever been invited. It's one night only, to benefit the American Society for French Medical and Civilian Aid. It will require some rehearsals and preparation, but you'll receive a small fee, and it's an important cause."

"Well, I'm incredibly flattered," I said. "And I can't really say no to that, given the cause, can I?"

"No, you cannot," Elise said. "Because I already told them you would do it."

"Why am I not surprised," I said, laughing and swatting her on the arm. "And now that I've *actually* agreed, you must tell me about these jobs. I need to stop sitting in my apartment wallowing. I think I'm driving my housekeeper, Nadine, crazy. I am far happier when I am working."

She paused, as if choosing her words carefully. "Bruce Steele, your former agent in California, contacted me," she said. "They . . . well, they want you for another *Charlie Chan* mystery."

"Elise . . . anything but that. I was so weary of those films. I am not . . ."

"Please just listen to what I have to say first," she said, holding up her hand. "There is a new actor playing Charlie Chan . . ."

"Given that poor Warner died, I expect it would have to be a new actor," I said. Elise ignored my sarcasm and kept talking.

"They are desperate to have you back for this one. And they are willing to substantially increase your salary."

I was about to protest, but the mention of salary stopped me. "How substantially?"

"Well, everything is up for negotiation, but Monsieur Steele suggested he could get double what they paid you for the last film."

I closed my eyes, rubbing my hand on my forehead, thinking about the money. After several bit parts in various films my first few years as a working actress, I had risen to midlevel stardom because of my roles as the "blonde heroine" in a string of films, each one about Charlie Chan, a heroic and honorable Hawaiian detective who traveled the world solving crimes. Chan had, rather inexplicably, been played by a Swedish American film actor, the late Warner Oland.

"The Chan series has kept the studio afloat during these tough years. The audiences loved you in them, as was evident with Monsieur O'Brien tonight," Elise said, watching me. "And I know you need the work."

I took a sip of my coffee and nodded. Elise knew I needed the money. The savings Jacques and I had in the bank were not going to last forever. Devastated after being turned down three times for the French military due to his poor lungs, Jacques had been determined to serve his country in some way and had finally been offered the position with the British Army. Unfortunately, the job paid hardly anything, a fact that had been a sticking point and remained of great concern to me. In the end, I knew that for my passionate, patriotic French husband, staying on the sidelines of this war was unacceptable, so I supported his decision to go. Right now, for my sanity as much as for our bank account, I needed to find work.

"But I would have to leave France," I said.

"You would," she said. "Most Americans have already fled the country for their own safety. You could go, make the film, get paid handsomely for it, and reunite with Jacques in a year or so."

"Do you really think it's only going to be a year?"

"No . . . not really," she said after a few moments.

"Me neither."

"Nobody knows," Elise said with a sigh. "That's why everyone is so worried."

"The thought of being that far away, not seeing him for however long it will be? It makes me ill."

I looked out at the bustling crowds on Boulevard Saint-Germain. A busker was playing a melancholy song on a saxophone in front of the majestic Église Saint-Germain-des-Prés church across the square. There were many reasons to go home, but one true reason to stay. The most important one.

"You must also remember, you are thirty-six years old," Elise said, lighting up a cigarette and offering me one, which I accepted, as the conversation was nerve-racking. "If you don't go back and take this role, another one might not come along for a very long time. If ever."

If ever. I knew she was right. At the beginning of my career, I had been constantly focused on the next role, on finding the bigger opportunity and becoming enormously successful and famous. And with the success of the Chan films, I had been on a path to achieve that. The "next Greta Garbo," the papers had called me; I was a starlet on the rise. But just as my star was rising, I was becoming disillusioned with Hollywood, and all of the grit and grime beneath the glamour. So, two years ago, when I was given the opportunity to perform on Broadway in the play *Green Grow the Lilacs*, I jumped at the chance. That experience had reminded me how much I adored performing in front of a live audience, the rush of being onstage in front of hundreds of people. And getting away from the West Coast had been good for my soul. When I was offered a role in a new play, *Golden Boy*, opening in London, I immediately said yes; I couldn't resist the allure of both another theater role and European travel. And that decision had changed the trajectory of my life.

I had met Jacques in London on my opening night. He had been standing at the bar at the Savoy when I walked into the after-party there. I glanced in his direction and did a double take at the Frenchman with the large, dark eyes and high cheekbones, the slicked-back black hair. He was gorgeous, even better looking than Clark Gable. When he smiled at me that night and raised his glass, I knew I was a goner. A half hour later, he came over and introduced himself and bought me a gin rickey. After I was finished greeting guests, we sat at the bar and talked until last call. After too many drinks, I had let him kiss me goodnight. Jacques said it was what the French called *le coup de foudre*—a thunder-clap, overwhelming love at first sight. And he was exactly right.

"Drue, hello, are you there?" Elise asked, waving a hand in front of my face. "You aren't offended, are you?"

"No, not at all. Sorry, just thinking about how much everything has changed. And I have definitely not forgotten my age," I said with a sigh. "Thirty-six is practically a grandmother by Hollywood standards. I know how fickle the studios can be about actresses. How quickly I could be forgotten."

Elise simply nodded.

"What if I stayed in Europe—are there no movie roles in England for me? Have you looked into any jobs there?" I asked.

"Of course I have," Elise said in a tone of mild indignation. "But I'm afraid, at the moment, most film production in the United Kingdom has been suspended due to the war."

"I'm sorry, I know you're always on top of opportunities for me," I said. "What is the other possibility you wanted to discuss, then? Is it here in France?"

"Yes—well, it is, but it's not so good," she said before signaling the waiter and ordering another coffee and some bread and cheese to share. "The hours are highly unusual, it is not in film or theater, and the money is just *tout juste correct*." She put her hand out and waved it, signaling "so-so."

"What in the world is it?"

"You would be working for the French Ministry of Information, doing radio shows. Broadcasting from a station behind Gare Montparnasse."

"Are you joking?" I said, laughing. "Radio shows for the French government? My French has improved a great deal in the past year, but it's not good enough for French radio."

"I am not joking," Elise said, amused. "And I agree your French still needs some work. But the Ministry wants you for English-language broadcasts. To America."

"To *America*?"

"Yes," she said. "To make broadcasts to the United States in the interests of France."

"Well, I have absolutely no radio experience," I said, trying to imagine myself in a radio studio. "Though I'm sure I could do it. After doing films, how hard could doing radio programs be?"

"I agree, I'm sure you could do it too. And the American public knows you from the movies, so your name came up as a possibility, *if* you are staying here," Elise continued. "You would, as they described it, be 'America's eyewitness to life in France during wartime.'" She motioned with her hands as if reading a movie marquee.

"And the unusual hours?"

"Broadcasts would take place five days a week, from midnight until six. You'd be working for the head of radio programming, Jean Fraysse.

He's around our age and a political star on the rise—he's also brilliant and passionate and blustery, but you can handle him."

Naturally, the hours would be overnight because of the time difference. It would be peak listening time in the United States.

"You know, out of the two opportunities, as your agent, my recommendation would be to go back to Hollywood, do the *Charlie Chan* movie, make lots of money, and be safe from the war."

"Yes, but you are not just my agent, you are my friend," I said, pointing at her as I grabbed a piece of baguette.

"This is true," Elise said, smirking as she held her cup to her lips. "And I will support whatever decision you make. Even if you go with the crazy choice and stay."

The crazy choice.

We sat for a minute, watching the crowds pass by the café. Two teenage girls in matching oversize white-rimmed sunglasses walked by arm in arm, laughing. There was a feeling in the air around us, like Parisians were determined to squeeze the joy out of life while they could, despite the simmering tensions of war that hung over the city like a faint sickness.

Though the money for the film role was tempting, I knew in my heart I couldn't leave. I couldn't be an ocean away from my husband or this place. A job like the one she'd described would be something else to tether me to my new life here. It would give me another worthwhile reason to stay.

"Elise, I'm sorry, but you're stuck with me," I said. "I will do this radio job until the war ends and Jacques returns. If I went back to the States, it might be a year or more before we could be reunited. I couldn't bear it."

"I haven't known you long, my friend," Elise said with a laugh, reaching across to squeeze my hand, "but I was certain you would stay. I'm glad; I would have missed you."

"Good," I said, swallowing the last drop of coffee in my cup. "It's settled. I'm going to give the crazy radio job a try. Let's order some Sancerre to celebrate."

Chapter Two

Elise scheduled a meeting with Jean Fraysse, the president of Paris Mondiale, at the end of the week, at their broadcasting studios behind the train station at Gare Montparnasse. The station, in the fifteenth arrondissement, was a large, dismal structure that reeked of cigarette smoke and urine. Following the directions Elise gave me, I found the low building directly behind the station. I opened the door to Paris Mondiale radio studios and walked into a dimly lit, chaotic scene inside. The frenetic atmosphere of people rushing in and out of offices and sound studios reminded me of a movie set, which was comforting, as I didn't know much about the inner workings of radio broadcasting. I stood and observed it all, perplexed about where to go and surprised there was nobody there to greet my arrival. The air inside was stuffy and the odor nearly as bad as the train station. I put my fist over my mouth and stifled a small cough.

"I coughed like that all the time when I first came here." An older woman with an American accent came striding toward me from the corridor of offices to my right. "You'll get used to the smell."

"I hope you're right," I said, grimacing. "I'm Drue . . ."

"Oh, honey, of course I know who you are," the woman said with a warm smile. She had silver-white hair, rosy cheeks, and a wide mouth. Her eyes peeked out at me from beneath a burgundy fedora that matched her suit. "Drue Leyton. The Hollywood actress. Jean Fraysse is expecting you. I was just heading out, but I'll show you to his office. I'm Dorothy."

"Thank you, pleasure to meet you. My married name is Drue Tartière. And my birth name happened to be Dorothy, but I've been Drue for a long time now." We shook hands. I liked her immediately and couldn't place where I might have met her—perhaps at an early-summer cocktail party at the embassy. "I feel like perhaps we've met before?"

"Jean just asked me if we had met. I don't believe we have," Dorothy said as she led me down the hall, people nodding their greetings to us as we passed—and there were lingering looks and double takes as well.

"The place has been buzzing about your arrival," Dorothy said in a low voice. "If you can't tell."

"Do you work here?" I asked. She glanced over at me with a look that was hard to decipher, a combination of amusement and annoyance.

"Um . . . no, dear. No, I do not work here. Here we are." We arrived at a glass-windowed door to a corner office. The man inside, whom I assumed to be Jean Fraysse, was sitting at his desk smoking a cigarette, completely immersed in some files he was reading. Dorothy knocked on the door, and he glanced up, bothered by the interruption. Then he looked at me and back at Dorothy and waved for both of us to come inside.

"I found her in reception, coughing terribly from the smell," Dorothy said, giving me a conspiratorial look. "I swear if I hadn't found her, she would have left and never come back. You've got to clean up this joint, Jean. Especially if you're going to have an American film star working here."

He rolled his eyes at the comments. I guessed he was in his midthirties, like me, tall and rangy, and ruggedly handsome, with thick brown hair, an aquiline nose, and at least a few days' worth of stubble on his face that highlighted his strong jawline.

"Ah . . . thank you, Dorothy," I said with a laugh, and then held out my hand to Jean Fraysse. "I'm Drue, and you must be Jean Fraysse? It's a pleasure to meet you."

"And you as well," he said in perfect English, motioning. "Please sit down. Dorothy, remember to think about my offer?"

"I'll consider it, if you will consider being open about the type of broadcasts I want to do," Dorothy said.

"Of course, *I* am," Jean said with a sigh. "It's my bosses at the Ministry who may not be."

"I know. Keep me posted. It was nice to meet you, Drue." She nodded at me.

I sat down in the cracked brown leather chair in front of Jean's desk, which was covered with newspapers and files and books, all piled high and haphazardly. Multiple tin ashtrays, most of them still full of old cigarette butts and ash, littered every surface. The state of disarray was giving me such a strong urge to start tidying up that I had to clench my fists to keep from at least moving a few things. A distinct cloud of smoke hung over the office like its very own weather system. One small rectangular window was cracked open behind the desk, but it did nothing to clear the haze. Jean took a cigarette case out of the pocket of his shirt and offered me one. I declined.

He sat back in his chair and studied me for a second, and then he twisted his mouth in an almost comical way.

"I can't quite believe you came today," he said.

"Now, why is that?" I said, crossing my arms in front of my chest.

"Your film career and your face . . . it is not exactly a radio face, as they say," he said.

"I'm sorry, what do you mean?" I asked, though I knew what he meant. I just wanted to hear exactly what his perceptions of me were.

"Miss Leyton . . ."

"It's Tartière now; I'm married," I said.

"Yes, yes, *Tartière*," he said, taking a drag on his cigarette and waving his arm in the air, dismissively. "If we put you on the radio, it will be Leyton, because that's who America knows. Forgive my directness, but you are an incredibly beautiful woman, a successful actress. I'm surprised you are here because of all that. You are sitting with me in this shabby studio building when you could be in California making another film, far away from the war. Elise told me you had that option. I'm trying to understand why you stay. Especially now."

"Oh . . . ," I said, opening my mouth and then closing it. "Mr. Fraysse, are you married?" It was my turn to be direct.

"I am," he said, a little taken aback by the question.

"Happily?"

"Yes," he said, without conviction. "Germaine and I have been married five years. It's my second marriage. And please call me Jean."

"We have that in common, then. I am happily married to Jacques, also my second marriage. He's in Brittany, working as a liaison for the British military. I am not going to leave this country and go half a world away for a film job. France is my home now. This job—well, it's in Paris, which is the most important criteria for me at the moment. I will resume my acting career when life returns to normal."

Jean let out a cynical grunt and nodded, thinking it over. Then he put out his cigarette and started digging a file out of one of his numerous piles, causing several to cascade to the floor around us, papers flying everywhere. I immediately jumped up and started gathering them, trying and failing to determine which papers belonged to which file because there was no discernible organizing system.

"Leave it, leave it for now; we have much to discuss," he said, and I was compelled to gather up one more folder before sitting down.

"All right, so you're staying in France," he said, sitting back again. "Do you have any experience in radio broadcasting?"

"No."

"Acted in any live radio shows?"

"Well . . . no. To be completely honest."

"Any journalism experience before you became an actress?"

"Not exactly. I mean . . . no. You must know that," I said, feeling my face grow warm. "But as you've mentioned, I have been an actress in the movie industry for a decade, and I've done live theater on Broadway and in London's West End as well. I am quite sure I can do radio programs. Do you . . . do you have reservations about me?"

I was incredulous. How could he have reservations about me doing a radio program out of his self-described dingy studio after all I'd done in my career? Did he realize what a step down this was for someone like me?

"Please, you misunderstand," Jean said, holding up his hand to interrupt me. "Of course the job is yours if you want it."

"Oh," I said. "For a minute there I thought you might be questioning my credentials."

"No, don't be silly," Jean said, taking a sip of coffee out of a cream-colored cup. He was clearly amused at my mild indignation. "I was just curious. I'm well aware of most of your career, and Elise filled me in on what I didn't know. How could I have reservations? The only person who should have reservations right now is you."

"Well, I must admit, it is going to be a very different type of work than I'm used to, but I'm sure I'll adjust," I said, giving him my movie-star smile and relaxing back into my seat. Would I adjust? At this point I could barely adjust to the smell of the place.

"You also know the US ambassador, correct?"

"Yes, Ambassador Bullitt. He's a friend."

"That's what I thought. You see, Miss Ley—" He paused and then continued, "Tartière, I need you, more than you would ever need this job, I assure you."

"Do you?" I said. "In what ways, exactly? I'm still trying to understand the role you have in mind for me."

"I need someone well known to an American audience for the radio broadcasts, but I also need someone with influence, to help me arrange all of this with the American embassy, so that the French Ministry of Information, through Paris Mondiale, can make broadcasts to the United States in the interest of France."

"Wait. You don't even have *that* part figured out yet? This whole idea, nothing has been arranged with anyone in the United States?"

"No, we do not," Jean said, shaking his head with a laugh. "We have some of the programming ideas decided. One is called *Letters from France: Life in Paris*. Also, I'm hoping Dorothy will agree to be a regular contributor, though my superiors are wary of her. If she does agree to come on, you would interview her, as well as other prominent Americans living in Europe—journalists, entertainers, people like that. We might do a show, like a play, about daily life in France that you could write and act in, for instance . . ."

As he continued to talk about possibilities, I had a sudden revelation that made me gasp.

"What? What is—?" Jean stopped talking midsentence.

"It just dawned on me. The Dorothy who brought me in here . . ." I closed my eyes and let out a small groan. "Please tell me that wasn't Dorothy Thompson."

"Yes. You didn't know? You didn't recognize her? How could you not *know*?"

"I knew I knew her from somewhere, but she didn't tell me her last name . . . and seeing her here, I should have known. Oh no. Oh my God. I'm completely mortified. She must think I'm an oblivious snob."

Dorothy Thompson was one of America's most prominent international journalists. She had famously interviewed Hitler for *Cosmopolitan* magazine and had been warning the world about the dangers of the Nazi regime in Germany since the early thirties.

Jean Fraysse just sat there, his lips in a tight smile, completely entertained by my embarrassment over not recognizing the most famous female journalist in the world.

"Don't laugh." I covered my face with my hands. "I just asked her if she worked *here*! I feel like such a fool."

Jean had to hold a hand over his mouth to keep from spitting out his coffee, and as soon as it was safe, he burst out in a deep, hearty laugh.

"You thought the legendary Dorothy Thompson was, what . . . my secretary?"

"Please stop," I said, my face burning with embarrassment. I just shook my head, leaned back in my chair, and stared at the ceiling.

"You do realize she's much more famous in Europe than you are?"

He continued to laugh, and I looked him in the eye and smirked at him, trying to remain serious. But something about his laughter was contagious, and I finally broke down and started laughing too. We sat there for a full minute laughing as I told him about the odd look that Dorothy had given me when I asked if she worked at Paris Mondiale.

And I realized at that moment, laughing in that smoke-filled office, that I could work for this man. He seemed messy and a bit frenzied, but he had a good sense of humor and was full of ideas. He would probably make a fine boss. And I would do my best to adjust to this odd wartime role that I was about to take on.

"Now, tell me," I said when we had both composed ourselves again. "What exactly do you need me to do to convince Ambassador Bullitt to help you broadcast? What is your plan for all of this?"

"Ah, very good questions," Jean said, pleased. "Why don't we go to the café across the street for a drink, and I will explain it all to you in detail?"

"Sounds perfect," I said, gathering my purse. "Let's go."

Chapter Three

November 4, 1939

Over a glass of wine at Café Montparnasse across from the train station, Jean Fraysse had, with passion and urgency, laid out his plans for this new radio programming, sketching it all out on a notepad he had brought with him. I would help produce variety programs, commentaries, and broadcasts, all aimed at the American audience, and I would take part in some of them myself. We would interview prominent American journalists, like my new acquaintance Dorothy Thompson, on a regular basis. He also wanted to do some sort of fictional series. The plans were both incredibly ambitious and half-formed. Over the course of our conversation, it had become clear that he cared as much about my embassy connections as my acting skills. And it was apparent to me that he desperately needed me to make all his grand plans work.

"So, what do you think?" Jean said, squinting at me as he stubbed out his cigarette and paid our café bill. "Can you persuade Ambassador Bullitt to let us broadcast?"

"I'm sure I can, yes," I said. "I would think it would make sense from his perspective. I'm afraid it's only a matter of time before America's pulled into this mess."

"I agree," he said with a nod. "And time is of the essence. So perhaps you can try your best to convince him, say . . . tomorrow?"

I thought he was joking about visiting the embassy the next day, but when I started to laugh and his intense expression didn't change, it was clear he was serious.

After Jean and I parted ways, I was fortunate enough to schedule a brief meeting with Ambassador Bullitt for the next morning.

I woke up at a little after seven. No one in the building needed an alarm clock, as Oscar and Titou's barking for their breakfast echoed through the halls at the same time every day. Nadine Cadieux, my housekeeper, knocked on my bedroom door as I was standing in front of my closet trying to decide what to wear to the embassy.

"*Bonjour!* Are you awake, madame?" Nadine said in her high-pitched voice. "May I come in?"

"Yes, come in," I said. "And please tell me you have a cup of coffee for me."

"Why, of course," she said with a smile as she walked through the door holding cups for both of us. Just twenty years old, she was slim, with fine, pale features and flyaway shiny black hair that resembled feathers she couldn't quite tame; Jacques had said Nadine reminded him of a sparrow. She moved like one too, flitting here and there, doing tasks around our apartment with speed, efficiency, and, most of the time, cheer. Every housekeeping chore was completed before I even had to ask.

Nadine smiled and handed me my cup, and we took a moment to have coffee together on the tiny balcony outside my bedroom. It barely fit a circular table and two wobbly rattan chairs. Watching our neighborhood come alive for the day had become part of our morning routine since Jacques had left, and it comforted me. A waiter at Café Rita across the street was setting up the tables and chairs under the restaurant's red-and-white awning, and Hugo, the owner of the cigar shop a few doors down, was washing its windows with meticulous care, singing to himself as he did.

After a minute, Nadine cleared her throat and sat up a little straighter in her chair.

"Madame Tartière, I am changing your sheets today," Nadine said with a firm nod, still looking out at the street. Nadine had only been working for me for a little over two months. She had moved from her remote family farm near Colmar, in Alsace, into one of our two tiny guest bedrooms. We were still getting to know one another, and with such different backgrounds, I knew it was going to take some time to settle into any sort of comfortable familiarity. I was a little taken aback by her command. But she was right. I hadn't changed the sheets since Jacques had left, because I could still smell his cologne on his pillows, a heady combination of cedarwood and vanilla that I adored. But I knew I was acting like a heartsick teenager; it was silly.

"Nadine, I . . ."

"Madame, it is time. They must be changed. I would be a terrible housekeeper if I did not tell you so." She still would not look in my direction.

"And I was about to say I agree with you," I said. "You can change the sheets, on one condition."

"Yes?" she asked with a quizzical look.

"You must stop calling me madame and start calling me Drue. You make me feel like an old lady when you call me madame. All I can think of is Madame Vachon upstairs."

Nadine's frown turned into a small, closemouthed smile.

"OK . . . Mad . . . *Drue*," she said, my name sounding awkward on the first try.

"Thank you," I said, smiling back at her. "Now, I must tell you about this meeting I have this morning. And I need your advice about what to wear."

Though she hadn't had much formal education, I had learned through our morning chats over coffee that Nadine was bright and inquisitive. We would take turns, some days speaking French so I could continue to improve and some days, like today, speaking English so she could become more fluent in the language. She was a fast learner. She was also fascinated by my new role with the French Ministry. And if I was staying in Paris, it meant that she would be too, which delighted her. But as I described Jean Fraysse's plans and my role in them in greater detail, her delight faded to a frown.

"You really think the American embassy will agree to something like this?" Nadine asked, skeptical.

"Honestly? I can't say for sure what Bill, the ambassador, will say, but he's a rational man, and he was a journalist here during the last war, so . . . I think he'll agree. If he's hesitant, I think I can work my charms and convince him," I said with a shrug.

The coffee churned in my empty stomach, because deep down I shared some of Nadine's skepticism. I had lain awake the night before thinking about the potential "what-ifs." The biggest one being—what if the ambassador balked at the idea because his superiors in Washington were holding so tightly to America's neutrality? Then what would I do?

"And these late-night hours? You really want to do that?" Nadine said, interrupting my thoughts.

"I know it will be an adjustment, but . . . I do want to give it a try, yes," I said, nodding multiple times as if to convince myself as much as her.

"But . . . *Drue* . . . but when will you eat dinner? You must have time to eat."

I had learned that Nadine loved food; she also had an enormous appetite, which was a surprise, given her birdlike frame. And unlike me, she was an excellent cook and had taken on grocery shopping and meal planning for the two of us with enthusiasm.

"I am sure I will find time to eat. I'll probably even be able to eat dinner here most nights, as we won't start broadcasting until very late," I said.

She looked at me over my coffee cup, still doubtful.

"What would Monsieur Tartière say about this new job if he were here?"

"How I wish he were here," I said. The ache of missing him had taken up permanent residence in my heart, a lingering affliction that I had adjusted to but that hadn't lessened with time. "I imagine he would not be happy about his wife being out all night working until dawn, but Jacques is away because of the war, and I am taking this rather unusual job for the same reason." I looked over at her and shrugged. "I have to give it a try."

"I understand," she said. "Just make sure you eat and sleep and do not exhaust yourself."

"Thank you," I said, touched by her concern. "Anyway, I won't even have this job until I persuade the ambassador to help us broadcast, so I'd better go get dressed and head over to the embassy."

"You should wear your violet dress to this meeting."

"Oh, you think so?" I asked. The simple peplum dress was one of Jacques's favorites.

"Absolutely. I have seen the way men look at you in that dress when we are out shopping." She gave me a pointed look. "It can only help your cause."

~

The American embassy was a grand four-story building on Avenue Gabriel on the northwest corner of the Place de la Concorde. It faced the gardens of the Champs-Élysées and, by design, had the same neo-classical architecture as the Hôtel de Crillon, a former palace commissioned by King Louis XV that now housed visiting diplomats.

I walked up the cobblestone path through the courtyard to the building's main entrance, past the statue of Benjamin Franklin, going over what I would say to Bill Bullitt and playing out his possible responses in my head, as if I were heading to an improvisational acting class instead of to a meeting with the American ambassador to France.

The receptionist, a warm and friendly young woman, greeted me in the foyer and brought me to the embassy's vast, oak-paneled library, where I had previously attended a few receptions with Jacques. Next to one of the room's dark leather sofas was a serving tray with a tea service including scones, clotted cream, tea sandwiches, and cakes.

"The ambassador asked me to apologize; he'll be a few minutes late for your meeting, Mrs. Tartière. He had to take a call with the president," the receptionist said. "May I pour you a cup of tea while you wait?"

"That would be lovely, thank you," I said with a smile.

She poured me tea, took my coat and beret, and left me alone to wait. When I had first begun auditioning for roles in Hollywood, I had felt like a huge impostor, like I had no idea what I was doing and didn't belong there at all. But even if I didn't feel confident as an actress back then, I found that the more I faked it, the more that false confidence gave way to an actual belief in myself. And that was when I finally started landing roles in the movies. I worked hard, hustled, and fought for roles, small ones at first, then larger ones over time. And I never looked back.

And that was why this radio job felt like a demotion. I had to keep reminding myself that it was temporary, and that I was doing it for my marriage and for a steady paycheck. After the war was over, I would return to my life on the stage and screen. I was sure of that, despite what Elise said. Hollywood wouldn't forget me.

"Drue." From across the library, the voice of Bill Bullitt made me stand up and put down my teacup. "How wonderful to see you. You look ravishing, as always."

Ambassador Bill Bullitt was in his late forties, over six feet tall and nearly bald, with pale-blue eyes. He had a magnetism that had charmed the French from the moment he was appointed. Parisians approved of his style—he could negotiate and flirt in flawless French, was always impeccably dressed, and had excellent taste in wine.

I had first met Bill two years prior, after he and his daughter had attended one of my performances of the play *Golden Boy* at the Group Theatre in London.

"How is Jacques holding up in Brittany?" he asked with a warm smile as he helped himself to a cup of tea.

"From his last letter, he's doing splendidly," I said. "The British officers he's working with seem to really like him. He's getting along well so far."

"Excellent," he said. "Send him my regards."

"I will," I said. "I have to thank you for meeting me on such short notice."

"You picked a good day, as one of my meetings was canceled this morning. I also had an interview scheduled with the one and only Dorothy Thompson, but she had to move it until the end of the week."

"I actually saw her the other day at Paris Mondiale," I said, blushing at the memory.

"Oh? What were you doing over there?" Bill asked, his expression curious.

"Well, it's funny you should ask," I said. "Because that is exactly why I am here today."

I took a deep breath and explained everything about the proposal for the new American radio programming to him in detail, from Jean Fraysse's vision and plans to my role in helping to oversee production both on and off the air.

"And finally," I said, "I need your help arranging the broadcasts. That is why Jean Fraysse asked me to meet with you."

Bill Bullitt put his teacup down and leaned back, a serious expression on his face. "I have to be honest, Drue. When I saw your appointment on my calendar, I thought you were making plans to go *home*," he said in a quiet voice. "As I advised every American in this city to do last month."

"I know you did, Bill. But the United States isn't my home anymore," I said. "I know I'm not the only American who feels that way." He gave me a sad smile and a nod.

"Unfortunately, there are a couple thousand others who also didn't heed my call," he said. "But I understand."

"So . . . do you think you might be able to help? With the broadcasting, I mean?" I asked.

"I might," he said. "But I don't think you and Jean Fraysse understand what a steep hill we've got to climb when it comes to changing American sentiment. Most of the country believes that the US should stay out of any European entanglement. Trust me, I discuss this with Roosevelt daily."

"I'm sure you do," I said. "And I don't mean to sound naive, but doing something like this, to offer a perspective on life in France, what we're up against, it . . . I feel, as Jean Fraysse does, that it can only help. Oh—and Dorothy Thompson might be one of our regular broadcasters too. That's why she was there yesterday."

"That's good," Bill said. "She understands what most of the country doesn't. That America is not going to be able to sit in our quiet corner while Hitler and the Nazis take Europe."

I nodded in agreement and waited for him to continue speaking, because it was clear he wasn't through.

Bill leaned on his elbows and put his fingers together as if in prayer, thinking it over. "The thing is, Drue, and please don't take this the wrong way, but Jean Fraysse is a savvy political operative and writer, and Dorothy Thompson is a seasoned wartime journalist. This will be the first time you've ever done anything like this. And when America is pulled into the war—and mark my words, that is a *when*, not an *if*—those red certificates we issued to Americans here will no longer protect you under international law. Have you really thought about this? You've traveled the world and lived well, as a beautiful, highly successful actress—far too beautiful for radio, in my opinion. Why not take an acting job back in America and be safe, live the more pampered life you're accustomed to? And then you can reunite with Jacques when all of this is over?"

"Have you talked with my agent? Because you sound just like her."

"I have not, but I fear you are somewhat naive about what's coming. You can still get out, Drue. It's not too late yet, but at some point, it will be."

I knew Bill's intentions were good, but I didn't appreciate his condescending tone or what he was saying. And I realized that though we were friends socially, he really didn't know me well at all.

I opened my mouth to speak, then shut it again, trying to control my frustration. For my entire life, I had been underestimated because of my beauty. Many men in my past—from directors to actors to doormen—had been surprised by my intelligence, my work ethic, and my ambition. Many . . . except Jacques. I was thirty-six years old, and I was so exhausted by men who misjudged me. I closed my eyes and pinched the bridge of my nose to calm myself.

It took much more than a pretty face to achieve the level of success in Hollywood that I had. It had taken grit and perseverance and brains to claw my way so close to the top. And if I could make it in Hollywood, I had no doubt I could handle a broadcasting job in a dingy radio studio in Paris.

"First, I *am* staying . . . for love," I said, my voice soft as I tried to keep my temper in check, though my flushed cheeks revealed a hint of what I was feeling underneath the surface.

"It's for love. It's that simple," I continued, helping myself to more tea. "While Jacques is away, I will work at Paris Mondiale and convince Americans to not be so apathetic to what is happening over here. I have followed the news reports about the Nazi Party's horrific crimes. If they can do it in Germany and Poland, they could do it here. I'm staying because I love Jacques, but also? Because I love France as much as you do."

At this, Bill Bullitt let out a big sigh, took out a cigarette case, and offered me one, which I accepted.

"There's one other enormous risk I don't think you have considered, and I want you to take the weekend to think it over. This is a program for America, but the Germans will be listening to every word of it. From your very first broadcast, they will know exactly who you are. And once they know who you are, you cannot undo that. At some point, you could be in real danger if they don't like what you're telling your American audience. Have you thought about that?"

"Yes, of course I have," I lied, my voice wavering as I looked away from him and took a drag on my cigarette. I hadn't truly considered it until that moment. I hadn't thought about the Germans knowing my name. It sent a chill through me and made me realize that maybe, on this point, I *was* a little naive.

"OK, but I want you to think about it this weekend anyway. You have other options. But if on Monday you decide you still want to move forward, call and I will have my secretary set up a meeting with the two of us, Jean Fraysse, and my new lieutenant here."

"That makes sense. Thank you so much, Bill." I gave him a grateful smile. I knew his intentions were good. And I tried to put aside the other comments, particularly those about being pampered. If only he knew I could end up evicted from my apartment if I didn't start working soon—hardly the definition of a pampered life.

"Thank you for your time, and for being so concerned for my welfare," I said, kissing him on both cheeks.

He got up and walked me to the door of the library, where the receptionist was waiting with my coat and hat.

"Always a pleasure, Drue," he said. "Please think about what we've talked about, and I will wait to hear from you on Monday."

We said our goodbyes, and I walked down the cobblestone path as the November sun was peeking out from behind the clouds. I inhaled the fresh autumn air and gave a nod to Benjamin Franklin's statue on the way out. Despite what I had told Bill, I didn't need to think a second more about our discussion. The meeting would happen next week, and he would help us make the radio programming to the United States become a reality. I would work at Paris Mondiale until the war was over and Jacques returned and I could pursue more acting roles again. And I would not be intimidated by Bill's warning about the Germans listening to our new radio programs. So many were sacrificing so much in this war; at the very least I could risk being famous in an entirely new way. Soon the Germans would know my name, as the premier American radio host in France.

Chapter Four

November 24, 1939

Dearest Mom and Dad,

As there's no longer airmail to America, I just hope that this letter reaches you sooner rather than later. Your cable came through early this week, and I went to the bank to transfer the five thousand francs you sent. Jacques and I are enormously grateful. He is happy to serve his country, but this role pays such a meager stipend. And we had to buy his uniform, shoes, and shirts, as well as a new raincoat.

I spoke with Jacques last night, and he is doing quite well in his new role as a liaison and translator for the British Coldstream Guards. He just started training and he's working with the most charming British officer, who is aware of Jacques's health issues and is keeping an eye on him. I don't think Jacques will be sent anywhere else for a while due to lack of training, so that gives me some comfort.

While movie roles here are scarce, I have been working for Paris Mondiale, the French government's radio station, for almost a month now, directing and hosting shortwave broadcasts to America. The work is chaotic and interesting, but it is the night-shift hours that have been the biggest adjustment.

I often go to bed at six in the morning, getting up around eleven to meet with the French government's Ministry of Information, where Paris Mondiale's director, Jean Fraysse, and I are given strict instructions on materials to be used and what should be censored. In the afternoon, I try to meet with any Americans who might be available to do broadcasts for us. I try to have a rest and dinner before I head back to the studio before midnight.

We broadcast several programs every night. This week, the esteemed French writer Colette wrote and delivered a beautiful causerie to Americans about how Parisians have become acutely aware of the precious beauty of their city, now that they live in fear of losing it all.

I have my own show every night at 1:00 a.m. I hope you will try to listen! I have been trying to arrange interviews with several Americans still living in the city. Tonight I am interviewing the one and only Josephine Baker, who is so beloved here I cannot even tell you.

It is hard and exhausting work, and I only hope it is generating some sympathy over there for the people of this country. There are blackouts every night and air-raid drills daily, and we've been warned to expect things to get worse unless some sort of peace terms are agreed upon. It is unbelievable to all of us here that America can't understand the urgency of taking immediate action. Instead, there's that new "damned neutrality bill," as Jean Fraysse referred to it yesterday.

On Saturday I have been invited to a Parisian American Thanksgiving dinner hosted by my friends Tudor and Kathleen Wilkinson. They have invited an eclectic bunch of American expatriates to join them, so it should be an interesting evening.

You are so wonderful and generous; thank you again, and please try not to worry too much about your daughter. I am happy to be as close to my husband as I can be, living in a city I love, even in these dark times.

I can hear the others arriving at Paris Mondiale, so it is time to start my "day" here at the station! Much love and kisses to you both —

Drue

Xoxo

I put the letter in my purse to mail on my way home. Both my parents and Jacques's were well off and happy to send money to help support us, but I was ashamed and frustrated that I had to accept financial help from them at my age. Before he had left, Jacques and I had had one of the only bad arguments in our relationship. I had understood his passion and desire to serve his country and how devastated he was at getting turned down by the French army due to his health. In his desperation to serve, he had jumped at the opportunity to work with the British Coldstream Guards in Brittany. But when they asked if he had an independent income to subsidize his small stipend and take care of most of his financial needs, he had lied.

When both of us were working, we lived a very comfortable life, and though we had a small savings, we did not have anything close to the independent wealth of many of the gentlemen officers in the Coldstream Guards. I knew it would become stressful for both of us if he made the choice to take the role, and I had been right. We now had to rely on the kindness of our families and my modest salary at the radio station to stay afloat, and I hated that fact. I had been financially independent since I divorced my first husband and moved to Hollywood at twenty-four, so our current reality felt enormously awkward and uncomfortable for me.

At least I had the radio job to keep me busy to the point of exhaustion, leaving less time to worry about Jacques and his safety. It had been a whirlwind month, but we had successfully come to an arrangement with Ambassador Bullitt, and we were able to broadcast from the radio station across the Atlantic into American homes. Jean Fraysse was brilliant and kind and, as Elise had said, a bit frenzied, with a mind that was sometimes as chaotic as his messy office. It had taken a great deal of work on my part to create a programming schedule that was organized and succinct and, I hoped, interesting enough to gain listeners in America.

The author Colette was a perfect ambassador in her weekly oratories, and the other programs were entertaining enough, but I was still left with a nagging feeling that we should be doing something more impactful. It was Ambassador Bullitt's words that were stuck in my head: "America is not going to be able to sit in our quiet corner while Hitler and the Nazis take Europe." And yet, with the latest Neutrality Act, that was essentially what America was doing.

We were being too safe on the broadcasts, talking mostly about French culture and not enough about the German threat to France. I had been meaning to bring it up with Jean Fraysse, but our schedules had been so mismatched I hadn't had the chance yet.

"Ah, it is our very famous American actress; how are you this evening? And why such a serious look on your face?"

I looked up to see Claude Molet leaning into my tiny, windowless office, coffee in hand, and I couldn't help but smile at his teasing me in his heavily accented English. Claude was the night director and Jean's right-hand man. He was a short, heavyset man in his early sixties with dense, wiry eyebrows and deep lines around his mouth, probably from smiling so much. He always wore a monocle and was a dapper dresser, even by Parisian standards, with an affinity for tweeds. I had met him my first night at the station and liked him immediately.

"I was writing a letter to my family and thinking about what we're *not* doing here." I waved, indicating the studio, and told him my thoughts. He nodded along, letting out an exasperated sigh when I quoted Ambassador Bullitt.

"You are both right," Claude said, taking the worn leather chair opposite my desk. "And Jean understands that. But he has to be very careful politically. We need to make sure we don't upset the Ministry of Information when we're just getting started. They think the focus should be cultural programming, not anything that could be perceived as propaganda."

"But it's not propaganda; it would be the facts about what is happening over here from French citizens and American expatriates. This month is the one-year anniversary of Kristallnacht. And we haven't even said one thing to mark it."

On November seventh of the prior year, a Jewish teenager named Herschel Grynzspan had walked into the German embassy in Paris and assassinated Ernst vom Rath, a Nazi working there. Grynzspan had said it was in retaliation for the deportation of his family in Germany to Poland. Two days later, the Nazis used Grynzspan's criminal act as a pretext for a night of horrific violence against Jews in Germany. It had since become known as Kristallnacht, the "night of broken glass."

"No," Claude said, shaking his head. "Absolutely not. Not yet. The Ministry would not approve."

"But *why* not? We have to start talking about more than what French families eat for dinner."

"Be patient," Claude said, reaching over to pat my hand. "You and I have gotten a great deal done together since you started. And you are doing a wonderful job on the air. We will do more, but for now we must hold off. And have faith in Jean; he knows what he's doing."

"I hope you're right," I said, standing up from my desk, still feeling conflicted. "He certainly knows how to navigate politics here much better than I do. Now, if you'll excuse me, I have to go pick up the news reports for tonight and start to prepare for Josephine Baker's arrival."

"Ah yes, La Baker is coming in tonight! I had forgotten. Everyone is so excited to see her. She is *magnifique*. The most beautiful and talented woman in all the world."

He started humming "J'ai Deux Amours," her most famous song, as he sauntered out of the office and attempted to mimic Josephine's famously sensual dance moves.

"I can't wait to finally meet her," I said, laughing.

I walked through the poorly lit hallways of our studios, greeting various members of the Paris Mondiale team. I still hadn't adjusted to the smells in the building, a cocktail of cigarettes and mold and stale air. Before going on the air every night, I picked up the evening's news reports from Jean Fraysse and went over the night's programs. He didn't even look up when I walked in, his elbows on the desk, a cigarette dangling from his right hand as he scanned the papers in front of him.

"Oh, I've got the news file for you somewhere here," he said, startled, as I sat across from him. There were dark circles under his eyes. The stubble on his face was there most days. The first week I had started working for him I'd attempted, and failed, to organize his office, and there were still piles of files and papers everywhere.

"Here, here it is," he said, distracted.

"And it's been reviewed by the censors?"

"Yes," he said, rubbing his hand over his face.

"What's worrying you?" I asked. "You're even more preoccupied than usual."

"What's worrying me?" he said. "The failed assassination against Hitler . . . whether these very young, ill-equipped soldiers that we are sending to the front can win a war . . . if the Maginot Line will hold. That's a few of many worries I have tonight."

"Of course the Maginot Line will hold," I said.

The Maginot Line was a 280-mile-long array of defenses—fortresses, bunkers, minefields, and gun batteries—along France's border with Germany.

"I used to think so, but I don't think anyone really knows for sure."

The comment chilled me, making the hair on my arms stand up. I was counting on Germany not penetrating the Maginot Line and invading France. I was counting on Jacques being safe in Brittany, on Paris being safe. Because the alternative was unthinkable.

He motioned for me to sit. "I am sorry. Let's focus on the tasks at hand. That is all we can do." He grabbed a notepad as I scanned the folder.

"We have the *Letters in France* program first," I said. "Followed by my news reports and interview with Miss Baker."

We went over some more details regarding programming, and soon it was time for me to head to the studio.

"And I will not be here for the broadcast," Jean said, crushing his cigarette in the overflowing tin ashtray. "I have to leave early."

There was a joke among the staff of Paris Mondiale that Jean lived at the station; he only seemed to leave when it was to go to another meeting, at the Ministry or elsewhere.

"You're going to miss Josephine Baker? Claude is so excited he's dancing in the hallways."

"I'm sure he is," Jean said with his charming, lopsided smile, the one that made all the young secretaries in the building blush. "But I have met La Baker on several occasions. If I don't go home at a decent time tonight, my wife, Germaine, may leave me."

"Oh," I said, unable to tell if he was joking. "I think you'd better go home, then."

"Yes. She believes I am having an affair," he said, lighting up another cigarette and rolling his eyes. "To be honest, I think she's having one of her own."

"I'm . . . I'm so sorry to hear that," I said.

He waved his hand dismissively. "It's fine; we are just very different people from when we first met. It happens in a marriage sometimes."

"Yes," I said, thinking of my first marriage. "I know that firsthand."

"What she doesn't understand is, I love her, but my passion for France's future is just as strong. There is no affair; there is only my work and the war."

Jean oversaw Paris Mondiale, but he was highly connected politically and involved in other government operations, including military intelligence.

"Jean . . . I was thinking . . . ," I started, but he looked so drained, his face pale and eyes shadowed, that I decided to heed Claude's advice.

"Yes?" he said, raising his eyebrows at me. "You are rarely at a loss for words, Drue Leyton."

"Oh . . . never mind, it can wait."

"Are you sure?"

"Yes. I'd better go get ready or I'm going to be late getting on air," I said, and hurried to do my final preparations before the broadcast.

I knew Josephine Baker had arrived in the station before I laid eyes on her because the energy outside the broadcast studio suddenly shifted. There was excitement among the staff, with more people milling about, craning to get a look at something outside my line of vision. Claude, never one to be subtle, looked at me through the studio window with a huge smile and mouthed, *She is here!* pointing behind him as his breath fogged the glass.

When I finished the news segment and the "On Air" light went off, there was a gentle knock on the door.

"Miss Baker is here," Claude said, beaming as he cracked open the door. "Are you ready for her?"

"Yes, please bring her in," I said.

Claude opened the door and led Josephine Baker into the studio. There was a crowd taking on the feel of an impromptu party in front of the studio window now, all smiling and waving at her. She let out a laugh, waved back at them, and blew kisses. She had luminous skin and enormous brown eyes with thick, dark, curled lashes. Under a light-gray wool cloche hat, her black hair was very short and slicked with a glistening pomade, sculpted curls framing her face, and she wore a charcoal wool coat with silver fox-fur trim and a navy-blue silk dress.

Josephine Baker had left America as a Broadway chorus girl and was now one of the most famous and successful American entertainers in Europe. Parisians had fallen in love with jazz and black American culture, and so they had fallen head over heels in love with Baker, who embodied both.

In Hollywood, I had been in the presence of many movie stars at various industry events and parties. Beyond their looks or personalities, the biggest stars shared one specific quality—a dazzling charisma—that couldn't be taught in acting class. When they walked into a room the air shifted, and it was hard for people to take their eyes off them. Greta Garbo. Fred Astaire. Cary Grant. But when Josephine Baker walked into my studio, she radiated a light and magnetism that eclipsed every star I had ever met.

"Drue Leyton, it is so wonderful to finally meet you," she said, kissing me on both cheeks and hugging me. She smelled of jasmine perfume. "I'm surprised that this is the first time our paths have crossed."

"Lovely to meet you, Josephine; I was thinking the same," I said.

We got settled across from each other at the large oak desk in the studio as Claude, a boisterous young producer from America named Smitty, and several staff members milled about, checking our audio equipment and headphones as we talked about various Americans in Paris we both knew, including my friends the Wilkinsons and Ambassador Bullitt. I explained my decision to stay in France.

"Do you think you'll go back to America after the war is over?" I asked.

"Oh no. No, definitely not," she said, and for the first time since she'd arrived, her smile faded. "I tried going back a few years ago. I was treated . . ." She stopped herself, turning on the charm again, and her thousand-watt smile returned as she added, "France is my home."

I nodded and was about to ask her more, but Claude called out from the studio's control booth, "Thirty seconds to air, mesdames!"

"*Bonjour* from Paris, America," I said when the "On Air" sign lit up. "This is your host, Drue Leyton. I am honored to have a very special guest tonight, one of the most famous entertainers in all the world, Miss Josephine Baker." A few of the staff members watching behind the glass started clapping and whistling until Claude shushed them.

Josephine was charming and vivacious throughout the interview, sharing funny stories about how she rose to stardom in France as Parisians flocked to her funny and erotic cabaret shows at the Folies-Bergère. Her revue, *Un Vent de Folie*, in 1927, had caused an international sensation, mostly due to her incredibly risqué costume, which consisted of only a tiny skirt made of artificial bananas and a beaded necklace over her bare breasts.

"You are one of the most beloved entertainers in France now. But was it hard to leave Broadway for Paris over a decade ago?"

"It wasn't hard at all," she said, shaking her head. "The freedom here, the acceptance, men and women kissing in the streets!

"And I was one of the first colored entertainers to move to Paris. After one of my first shows here, it was the only time in my life that I was ever invited to sit at a table and eat with white people. *Ever.* It meant everything to me. The Parisians gave me their hearts. And France made me what I am. I would give my life for this country, because of everything it has given me."

We continued talking, and I wasn't sure how Americans listening back in the States would react to her answer, but the Paris Mondiale office was hanging on to her every word. As we approached the hour mark, Josephine Baker looked out at the audience of staffers, including Claude, watching behind the glass, and blew them kisses as they broke out into applause again. Claude seemed to have something in his eye.

"And you can tell just by the expressions in the studio tonight how much the people of France love you. Thank you so much for being my guest; it's been an honor to meet you."

I was moved by this woman's passion for her life and for this country, and the type of obstacles she had to overcome to achieve her extraordinary success, obstacles I could not even begin to imagine. On impulse, inspired by her bravery, I made a decision.

"As we say goodnight from Paris, I want to add that this month marks the one-year anniversary of Kristallnacht, the so-called night of broken glass. One year ago, the Nazis launched an attack on German Jews, their own citizens. They burned hundreds of German synagogues, vandalized thousands of Jewish businesses, and murdered ninety-one people. I want to leave you with a quote from the revered journalist Miss Dorothy Thompson's radio broadcast from exactly one year ago tonight:

"'This crisis is not a Jewish crisis. It is a human crisis . . . We who are not Jews must speak, speak our sorrow and indignation and disgust in so many voices that they *will* be heard.'"

I could feel Claude's eyes boring into me, but I refused to so much as glance in his direction as I concluded my broadcast.

"It is a human crisis. And since that night, the Nazis have continued their reign of terror and have only grown more emboldened. As Americans, we must remember the evil our allies, Britain and France, are up against in this war. This is Drue Leyton broadcasting to you from Paris, France. *Bonne nuit* and goodnight, America."

Chapter Five

November 25, 1939

The next day, Saturday, was a precious day off from the station, and for the first time that I could remember, I slept so soundly that even Oscar and Titou's early-morning barking did not wake me. Nadine had taken the day to go see her family in Colmar, so I made my own coffee, wrapped myself in a blanket, and took it to my tiny balcony, enjoying it in the fresh air.

I spent the morning memorizing my lines for the charity production of Molière's *The Misanthrope* at the Comédie-Française that I had agreed to do the weekend after Christmas. Mercifully it was in English, for a mostly English audience, and the two actors I would be working with were inexperienced but lovely young Parisian men.

I was going to the Wilkinsons' American Thanksgiving dinner party that evening, so I planned to go to one of the markets to buy a bouquet of flowers to bring, along with a bottle of wine. As I was getting dressed, my phone rang, and I nearly tripped on my robe rushing to answer, thinking it was Jacques.

"Hello, is this Mrs. Tartière?" a man with a British accent asked when I picked up.

"It is. Oh my God. Is this about my husband?" I said, sitting down and gripping the phone with both hands, terrified.

"Yes, yes, it is, but everything is fine, I assure you. This is Officer Partridge. I was passing through Paris and your husband asked me to call you, because he won't be able to call for some time, due to security reasons. Jacques is doing quite well and is one of the most popular men in the department."

"Oh. Thank you," I said. My terror receded, but my heart sank. He wouldn't be able to call, which meant he was on the move.

"He may not be able to write for a while either, so he wanted me to tell you he has received the coat, as well as the money you sent. And that he still hopes to take a two-day leave at the end of December."

"Hopes to? Do you think he will be able to, Officer?"

"Mrs. Tartière, I wish I could tell you definitively, but the fact is, things are changing day to day."

"I know," I said. "Thank you for the update."

"I wish we had more translators like him; we are most fortunate to have him with us."

"Yes. You are," I said in a soft voice.

We said our goodbyes, and I sat in the quiet apartment trying not to cry. Jacques would not be coming back to me permanently anytime soon. And things were getting more dangerous in Europe every day. The uncertainty of it all made it hard to breathe.

I closed my eyes, thinking back to the day we had moved into this apartment as newlyweds, a little over a year ago. After we were settled, Jacques and I had packed a basket—with a bottle of rosé and snacks and a cotton blanket—and walked down to the park in front of the Eiffel Tower for a picnic. It was a beautiful September evening, and we sat and sipped wine, taking in the scene—families and lovers lounging on blankets like we were, children running around playing tag, and more than a dozen family dogs romping or rolling in the grass. The setting sun bathed the tower in gold and transformed the evening sky into a dazzling canvas, brilliant shades of pink and orange.

"I can't believe I get to live here, in this beautiful city, with you," I said, smiling up at Jacques as I leaned against his chest. My voice overcome with emotion, I added, "I didn't know it was possible to be this happy."

He leaned down to kiss me, and I tasted the rosé on his lips.

"I've loved you since that moment I saw you on that stage in London," he said, wrapping his arms around me. "And I can't wait to show you all of my favorite places in Paris. Seeing them through your eyes, it will be like experiencing them again for the first time."

The memory made my chest ache, but I opened my eyes, took a deep breath, and forced myself to finish getting dressed, tucking my curls under my hat and grabbing my raincoat, as the skies were now a murky gray that matched my mood. As I opened the door to the apartment, I was distracted, deciding whether to walk or bike to Marché Président Wilson, one of my favorite open-air markets, and I jumped when I saw Jean coming up the staircase.

"Oh! What in the world are you doing here?"

Though I knew exactly what he was doing here. After my impromptu sign-off about the anniversary of Kristallnacht the evening before, Claude had warned me that Jean would not be happy. As soon as we had said goodbye and thank you to Josephine Baker, Claude had stormed into my office, exasperated, his round face flushed.

"You are supposed to stick to the *script*—the news, the programming approved by the government. I told you to be patient."

"I know, but I told you, I'm feeling like we no longer have the luxury of being patient," I had said, trying to seem strong even though my stomach was in knots over what I had done. "We are running out of time for what we say on air to matter at all."

"It is not up to *you* to decide. It's up to Jean, as the head of Paris Mondiale. He is going to be furious," Claude said.

"I will talk to him," I said. "I should have talked to him tonight, but he . . . I didn't feel like it was the right time."

Now it was Saturday afternoon, and here was Jean, standing in my hallway, in black pants, a beige cashmere overcoat, and a plaid scarf, a grim expression on his handsome face.

"Are you going to talk to me or just stand there looking angry?" I asked, hands on my hips, trying to figure out what in the world to say that would help my cause.

"Where were you going?" he asked.

"To Marché Président Wilson, to get some flowers for a dinner party tonight."

"Why don't we walk there together, and you can convince me why I shouldn't fire you for going off script last night."

I nodded, nauseous at the thought of losing my job. I studied his face, trying to determine whether he was bluffing. I'd been around many actors in my life, but it seemed that Jean was among the best.

"OK," I said. "Let's go. They still have a good flower selection, even in November."

The elderly concierge of our building was sitting, hunched, on a wooden stool near the front doors. She was never friendly to me, but gave a cheerful goodbye to Jean, who had apparently worked his charms on her to get into the building.

We walked in silence down Rue Saint-Dominique in the direction of the Seine, and I bit my lip, resisting the urge to speak first. He made me wait a full five minutes before speaking.

"You know that everything we do, every interview, everything we say on air must be approved by France's Ministry of Information *and* its censors. They determine material to be used and material to be censored."

"Yes, I know. But—"

"No," Jean cut me off, frustration in his voice. "I know why you said what you said, and I do not disagree with the sentiment, of course, but it's not up to me to decide."

"I just don't understand what we're doing, Jean," I said, throwing up my hands. "The shows we've done so far are entertaining, and I guess they give a glimpse into French life today, which is . . . *nice* . . . but none of it is going to change American minds."

Jean didn't say anything for a moment. We had reached the Pont de l'Alma, and he offered me a cigarette, which I silently accepted. At the midpoint of the bridge he stopped and leaned against the railing next to one of the lampposts. The Eiffel Tower loomed in the distance, against a backdrop of darkening clouds. I wrapped my raincoat tighter around myself.

"So this is what you wanted to talk to me about last night?"

"Yes," I said, letting out a deep breath.

"Drue," he said, "I understand . . . no, I *share* your frustration. I have been pushing the Ministry on this myself, you have no idea how much. But politically? I must tread carefully here. The bureaucracy doesn't want us directly attacking the enemy."

"But I thought that was part of our job," I said.

"I thought it would be too, but so far they think presenting France as a 'cultural beacon to the world' is enough." He let out a cynical laugh.

We stood side by side in silence for a few minutes, smoking and leaning against the rail on the bridge, so close that I could smell his now-familiar cologne, notes of lemon and bergamot, so very different from Jacques's.

"I'm really sorry I said those things without running them by you first," I finally offered.

"But you're not sorry you said them?" He gave me a smirk, eyebrows raised.

"No. I'm not. And I get the impression you're not sorry I did either."

"Not entirely, no," he said as we started walking again. "But if we are going to do this, to weave in some actual political commentary and truth telling? We have to walk a fine line with the Ministry. You absolutely must run anything you plan on saying or doing by me first. Do you understand?"

"I understand," I said, smiling at him. "Completely."

The sun was still behind the clouds, but my entire disposition changed as soon as he said this. I took a deep breath of relief. He was on my side, and I could keep this job, one that in a short time had come to mean a great deal to me. The work had given me a purpose and an escape from the loneliness of missing my husband.

"So does this mean you're not going to fire me?"

"No, of course not," he said, rolling his eyes at me. "The truth is, you are a well-known American, and that will always allow you to get away with saying things on the air that I, as a Frenchman in the government, cannot. And besides, there would be outrage if I fired Drue Leyton, 'America's sweetheart in France,'" he said, referring to a recent article about my radio work in the *International Herald Tribune*.

"That article was nonsense," I said with a laugh. "But I'm relieved. When I opened my door this morning and saw your face, I thought I was a goner."

"No, not a goner. But if you do it again, you might be," he said.

"OK, boss," I said, wiping my brow dramatically. "Thank you."

He chuckled at this and shook his head at me.

We had reached the bustling Marché Président Wilson. On Wednesdays and Saturdays, vendors from all over the region set up stalls to sell the most amazing selection of epicurean delights, produce, and avalanches of in-season flowers—today, there were deep-violet anemones and pale-pink camellias. We strolled through the crowded market, past stalls selling cheeses and truffles, prawns and oysters just plucked from the ocean, and enormous buckets of freshly ground spices.

Jacques and I had loved to browse here on Saturdays. It didn't feel the same without him, but it wasn't only because he wasn't with me; it was because there was a pall over Paris, an anxiety that rippled in the air and revealed itself in people's faces. Jean and I, and the entire city, were trying to go about our daily lives while collectively holding our breath, wondering what would happen next.

"How's your wife, by the way?" I said as we passed a *fromagerie* stall and the gray-haired man behind the case handed us both samples of *chèvre*.

"She's no longer mad," he said with a shrug and a grin, popping the cheese into his mouth.

"I am so very glad to hear it."

"How is Jacques? Have you heard from him?"

I told him about the call from his officer that morning.

"But if he's a translator with the Coldstream Guards, that means he doesn't really get paid much at all, does he?"

"No, he doesn't," I said, bristling at the personal question, but also wanting to talk about it, especially after the call. "After officer training, he'll make a little more, but not much."

I went on to explain about his lungs and the shame he felt being turned down by the French military, and how much it meant to him to find a way to serve his country.

"Still, not easy when you are newly married," Jean said, looking at me with empathy.

"No, none of it is," I said. The separation, the worry about his safety, the financial concerns—it weighed on me more than I admitted to anyone. It felt good to talk to someone about it. "But there are many in much worse situations. Where is your wife today?"

"Germaine said she had to go out of the city today to see a sick friend. Which I think means she is meeting her lover for a rendezvous."

"Oh, really?" I said, feeling sad at the thought of a betrayal like that.

"Yes," he said.

"I'm so sorry. Are you . . . are you OK?"

We were standing in a cloud of powdered sugar and orange liqueur coming from a stall making fresh *crepes*.

"Like I said, we are different people now." He shrugged, looking more resigned than upset. And then, seemingly wanting to change the subject, he added, "Are you hungry?"

"Ravenous," I said. "The smells here aren't helping."

"Me too," he said. "After you pick out your flowers, let's get something to eat."

Chapter Six

The Wilkinsons lived at eighteen Quai d'Orléans in a stunning three-story apartment located on the exclusive island neighborhood of *Île Saint-Louis*. Elise had been invited by them as an "honorary" American, and she agreed to be my date for the evening. On our way over on the metro, I told her about my call from Jacques's superior that morning, and also about what had transpired with Jean and Paris Mondiale.

"I am very glad he didn't fire you, because I don't think I could find you another film job, or any job, given the state of the world right now," she said as we walked along the Seine.

"Yes, that had occurred to me too."

I hooked arms with her and took a deep breath, inhaling the scent of the bouquet I was carrying.

"Thank you for coming tonight; I almost canceled," I said.

"I knew you might. I would have dragged you out," she said, squeezing my elbow. "Better not to wallow."

I nodded and sighed. She was right.

"Tell me, how are the rehearsals for *The Misanthrope* going?"

"We've only had a few, but well so far," I said. "The young actors I'm working with are very green, but they'll do well enough. And I'm looking forward to being onstage again."

"Perfect," Elise said, squeezing my arm. "Because the guest list is growing, and I think the charity will raise a great deal of money. Charles and Fern Bedaux just purchased six tickets. Have you met them before?"

"I have, and though I am grateful for their generosity, I could do without them, honestly," I said. "He always looks angry. She has that high-society snobbery about her. She clearly thinks actresses are quite beneath her."

"They are not my favorite Americans either, but please make a point to thank them that night."

"Do I *have* to?" I asked, though now I was teasing her.

"Drue, as the star of the show, you know you do. And there's a cast party afterward at Maxim's. That Fern Bedaux loves a good party."

"I was only being sarcastic. I'll do what I must for the worthy cause."

"I know you will, *très chère amie*, that's why I adore you," she said as we rang the bell of eighteen Quai d'Orléans.

The Wilkinsons' concierge greeted us with a smile, took our coats and hats, and led us through the dazzling marble foyer and up the stairs to their apartment. The couple's home was gorgeously appointed, furnished in Gothic style, with timber beams and delicately carved mantelpieces. Tudor's impressive art collection was showcased throughout, and all three floors had balconies with stunning views of the Seine, though nobody could enjoy them tonight.

We opened the door to the sounds of clinking glasses, laughter, and a jazz quartet. The party was in full swing, and much larger than I had expected, at least thirty or so people. Due to the city's recent blackout regulations, the home's dark-green velvet curtains were drawn tight, the rooms lit only by scattered candles. Their diffuse glow gave the party a warm, festive, nostalgic feel, like a party from a past century.

"This is how you do American Thanksgiving?" Elise asked, amused.

"Um, not exactly," I said in her ear. "I think this is how the *Wilkinsons* do Thanksgiving."

As if on cue, Tudor and Kathleen Wilkinson appeared behind us, and Tudor was already signaling one of the waiters carrying trays of champagne flutes.

"Ladies! So wonderful to see you, thank you for coming; you look beautiful, as always," Tudor said as the couple greeted us with kisses. In his late fifties, he was tall and thin, with slicked-back salt-and-pepper hair and an aristocratic bearing. Born into one of the wealthiest families in St. Louis, Tudor had never had to work a day in his life. His passions were his art collection and his wife, with entertaining friends coming in a solid third. The consummate hosts, the Wilkinsons' social gatherings were always the talk of Americans in town.

"Bigger crowd than we expected this evening, to be honest," he said. "I think a lot of our American friends are craving a sense of home right now. I know I am."

"My darlings, I've missed you. We need to have drinks soon. I hope you have both been holding up well," Kathleen said. She had once been called the most beautiful showgirl in the world, with her porcelain skin and pale-blue eyes. Now in her forties, with her platinum-blonde hair cut very short, she was still the most striking woman in the room, wearing a silvery-charcoal-gray men's pantsuit that fit her to perfection, as was her style.

Tudor hurried over to greet Sylvia Beach, owner of the iconic Shakespeare and Company bookstore, and her partner, Adrienne Monnier.

"Have you met Sylvia and Adrienne before?" Kathleen asked, clinking glasses with us. "They are delightful."

"I have, and I agree," Elise said.

"I have not, but maybe Sylvia will come on Paris Mondiale for an interview," I said, watching the petite Sylvia talking and laughing with Tudor.

"Speaking of," Kathleen said, "excellent job last night; I couldn't sleep, so I turned it on."

"Thank you very much," I said. "It's been an adjustment, the radio work, but I'm getting there."

"And tonight's party is perfect timing, because you'll never believe—" She was interrupted by a bell ringing. "Oh shoot; if you'll excuse me, I have to announce dinner."

She made her way to the staircase to the second floor and climbed up a few steps so everyone in the room could see her.

"Ladies and gentlemen, thank you so much for coming to our valiant attempt to have an American Thanksgiving in Paris. If you would please make your way to the dining room, where we have two dinner tables set, and find the place card with your name on it."

As the party made its way into the candlelit dining room, I felt someone tap me on my shoulder and turned to see Bill Bullitt.

"Ambassador, so lovely to see you," I said as we kissed each other in greeting.

"And you, as always, Drue," he said. "Can you give me a minute before we go sit?"

"Yes, of course; how can I help you?"

"I heard your broadcast last night—the interview with Josephine Baker, and the commentary about Kristallnacht. Both were very well done."

"Thank you," I said, bracing myself for criticism, given his initial reaction to my taking on this role.

"And Jean and the Ministry approved it?"

"Well, no, to be honest . . . ," I said, and I explained my decision to go off script and Jean's visit that afternoon.

"Ah, well, that's good he said he'll be more open. You know, I appreciate the delicate position that Jean is in, but I thought by now you would be doing more programming to actually try to *change* Americans' minds."

"And that's exactly why I did it," I said, relieved that he understood. "If the Germans are listening anyway, might as well give them something to be mad about."

"Oh, my dear, be careful what you wish for there," Bill said as he took a sip of wine. "But, to your point, you're in it now with the broadcasts; America is listening, including the president. Make them count. I'm on your side; keep pushing Jean."

"Thank you; I intend to," I said, encouraged by the support of a man who had originally doubted me.

The Wilkinsons' dining room had grand beamed ceilings and an enormous stone fireplace at the far end, decorated with overflowing cornucopia baskets and pumpkins. The tables were draped in autumn-colored linens and beautiful floral arrangements, and I felt a pang of nostalgia for Thanksgivings past, mingled with the longing for Jacques to be there with me.

Elise and I were seated at the end of the table, with the ambassador and some of his staff that I had gotten to know over the past year, including new staff member Richard O'Brien, whom we had met at the café in October. There was an empty seat to my right.

"No surprise that she's late. She's always chasing the next story, that woman," Bullitt said with a shake of his head.

The place card in between us read "Dorothy Thompson," and my face grew warm as I tried to think of what I would say to her. I was still mortified for not recognizing her that first day in the studio.

"That's why she's a national treasure," Richard O'Brien said as the waiters poured red wine. "Even if Lindbergh and his ilk think she's a thorn in the country's side."

Lindbergh was a national figure, after becoming the first pilot to fly his plane from New York to Paris. He had political aspirations and had come out strongly against America entering the war.

"Oh, to hell with Lindbergh," I said.

"Thatta girl, my thoughts exactly," Bullitt said.

"Mine too," said a voice behind me, and I looked up to see Dorothy Thompson, graying hair swept up in a simple chignon with a rhinestone hairpin above her ear, wearing a deep-sapphire silk dress that flattered her fuller figure and brought out her eyes. Richard O'Brien jumped up and pulled out her chair for her, and when she first sat down, it seemed every guest in the room came up to greet her and talk about how much they admired her work and her writing.

I had rarely been intimidated by other women, but Dorothy Thompson, with her undeniable brilliance and boldness on the world stage, was the exception.

"Hello, Dorothy," I said. "It's so good to see you again."

"And you as well, Drue Leyton," she said, raising her glass of red wine to me. "You and I have much to discuss."

"Oh, do you two know each other?" Bullitt asked.

"Well, not—" Dorothy started.

"Please, Dorothy, let me explain and also finally apologize," I said, holding up my hand. I proceeded to tell everyone at our corner of the table about our meeting at the studio and was relieved that Dorothy was amused and not offended.

"Please do not give it a second thought," Dorothy said, waving her hand in the air with a laugh. "I am known more for my words than my face, whereas you are known more for your face than your words."

At this comment, Elise almost spat out her wine, and now it was Dorothy's turn to blush.

"Oh my God, as soon as I said it, I realized how awful it sounded. I'm a prize idiot. Drue, I didn't mean it like that. Only that you're a famous film actress, and . . ."

"Say no more," I said with a smile, though the comment stung because it was true. "I understand what you meant, truly. Maybe both of us should just start over from here?"

"Thank you, that sounds perfect."

For the rest of dinner, I found myself enjoying being surrounded by other expatriate Americans. I hadn't socialized much since the war started. Dorothy shared some fascinating stories of her adventures in Berlin and Prague, while I regaled them with some of my funniest off-camera moments filming the *Charlie Chan* movies. The Wilkinsons' Thanksgiving feast was one for the ages, as the waitstaff brought out Thanksgiving dishes with a French flair—*ratatouille* replaced green beans, with potatoes *au gratin* in place of mashed potatoes. The conclusion of the meal was a course of incredible cheeses, American-style pumpkin pie, and a French apple tart.

"I cannot eat another bite," I said, sitting back in my chair and taking a sip of red wine after finishing my tart.

"The Wilkinsons have done it again," Dorothy said, scraping up the last bit of pumpkin pie from her dessert plate. "Drue, can we duck into the salon for a minute before I have to go? I wanted to have a word alone."

"Yes, I'm happy to," I said, feeling that twinge of intimidation again.

Dorothy and I took our glasses of wine and made our way to the little salon, which was also candlelit and inviting.

We sat across from each other on the velvet sofas. "Dorothy, is this about my quoting you on the broadcast the other night? I hope you were OK with that."

"I was more than OK with it," Dorothy said. "And it's about damn time. I have been wondering when Jean was going to get to the real stuff."

"I actually added that piece at the end without the Ministry's approval," I said, explaining the situation to her in more detail.

"Well, good on you," Dorothy said with a laugh. "Paris Mondiale has been playing it far too safe."

"I agree, and so does the ambassador. Will you come in and do an interview with me?" I said.

"I absolutely will," Dorothy said. "That's why I wanted to talk to you. I'll be back at the end of December. I must go back to the States tomorrow, to attempt to deal with my divorce and my . . . my son. My son by my *second* husband." Her voice grew softer and faltered on the word "son," and, for a moment, this strong hurricane of a woman showed a glimpse of vulnerability.

"He's nine and has some problems, although my soon-to-be ex-husband, Sinclair, has issues of his own. And with what I do, my work and travel . . . I haven't been the best mother or wife. That's an understatement, if I'm being honest."

Her volatile marriage to the famous playwright Sinclair Lewis had been splashed across the newspapers since their honeymoon.

"I'm divorced too," I said, looking down at my glass, wondering why I still felt shame when I admitted it to people. "My first husband lives in California."

"Oh? I didn't know," Dorothy said.

"Since I was a girl, I had always dreamed of going to Hollywood and becoming an actress. I married far too young. My ex-husband didn't approve of my wanting to be an actress, and wanted nothing to do with Hollywood. So . . . I outgrew the marriage, but not my ambition."

"I understand your career ambitions more than I can say," Dorothy said with a sad smile. "You and I? It seems we have more in common than I thought."

"We do," I said as she offered me a cigarette that I gratefully accepted.

"When I first saw you breeze into Paris Mondiale? You carry yourself like this glamorous Hollywood creature without a care in the world."

"Huh," I said with a laugh. "If *only* that were true. But I guess that makes me a halfway decent actress."

"More than halfway decent," she said.

"So you'll do an interview when you get back?"

"Absolutely," she said. "But let me find a pen and paper, because I have some ideas for programming this month, some other journalists you must try to interview if at all possible. The ambassador is right; we've got to push Jean to do more. We can't wait a month to get started. We can't afford to wait another day."

Chapter Seven

Friday, December 29, 1939

I heard the ringing as I was coming up the staircase, and I lunged up the stairs to make it to my apartment door, frantically searching for my keys at the bottom of my purse. The phone kept ringing as I rummaged. Fumbling to open the door, I felt the keys slip out of my hand, and, when I kneeled to get them, the bag of vegetables I was carrying in my other arm spilled over, potatoes and onions rolling down the hall.

The ringing stopped before I could even unlock the door. Groaning in frustration, I gathered up the produce near the staircase and went inside. I had not heard from Jacques in over a month.

"My darling, I am doing everything I can to come home for a few days; if not Christmas Day then soon after," he had said at the conclusion of our last phone conversation in late November. "And you mustn't worry if you don't hear from me; I may not be able to get to a phone for some time, and the censors are becoming stricter about the mail every day."

"Please promise you can get home even for a day or two," I said, my heart aching at the sound of his voice. "I miss you more than I can say."

"Me too," he said. "Don't work too hard and exhaust yourself. You know you tend to do that. Remember England."

He was referring to my schedule in London when we first met. I had been filming a movie while also performing in *Golden Boy* seven days a week, twice on Sundays. I had nearly been hospitalized for exhaustion. "I know I do," I said. "But I find I am enjoying the radio work more than ever."

"You are the most extraordinary woman I've ever known," he said, his voice a whisper. "I love you with my life."

"And I love you more," I said, swallowing back tears. "Be safe, my darling."

"*Je t'embrasse et à bientôt,*" he had said as we hung up the phone.

And since then I hadn't heard from him, nor from anyone in his unit, not even on Christmas Day, which I spent at a dinner club in Montmartre with Elise and some other friends. And that was the day the worry started making me slightly crazy. I was smoking more cigarettes than I ever had in my life, and my appetite was almost nonexistent. Now there were only two days left in the month, so my hope for Jacques coming home for a visit was waning.

The only saving grace was how incredibly busy my schedule had become. After attending meetings at the Ministry in the morning, I would head straight to play rehearsals in the afternoon. In the evening I would have dinner with Nadine and take a nap, then head to the studio before midnight. It was a grueling workload, but it helped me compartmentalize my increasing anxiety about Jacques's safety.

There was one more rehearsal until the charity performance of Molière's *The Misanthrope*, which would be performed to a sold-out house. It was a relief, because, as much as it had all been a much-needed distraction, I was looking forward to my life being a bit less chaotic.

And I needed to focus solely on Paris Mondiale. Since the morning he had shown up at my apartment, Jean and I had been in an ongoing debate about just how much political commentary we should weave into the programming, but I was forging ahead with plans to do as much as possible in the new year.

And Dorothy Thompson had kept her word. She had called me earlier in the week, the day she returned from the States. Tonight was the night we had scheduled her to do an on-air interview.

I was still putting away the vegetables when Nadine returned from her errands. She was breathless, her cheeks flushed and her flyaway black hair wild and windblown, making her look even more sparrowlike than normal. She placed her bags on the table and set the olive-green kettle on the stove for tea.

"It is freezing out," she said, holding her hands up to the stove and rubbing them together. "Be sure you dress warm tonight, because it will be a very cold bike ride to the radio station. And it's supposed to rain again. The river is almost up to the bridges."

"I just missed a phone call," I said.

Nadine swore under her breath as she got teacups out for both of us. "I'm so sorry. There is not anyone you can contact?"

"I've tried," I said.

"I went to the *viennoiserie*," she said, putting some *pain au raisins* and *brioche* on a plate for us. "You're looking too thin. You need to eat."

I picked at a *brioche* bun as she poured us tea, frowning and still out of breath.

"Are you OK?" I asked. Over the past few months, Nadine and I had developed a sisterly rapport. I had learned that her sense of humor was as great as her cooking. She had also befriended a couple girls in the building close to her age, and, after spending her entire life on a farm outside Colmar, she had embraced city living.

"Yes, just . . . well, it almost seems ridiculous to even tell you," she said, waving her hand in dismissal, though her expression was nervous.

"What is it?"

"There was a man in line at the *viennoiserie*, his cap pulled low over his eyes, just a little taller than me."

"And?"

"Something about him made me uncomfortable," she said. "I felt like his eyes were fixed on me the whole time I was in the shop."

"Did you recognize him at all?" I said, feeling uneasy about this stranger she had encountered.

"No," she said, shaking her head. "And when I left the shop I hurried home because the weather was terrible. But at one point I turned before crossing the street and I spotted him a block behind me."

"It's possible he was just heading in the same direction," I said.

"I thought that too, but the weather was just miserable and so—because, again, there was something odd about him—I started running when I turned on our street. I rushed into our building and asked the concierge to look out for a man of his description walking by—short, stocky, with a light-brown mustache and black cap. And two minutes later, he did. I waited away from the front windows as the concierge described him pausing in front of our building to light a cigarette, taking a long look at it before he left."

"Why would he follow you?" I asked, frowning.

"I have no idea," she said. "Maybe he wanted to steal from me? I told the concierge to let us know if she sees him again."

"I will be sure to pay her a little something extra so that she does," I said. "Though I doubt you'll ever see him again."

"Hopefully not. But you are riding through the city at all hours of the night; you need to stay safe . . ." Preoccupied with her thoughts, she trailed off.

"What else were you going to say?"

"I have been thinking that maybe he was just a common thief, or maybe he was a spy. I can't think of a reason he would want to spy on a girl like me, but I can think of a few reasons why he'd want to spy on an American actress working for Paris Mondiale radio."

"Oh, I doubt that," I said with a laugh, though again, a nervous feeling gnawed at the pit of my stomach. "I don't think what I'm doing is important enough for the Germans to have anyone following me, or spying on me."

"And I think you underestimate your importance," she said. "Just promise me you will be extra careful biking so late at night?"

"I promise you."

~

I arrived at the station that evening drenched from head to toe. It had been the rainiest month that I could remember, and as a result, bicycling in the ink-black darkness was miserable because the roads were slippery and dangerous to navigate. I did my best to pay attention to my surroundings, but I didn't see anyone following me, though it was almost impossible to see anything at all.

"Madame, you look like a drowned cat," Claude said to me as I walked into Jean's office, which was filled with a cloud of smoke per usual.

"Why thank you, Claude, you're looking well yourself," I said, giving him a fake scowl.

"Have you heard from Jacques?" Jean asked, looking up from the papers he was reading, compassion in his eyes.

"I have not," I said, unable to hide the strain in my voice. "Not a word."

"I am certain he is just fine," Claude said, stubbing out his cigar as he got up and helped me take off my raincoat. "I have some towels in my office. I'll go get one for you. And something hot to drink."

I was touched by their kindness. I sat down across from Jean.

"Something odd happened today," I said, and told him the story about Nadine and the stranger.

Jean's expression grew more serious as I told him.

"It's quite possible someone's monitoring you and, because she lives with you, Nadine, for the Germans. I've definitely been followed at various times over the past few months."

"Yes, but you deal with military intelligence. You don't really think they'd be watching me just because I work here?"

"Of course," he said.

"So what should I do?" I said, feeling uneasy now that Jean had validated Nadine's concerns.

"For now, just keep an eye out, let me know if you see him again," he said. "The number of spies and Nazi sympathizers will only grow as Germany advances. Get used to looking over your shoulder; I think it's going to become a part of both our lives."

"OK," I said, and I took out programming notes to review, trying to focus on the evening's work and not think about adjusting to a life where I was spied on on a regular basis.

"When is Dorothy expected to arrive?" Jean asked.

"In a half hour," I said. "Here are the questions I've prepared for her."

I handed him my sheet of questions, gritting my teeth as he looked them over.

"I can tell by the look on your face you're worried about her. And I'm sorry I didn't have these ready for the Ministry to review earlier," I said, though that was somewhat by design on my part. I thought Jean would be more lenient with approving questions than the rigid government officials who normally handled such things.

"I am concerned," he said, leaning back in his chair. "She's brilliant, but she's also fiery and bombastic, and, well, frankly, these questions you want to ask her—about Lindbergh, for instance? The Ministry would never approve. We can't directly counter Germany's propaganda with our own . . ."

"But we're telling the truth. Not the propaganda and lies the Germans are spouting on French-language radio—mocking France's leaders, questioning Britain's motives. Ninety percent of Americans are still against US involvement. Ninety. Isn't it time we *really* tried to change some minds?"

"I have tried to get the Ministry to let us do more, say more, but this is France, this is the French government. Things work differently here." He put his hands behind his head and leaned back in his chair just as Claude brought me a cup of coffee and a threadbare gray towel to dry off.

"He's right, this is France," Claude said with a nod and shrug as I thanked him and attempted to towel dry my curls. "See you in the studio."

"What does that even mean?" I said, throwing the towel up in exasperation. "Things work differently here?"

"It means sometimes things don't work at all," Jean said. "They barely approved her interview tonight, but I did convince them to allow her on. Just keep it short."

"Jean, are you serious? When you came to my apartment a few weeks ago, you said you would allow more political commentary. And this is the *best* political commentator in the world, here, tonight, with us. If you're so passionate about the future of France, why wouldn't you have her speak about the war like only she can?"

"Nobody is more passionate than I am about the future of France," he said. "But as hard as I've pushed back, the Ministry still wants us taking the higher ground."

"They are absolutely wrong," I said, crossing my arms in front of my chest.

"I know they are! But I am trying to make sure they allow us to stay on air," Jean said, his voice rising, and I could feel his frustration. "They are politicians, and I report to them. And as head of Paris Mondiale, I must be political with *them*. I promise you I am doing all I can for France's future in . . . in . . . in ways I cannot discuss."

"Oh . . . ?" I frowned at him, waiting to see if he would offer more details.

"Like I said, I can't discuss it," he said. "You must promise me, short and sweet interview, yes?"

At that moment, one of the young assistants knocked on Jean's door to tell us that Dorothy had arrived and was waiting in the studio for me.

"Oh. It's already time. I need to go greet her and prepare," I said, taking my notes and my coffee.

"Drue, promise me!" Jean yelled as I breezed out of the office without answering him.

"All right, all right, I promise!" I hollered back, beyond aggravated with the tight rein that France's Ministry of Information had on Paris Mondiale. It was a bastion of dysfunction. I was disappointed in Jean too; I had thought he would be taking more risks by now.

"Drue, so wonderful to see you again." Dorothy greeted me with a warm hug as members of the staff milled around us doing last-minute checks before the broadcast. She was wearing a smart-looking red-and-black plaid suit and a red-brimmed slouch hat with a silk flower.

"I love your hat," I said.

"Thank you. I was never allowed to wear red when I was younger, but I must have a dozen different red hats now. I like the way they look against my hair."

"How was your trip to the States?" I asked as we sat down.

"Well, my divorce is getting uglier, which is hard to believe, and my son barely speaks to me," she said in a resigned tone. "Let's just say I'm happy to be back in Europe working."

"I'm happy to have you here. Thank you for agreeing to do this."

"Of course. So tell me about the format for this interview; I know we don't have a lot of time."

I relayed my conversation and my frustration with Jean about a "short and sweet" interview.

"I'm sorry, I hate wasting your time to come down here in the middle of the night," I concluded. "I guess he wants me to just ask you about your Christmas dinner . . . I don't know . . . To be honest, I'm beside myself that he said no to the way I wanted to do it."

She sat for a moment, tilted her head, and looked at me. "Aren't you tired of men always telling you what to do?"

Something in the way she asked the question hit me like a punch to the gut. It was so true it physically hurt.

"Yes, as a matter of fact I am," I said, thinking back on all the male casting agents and directors and producers who would try to tell me what to do, thinking they knew what was best for me, underestimating my intelligence and business savvy.

"Me too. Even though, at this point in my career, it happens far less than it used to."

"That must be refreshing," I said. "But in this case, the man isn't just anyone. He's my *boss*."

"Yes, yes," she said, waving her hand in front of her. "Details. Tell me something, how did you want to do it? If you could ask me anything at all in this interview, what would you ask me?"

"Oh, well, here are the questions that Jean said I cannot ask . . . ," I said, rifling through my papers.

"Ah, these are pitch perfect." She looked back up at me after reading them, a twinkle in her eye. "You have a knack for this type of work."

"Thank you," I said. "That means a great deal coming from you."

"Let's do it."

"Are you serious?"

"Completely serious. We have to. You know how important it is to counter the toxicity of people like Lindbergh. Americans still haven't grasped what is going on here in Europe and why getting involved is a moral imperative."

"Jean will kill me; I promised," I said, cringing at the thought of him showing up at my apartment again to fire me for real this time.

"In the words of St. Benedict, it is easier to beg forgiveness than ask permission," she said. "Jean *must* be political. The question is, do *you* have to be political? Truly?"

"Now that you mention it, no, I don't," I said. I thought of what Jean had said at the market that day—how he couldn't do certain things on air and get away with them the way I could.

"And you have to remember, you have power here too," she said, as if reading my mind. "You're a well-known American actress, the voice of America in France."

"I'll probably get fired. I nearly did the last time."

"But that's the thing. This is bigger than this job; it's a chance to do something that might make a real difference. Isn't that worth the risk?"

She was right, of course. It was what I had been feeling, what I had tried to explain to Jean earlier. I was worried about the money if I got fired, but like Dorothy said, I was able to do something that few were in a position to do.

And here was this woman who had given everything, her entire life and career, to fight for what was right. Certainly I could be bold enough to take this one risk, to do something she had been doing all her life.

Claude gave us the one-minute countdown through the glass, and a jolt of adrenaline rushed through me as I made the decision.

Dorothy raised her eyebrows at me. "So?" she asked.

I knew our mics were on and people could hear us in the booth, so I whispered in her ear, "OK. I'll beg for forgiveness."

"Thatta girl," Dorothy said, smiling back. Out of the corner of my eye I saw Claude watching me, one fuzzy eyebrow raised.

The "On Air" sign flashed, and I took a deep breath.

"*Bonsoir* from Paris, America. This is your host, Drue Leyton, and I am absolutely thrilled to introduce my guest this evening. World-renowned journalist Dorothy Thompson is in the studio with me tonight. Most of you know she was one of the first journalists to ever interview Hitler, and wrote a book about that experience. Her On the Record column for the *New York Herald Tribune* is now syndicated in over one hundred newspapers around the United States, and she was recently named one of *Time* magazine's most influential women, second only to First Lady Eleanor Roosevelt. Welcome, Dorothy, it's an honor to have you on the program."

"Thank you for having me, Drue; I'm delighted to be here."

"You have been warning the world about Hitler and the Nazis since the early 1930s, and they forced you to leave Germany because of your writing."

"Yes," she said. "And now the world knows that Hitler is a madman. But I think I was kicked out of Germany because I called him an *ordinary* man, a small man who lifts his finger when he drinks his tea. And calling Hitler ordinary is a crime against the reigning cult in Germany that says he's a messiah sent by God to save the German people."

I glanced over at the booth to see Claude, hands covering his mouth, warning me with his eyes.

"And now that the Nazis have risen to power, much of what you predicted has transpired—their conquests of Czechoslovakia, Austria, and now Poland."

"I did say that, but I've never gloated about those predictions," she said with a sigh. "I think it's one of the most incredible stories in history that a man could sit down and write in advance—as Hitler did in *Mein Kampf*—exactly what he intended to do and then put his plan into operation. And the statesmen of the world continue to say, 'He doesn't really mean it! It doesn't make sense.'"

She said the last part using a comical male voice, whiny and desperate.

And then we were off, on a fascinating and engaging interview in which I asked Dorothy the kinds of questions that allowed her to passionately condemn Germany and pontificate to the Americans listening about why the beleaguered Europeans desperately needed our help and support. I was not sure how our audience in America was responding, but the audience in the studio was completely mesmerized, captivated by her passion, frankness, and humor.

Claude was pacing the production booth, and I had not yet seen Jean, but I tried to just remain focused on the interview.

"You have voiced frustration in your columns about America's strong isolationist tendencies," I said, now halfway through. "And you've been quite critical of leaders like Fritz Kuhn of the German American Bund and Colonel Charles Lindbergh."

"It's true. Lindbergh is not only an isolationist but an anti-Semite, a fallen hero who will not be satisfied until the United States bows down to the Nazis. Or he becomes the American führer." Dorothy made an audible tsk at this.

Claude threw up his hands this time. I knew none of this part of the conversation would have been approved by the Ministry, but it was too late now.

"You dropped in uninvited on the pro-Nazi Bund rally earlier this year at Madison Square Garden in protest, causing quite a commotion. Tell me more about that night."

"I'll never forget it," she said, looking past me, as if visualizing it. "Over twenty thousand Nazi sympathizers, sitting under flags with giant swastikas and huge portraits of Hitler. In *America*. It was one of the vilest displays of organized bigotry I've ever seen. I *had* to go, to heckle, to make these men look as small as Hitler. The gangsters are among us now, Drue. And this rise in anti-Semitism in America? It's a direct attack on everything that American democracy stands for."

Claude had started signaling me to wrap up the interview when the door to the production booth swung open behind him and Jean walked in, glaring at me behind the glass as I asked my last question.

"Some . . . some in America have labeled you a warmonger. What do you say to that?"

"That's nonsense," she said, rolling her eyes. "If my *life* would end this war, leaving Europe in decent shape? I would die gladly. I mean it! The American people need to understand that 'peace' is not simply avoiding conflict at all costs. Cities and towns have been bombed, great capitals of Western civilization have been evacuated, and millions of *children* have been put into gas masks and forced to flee their homes. The Nazis are a *world* problem, not a European problem, and it's about damn time America started acting like it."

Some of the Paris Mondiale staff watching burst into applause.

"Living in Paris, with a French husband who is off to war, I could not agree more," I said.

"Thank you for letting me come and speak tonight. And God bless your husband," Dorothy said, reaching across to pat my hand.

"Thank you for the honor of this interview," I said. "This is Drue Leyton broadcasting to you from Paris, France. *Bonne nuit* and goodnight, America."

The "On Air" light went dark, and Jean burst into the studio just as Dorothy and I stood up.

"You promised me," he said, his raspy voice louder and angrier than I had ever heard it as he pointed at me. "You promised you wouldn't do exactly what you just did."

"Now, wait—" Dorothy stepped closer to me, trying to defend me, which I appreciated, but I interrupted her. I had made the choice; these were my consequences to deal with.

"I did, Jean, because it was the right thing to do, and deep down you know that too," I said. "It was absolutely the type of interview we need to be doing here, and I'm sorry. I know I said that I wouldn't ask the questions I'd prepared, but I just . . ."

"You *promised* you wouldn't. I can't trust someone who lies like you just did," he said, pacing the studio. He swore under his breath and kept talking.

"You do not know what I am dealing with. *My* superiors at the Ministry are going to be outraged that we didn't have any of this approved by the censors; you completely crossed the line. And now I have to go there first thing tomorrow to convince them not to pull us off the air completely. You have no idea what trouble you've caused for me and everyone who works here. Don't come in to work on Monday night."

"But . . . ," I started. It was a shock to hear him say it, even though I was partly expecting it. "Are you firing me, then?" I said, my voice wavering, my face flushed as Claude and the others who had been quietly watching our conversation started to exit, uncomfortable witnessing the exchange.

"Oh, Jean, come on now, you can't—" Dorothy started, and Jean held up his hand.

"I am too furious right now to speak anymore to either of you," he said. "Do not come in Monday. That's all."

He turned on his heel and walked away, slamming the door behind him.

My exhilaration at what I believed was a powerful interview was now eclipsed by Jean's anger and my being fired. I felt nauseous, and the sour smells of the studio were not helping.

"Men," Dorothy said, rolling her eyes at me, seemingly unfazed by it all. She put her hat back on and smoothed her hair.

"I am not sorry we did the interview," I said, my hands shaking a little as I grabbed my files. "But I am sorry that I'm unemployed. And I should have convinced him ahead of time. He's reasonable and on our side—well, maybe not on *my* side right now."

"Don't second-guess yourself. Remember what I said? Give him some time to calm down. And then beg for forgiveness."

"I know, I know. I will try. But what if he thinks it's unforgivable?" I said, with a grim laugh.

"It was an incredibly important interview that might just change some American minds. We did brilliantly, and you should be proud of it. Now, grab your things and let's go to the Ritz. I'm going to buy you a drink. Everything will feel better after a martini."

Chapter Eight

December 30, 1939

The next evening, the audience's applause, cheers, and whistles were deafening as I stood behind the red velvet stage curtain at the Salle Richelieu theater, holding hands with my fellow cast members of *The Misanthrope* at the Comédie-Française, the national theater company of France. We looked at each other, smiling, delirious with exhilaration as only performers can be at the end of a dramatic performance that was pitch perfect. I have never known a drug as powerful as performing in front of a live audience, and I had forgotten how blissful it was when every role, every facet of a production came together in an almost symphonic fashion.

The cheers went from deafening to overwhelming, and people's thirst for art and community during wartime was apparent in the joy of the crowd. As the curtain was raised, the audience leaped to their feet, and we walked up to the front of the stage to take our bows. As the very first foreign guest performer in the leading female role of Célimène, I was the last to bow. As I looked out at the audience and blew kisses, the lead actor, who played Alceste, the play's title character, brought out an enormous bouquet of deep-pink American Beauty roses that brought me to tears. Tears of joy for the honor of being able to perform with such a hallowed theater company in front of a warm and enthusiastic audience, though a few were tears of exhaustion over the current state of my life.

I had woken that morning with a slight headache that I blamed on the two very dry martinis I had drunk before last call at the smoky, wood-paneled bar at the Hôtel Ritz Paris, which felt more like a private men's club. Dorothy, like many international journalists, was a regular customer and knew the white-coated bartender well. He stayed open past 2:00 a.m. just for us, as she paid for the drinks and gave me a reassuring talk. But I woke up feeling more anxious than ever about my current employment situation, and about facing yet another day with no word from my husband. And between the martinis and my racing mind, I had had a fitful, disrupted sleep. Here I was, most likely unemployed, again, with no real acting prospects in a foreign country at war.

But as I drank my coffee that morning and tried to calm myself, I realized I truly had no regrets about doing the interview the way I had done it. I did, however, regret being so dishonest with Jean, as well as losing my income and a job I had grown to love.

When I had arrived at the theater that afternoon to get ready for the performance, it had taken every ounce of acting ability to pretend I was in good spirits. Pushing through my emotions and exhaustion, I had given the audience and my fellow cast members the best of me. Ultimately my faked enthusiasm evolved into the real thing, as the excitement of the cast and crew was contagious.

And as I stood on that stage, holding my flowers in front of the crowd, I closed my eyes for a moment, grateful that we had pulled off the play in such a short time, raising thousands of francs for the American Society for French Medical and Civilian Aid. Now I just had to get through a dinner, in my honor, at the iconic Parisian restaurant Maxim's, before I could collapse into my bed. Kathleen Wilkinson had insisted on planning the after-party, renting out the entire restaurant for the occasion.

Needing fresh air to clear my head postperformance, I walked with Elise from the theater down the Rue di Rivoli to Maxim's. Thinking of Nadine's stranger, I found myself looking behind us a few times, but there was no sign of anyone following us. It was bitter cold and overcast, and the air smelled like snow, so we huddled against each other and didn't speak much. I had already decided to not confide in her yet about what had happened at the station. We would have to discuss it soon enough. Tonight, as the guest of honor, I had to put my worries in a black box in my mind and focus on getting through the rest of the evening.

"Well, you certainly look the part of the movie star," Elise said just before we arrived at Maxim's.

"Do you really think so?" I said, looking down at my chosen outfit. "I'm feeling a little out of practice."

Under my camel cashmere coat, I had chosen to wear a cocktail dress by the Parisian designer Lucien Lelong that I had not worn in over a year. It had a velvet bodice with intricate silver-and-gold beading and a flowy black tulle skirt. My blonde curls were styled in a side chignon, and I was wearing a silver-and-gold beaded headband.

"You are breathtaking, Drue. If only Jacques could see you tonight," Elise said, giving me a hug. "I know it's been very difficult not hearing from him. And you know I understand more than I can say. But maybe let's try to have fun to celebrate a wonderful performance?"

"I will try," I said. "What would I do without friends like you? Thank you."

The *maître d'* took our coats as we walked into Maxim's. Its gorgeous art nouveau decor was elegant, warm, and sensuous—with stained-glass ceilings and whimsical murals featuring dragonflies and butterflies, forest nymphs and fauna. When we walked into the candlelit main dining area, the fifty or so guests had arrived and were milling about, socializing and having cocktails. It had been some time since I'd had to be "Drue Leyton, film actress," and I was thrown off-balance by being the center of attention again after living a more anonymous life here, one where I was rarely recognized for my movie roles.

A waiter handed me a glass of champagne, and I made my way through the crowd, greeting the guests, introducing myself to those I had not met, reacquainting myself with others.

"Drue Leyton, that was a wonderful performance, my dear." Charles Bedaux came up to me, kissing me on both cheeks, his wife, Fern, right behind him.

"It's nice to see you both again," I said, though this was not exactly true.

Charles and Fern Bedaux were an odd couple. I had met them on several occasions at parties at the American embassy and elsewhere. A self-made millionaire with questionable international business connections, Charles was in his early fifties and of slight build, with wavy, dark hair and a weathered face. His wife was a Midwestern socialite, younger than him by a few years and noticeably taller, with thin lips and a general air of haughtiness about her.

"I could not agree more with Charles," Fern said. "You were letter perfect."

"Thank you both; you're far too kind," I said.

"Is that ravishing dress a Lelong?" she asked, stepping back and examining it like I was a show horse.

"Yes, it is, thank you," I said.

"I know my French fashion," Fern said, and then pointed at the dress she was wearing. It was a striking ivory silk organza frock with an oversize black sash embroidered with large black orchids. "This is Chanel. Dear Coco is a friend; have you met her?"

"No, I can't say I have," I said.

"And where is that charming husband of yours? Is he here?"

"No, in fact he recently started working as a liaison for the British in the north," I said, and I explained his role.

They asked me some polite questions about the cast of the play and some of my more recent movie roles. Fern also invited me to their villa in the South of France as I silently wished Elise would rescue me from this conversation. Mercifully, it was time to be seated, and I politely excused myself.

I smiled greetings to my guests and was just about to go down the stairs to the ladies' room when Bill Bullitt stopped me. We exchanged kisses, and I was grateful and touched that he had attended both the play and the dinner.

"You must be exhausted," he said, and it was good to see an old friend. "Mind you, you do not look it at all, but with the schedule you've been keeping. And to have to be the belle of the ball tonight— I'm not sure how you're still standing."

"Neither am I, to be honest," I said, laughing.

"I won't keep you, but I wanted to have a quick word about your interview with Dorothy last night."

I groaned and looked down, pinching the bridge of my nose.

"Bill, before you say anything, I'm very sorry I crossed the line with what we discussed on air," I said, holding up my hand, wanting to explain my actions before being reprimanded. "It wasn't approved by the Ministry. But Dorothy and I both felt it worth the risk, and I'm proud of it, and I think it's good for the country. Now, you're the ambassador, and maybe you disagree, but if you don't want me to do it again, you don't have to worry, because Jean fired me right after it ended."

"No, he didn't," Bill said.

"What?" I said, frowning at him. "Yes, he did. He said not to come in on Monday."

"Well, maybe he did, but either way you still have the job. He's going to give it back to you."

"How do you know? What are you talking about?"

"Let me explain. As Jean expected, the French government was very unhappy about your interview. They not only wanted him to fire you—they were going to let him go also. And shut down the entire operation."

"Oh," I said. "But . . . ?"

"But I got a call today from someone who was listening in the United States that was delighted with the interview. Thought it was perfect in every way."

"Where are you going with this, Bill? Why would that matter?"

"It matters because the person listening was the president. Roosevelt liked what he heard, he thinks it's important, so I intervened on his behalf and smoothed things over with the Ministry."

I stared at him, stunned at this news. "You are kidding me."

"Drue, why would I ever joke about this?" he said with a laugh. "They're going to give you much more leeway in terms of commentary and political programming. Per the urging of the *president of the United States.*"

"This is the best news I've heard in a while," I said, giving him a hug. "Thank you; I needed this tonight. Truly."

"Thank Roosevelt. And you're welcome," he said. "Tell you what, come to the embassy Monday afternoon at four for tea and we'll talk more, but bottom line is, your instincts so far have been right, and you still have the job."

I reassured him that I would and made my way down the narrow staircase to the ladies' room to freshen up before dinner, my mood much lighter, as I considered what kind of gift I could get for Jean as an apology, an apology I prayed he would accept.

Chapter Nine

The dinner party at Maxim's went by in a haze as I attempted to be the perfect guest of honor while also trying to absorb Bill's news that I would still be broadcasting thanks to the president. The backdrop of the art nouveau restaurant, candlelit and overly warm with the windows covered, made it all feel surreal. To my great relief, I managed to avoid Charles and Fern for the rest of the evening, as they were seated at a table on the far side of the room.

Elise sensed that I was preoccupied on the taxi ride home and asked me why, but I was too tired to explain and told her we should meet at Les Deux Magots later that week to discuss. A light snow had started falling, and the air was bitter cold as I fumbled to open the door to my apartment building. It was past midnight, so the hallways were dark, and the building's concierge was not on her usual perch.

I took off my heels to climb the stairs, needing a hot bath before bed to soothe my aching feet. When I reached my floor, I stopped short at the faint sound of jazz music coming from inside my apartment. Nadine was supposed to be away at her family's home for two more nights. And why was she playing jazz after midnight?

"Nadine?" I said as I turned the key to open the door. "Is everything all right? I didn't expect you until—"

"Everything is fine, darling. My beautiful wife," Jacques said, his voice deep, and thick with emotion. He was standing in the middle of the apartment, surrounded by candles and flowers, arms reached out to me, looking more beautiful than I had ever seen him. My French Cary Grant, more handsome than the original.

"I tried so hard to get here in time for your performance, but the trains were all running late. I am sure you were brilliant."

The shock of him standing in the middle of our apartment made my knees buckle.

"You're here, my God," I said as the tears started to fall. I ran to him and collapsed into his tall, solid frame, inhaling the smell of his vanilla-and-cedarwood cologne, feeling at home in his arms. "I . . ." I let out a sob, and he wrapped me in his arms and held me tighter as we sank to the floor.

"I'm so sorry, Drue," he said, stroking my hair. "I wanted to get word to you, but it was impossible. I hope you'll forgive me."

"I thought you were . . . you might be . . ." I breathed deep, trying to get my emotions in check, but it was like the dam had finally broken, my fatigue mixed with all the anxiety of not knowing where he was, and now he was back and safe with me. I put my hand on his damp cheek and looked up at him.

"I know, and it has been torture to not even hear the sound of your voice," he said. "I'm here and safe and alive with you. I love you, and I am so incredibly sorry to cause you so much worry."

"I love you, my darling. It is such a relief to have you back."

He helped me with my coat, all the while kissing me, at first long and slow, and then we held each other tighter, to remind ourselves that we were real and together in this moment. As our kisses became more urgent, he scooped me up off the floor, kissing my neck as he carried me toward the bedroom.

"You are exquisite," Jacques whispered in my ear as he placed me down on the bed and unzipped the back of my dress while I started unbuttoning his shirt. "I have been dreaming of a night like this with you for weeks."

We undressed each other frantically, with a desperate passion that had been building up since the last time we were together. My dress and stockings and undergarments were tossed to the floor with his shirt and pants as we fell back onto the bed and I wrapped my legs around him, his breath ragged as he pulled me into him, and I let out a gasp as he left a trail of kisses down my neck to my breasts.

Sometime just before dawn, we finally fell asleep, satiated and exhausted in each other's arms.

Late the next morning, I woke up and reached for him, but the bed was empty, the smell of coffee coming from the kitchen. I put on my silk robe and found him sitting at the kitchen table, writing a letter and sipping his coffee. It felt so wonderfully normal to see him there, his black hair disheveled from sleep, stubble on his cheeks. I tried to capture it like a photograph in my mind that I could conjure when I missed him.

"Good morning, my love," I said, leaning over to kiss him on the forehead. He pulled out his chair so I could sit on his lap.

"Good morning," he said. "I was just writing a letter to my father; I hoped you could mail it for me. I'm asking him to send me a waterproof sleeping bag, as they're impossible to get here now. And I am going to need to have you send me some money from our savings."

"That's fine," I said, my heart sinking. "I didn't want to ask last night because I knew I would hate the answer. How soon do you have to leave?"

"I have to be back by tomorrow," he said. He looked up at me, his eyes mirroring my own sadness.

"But that's . . . that's no time at all."

"I know," he said, running a hand through his hair, making some of it stand up in random spikes that made him look younger than his years. "I tried to get a couple more days, but too much is happening. I think . . . I think we're going to be on the move soon."

"Oh no," I said, standing up, rubbing my face with my hands, trying to absorb the news and wake up. "Moving where? How soon? I wanted you to be with the British, with the Coldstream Guards, because you would be safe."

"Darling, I am safe enough," he said, getting me a cup of coffee. "And I will do my best to continue to be, but it's wartime. Nobody is truly, completely safe, are they?"

"Where are you going? You didn't answer my question," I said, my anxiety about his safety creeping back.

"Northern Europe," he said as he handed me a cup. "That's all I know."

We sank down onto the sofa next to each other; he took my hand and stroked it. I looked out the window at the light flurries dancing past it, and I tried very hard not to cry.

I asked, "Tell me, are you still happy with the work you are doing?"

"I truly am," he said with a smile. "I am incredibly busy, and I am now a translator for several divisions. The officers are all fine men, both French and English. We are next going to be barracked at a hotel with good food and warm beds, and how much more can I ask for? I needed to do this, to serve my country and to travel—I have wanted to do something like this my entire life. Now I finally have the chance."

"I know," I said. After his third rejection from the military, he had been so depressed, restless, and angry that he could not serve like so many of his friends and family members had. This opportunity had, in many ways, saved him. I couldn't deny that.

"The only part of all of this that I hate is being away from you. That and the fact that I am not making enough money and we must rely on your work and the kindness of our families. Thank you for your sacrifices in letting me do this. I don't deserve you. Truly."

He pulled me over to him, and I settled into the crook of his arm.

"You're welcome," I said with a dramatic sigh. I had been feeling a little resentful and stressed about our money situation. "Why do you have to be so noble, so *good*, and understanding? With your lungs you had a perfect excuse not to serve, and yet that didn't stop you. How are you feeling, by the way?"

"Very well," he said. I looked up at him to see if he was telling the truth, and I felt his body tense. "I am fine, the picture of health. I should be asking you that question. How are you? I told Nadine to make sure you weren't working too hard."

"I'm fine now that you're here. And Nadine and I have become closer since you left," I said with a smile. "I'm fortunate we can keep her on; she's a huge help and great company too."

I told him everything that had transpired in the past month, all about my role at Paris Mondiale, about Claude and Jean and the controversies over programming, about our fascinating guests like Dorothy and Josephine. He listened intently and asked me thoughtful, curious questions all along, a reminder of one of the many reasons why I loved him. He was interested in my pursuits in a way my first husband never was. In a way no man ever had been. At the end of the day, I thought, every woman just wanted someone who believed in them, who shared in their joys and supported them in their sorrows. But I knew men like Jacques were rare. I was one of the lucky ones.

"I am immensely proud of you and what you're doing at the station, your radio broadcasts," he said. "You're incredible."

"I don't know about that," I said with a laugh. "But I'm doing the best I can; thank you."

"And you need to tell me all about the play," he said.

I told him about the young actors I worked with, the standing ovation, and the dinner party. He was impressed to learn Bill Bullitt's news about President Roosevelt listening in and thus saving my job.

"But the best part of the night was finding you here," I said, kissing his cheek. "What would you like to do for the rest of the time you're home?"

"It's already midmorning; let's try to enjoy it to the fullest," he said. "We'll go to a café or two, drink champagne and toast to our marriage at midnight. Let's forget tomorrow until it's here. Do you think you can do that?"

"But what about seeing some of our friends? Elise, at the very least?"

"Let's just see where the day takes us. Our time together is precious, and we need to fit a month's worth of memories into hours. Sound good?"

"OK, sounds good," I said, smiling, trying to push down the feelings of sadness from knowing he would be leaving so soon. I knew he was right. Elise and many other wives had not seen their husbands for months, had barely received a letter. I was greedy for more, but I needed to be grateful for *this*. "On that note, come, let's not waste another minute."

I wrapped my arm around his and led him into the bedroom.

Chapter Ten

Darling,

You are asleep next to me as I write this, and very soon I will be on a train back to Brittany. This precious time with you has made me wistful about what our newly married life would have been like had the war not happened. Thank you for the wonderful memories of this weekend; they will keep me warm on my nights away from our bed.

I thank you for understanding how important it is for me to serve my country, but as I said yesterday, I'm so sorry for the sacrifices it has required of both of us. It is a lot to ask of a new bride living in a foreign land, and yet you do it willingly because you know what it means to me as a Frenchman. Because you love me. And that means more than words can say, my darling.

Please try not to worry too much; I am in a good position and safer than most.

You are always my lucky star. I have no fear in my heart, and you must not be afraid either. I will come back to you. No matter where you are or how long until I reach

you again, you know what there is between us. Je t'em-
brasse, je t'embrasse, je t'embrasse.
   All my love,
   Jacques

I reread the letter for the twentieth time since his train had left the station at six that morning. He had looked so handsome in his new black cashmere overcoat and uniform. With a passionate kiss and embrace, he handed me the letter, his eyes watering.

"I love you," he said as he walked away backward, blowing me a kiss.

"*Je t'aime tellement. J'attendrai,*" I said, the second phrase being from the song he had sung to Elise's daughter the night before. *I love you so. I will wait.*

He turned to go and waved once more before stepping onto the train.

I had gritted my teeth and held back the tears until I knew he couldn't see me.

It had been a wonderful New Year's Eve day and night with Jacques, so lovely and magical that the goodbye was that much harder and bittersweet. We had bundled up and taken a long walk through the city we adored, ravenous when we finally arrived at Les Deux Magots. Jacques was thrilled the portly gray-haired waiter remembered us and brought us to our favorite table, inside near the windows. And there we had lingered over a late lunch of salad and omelets and warm goat cheese on sourdough bread and a full-bodied red wine.

A little before five, the sun already setting for the last time in 1939, we paid a quick surprise visit to Elise, her mother, Yvonne, and Elise's eight-year-old daughter, Corinne, and they all whooped with joy at the sight of Jacques, hugging and kissing us both. Yvonne brought out champagne to toast our brief reunion. At one point, Jacques picked up Corinne, singing the popular song "J'attendrai" and dancing her around the apartment until she was laughing so hard she couldn't breathe.

Later that evening we sat by our tiny fireplace filled with candles, a tray of cheeses and bread between us, toasting to an uncertain future and trying to pretend we had days and not hours left to spend together. We made love until long past midnight, falling asleep tangled in each other until it was time for him to leave.

I didn't know when he'd be able to come back to me again, but I knew that it might be a very long time. And I needed to figure out a way to handle his absence better than I had been. I needed to get through these weeks or months without being a constant nervous wreck. Working hard would be one way through. There were refugees pouring in from other countries every day who required food and shelter and medical care, and Kathleen had started volunteering to help with those efforts. Now that the play was over, I thought I could help too.

My tea with Bill was in an hour, and then I would learn if I truly did still have a job. Thinking back to how furious Jean had been, I still had my doubts, despite the approval of the president of the United States.

I blotted my eyes with a cold, damp cloth and put on my makeup, failing to completely cover up the puffiness and dark circles. I chose my favorite wool suit. It was a deep charcoal gray and felt businesslike enough for the meeting, but at the cuffs and collar it had a delicate pink silk trim embroidered with silver butterflies, details that appealed to my dramatic side.

As I was looking for my gas mask, there was a knock at the door followed by a feisty bark.

"Drue? I am home," Nadine said as she opened the door.

Nadine was standing there with her gas mask and overnight bag. At her feet, next to her bag, was a dog with wild black curly hair, a little over a foot tall, with large watery eyes that made him look cartoonlike.

I looked at the dog and back at Nadine. "Oh," I said, tilting my head. "Who do we have here?"

"This is Ondie; he is a five-year-old poodle," she said, her voice nervous and even higher-pitched than normal. "My family's elderly neighbor passed away last week. This dog has no one left. He doesn't have to stay forever. He is a *très bon chien*. A very good dog. If you allow him to stay, you will not have to worry; I will take care of all his needs."

The dog looked up at me, his eyes sad and imploring, as if waiting for my verdict.

I kneeled, and he covered me in kisses and nearly toppled me in his excitement. "OK, Ondie, I suppose you can stay . . . at least for now. Long term, we will probably have to figure out something else."

I stood up, and this time it was Nadine who almost bowled me over with her embrace.

"Thank you so much," she said, and I laughed as Ondie let out a little yelp of joy of his own, and I helped her bring him and her bags into the apartment.

"Oh, Nadine," I said as we hugged each other tightly and the dog jumped up on us and tried to join in the affection. "I am so happy to have you back, and I have so much to tell you."

I gave her a brief overview of what had happened while she was away as I put on my overcoat and gathered my things.

"I have to go, but I will be home for dinner after my meeting at the embassy, and I can tell you the rest then," I said. "And I might be going to the station tonight as usual, but I won't know for sure until I talk to the ambassador."

I patted Ondie on the head and smiled.

"I'm just so grateful you're here. Both of you."

"Me too," she said, giving me a gentle push out the door. "Now go before you're late."

I waited in the library of the American embassy, sitting on the same sofa and drinking Darjeeling tea as I awaited Bill. A few minutes after I arrived, he walked into the library with Richard O'Brien, and my stomach lurched, because behind Richard was Jean, his eyes neutral when he saw me, his demeanor cool, like I was a stranger. I hated it.

"Drue," Bill said, kissing me on both cheeks when he reached the sofa, "thank you for meeting with me on New Year's Day; it was just too important to wait."

"It's not a problem at all, Bill," I said.

"Hello," said Jean in a quiet voice as he greeted me with kisses as well, his body language stiff and guarded.

"Hello, Jean," I said, my voice tight. "I wasn't expecting to see you here. Nice to see you again, Richard."

"You as well, Miss Leyton," he said. "I've been meaning to tell you, my father was absolutely thrilled with the autograph. Thank you again."

"You're very welcome," I said, wondering why Bill had invited him to the meeting.

One of the embassy's staff came in and poured tea for the men while another brought out a tray of tea cakes and sandwiches.

"Excuse me," I said, standing up. "It's just that I wasn't expecting Jean and Richard to be joining us. Before we begin, I'd like to step outside the library to have a word with Jean. It will only take a minute."

I didn't ask permission, which was something I would have done when I was a young, eager actress just starting out. Now I had no time for it. I needed to make things right with my boss.

"Of course," Bill said. "By all means."

We closed the door of the library behind us and faced each other in the hall. Jean had his arms crossed, a few days of black stubble at his jawline. I took a deep breath and begged for forgiveness, per Dorothy's advice.

"Jean, I am truly sorry," I said. "For going ahead with the interview the way I did, for going against your wishes. I was just so inspired by her passion, and you know how I've been feeling about wanting to do more. And all I've got are these radio broadcasts, so, on impulse, I went ahead and asked those questions. But I know it was wrong to betray your trust like that, and I promise you I will never do that again."

"Thank you for the apology," he said. He looked up at the cathedral ceiling of the embassy hallway. "I suppose you have to stay on, now that you've got a fan in President Roosevelt."

"That was unexpected news, I'll admit," I said, my body relaxing.

"Unexpected but welcome," he said. "Now we've got the president *and* the ambassador on our side. So, to be clear, I was furious with you the other night. And I did feel betrayed, not only because you work for me but because . . . I consider you a good friend now."

"I consider you a friend too," I said in a soft voice as we looked into each other's eyes. Jean had become a dear friend these past months, and my heart ached because I had hurt him personally. "Again, I am so sorry."

"I know," he said. "At least you've made up for it in a way. Because now we have the most powerful person willing to defend what we're doing to the Ministry. And this is what I've wanted all along."

"Does this mean I still have a job?"

"Yes, you still have a job. Unfortunately, I cannot do this without you," he said, shaking his head, and I studied his solemn expression with worry until he broke into his lopsided smile.

"Thank you," I said, so relieved that I couldn't help but give him a hug, the tension leaving my shoulders as we embraced. "Thank you. I will not let you down."

"I know you will not," he said, still smiling as he pulled away, and I was surprised to see he was now blushing. "But from now on, no more of this American rebel-cowboy nonsense, doing your own thing. We must communicate and make decisions together."

"Of course, absolutely," I said, biting my lip.

"Is there anything else, Drue?" he asked. "Are you OK?"

"I'm a little out of sorts this afternoon," I said, touched that he'd noticed. "Jacques made it home this weekend."

I told him about the thirty-six-hour visit and the difficult goodbye.

"Ah, that's why your eyes are so red," he said, his smile fading. "I knew it was something. I'm sorry, but I am glad that you got to see him and he's well."

"Thank you," I said as we headed back into the library, enormously happy that our friendship was still intact.

"Oh, good," Bill said as we joined them on the sofas. "So, I wanted to meet with you both today to make sure you understand that I've intervened with your superiors at the Ministry and you now, finally, have air cover from the US president, and therefore much freer rein to broadcast the types of programs and interviews that we all want."

"Yes, we were just discussing that," Jean said. "This is incredible news."

"The other reason I wanted to meet with you is to introduce you to Richard for redundancy, as another contact here if ever you can't get in touch with me." Bill sipped his tea and paused. "Just between us, the latest war intelligence points to things getting much worse here in the coming months. We all need to be prepared for it."

"Worse in France overall or worse in Paris?" I asked, wrapping my arms around myself, thinking of Jacques.

"Both, I'm afraid," he said. "And I'm not being an alarmist; I'm being a realist. Nobody believes Germany will attack France but me and Colonel de Gaulle, but it's coming. I've been working with the American Hospital; we're transforming it into a military facility, with a unit for blood donations and the ability to treat shrapnel wounds, gas attacks, or damage from bombs."

I shivered, and Jean and I looked at each other, both of us absorbing the gravity of what Bill was saying.

"When things take a turn, I want you to report on absolutely everything that is happening here—in the government, in the streets, anything—for as long as you possibly can. Hire more English-speaking reporters and writers if you must; just do it. Promise me you will do that?"

"Absolutely," Jean said.

"We'll do everything we can," I said.

Chapter Eleven

Wednesday, April 24, 1940

Dearest Raymond,

I'm writing to you from my apartment balcony on a warm April afternoon; our new poodle, Ondie, is sleeping next to me on his back, so he can feel the sun on his belly. After the coldest winter ever recorded in France, you can imagine how good it feels to have a real spring day in Paris. People are out at the parks and sitting outdoors in the cafés for the first time in ages — a gift from the weather gods in these dark times.

On the surface, things appear somewhat normal. We have all had to adapt to the food and gas rations and the air-raid drills. Charles and Fern Bedaux and the Wilkinsons have thrown some extravagant parties, and the other night I went to the premiere of a spectacular new song-and-dance revue starring Josephine Baker and Maurice Chevalier. I had them both on for an interview the night before the show, and they were delightful. Perhaps you heard it?

But, of course, the relative normalcy is an illusion; with Germany's occupation of Denmark and increased fighting on France's northern border, anyone paying attention is holding their breath, wondering what in the world is to come next.

In my last call with Jacques, he told me that all military leaves had been canceled and that his unit was on the move, but he could not say to where. I worry constantly about his safety, of course. I begged him to come back to Paris, to use his lungs as an excuse. But in the end, I know he needs to satisfy his yearning to serve his country and his sense of adventure — oh, how I wish he had been able to do both before we met!

I have been working harder than I ever have before in my life, as it's the only way to maintain my sanity with Jacques away at war, and I hope you and Gladys are well and coping in whatever way you can.

I spend most nights at the radio station interviewing American expatriates and Frenchmen and anyone who can give Americans perspective on what's really going on here. And in every single letter I receive from my American listeners, they express sympathy and a strong desire to aid France. It is the political fighting in Washington that is making it impossible. The many letters coming from the States tell me our radio programs are making a difference, that we are changing Americans' perspectives about the war, but the news reports about Congress and Roosevelt tell me it's still not enough.

I am spending many of my daytime hours volunteering, sending much-needed supplies to prisoner-of-war camps and aiding refugees heading south out of Paris. My dear friend Elise has volunteered to drive ambulances to the front, transporting wounded French and British soldiers from the battlefield. In an hour, I am attending a ceremony to honor her and the other volunteers before the units begin their work.

Thank you for your last letter, and for your very generous deposit into our Chase Bank account. It seems it is taking much longer to send and receive mail from the US. But *writing home to you all gives me some peace, and receiving your letters means more than you know.*

I will continue to keep you updated on Jacques. Please pray for him and for a quick end to this war. Bless you.

All my love—

Drue

I mailed the letter to Jacques's father on the way to the ceremony. Jacques's stepmother, Gladys, was American, so they had made the decision to leave for the States in August. As I rode my bike for the first time since December, the sun was warm on my face and the wind wasn't blowing through my every layer of clothing. The ceremony was to take place in the massive courtyard in Les Invalides, an impressive collection of seventeenth-century buildings that included museums and monuments to France's military history as well as a veteran's hospital. It also included the dome church, whose glittering golden roof was a Parisian landmark that never failed to impress, particularly on a day like today, where it glistened against a cloudless blue sky.

I spotted Jean waiting out front for me at the ornate black-and-gold wrought iron gate on the north front of the complex. He was leaning against a wall, wearing dark pants and a white button-down shirt, unshaven per usual. Distracted and writing in a notebook, he didn't even notice me until I stopped my bike right in front of him.

We exchanged greetings, found a place to lock my bike, and headed toward the entrance.

"I thought we could split up; if you could interview some of the drivers before the ceremony starts, I'll interview some of the Red Cross administrators," Jean said.

"Sounds good, I . . ."

I heard someone yelling my name and looked up to see Richard O'Brien in a beige suit, jogging toward us, waving frantically.

"What on earth?" I said, frowning at Jean.

"Drue, Jean, I can't believe I actually found you," Richard said when he finally reached us, hands on his knees, breathless. "You need to come with me to the embassy right now."

"The ceremony is starting very soon. We had interviews planned. Could we just wait until this is over?" Jean asked.

"No, sorry, it's too important. I promised Bill I would find you and bring you back."

"Can you at least tell us what this is about?" I asked, and then, starting to panic a little, I asked, "Is it about Jacques?"

"No. And I cannot discuss this with you in such a public setting; it's classified," Richard said, a bead of sweat dripping down his hairline.

"Classified?" I said, squinting at him in the sun, trying to guess what could be the source of such urgency.

"*Yes*," Richard said, clearly aggravated. "You must come with me now, and all will be explained."

"Oh." I nodded. "OK, I'll just unlock my bike over there and we can go."

"Classified cannot be good news," Jean said when I returned. Richard was already walking ahead, motioning for us to follow.

"Probably not," I said, and we looked in each other's eyes.

"Let's go find out," Jean said, putting his notebook away. "Whatever it is, we'll face it together."

∾

This time, our meeting with Bill and Richard O'Brien was not over tea in the library but in Bill's wood-paneled office. The sun was close to setting, and Bill pulled all the curtains as Richard went through the room looking under lamps and tables and examining electrical outlets.

"What are you doing?" I asked Richard.

"Looking for bugs," he said.

"You think the Germans are bugging the embassy?" Jean asked.

"Yes," Bill said. He had placed four crystal snifters on his mahogany desk and was pouring cognac in each of them. "We're not sure who or how, but we've found them on two occasions now, so we're checking regularly."

He passed out the snifters as Richard sat down in the lone empty leather chair next to Jean and me.

"Unfortunately, the Nazis have far too many friends in this country," Bill said, raising his glass in a toast. "But it appears that you, Drue Leyton, are not one of them, and that is why we are here now."

"Bill, I'm sorry, what?" I asked. I had frozen, holding my snifter in midair, bracing for what he was about to say.

"We have staff that monitor German radio constantly," Bill said. "In their French-language broadcasts these past few days, they have issued a death warrant. For you."

"But . . . what does that even mean?" I asked. "I mean, obviously it's nothing good, but . . ."

"You have been added to the long list of people the Nazis plan to execute when they conquer France," Richard said. It was clear he hated to be the bearer of this news.

"And they named me. Specifically *me*?" I looked at Richard and then at Bill, blinking, trying to wrap my head around the words he had just uttered.

"Yes," Richard said. He paused before he continued to speak. "They've issued a death warrant for, to quote, 'the American actress, Drue Leyton,' citing your 'pro-British, anti-German radio broadcasts.'"

"When did they say this?" Jean asked, anger in his voice. He downed his cognac and slammed the snifter on Bill's desk.

"They have announced it in at least five separate broadcasts," Bill said, speaking very carefully. "That we know of. Probably more."

"Death warrant. Well, this is . . . this is a first for me," I said, putting my glass down. A wooziness came over me; it felt like the room was swaying.

"Drue?" Jean said, grabbing my wrist. "You are ghostly white. Are you OK? Drue? Answer me."

It was like his voice was coming from the other end of a tunnel, and I stood up, seeing the dark spots in my vision that always preceded fainting. Jean stood up with me, his arm around my shoulders, holding me up.

"Just . . . I think some air . . . ," I said. And then everything went black.

~

I woke up to the smell of books, lying on a leather sofa, a cold cloth on my forehead. I kept my eyes closed as I listened to Jean, Bill, and Richard speak of me as if I weren't in the embassy library a few feet from them.

"Should we take her to the hospital?" Richard asked in a soft, nervous voice.

"No, that's not necessary," Jean said. "She should be fine in a minute. She just had a bit of a shock, as anyone would to hear that news."

"I'm going to suggest she leave the country immediately," Bill said, an urgency in his voice. "She should change her name to Drue Tartière permanently."

"I agree," Jean said, though there was a hesitancy in his tone.

I breathed in and out, eyes still closed, absorbing the fact that the Nazis had a target on my back. In life, I had always thought there were "before and after" moments. My first film role in Hollywood. My first marriage. My divorce . . . Meeting Jacques. Taking the job at Paris Mondiale. These were all moments that changed my life in monumental ways, for better or for worse. Having the Nazis announce their plans for my execution was certainly a pivotal before-and-after moment for me. The question was, How was I going to handle it?

I could let the fear of this threat consume me, as I had been letting my fear for Jacques's safety fill me with constant anxiety since September. But I knew that it would lead to a nervous breakdown if

I didn't find the strength to change my perspective. If I was going to stay in France, continue to work in radio, have a husband off to war, I was going to have to stop living—or sometimes drowning—in perpetual terror and anxiety about the future, because I wouldn't survive. I thought of Dorothy Thompson's words at the Ritz when I had asked her if she was afraid of the Nazis' retaliation for her actions, her writing, and her criticisms, if they were to get to her.

"Afraid? No," she had said with passion, her red hat shadowing the fierce determination in her eyes. "I am not afraid of them. I realized a long time ago that you mustn't surrender to fear. I am a little bit older than you, and I've gone through some things, so here's a bit of advice—it's only when we are no longer afraid that we truly begin to *live*. I am not afraid of them, and you shouldn't be either."

Her words seemed prescient now. It was time for me to take that advice. Love and hope over fear. Courage over all-consuming worry. There was no alternative. I opened my eyes. The three men were standing by the window, drinks in hand, the late-day sun outlining their silhouettes as they tried to determine my future for me.

"Can one of you get me another glass of cognac now?" I said in a loud voice, sitting up.

Jean hurried over and sat next to me, hand on my arm. "Are you OK?" he asked, examining my complexion. "Take it slow. Do you need something to eat? Have you had any food at all today?"

"They just brought in some cheese and bread and fruit," Bill said, pointing to a platter on the coffee table. "But if you need something more, I can ask the chef."

"We could also get you some aspirin, or coffee?" Richard said.

"Gentlemen, thank you all for your concern, but I am fine," I said as Bill handed me the cognac. "It was just a bit of a shock to hear that the Nazis want to kill me, that's all."

"That's an understatement," Richard said with a smile. "I am so very sorry I was the bearer of bad news. And I am relieved you are awake and well. If you all will excuse me, Bill and I have another meeting starting in ten minutes about those other expatriates."

We said our goodbyes to Richard and settled into the couches. Jean put a small plate of Camembert, sliced baguette, and grapes in front of me, and I helped myself to some.

"Tell me, Bill, have they mentioned anyone else from Paris Mondiale?" I asked. "What about Jean?"

"They've had Jean in their sights for some time now," Bill said. "So you're in good company."

I patted Jean on the shoulder and smiled, and he just shrugged.

"I heard you talking about my leaving," I said. "I decided, lying on the couch just now, that I am not going anywhere."

Jean looked at Bill as if to say, *I told you so.*

"They've issued a death warrant for me," I said. "So now I just . . . stop doing my job? What more can they threaten me with beyond *killing* me?"

"You'd be surprised," Bill said. "I've heard some horrific stories of other kinds of threats they've made good on."

"Don't tell me," I said. "I don't want to know. In the meantime, Jean and I might as well keep broadcasting for as long as we can."

"I actually have to agree with you," Jean said.

"Good," I said, and this time he smiled back. "Thank you."

"Now wait a minute," Bill said, holding his hand up. "What would Jacques say about this?"

"I think he would also agree," I said. "But I don't even know where Jacques is right now, so I need to make this decision for myself."

Bill put his drink down and leaned over, elbows on his knees, rubbing his face. He had aged this past year—more gray hairs, new lines on his face. I didn't envy his role.

"I have a hundred other things I need to get to today, and I know how stubborn you are. I anticipated this might be your reaction. You can keep broadcasting; your programming to America is the best we've got right now."

"Thank you, and I appreciate you looking after me, I do," I said, feeling pride at his words. "But, like you, I can't leave."

"I know," Bill said, giving me a sad smile as he picked up his glass and swirled his cognac. "As I said, you both need to be more alert, because you are both most definitely being monitored by spies for the Germans."

"But . . . Will they *do* anything to me? To us? More than keep tabs? Could they make good on the death threats?"

"At the moment, no, I truly don't think so," Bill said. "But that could change quickly. So you need to have a contingency plan, should France capitulate to Germany. If that happens, you *must* change your name to Tartière—Drue Leyton is no longer in the country. And you need to find a place outside of Paris to live quietly for a while if the city gets too dangerous. Promise me you will do that? Come up with a plan and be ready?"

"Yes, of course," I said.

"I have already been thinking about all of that too," Jean said.

"And you still think France will fall to Germany?" I asked, though I was certain I knew the answer.

"More than ever." Bill's expression was grave. "The fever dream of this so-called phony war is about to break."

Chapter Twelve

May 21, 1940

For the month of April and into May, Jean and I had continued to broadcast the exact kind of programming that had led to the death warrant the Nazis had issued for me. There had been something freeing about that day at the embassy when I had first learned of it. After accepting that I was on the Nazis' most-wanted list, I had let my anger about it fuel my passion to do more to fight against them. Jean and I worked long hours to put out the best, most persuasive broadcasting to the American public that we could. We had Dorothy Thompson on whenever she was in France, and several of her friends in the newspaper business, including acclaimed journalist Vincent Sheean.

But by mid-May, all of France was mobilized, as Bill Bullitt's ominous prediction came true in a way that shocked the world. On May 10, Germany had invaded the Netherlands, Belgium, and Luxemburg, launching a vicious, strategic, and prolonged attack on France through these Low Countries and the dense and rough terrain of the Ardennes Forest in the south.

The false veil of security that the so-called phony war had provided Paris fell away, and within days it was as if it had never existed. French soldiers returning from the front told tales of disaster and disorganization, even as thousands of young men were heading there, demoralized before they even left their homes and families. One evening at the station, Dorothy Thompson shared a heartfelt piece about the soldiers' departures:

> Nobody smiles. Nobody sings. . . . The whistle blows. The officer holds his girl's cheek to his. The soldier kisses his girl on the mouth. Just once more!
> *Nobody watches anyone else. No one pretends. No one is pretending anything. "Kill a Boche for me, darling." Didn't they say that in the last war? No one says a word about Boche or killing. Not a word. Not a flag. Not a salute . . . not an "au revoir." They pull apart and the men crowd into the cars . . . They look through open windows—a thousand different faces, not one like another, not one common expression, not one replaceable face . . .*
> *The train begins to move. The men wave. The women wave and, weeping, smile. No one calls "Viva la France!"*
> *There goes France.*

And as the young soldiers left, the refugees arrived. We had experienced war refugees coming into the city before, but this time a sea of humanity descended as thousands of people from invaded Belgium flooded into the city by train; others came in old-fashioned automobiles and trucks, farm tractors and private cars, many of them covered on top with grass and flowers for camouflage. They had been forced from their homes at a moment's notice, taking only what they could carry. Many of the trains and cars had been bombed by the Germans, and there were horrific stories of refugees being mowed down by machine-gun-toting Nazis.

On the third Tuesday morning in May, Nadine and I went to volunteer to help the refugees that were temporarily housed at Gare Montparnasse. We found ourselves speechless as we arrived at the dirty gray train station. The stench in the air was so overpowering you couldn't help but gag, and grief and misery blanketed everything.

An elderly woman with long, greasy gray hair, in a shawl splattered with blood, was sitting in the middle of the chaos, inconsolable and wailing about her missing son and her unfed dogs she had to leave behind. The echoes of babies crying bounced off the walls in a tragic chorus. A raven-haired girl in a dirty blue dress with cuts and mud all over her legs sat in a corner nearby, singing a lullaby to a doll she had wrapped in an old rag.

"Excuse me, excuse me." A tall middle-aged woman grabbed my hand, speaking French with a strong nasal accent. "I must find my daughter, she is eighteen. She said she would meet me here. She must be here. Who is in charge? Someone must know where she is! Please help me."

Her eyes were red-rimmed, and her voice kept rising as she spoke, manic with grief and fear for her daughter's safety.

"I . . . I will see if I can find someone to help you," I replied in French, looking into her eyes, trying to convey the empathy I felt for her. "I hope you find her safe."

"Thank you," she whispered as a stream of tears made a trail through the dirt on her face. She shook her head and wandered away in a daze.

"I have to get two of the station's reporters down here," I said, choking out the words, almost too emotional to speak. "America needs to know what is happening. And so many children."

There were hundreds of children of all ages, some staring into space and rocking themselves for comfort, some sleeping, crowded together on benches.

"How could God let this happen?" Nadine asked as she took out a handkerchief and tried to compose herself.

"We can't blame God for the evil of men," I said, looking out, trying to find the woman looking for her daughter, but she had already disappeared into the crowd. "God had nothing to do with this."

"Oh, Drue, Nadine." Kathleen Wilkinson came hurrying up to us, a medical apron over her gray pantsuit, her hair covered in a kerchief. "Thank you so much for coming. I feel like we're not even making a dent in terms of helping these poor souls. More volunteers are coming this afternoon. We're setting up a food line—Nadine, would you please help with that? You know your way around cooking. Drue, we've received many donations of fresh clothes for the children; would you help me distribute as many as we can? Oh, and diapers, many of these babies need diapers and canned milk."

We got to work. Nurses arrived from the American Hospital to help tend to the wounded; more female volunteers from all walks of Parisian life came to do whatever they could to help. We sorted clothes into sizes for adults and children and distributed them to families. I helped the nurses, getting bandages and other supplies and helping triage patients, determining the urgency of their need for treatment. The work was exhausting and heartbreaking—the metallic smell of blood mingled with even more overpowering odors—and after several hours I had to take a quick break for a cup of coffee and a cigarette and a breath of fresh air outside the station.

"How are you holding up?" Kathleen Wilkinson followed me out, looking as frayed as I felt.

"Better than anyone in there," I said, nodding back to the station, then looking up at the sky and blinking back tears. "I'm going to need to go home and have a good cry after this. It's hard to even process so much suffering."

"I know," she said, her voice quiet. "It's too much to bear."

We stood there in silence, smoking, trying to compose ourselves so we could go back inside and keep helping.

"I hope you're going home for some rest soon," I said. "You've been here longer than anyone."

"I will," she said. "Tell me, if the Germans invade and get close to the city, will you stay?"

"I don't know," I said. I had told her about the Nazi death warrant. "I'd like to try to stay in Paris for as long as I can, but I'm not sure if that will be possible. Even if I do change my name to Tartière, it's not like I can easily hide here. How about you?"

"Tudor wants to go to our home in the South of France, in Antibes," she said. "I want to stay. But if we do go, I will of course let you know. You and Nadine are welcome."

"Thank you," I said. "I have been considering Barbizon if we need to get out. There's a villa on the main street owned by friends of Jacques's parents that I stayed at a couple of summers ago. Villa L'Écureuil. It was lovely, with a private courtyard and cottage out back. I was going to see if it was available to rent."

"Villa Squirrel." She said the English translation of the name with a smile, tossing her cigarette and stepping on it with her heel. "I love the sound of it. Are you going to the studio tonight?"

"I am. I can stay for about another hour, and then I'm going to go home and change and grab a quick bite to eat with Nadine. We can come back tomorrow to help."

"Thank you," she said with a sigh. "Thousands more are expected."

"Thousands?" I gasped. "I'll make a plea to Americans tonight on the broadcast, reporting about the refugees, asking for donations. It can't hurt."

"No, it can't," she said. "For God's sake, if Americans could just witness what we're seeing."

～

After I had a quick nap and a dinner of potato-and-leek soup with Nadine, the evening weather was so pleasant I took a bike ride through the city to try to clear my head of all I had witnessed earlier in the day. Riding down the Champs-Élysées, I drove by street sweepers lined up like oversize sentries down the center of the grand boulevard, placed there to block small planes from landing. Other wide streets had garbage trucks and various large vehicles parked for the same purpose. This was what it had come to for the city that I loved. What would come next?

By the time I walked into Jean's office a half hour later I was tired but at least refreshed from the cool night air and the brisk ride. He was staring out the dirty window smoking a cigarette, per usual, the cloud over his desk particularly thick this evening.

I knocked on the doorframe, and he jumped.

"Oh, come in," he said, waving me to the seat across from him. "Sorry, I was lost in thought. Claude is going to join us too. We have much to discuss before we begin broadcasting tonight."

I took off my navy windbreaker and my beret and hung them on the hook on the office door before I sat. Jean looked exceptionally pale tonight.

"Are you feeling all right? You look tired."

"I could say the same about you," he said, and I knew he was right. "I'm having some stomach pain lately. It's the stress of these times; it's getting to all of us."

"That is why I brought refreshments," Claude said, swooping into the office with a bottle of red wine under one chubby arm and holding three wineglasses upside down in the other hand. "Very stressful times call for excellent Burgundy."

"I shouldn't; we have a long night ahead," I said, holding up my hand, which Claude batted down.

"Nonsense, you'll be fine, *ma fille*, and I have a feeling we'll need it for whatever Jean has to tell us," Claude said as he handed a glass to Jean. Jean just nodded, and so I took the third glass.

"A toast," Claude said, holding up his glass as he sat down next to me in the twin cracked leather chair. "To all we have accomplished at Paris Mondiale and all that we will continue to do, however long it lasts."

We clinked glasses and sipped.

"First," Jean said, "on French-language German radio, there was yet another call for your execution. I just, well—the Ministry thought you should be aware."

I took a big gulp of Burgundy and slammed my hand down on his desk.

"Oh for God's sake, you know what? Good. That means we're doing our job. Today I worked with refugees and saw the aftermath of what they did in Belgium. I'm too furious and sickened to be afraid anymore; I'm willing to do or say anything against them. They are monsters."

I hadn't realized I felt that way, truly, until I said it out loud. It was completely liberating.

"Yes, I like this feistiness," Claude said, raising his glass to me. "To hell with the Boche bastards."

"Indeed," Jean said, amused. Then, looking in my eyes, he said, "You've certainly recovered from your initial shock about it."

"I have," I said. "And then some."

"I'm glad, because the other thing I wanted to discuss is what happens next here at the station. The news from the front just continues to get worse," Jean said. "There are a total of forty-two staff members here. Starting tomorrow, we will keep automobiles and a bus out front, so we are ready to evacuate at a moment's notice. I suggest you pack a bag and either keep it here at the studio or bring it back and forth. The Ministry will let us know when it's time to evacuate; we will keep broadcasting in the meantime."

"Ha! I am not going anywhere," Claude said with a snort, laughing.

"What are you talking about?" Jean asked. "Of course you are coming. And we need you to continue broadcasting."

"I am a fat sixty-one-year-old man," Claude said, pride in his voice as he balanced his wineglass on his belly. "The Germans will not bother someone like me. I will be your eyes and ears while you're gone. I'm not leaving. Smitty knows enough about what I do; he can do my job."

Jean rested his elbows on the desk and rubbed his hands over his face, thinking.

"OK, fine," he said. "But I know you; you get into heated discussions at the cafés all the time. You need to be more discreet."

"Jean's right," I said. I had seen some of Claude's antics.

"*Ma fille*, don't worry about me," Claude said, patting my hand. "I have lived in this country much longer than you have. In France, we argue bitterly and then always kiss at the end."

"I have also lived in this country a long time, and you are more combative than most," Jean said. "Please, take care and listen to us."

"Yes, yes," Claude said, rolling his eyes.

"May I bring Nadine with us? And our puppy, Ondie?" I asked Jean. I couldn't imagine leaving the two of them behind. They had become my little Parisian family since Jacques left.

"The dog? Really?" Jean said, making a face.

"Yes, the dog," I said. "What else would I do with him?"

"Have you no soul?" Claude looked at Jean, aghast. "She brings the dog. Why would you even question it?"

"All right, all right, the dog can come," Jean said, cracking a small smile. "And I guess Nadine can too."

"Will Germaine be coming?" I asked. I had grown curious about Jean's mysterious wife, as I still had yet to meet her.

"No, are you kidding?" Jean said. He looked away from me, his tone cynical with a hint of bitterness. "She would rather die than leave this city."

I couldn't imagine being away from Jacques if I didn't have to be. It made me sad for the state of Jean's marriage.

"Have you heard any more of Jacques?" Claude asked.

"He's still somewhere in Northern Europe, as far as I know," I said. I had been trying to compartmentalize my heartache and worry and had been doing a better job at it than I had at first. But the thought of leaving the city where we had spent our happiest days of marriage stirred up all my emotions again. "And I know he won't be taking leave anytime soon."

"I imagine not," Claude said, sympathy in his eyes as he looked at me. "But when you leave Paris, I will keep an eye out for him too, just in case."

"Thank you, my dear friend," I said. Then, looking at the clock, I added, "Regarding tonight, Smitty is writing a piece about the refugees at Gare Montparnasse as we speak. I need to make a plea for donations as well."

"Yes, time to get to work," Jean said, pulling out the programming schedule for the evening. "That's all we can do."

Chapter Thirteen

June 3, 1940

It was a perfect June day, the sky a cloudless blue, and Elise and I were sitting on the terrace at Brasserie Lipp, catching up over glasses of Sancerre. She had the afternoon off for the first time since she had started volunteering as an ambulance driver, and I had a couple of hours in between helping with the refugees and going to the station. The streets and cafés were vibrant and colorful and packed with people. But the only topic of discussion was the war.

There was a palpable collective anxiety in the air, as strangers debated in the streets and café patrons shared whatever new information they had with their fellow diners. Every day, people lined up in front of the newsstands before the newspaper couriers had even arrived. And then there were the ever-present radios, in courtyards and offices, in restaurants and even in theaters—you could not escape the relentless reports on French radio. It was like the whole city was listening with bated breath for some snippet of positive news. I had been told on more than one occasion by a neighbor or acquaintance that they had started waking up to listen to my American broadcasts, trying to find something hopeful amid all the dark reports.

"If I do end up going to Barbizon because it's not safe here, you're welcome to come with me and Nadine—your mother and Corinne too, naturally," I said to Elise as we shared possible future scenarios and plans. People had started to flee the city, and Jean had cars and trucks ready for us in front of the station at all hours, but so far, the government had told us to remain where we were.

"That is very kind of you," she said. "Though my mother told me the other night she is not going anywhere no matter what happens."

"Have you had any word from Philippe? Any updates on his whereabouts?"

"No, not since the note I told you about a few weeks ago," she said, resignation in her eyes as she talked of her husband. "I am sure he is at the front. I can feel it in my bones that he is not safe. I keep thinking I will see him, praying by some miracle I'll find him on one of these ambulance runs, which I realize is ridiculous."

I reached across and squeezed her hand. "These are not easy times for wives."

"These are not easy times for anyone," Elise said, offering me a cigarette.

"That is true," I said, watching the people passing by, trying to forget for a moment.

"I've been worried about you; you seemed quite fragile for a while, like you were always on the verge of breaking, but now you seem better to me. Are you, despite the German target on your back?"

"I am," I said. "After saying goodbye to Jacques the last time he was here, I was in such a state. And learning about the Nazi threats against me didn't help, of course. But I realized I was not going to survive this war living on the constant verge of falling apart. And helping the Belgian refugees has given me some much-needed perspective."

I shuddered, recalling the images of Gare Montparnasse, of mothers losing their minds from grief, of children with life-altering injuries.

"I feel the same after driving these soldiers," Elise said.

The air-raid siren started just as the waiter brought out our *salade Niçoise*.

"Not again," Elise said, cursing. The sirens were blaring at least once a day, it seemed, but mercifully nothing had come near Paris yet.

The black-vested waiters on the patio, many of them exasperated, threw up their hands and groaned as they filed into the restaurant.

"Mesdames, I am so sorry," our waiter with the silver mustache said as he passed our table. "It's required of us."

"What do you want to do? There is a shelter right over there." Elise pointed her finger at one of the city's many covered trenches, pouring me more Sancerre with her other hand. "Or we could ask to go to the basement with the staff."

"I don't know; we weren't invited," I said, taking a sip of wine, looking around the patio. A few patrons got up and left, but many were like us, still sitting, contemplating what to do next; some had just continued to eat and drink and ignore it entirely.

Then the glasses on our wrought iron table started vibrating, and I heard the sound, like thunder but more menacing, as there wasn't a cloud in the sky.

The thunderous roaring sound became deafening, and then the sky was dark, not with clouds but with planes. Dozens and dozens of planes, as far as the eye could see.

"Are they ours? Are they *ours?*" a young woman in a white polka-dot dress asked in a panicked voice as chaos erupted and everyone on the terrace got up, knocking over tables, glasses shattering as people scrambled to find shelter.

"No. They are not ours. Those are Luftwaffe planes," Elise said to her, her voice flat. She looked up at the sky and let out a streak of curse words.

We decided to go inside the restaurant and sit halfway down the narrow staircase leading to the basement, invited or not. I had gotten so careless about my gas mask I had left it at home that morning; Elise didn't have one either.

The roaring continued, and part of me wanted to be outside, to see what they were going to do, to see if the French would counterattack in any way. I wanted to bear witness, so I could report it that night to the rest of the world. Paris itself was now under siege; would America even care?

Then came the sounds of explosions, somewhere not in the immediate area but not too far away, and then even more planes. The first explosion made me jump, and I grabbed Elise's arm as we braced ourselves for more. The deafening chaos went on for an hour, although, sitting on the cramped staircase with my knees up to my chin, it had seemed much longer. Finally, it was silent, and after about twenty minutes, the waitstaff started to come up the stairs, even though the all-clear siren had not sounded.

Everyone in the restaurant hurried outside to see what, if anything, we could see. We weren't the only ones, as people started coming out of buildings and shelters, looking up to the sky, trying to get a sense of what the hell had just happened. There were dark clouds of smoke rising from the direction of Montmartre, and from Neuilly, where the American Hospital was. The woman in the polka-dot dress was leaning against a lamppost weeping. Some restaurant patrons returned to their tables on the terrace; people in the streets resumed walking to wherever they were headed. Someone turned up the volume on a nearby radio, and several of the customers and staff crowded around it to see what they could learn about the attack.

"They are going to need me back at the hospital, ready to drive," Elise said. "If it's still standing, that is. It looks like some of the bombing was in that area."

"I'm going to check on Nadine; she was meeting a friend this morning in Montmartre," I said. "Then I'm going to get Smitty and view the damage so we can report this."

"Good," Elise said, her voice simmering with anger as her eyes filled with tears. "Tell the world. I'm so filled with rage right now I could scream. How dare they do this to my city."

"How dare they," I whispered. "Be safe and stay in touch, my friend," I said, my voice cracking as I gave her a tight embrace.

We said our goodbyes, and I biked home as fast as I could. By the time I got to my apartment building, my blouse was sticking to me with sweat. I ran up the stairs, yelling for Nadine, praying she was home safe with Ondie and not still in Montmartre. I heard barking as I reached the door, and Nadine opened it before I knocked. We hugged each other as Ondie jumped up and tried to get in between us with his black poodle paws.

"Thank God, I saw the smoke from Montmartre and . . . ," I said, letting myself relax. They were safe.

"I was home by noon, and I wasn't sure where you were," she said, distraught. "Ondie and I went into the coal cellar with everyone who was here in the building. I've been listening to the radio since I came back up. Bombing in Montmartre and Neuilly. Including a school. It's horrific."

"Oh no," I said with a gasp. "I need to change my clothes and head out to survey the damage so I can report on it tonight."

"Would you like a cup of tea before you go?" Nadine asked.

"A quick one, please; thank you so much," I said, and she put the kettle on our stove.

I splashed water on my face and changed into a fresh blouse and my black culottes, which were better for biking, and pulled my curls back into a low bun to tame them from the heat of the day.

Nadine brought out cups of tea. It was almost four o'clock, and I had so much to do, but I sat and took a deep breath in, trying to calm myself and prepare for the long night of work ahead of me. And after today, I needed to have a conversation with Nadine.

"I expect after what's happened, the government, including the Ministry, will be leaving the city soon, days if not hours from now, and the broadcasting staff will follow them wherever they go."

"I have my bag, and Ondie's packed and ready whenever that happens," Nadine said.

"That's good," I said, clearing my throat. "But listen—your parents, I know you said they went somewhere south?"

"Yes," Nadine said, frowning at me. "They are with my mother's sister in Collioure, near the border with Spain. Why?"

"I need to say this. When we hired you as a housekeeper, I never knew that we would become such dear friends," I said. "I have made peace with the fact the Germans want to kill *me*. But if you stay with me, you'll be in danger too. So, please, go to Collioure instead. For your own safety."

"You . . . you don't want me to go with you?" she asked, her eyes growing wide, her voice full of indignation. She put her teacup down.

"No, I'd actually love for you to come with me," I said. "I'm going to be with a group of mostly men on the road, and the only two I am friendly with are Jean and Smitty. But I think you should consider going to be with your family. I don't want to put you in danger. What if the Germans do track me down at some point? You will be at risk too."

"Ha—there is nowhere to hide from the war," Nadine said with a cynical laugh. "Not even in Collioure. You have given me the chance for a life in Paris that I never thought I would have. And . . . unless you are firing me, I would like to stay. I'll go wherever you go."

Ondie came onto the balcony at the exact moment she said this, as if on cue. He curled up and sat on my foot. With Jacques away, I needed them both to come with me, more than I had been willing to admit to myself.

"I'm not firing you," I said with a smile, blinking back tears. "And I'm so grateful to have you here. I don't know how I would have managed without you these past months."

"Me neither," she said with a laugh.

We looked out at our street. People were drinking and laughing on the terrace of Café Rita; Hugo was sweeping outside of his shop. All around us, Parisians, at least in this neighborhood, carried on with their day as if it were any other. But we both knew nothing in the city would ever be the same.

Chapter Fourteen

June 10, 1940

It was hard to overstate how fast things deteriorated after the bomb-ings. News from the front was dire, and many of the French troops that had been in Paris began to leave as the German military edged ever closer to the city. During the days that followed, to keep the fuel out of Germany's hands, the Standard Oil petroleum reserves on the outskirts were set afire, filling the sky with a pervasive black smoke that left a sooty residue on everything and added to the miserable atmosphere.

Exactly a week after those first bombs hit, Paris was declared an "open city," waiving its right to resist in exchange for a peaceful occu-pation with no destruction. The French government fled to Tours, and, despite being an American, Bill Bullitt was effectively appointed the de facto mayor of Paris in their absence.

Jean and I, as well as the rest of Paris Mondiale, wanted to follow the government to Tours, but we were told to await word from the Ministry of when we should leave. But the next day when we went to see our superiors there, the building was completely empty, the doors and windows wide open, with evidence of many small fires from the thousands of papers that had been burned. The government, including the Ministry, had abandoned us, with no instructions or warning, no plan for what the future of Paris Mondiale operations might be.

Furious, I went to see Bill Bullitt to find out what he knew. Meanwhile, Jean went to inform the staff that we would be leaving the following morning. When I arrived at the embassy, it was eerily quiet— no secretary to greet me, no bustling frenetic energy of expatriates doing America's business in France.

The door to Bill's office was open, and he didn't notice me as he sat at his desk on the other side of the room, staring out the window, smoking a cigar. He was dressed to the nines as usual in a light-gray summer suit and patriotic tie, but he looked drained and pale; the past few weeks had taken a toll. I knocked on his door just loud enough that he could hear it, and he jumped.

"So sorry, Bill, I was trying not to startle you," I said. "And do I call you Ambassador Bullitt or Mayor Bullitt now?"

"Both? Neither?" He gave me a tired smile. "I'm surprised you're still here. Weren't you supposed to be on the road by now?"

"Yes," I said, "but the order never came." I explained how we had been left behind, and he put a hand over his mouth and groaned.

"The incompetence," he said. "No wonder it's all gone to hell. I hope you're leaving soon?"

"Maybe. I think to Tours? That's why I'm here," I said. "Are you?"

"Leaving? No, absolutely not," he said, shaking his head. "I told FDR no American ambassador has ever cut and run since 1870. I'll be damned if I'm the first. I'm staying. Someone has to be in charge now that the entire French government has left. Prime Minister Reynaud asked me to stay on in the interest of public safety, for when the German troops arrive. So . . . here I am. And on that note . . ."

He reached behind his desk to his liquor cabinet and took out two glasses and his favorite cognac and poured some for both of us. It was barely noon, but I accepted. If nothing else, it was good for my nerves on one of the more surreal days of my life.

"I'm here to get your advice. What should we, as Paris Mondiale, do? What happens now?"

He sat back in his chair, holding his cognac, and looked at me.

"I'm not even going to suggest you leave France . . ."

"Don't; that ship has sailed, and you know it," I said, pointing at him.

"In more ways than one," Bill said with a short laugh. "They aren't going to bother with most Americans still here, but you might be the exception."

"I'm aware of that," I said, taking a deep breath. "I'll be careful."

"So you'll no longer broadcast? Because that's one way of truly being careful."

"I'm still going to broadcast, but I'll go by Tartière outside the studio," I said. "I'm an American citizen married to a Frenchman. I should be fine."

"You really don't think they'll put two and two together—American citizen, blonde curly-haired actress with the same first name as the actress broadcasting for Paris Mondiale?"

"I hope that my death warrant is very low on their priority list for the foreseeable future."

"Hope isn't a survival strategy," he said, eyebrows raised as he looked at me over his glass.

"Maybe not entirely, but it's part of mine," I said. "Otherwise, I'd be curled up in a ball on my bed, paralyzed by fear about Jacques's well-being, about my fate, about how this all ends. I would have fallen apart weeks ago."

"I'm glad you didn't," he said. "Fall apart, that is."

We quietly sipped our cognacs for a moment, and then he spoke.

"Do not go to Tours," he said, waving his arm dismissively. "Trust me when I say it's a waste of time. Head to Bordeaux. My sources tell me the French government will be relocating there soon. There is a powerful radio station outside the city where you can broadcast. And then get on the air and do what I've been doing with Roosevelt—beg America to come to France's aid, describe all of it, all of the ugliest and most horrific parts. Schools bombed . . . little children . . . children killed." Bill swallowed hard and composed himself. "I cannot believe it's come to this. I cannot believe our country still refuses to do more."

I nodded, moved by his emotion.

"You surprised me, you know," he said after a moment. "You left the dazzle of Hollywood behind to marry this dashing Frenchman who, let's be honest, every unmarried woman in Paris wanted. And then he goes to war, and you come to me with this radio-broadcaster idea. I thought you'd last a week—only because the role seemed beneath you and not something you'd be interested in, frankly. I'm proud of you, Drue Leyton."

"I think you mean Drue *Tartière*. And thank you; that means a great deal," I said, giving him a small smile. "I knew I could do the job, as I told you last November. But it evolved into something I didn't expect. I am quite proud of the work we've done, damn the consequences." I winked at him, and he raised his glass.

"You've done a top-notch job. As good as the seasoned journalists you've worked with. Sometimes even better than them."

I leaned over and clinked glasses with him, feeling my face grow warm. I would take the compliment.

"Speaking of journalists, our friend Dorothy sends her regards," Bill said. "She's following the army to the front, to the Maginot Line."

"What?" I gasped.

"You aren't really surprised, are you?" he said, eyebrows raised over his glass.

"No," I said with a laugh. "I'm not. I just hope she makes it back alive."

He nodded in agreement and we sat quietly for a moment, and I imagined Dorothy with a helmet on instead of one of her fashionable red hats, bombs falling as she furiously scribbled in her notebook about the history she was witnessing.

"Do you have any idea what's going to happen now?"

"I have no idea. The government is in chaos," he said, exasperated as he refilled his glass. "Go to Bordeaux, report on everything you can. And, as I said to Dorothy, for God's sake stay safe."

Chapter Fifteen

June 12, 1940

My darling Jacques,

I just received your last letter, and I hope that you are as safe as you can be in Norway. I'm leaving Paris today for Bordeaux in the hopes of setting up a broadcasting station there with the rest of the Paris Mondiale team. It hurts my heart to leave our apartment, for it is like saying goodbye to you all over again. I'm enclosing a letter from your father I recently received, and I hope that it cheers you at least a little to read it.

My friend and coworker Claude Molet, whom I have told you about, will be staying at our apartment to keep an eye on things while Nadine and I are gone. He promises that he can get this letter to you. He's a gregarious older gentleman whom I wish you could meet, as I think you two would get along well. Maybe someday when this is over.

Sweetheart, I don't know what is to happen next, but talking to Ambassador Bullitt left me with a growing sense of dread. If you saw Paris right now you would understand that it's hard to be optimistic. And the exodus of people fleeing — thousands and thousands of people heading south as the Germans get ever closer to the city.

Would you believe Bill Bullitt is currently Paris's temporary American mayor since the French government fled the city? They left with no one in charge. Speaking of Bill, you should send any correspondence care of the American embassy. For now, I think that is our best chance of trying to stay in touch.

Stay safe, my darling. Je t'embrasse. Je t'embrasse. Je t'embrasse.

All my love —
Drue

I handed the letter to Claude and took one more look around my cozy apartment, making sure I hadn't forgotten anything important.

"Nadine and Ondie are waiting downstairs. I'd better go, or Jean might leave without us," I said, joking, as I tucked my hair under my straw hat. It was only eight in the morning, but it promised to be another hot and humid day.

"Jean would never leave without *you*," Claude said.

"Oh, I think he would," I said. "He's not always the most patient and understanding these days."

"Are you OK, *ma fille*?" he said, tilting his head, examining my face. *Ma fille* was French for *my daughter*, and I was touched by my given nickname.

"No," I said, giving him a fake scowl. "But thank you for asking."

He came over and kissed me on both cheeks, and I gave him a tight hug.

"Take care of my little home, please," I whispered in his ear. "And try to enjoy it; someone has to."

"Oh, I will," he said, with a mischievous grin. "Your saucy concierge is coming over for a drink tonight."

I burst out laughing, said a final goodbye, and left my apartment on Rue Saint-Dominique, unsure of when I would return.

An hour later, the forty-two staff members of Paris Mondiale, along with Nadine, Ondie, and three wives of staffers, left our station in a caravan of several cars we had requisitioned, as well as one bus. In the blazing heat, we joined a mass exodus of Parisians who were leaving by any means they could find—some by train or car, others by bicycle, even others by oxen and wagon. The bravest were leaving on foot, carrying their children and their suitcases in their arms, pushing their elderly family members in carts meant for toddlers. The looks on people's faces ranged from resigned to panic-stricken and miserable, and the summer heat became more oppressive as the day wore on.

Farther outside the city, we drove past scenic fields of golden wheat and scattered patches of wildflowers—of red poppies and blue cornflowers—like a Renoir painting come to life. The natural beauty of the landscape stood in devastating contrast to the man-made horrors we witnessed—the dead bodies and the wretched, grief-stricken survivors who mourned them.

The journey proved to be even more difficult than we expected, with abandoned cars and belongings making the drive even harder to navigate. By nightfall it was pouring rain, and we camped in an apple orchard for the night, sleeping in our cars and getting on the road the next morning at dawn.

Many hours later we finally reached Bordeaux, which was now the latest temporary capital of France, as Bullitt had predicted, since the French government had fled Tours and arrived in the city shortly before we did. The atmosphere was a thick stew of humidity, panic, and confusion as thousands of people kept arriving from the north. People were packed into the three most popular cafés in the Place de la Comédie, the picturesque square where the main streets of the city converged, flanked by the architectural beauty of the twelve-column Grand Theatre and Grand Hôtel. Many more were milling around outside, walking up and down the streets, heartsick, restless, and waiting for news, hoping they would somehow be able to return to their homes.

Nadine and I had managed to find a table on the terrace at one of the cafés. After checking out our temporary broadcasting studio, Jean joined us for our first decent meal since we'd left Paris. Ondie wrapped himself around my feet, hoping a piece of cheese would fall his way.

"Oh, hello, Drue, I can't say I'm surprised to see you here."

I had not been paying attention to anything but my plate of food, so I heard the American-accented greeting and looked up to see Fern and Charles Bedaux standing in front of our table. He was wearing a dark short-sleeved shirt and a sour expression, and she was in a pale silk dress, clutching an oversize purse, with multiple strands of pearls around her neck.

"Darling, how are you?" she said, as if we were the best of friends. I stood up to greet her, kissing her on both cheeks, and introduced her and Charles to the table. I was surprised when Jean acknowledged that he knew Charles through mutual friends.

"Isn't this all just dreadful? It's just terrible. All those poor people on the roads, so much suffering I could cry. I have cried, I tell you."

"Yes, it's all too awful for words," I said. "When did you get here?"

"Just this morning. Charles has a few meetings, and then we are heading to Château de Candé, our place in the countryside, isn't that right, Charles? I cannot wait to get out of this place." She said this and looked around, unable to hide her revulsion of the masses, then looked at him as if afraid he might change his mind.

"Yes, we're only here one night," Charles said. He was distracted, barely listening to her. Jean was watching his every move.

"And Charles just sent a cable, offering our estate to Ambassador Bullitt and his staff," Fern said. "If they need to evacuate Paris, they can work and live at the *château*. It will be quite fun if they take us up on it."

"What a generous offer," I said. "But from what the ambassador said to me, he's not leaving anytime soon."

"Oh, I think he might have changed his mind since then," Charles said, focusing back on us. "Or may be given no other option."

I frowned at this, studying Charles's face, wondering what he knew and how.

"And I just wanted to tell you all, you're welcome to stay with us too," Fern gushed. "We have *plenty* of room for guests, and you have an open invitation. We have gardens and tennis courts and a pool—we will have a cocktail hour every evening. It really is quite lovely; if you must evacuate Paris, think of it as a vacation."

Nadine started to cough, and with one look at her I knew she was laughing behind her clenched fist, so I kicked her under the table. Fern did sound ridiculous. She made war sound like a minor inconvenience, an excuse to have a country garden party. For the incredibly wealthy, maybe that was all it was.

"Thank you, that's very kind of you," I said, and Nadine and Jean nodded and said thanks as well.

"Anything else new we should know about, Charles, since leaving Paris?" Jean asked. The two men exchanged a look I couldn't quite decipher.

"Perhaps," Charles said. "Are you broadcasting tonight?"

"In a few hours," Jean said. "At Bordeaux-Lafayette PTT; it's a little bit of a ride outside the city."

"I will come by the studio, then," Charles said. "After my meetings this afternoon I will know more."

"OK, darlings, we are heading to the hotel for a meal now," Fern said. "So we should go. Toodle-oo!"

"Toodle-oo!" Nadine said, imitating her as soon as she was out of earshot, and I couldn't help but laugh because it sounded just like Fern.

"Exactly whose side is Charles Bedaux on in this war?" I asked, watching them disappear into the crowds.

"Oh, I think you know that already," Jean said. "Bedaux is on one side—his own. He will do whatever it takes, work with both sides, as long as it lines his pockets. You cannot trust him entirely, but you can trust the information he provides. He is rarely if ever wrong in his own intelligence gathering."

"So whatever he tells us tonight, what will you owe him for that intelligence?" I asked Jean.

"He mainly deals in favors when it comes to these things," Jean said. "I will owe him a favor in return."

"I don't like the idea of owing that man anything," I said. "Are you sure it's a good idea to be dealing with him at all?"

"Do I think it's a good idea?" he said, raising his eyebrows at me. He had turned pale again, and his voice was aggravated. "I don't think we have a choice. Our government isn't sharing enough with us, and I think we need someone to enlighten us as to what the hell is going on. Don't you?" Jean said this and then winced and clutched his side.

"You're still having those stomach pains? Are you sure you don't want me to track down a doctor for you?" I said.

"Or I could," Nadine said. "I am not working tonight like both of you; let me find one that will see you."

"No, I am fine," Jean said. "It will pass."

"OK," I said. "But let's get the bill. So you can go back to the apartment and rest before tonight."

When he reached down to get his cigarettes out of his pocket, I gave Nadine a look and mouthed, *Find a doctor*, and she gave me a slight nod back. If we were to accomplish anything, we needed Jean in charge and healthy.

Chapter Sixteen

Bordeaux-Lafayette PTT, the radio station outside of Bordeaux, was a massive facility and an engineering marvel. After ocean-bed telephone cables had been severed during the Great War, both the US and France understood the critical need for an alternative means of long-distance communications and had collaborated in the building of Bordeaux-Lafayette. The station's manager proudly informed us that it was one of the most powerful radio stations in the world, with gigantic radio pylon antennae that provided the capability for broadcasting across the globe.

All of us on the Paris Mondiale team would have settled for far less; we were just thrilled and relieved to be able to work again, at least for the time being. I wasn't alone among the staff in feeling that my job was the one thing keeping me from wallowing in utter despair for the state of the country.

As the sound engineers prepared for us to broadcast at our usual time in America that evening, Jean and I found an empty conference room to brainstorm what we should say to our American audience.

"We have news reports and eyewitness accounts of what is happening, and, since you have nobody to interview, Smitty said he'd like to come on and offer up his perspective as a soldier of fortune and citizen of the world," Jean said, giving me a wry smile.

"Oh, that will be interesting," I said with a laugh. "I have some remarks prepared, a plea to America. This will be of a little more of a personal nature than my usual. But desperate times call for desperate measures, as they say . . ."

"Have you written those remarks yet? I'd like to read them before you go on air," Jean said. He was still pale but looked better after our meal at the café and a few hours' sleep.

"I've got some notes, but nothing more than that," I said, though I barely even had that much. "If you'll allow me, I'd like to be a little more off the cuff . . . more authentic."

He looked at me, tilting his head, dangling his cigarette over the tin ashtray between us.

"All right," he said with a sigh. "Desperate times."

"Thank you for trusting me," I said. "I will do my best."

There was a knock on the conference room door, and I looked up to see the freckle-faced young man who had greeted us when we arrived at the station. He lived nearby and was obsessed with radio and had become a sweet ambassador to our team.

"Monsieur? Madame? There is someone here to see you," he said. "A Charles Bedaux."

Jean told him to bring Charles in.

"This will be interesting," I whispered.

Charles didn't bother to knock; he just sauntered into the conference room and pulled out the leather chair at the head of the table on our end. Always impeccably dressed, even he looked beaten down, rings of sweat staining his shirt, his pants wrinkled.

"I know you are going on the air soon, but confidentially, I want to share what I know with you, because things are changing very rapidly."

"I appreciate that," Jean said, and I just nodded.

"It's a good thing you're sitting down."

I crossed my arms, noticing the goose pimples breaking out at these words.

"Paris will be occupied by the Germans in a matter of days, if not hours."

"Oh no," I said, feeling physically nauseated at this news. "Bill knew it was coming. It's unimaginable."

"But it's happened," Jean said, his face grim. "So now what?"

"Well, it's an open city, and so *your* ambassador has single-handedly prevented it from being destroyed." Bedaux nodded at me when he said this, and I thought of Bill Bullitt in that empty embassy building, trying to keep the enemy from decimating the most beautiful city in the world.

"That's not the only news I have, unfortunately. Prime Minister Reynaud had promised the country he would fight to the end," Bedaux said, elbows on the table, making a steeple with his hands.

"And now . . . ?" I asked, holding my breath.

"He cannot make good on the promise," Charles said with a shrug. "He is resigning."

I gasped, and Jean let out a string of curse words.

"So who is going to be in charge?" I asked. "This is madness."

"Indeed," Charles said, though he seemed nonchalant about this turn of events. "Maréchal Philippe Pétain, the current vice premier, is about to take power as president of the republic."

"Pétain?" I said. "How old is he?"

"Eighty-four," Jean said, shaking his head in disbelief.

Pétain was an icon in France, a revered hero of the Great War who had recently served as ambassador to Spain.

"Yes, he is an old man," Bedaux said. "He has a small circle advising him, and it's rumored they are calling all the shots, given his age. And given that the circle is heavily pro-German, you can imagine who is advising *them*."

"So what happens now?" I asked. "What is Pétain going to do?"

"In the short term? He is coming here to give a speech to the nation," Bedaux said.

"Here to the station?" I asked.

"Yes," Bedaux said. "I thought you should know."

"Do you have any idea what he's going to say in this speech?" Jean asked. He was taking notes, and I could see the wheels turning in his brain, trying to figure out what our next move would be.

"No, I wish I did," Bedaux said, standing up from the table, looking at me, then Jean, and back again. "The situation is fluid, and I don't like the direction things are going. I am a transactional man, loyal to no nation. But I, like both of you, love this country. We need to prepare ourselves. Now, if you'll excuse me, I have more people to inform."

We said our goodbyes, and Jean and I sat there, absorbing the news.

"So many questions," I said, my stomach churning.

"Yes, too many," Jean said. "But understand that tonight's broadcast to America? It's possibly our last."

It was a somber atmosphere in the studio before airtime. Smitty and I were together; both of us had our mics set up and were ready to go. After my initial commentary, he was going to read the news and then have an on-air discussion with me. I thought he might be a little too volatile to be on air, but we had no other option.

One of the engineers gave us the one-minute warning from the sound booth as I was still furiously taking notes, debating how and what to say, still contemplating the news that Charles Bedaux had shared and what it all meant.

"You OK there, Leyton?" Smitty asked in a whisper. "Want me to go first?"

"No, no, it's all right," I said, straightening myself in my chair and taking a sip of water. "Thank you, though."

And then the "On Air" light started flashing, and I swallowed my nerves, took a deep breath, and began to speak.

"*Bonjour* from Bordeaux, America," I said, turning on my "radio voice." "This is your host, Drue Leyton. And tonight, sadly, Paris

Mondiale has a new home. If you have read any newspaper or listened to any radio these past few weeks, you know why. France is in trouble, America. It needs—*we* need—your help.

"Like thousands of other Parisians, I and the rest of the Paris Mondiale team had to flee Paris because of the German troops advancing. French families left the city on foot and bicycle, some even in cars—though gas is so scarce, and the roads so crowded, many vehicles were abandoned. I saw elderly men and women passed out on the side of the road from the heat and lack of water. I saw babies, miserable and sunburned and hungry.

"And during this exodus, low-flying German planes known as Stukas swept over the roads and machine-gunned down these innocents. So many . . . so many innocent people murdered." My voice caught as I relived the sights in my mind.

"I saw a little curly-haired boy in brown shorts, no older than five, who had been killed. His mother lay next to him, wailing, crazy with grief, refusing to leave him." I paused and wiped the tears off my face. Smitty nodded at me, encouraging me to keep going.

"I'm trying to paint you a picture of the wretchedness, of the panic and confusion here. And you've listened to my broadcasts; you know I've spoken out against the Germans many times. What you might not know is that they want to kill me for telling you the truth."

I had been so focused on my commentary that I didn't notice the commotion outside the studio until Smitty tapped me and pointed. Jean held up a paper against the glass that read "AIR RAID."

I took another sip of water and nodded, the ground beneath my feet vibrating from the noise outside that was not yet audible in the studio.

Smitty slid a paper across to me that read "Time to go!" Jean was signaling like crazy outside the window; everyone else had evacuated. The floor started to vibrate, and the roar of planes was now loud enough to hear in the studio.

"When children are murdered in broad daylight, this is not the time for what my brilliant friend Dorothy Thompson calls ostrichism," I said, raising my voice over the increasing roar of the planes. "Americans can no longer bury their heads in the sand. Pray for us. Send *help*. This is Drue Leyton broadcasting from Bordeaux, France. *Bonne nuit* and goodnight, America."

Smitty pulled the microphone away from me as the sound became deafening and yelled, "Hear that, America, the sons of bitches are bombing us right now!" as he rushed me out of the studio. Jean grabbed me by the hand, and the three of us sprinted, breathless, through the cavernous station. We made it to Bordeaux-Lafayette's air-raid shelter just before the bombs dropped.

Chapter Seventeen

June 17, 1940

The station and everyone in it were miraculously spared during the bombings the night of our first broadcast from Bordeaux. The next night, on French radio, Prime Minister Reynaud himself made a desperate plea to Roosevelt, asking America to come to France's aid with "clouds of planes." He admitted to the people that France was losing the battle and that it must prevent Hitler from installing a "puppet government."

People in Bordeaux listened in anguish at cafés and on the streets to the prime minister's desperate speech. The reactions ranged from fury and grief to disbelief and denial. "This can't be happening" were the words I heard most. France could not be losing the war; surely *something* would happen to turn things around.

But no silver linings, no glimmers of salvation came for France. On June 14, Bill Bullitt, in his dual role as American ambassador and Paris's mayor, had been the one to declare to America and newspapers around the world that, though the city was quiet, the Nazis were "inside the gates of Paris."

Bullitt's news was followed three days later by loud knocking on the door of our rented flat at seven in the morning on Monday, June 17. It was a disheveled young messenger from the Ministry of Information, which had finally started paying attention to the Paris Mondiale team again since we had begun broadcasting in Bordeaux. Breathless and sweaty, the messenger informed me that Jean and I needed to come to the station immediately.

"I don't understand—what do you need us for at this hour?" I said, frowning at him.

"Marshal Pétain has taken power in France," the messenger said, wiping his brow. "He wishes to make a speech to the nation on the radio this morning."

"And so it appears Bedaux was right," Jean said grimly after the young man left. "The old warhorse is leading the country now."

A little while later, Jean, Smitty, and I were in the studio with a few engineers when Marshal Philippe Pétain entered with an entourage of a half dozen men. He was both shorter and much older looking than I expected, with a bushy white mustache and hooded blue eyes, and he walked erectly but slowly, with a distinct military air.

We made introductions, and, when I came face-to-face with him, he shook my hand, his fingers clammy and knotted with veins.

"I am surprised at the number of Americans still here," he said, sizing me up; though my French was at this point very good, my American accent still gave me away.

"My French husband is here; I could not leave him," I replied.

He grunted at this, not impressed. I gave him my biggest, phoniest Hollywood smile, but he had already turned to Jean.

"There will be many changes in the weeks ahead, including with your radio programming. My deputy will be in touch and let you know what the plans are." Pétain said this in a tone that made it clear it was an order, not a request.

"Yes, sir," Jean said, his voice tight. His color was pale again, but the day before he had refused to go to the local doctor Nadine had found.

Jean led Pétain over to the table where he would give his address, and our new young helper ran over to adjust the microphone, his face red, his hands shaking from nerves. After a minute, Pétain was clearly frustrated with the boy for not moving fast enough.

"*Merde!*" Pétain said. He swore once more and then gave the boy a kick to the leg, so hard that the child let out a yelp like a puppy, his eyes watering.

I ran over to help with the microphone and ushered the poor boy away from the marshal's reach, biting my lip to keep from cursing at the new leader of France. Smitty, who had taken a liking to the boy, looked like he was going to leap over the table and punch Pétain himself. I motioned with my hands and mouthed, *Calm down.*

Nadine was outside the studio window watching with several staff, and I knew that dozens of others throughout the building stood or paced in the hallways, waiting to hear the old man's words over the loudspeakers, knowing that France's fate hung in the balance and with the power of this one man. The "On Air" sign flashed, Jean gave Pétain the sign to start, and, with a pounding in my chest, I listened to history unfolding. His talk was full of flattery and bluster, but it was what he said at the end that devastated everyone listening:

"It is with a broken heart that I tell you today it is necessary to stop fighting. Last night I addressed the adversary to ask him if he is ready to seek with me . . . after the actual fighting is over, and with honor, the means of putting an end to hostilities."

He finished his remarks, got up, and walked out of the studio without saying another word, as his entourage of sycophants hurried to fall in behind him. I seethed as I watched them leave.

Nobody in the room spoke, the faces around me stunned and silent. The little boy had decided to let the tears fall, and one of the engineers started wiping his own eyes. It took me a moment to realize the meaning of Pétain's words. Up until then, France had not given up the fight against Germany, but it seemed, from this address, that its new leader had decided to quit, forcing the country to do so along with him.

"Wait, did that old codger just call for peace with the Nazis? Does he . . . does he want to *negotiate* with *them*?" Smitty said to nobody in particular. "What the hell happens now?"

"I'll say one thing: that man showed no sign of a broken heart," I said.

I thought of Jacques and all the soldiers who had fought and sacrificed so much. I thought of the thousands of scared and desperate refugees packed into the city and beyond. This man was not the leader that would guide France out of one of its darkest moments in history.

Jean was frowning, staring at the floor, arms crossed, cigarette in hand. I could see him considering all the angles, what it all meant.

"I need to talk to some people to get more information," Jean said. "You and Smitty meet me at the café at the Place de la Comédie this evening to figure out next steps. And we must get the members of the team that are now in danger of imprisonment out of the country immediately."

He listed two British sound engineers and an assistant, and two other Jewish staff members.

"Drue, please inform them that they need to have their things packed to go at a moment's notice."

"Of course," I said.

"I will see you at the café tonight," Jean said as he rushed out of the studio, slamming the door behind him.

∾

That evening, after Pétain's speech, at the packed cafés in the Place de la Comédie, there was an indescribable sadness and world-weariness that permeated the atmosphere. A light rain started to fall at dusk, and it fit the gloomy mood so perfectly it almost felt clichéd.

Nadine and I were the first to arrive at the café, so we found a table and waited for Jean and Smitty. On the way we had passed a bar with a group of soldiers gathered outside. It was apparent they had been there for hours because their tables were littered with beer bottles and ashtrays.

"How could we fight?" one of them had said, belligerent and red-faced as he talked to his friends. "The filthy government wouldn't support us! The Boches just mowed us down!"

"This is the worst day in the history of France," Nadine said. She had finally stopped crying, but her eyes were still red, and she blotted them with a handkerchief.

"It might be," I said, and a wave of homesickness for Jacques and our brief married life before the war swept over me. I closed my eyes for a second and pictured him in the moment that he had surprised me in December, standing in the middle of our candlelit apartment, looking more handsome to me than ever. In these hardest of times, I longed to be sure of him. I thought of those soldiers we passed and wondered what in the world he was feeling right now.

"You must be worried about Jacques," Nadine said, patting my hand, seeming to sense my feelings.

"Worrying about him is a constant," I said. "But at this terrible time, I'd give anything just to be in his arms for one moment."

I spotted Jean and Smitty on the street. I called out and waved them over, swallowing my emotions.

"I am sorry, my friend," Nadine said, giving me a tight hug. "I will keep praying for him. I think I'll go take the dog for a walk. Let me know where in the world we are going next."

After they sat and ordered drinks, Jean got down to business. His complexion was gray again, and he winced when he shifted in his seat, but I knew he was not going to listen to reason right now.

"I've talked to some contacts, and the American authorities in Hendaye, on the Spanish border, will aid our team members who need to leave the country. They'll leave at midnight tonight from the radio station."

"And I'm driving them out," Smitty said.

"What do you mean?" I asked, looking at him in surprise.

"The truck can fit seven, and I'm the best driver of the lot. Also, I'll be armed just in case," Smitty said, patting his back pocket. "And I've decided to try to enlist. I want to go fight with the British."

"We'll miss you," I said, squeezing his hand. "Keep an eye out for my husband."

"Will do, madame," Smitty said, tipping his glass to me.

"And what's next for the rest of us?" I asked, surveying the café and the groups of family and friends and coworkers crowded around tiny wrought iron tables. Some people were crying, others talking loudly, their voices frantic as they considered the questions on everyone's mind. *What do we do now? How do we stay safe in a world turned upside down?*

"Tonight, I'm going to tell the rest of the team to take this time to see to their families," Jean said. "Word is Pétain is going to establish his new government in Vichy. I have been asked to go there to meet with his second-in-command, to determine my 'role, and the role of the Paris Mondiale station.'"

"Oh?" I asked, raising my eyebrows. "I wonder what they expect. I highly doubt we'll be broadcasting to America ever again."

"No chance," Smitty said with a laugh. "If anything, he'll want you to broadcast to Germany."

"I don't know what they expect," Jean said. "But I need to understand this new Vichy government and the players. We are to be very careful from now on; nobody knows who is on whose side anymore, or who is really in charge."

"You'd be wise to start carrying a gun too," Smitty said. "Things are going to get more dangerous."

"Yes, I agree, and I will," Jean said with a sigh. "In the meantime, Smitty, please go gather your things. We will see you off in a few hours."

"Can I make a toast before you go?" I said, holding up my glass of wine. "To unexpected friendships in troubled times. Thank you both for helping me muddle through."

"Here, here," Smitty said, clinking his glass against mine.

"*Vive la France!*"

They echoed my toast, and as we clinked, several tables of patrons around us lifted their glasses and repeated my words.

"This war is just a never-ending trail of goodbyes," I said, watching him walk away after we had finished our drinks.

"It is. But a few lives will no longer be in danger if they get out tonight. That's worth it."

"True," I said. I sat back in my chair and accepted a cigarette from him. "I'd like to attend the meeting with you in Vichy."

The waiter stopped by our table at the same moment, and Jean ordered another bottle of wine. He lit up his cigarette, and I thought his hesitancy meant he didn't want me to go.

"That's good, because I'd like you to attend too," Jean said, smiling.

"Oh," I said, surprised. "I thought you might object."

"Not at all," Jean said. "I know you're aware of the dangers at this point. And you've proved your worth as a broadcaster. And as a friend, Drue *Tartière*. I . . . I need you. There with me."

We looked at each other and the intensity of his gaze caught me off guard, and I felt my cheeks grow warm. I was the first to look away.

"Well, thank you," I said, touched by his words as the waiter refilled our glasses. I had depended on Jean's friendship more than I cared to admit. I needed him too. But as a friend, nothing more. My heart belonged to Jacques, and our time apart had only strengthened my love for him.

"When do you want to leave?" I asked, eager to move on from the moment.

"We should head out tomorrow afternoon. Before that I will see that doctor Nadine tracked down. The pain in my stomach is . . . well, it's almost unbearable."

"I knew it," I said. "You haven't been well for a while now. Your color has been terrible."

"Why thank you," he said with sarcasm.

"Do you want me to go to the hospital with you now?"

"No, no," he said. "I can make it a few more hours. I'll head over to the hospital after we see the truck off from the station."

"OK," I said. "And we don't have to leave for Vichy right away if you need any tests or treatment. It's important you get well."

"It's more important we get to Vichy for the meeting and see what the expectations are for us. You should know—for me, one thing is for certain: Pétain may be done fighting the Nazis, but I'm not."

Relief washed over me; this was exactly what I had wanted him to say.

"Good," I said. "Neither am I."

Chapter Eighteen

August 18, 1940

Vichy, France

Dearest Mother and Father —
I finally arrived in Vichy yesterday with the head of Paris
Mondiale, Jean Fraysse, my maid, Nadine, and our dog,
Ondie. I am safe and well. We were supposed to arrive here
weeks ago, but just before leaving, Jean ended up requir-
ing emergency surgery to remove his appendix. He had an
infection and was quite ill, so we stayed in Bordeaux for
several weeks until he recovered. Thank goodness he is finally
on the mend.

I wish I had news to share of Jacques's whereabouts, but I
haven't heard from him since I left Paris. It's difficult for us to
communicate at all because I have been on the move, and I know
he must keep his locations a secret, even from me. I would give
anything to know that he's alive and safe. My dear friend and
agent Elise just learned her husband, Philippe, an officer in the
French military, was killed in a bombing. He leaves behind Elise
and their beautiful daughter, and I am devastated for them.

At the moment, I'm sitting outside a beautiful villa that is the temporary home of the American embassy in this nascent capital of the brand-new French government. I'm waiting to meet with my friend the ambassador Bill Bullitt. Dear Bill has assured me he will bypass the censors and take this letter home for you, delivering it personally if he must, as he is leaving for the States soon.

The atmosphere in this city is one of confusion and paranoia, with the German occupation looming over everything like a dark and unpredictable storm. I can hardly grasp the fact that Europe is being dominated by the horrible Nazi regime, and that even Paris has fallen to them. Here in Vichy, there is a palpable undercurrent of suspicion since Marshal Pétain was basically given carte blanche to rule by decree. France's so-called zone libre, or free zone, that I am in now, doesn't truly feel free.

For many, the only glimmer of light in these incredibly hard times has been the series of speeches from London by General Charles de Gaulle, leader of the Free French movement, asking the French people to join him and resist. His broadcasts to the people of France from London are like a life raft after so much hopelessness and misery.

As to what is next for me? The Paris Mondiale team had its last broadcast to America from Bordeaux last month, and now I miss my radio work more than I ever imagined. I hope our programs made at least a dent in America's perceptions about the war here. Tonight, Marshal Pétain's right-hand man, Pierre Laval, has requested a meeting with Jean and me, and we'll learn if this new Vichy government will let us go back on the air and in what capacity.

So, you see, it is impossible for me to return to the US, as I may have more broadcasting work, and I have personal affairs to attend to back in Paris. And, as always, I must be as close to wherever Jacques is as I can.

This may be the last letter you receive from me for some time, my darling parents. I love you and miss you and will keep trying to get letters through to you in any way I can. I promise I will take care. Hugs and kisses and . . .

All my love,
Drue
Xoxo

I reread the letter once more before putting it in the envelope, fanning myself with it as I sat on a wooden bench across from the villa. There was so much more I could have said, but I didn't feel the need to feed their anxiety about my being in the middle of a country at war. I left out the number of bombings that had taken place while we were still in Bordeaux, including one night when Nadine and I sat in the basement of our apartment building there, both hugging Ondie, convinced the building would be destroyed by morning. I didn't tell them about sitting vigil at Jean Fraysse's hospital bedside on a hot July night, listening to the air-raid siren, unable to move him to anywhere safer.

Just before three, I grabbed my purse and adjusted my black straw hat, making my way to the door of the grand limestone townhouse. I was surprised when the young receptionist from the American embassy in Paris opened the door, and we greeted each other like old friends before she led me into an expansive parlor with ornate molding, pale-blue silk wallpaper, and floor-to-ceiling blush-colored drapes. I had just sat down when Bill entered the room, arms wide, eyes sparkling.

"So good to see you, Drue, so relieved that you made it here safely," he said, embracing me in a warm hug.

"And you as well," I said, adding as I handed him the envelopes, "I finished the letters; thank you for taking them home with you."

"Happy to do so," he said. "And I'm glad we were able to meet one more time before I leave. Especially because I received a letter for you. From Jacques."

"So he's OK? He's safe?" I felt the color drain from my face, and I reached for the sofa. Seeing my alarm, Bill put his arm around my shoulder and steadied me as I sat down, and he took the letter out of the breast pocket of his pale-gray suit.

"He's fine. He is back from Norway, and in England. For now."

"Thank God," I said, taking a deep breath and closing my eyes. "Thank God."

He poured me tea from the set the receptionist brought in, and I ripped open the envelope and gripped the thin paper with both hands as I read Jacques's familiar handwriting, hearing his voice speak to me through the words. His division had evacuated Norway after Britain had utterly failed to prevent a German invasion. But it was his final words that shook me:

> I believe that France will not go down. You must believe that too. De Gaulle is right—France has lost a battle but not the war.
>
> Darling, I've received frantic cables from my family and yours in America, urging me to persuade you to leave at once. So I am sending this letter to the embassy because I believe you must still be in France. I agree that you should go home to America and wait out the war. I will come to you as soon as it is over.
>
> I will be leaving Britain soon for far-flung places, and it may be some time before we can be in contact again, but please have faith and try not to worry. Our mission and duty are so clear in this war that there is no fear in my heart. We can never be anything but

victorious. And you and I will be together again at the end.

I love you with my life. Je t'embrasse, je t'embrasse, je t'embrasse.

All my love,

Jacques

"All my love," I said in a soft voice, tracing the words with my finger. "He wants me to go to America. I never thought he'd want that."

It hurt my heart to say it, like a betrayal. And more than ever before, it made the time and distance between us seem like a chasm. He didn't understand where I was in my life now, how I loved this country so much that I wanted to fight back too somehow.

"These are unprecedented times," Bill said. "He just wants you safe."

"I know . . . Still. When are you leaving?" I asked. I stared down at the letter, trying to think.

"In two days. The US will continue to recognize the Vichy French government, but that doesn't mean I have to work with them. I'm going home to help Roosevelt with his campaign. And I am only going to ask once because Jacques suggested it. I can get you out with me. This will probably be your last chance for a long time."

I put my elbows on the coffee table and rubbed my hands over my face. It would be so easy to leave it all behind.

Going back home, taking on some film roles, and waiting out the war until Jacques returned? That would be the simple, uncomplicated choice. But my former life on the stage and in motion pictures no longer suited me the way it once did. I wanted to keep living in France and doing whatever I could in the Resistance. And hopefully, someday, Jacques would understand.

"Once again, I'm staying. I also refuse to believe France is finished," I said. "But I appreciate the offer, Bill. Thank you for everything you've done for me here. Jean Fraysse and I are meeting with Laval tonight. I want to see what he has to say. And, frankly, I'm thrilled with the work I've been doing, despite everything. I will cable Jacques and my family in the States telling them it's impossible for me to leave at this time."

"I assumed that would be your answer," Bill said. "A bit of advice? Be cautious meeting with Laval tonight; he can't be trusted. Keep your thoughts to yourself and mostly listen."

"So I'm supposed to just shut up and smile no matter what he says?" I asked, crossing my arms and leaning back in my chair.

"Something like that, though I know that doesn't come easily to you." Bill laughed. "Just . . . please. Try your best."

"I will. Now, do you have any guess as to what Laval wants to meet with us about?"

"I am sure they have a new role in mind for Jean, and whatever it is involves you and the rest of the Paris Mondiale staff."

"That was my guess too," I said. "But whatever it is, I don't think I'm going to like it."

I left the villa and walked back through the tree-lined streets of Vichy to the charming inn on the banks of the Allier River where Nadine, Ondie, and I were staying. Under other circumstances, Vichy would be a beautiful spa town to visit, with its delightful string of parks along the river featuring luscious gardens, as well as its art deco architecture and world-class hotels and restaurants.

But there was something surreal about it all in this moment. For one thing, the population had surged, due to the war, with thousands of people arriving daily—refugees and journalists, soldiers, legislators, and diplomats, all needing a place to sleep, wash, and eat. Meanwhile, the offices of the new French government were set up in gambling casinos and music halls and hotels, places meant for tourists escaping the city, not an entire government fleeing the nation's capital. And in the beautiful town park, you would see groups of two or three men talking quietly, on a bench or behind a group of trees, meeting outside instead of in offices because of the constant fear of espionage.

Nadine and Ondie went out for a long walk through the city, so I took a nap before dinner. When I woke, I changed into a white cotton eyelet dress that I had picked up in Bordeaux. My curls never cooperated in the heat, so I pinned my hair up in a bun, letting a few strands frame my face. I took my time with red lipstick, rouge, and mascara. It seemed like years since I had dressed up, and it was a refreshing change from my tired dull culottes and blouses. I only wished I was going out with my husband and not the new government of France.

Jacques. I closed my eyes and pictured his handsome face, the last time I had seen him in his uniform, the smell of his cologne. All this time, I thought I had been staying in France for him. But after reading his letter, and being away from him for nearly a year, I knew I was also staying in France for *me*.

I thought back on my former life in Hollywood—the way I had competed with other actresses for roles, how I would obsess about press coverage and film reviews; things that were so important to me back then seemed so trivial now. My new life began the day I met Jacques Tartière. And now I had plans of my own as I awaited his return.

I tried to imagine him reading the cable, wondering how he would react. Did he know me, his wife, well enough to understand?

I lost track of the time getting ready and had to hurry down the street to meet Jean in front of the Hôtel du Parc, where much of the new government now had offices.

"Sorry I'm a tad late," I said, coming up behind him, blotting my face with my hands; I was already sweating and realized I should have foregone the rouge. His color was much better than it had been prior to surgery, but he had lost a great deal of weight during his hospital stay, so his pale-blue linen shirt hung loosely on his frame. Still, he had a rugged sort of handsomeness, and it was wonderful to see him in better health. He turned around at the sound of my voice and raised his eyebrows and gave a short whistle.

"You look stunning this evening," Jean said, his voice low, with an undercurrent of emotion.

"Oh, thank you," I said, smoothing out the damp curls sticking to my face.

"If your goal is to distract Pierre Laval with your beauty, you will no doubt accomplish it."

"Ha!" I said. "I am sure that Laval is too smart to be distracted by a woman."

"Yes, but you're not just any woman," Jean said, looking in my eyes with affection, and I couldn't deny the warmth I felt in return as we stood there, neither of us wanting to be the first to look away. I cared for Jean; he was one of the people I had become closest to in France. And I knew many married women in both Hollywood and France who had affairs with abandon, never letting it affect their conscience. I wasn't one of them. I still loved my husband madly, despite so much time apart.

"That's right, I am Drue Tartière, *married* to a Frenchman." I gave him a pointed look. He immediately understood and laughed. I was going to bring up Germaine but thought better of it.

"Point taken, Madame Tartière," he said, beaming as the doorman opened the hotel door, and with his hand on my elbow he led me inside. I tried to ignore the slight thrill at the touch of his warm hand on my skin, because it felt like a betrayal of Jacques, albeit a very small one. "We have time for a quick drink before dinner; tell me about your meeting with the ambassador."

We sat at the bar and ordered glasses of champagne, and I told him about my meeting with Bullitt, including the letter from Jacques.

"If I were your husband, I would also want you far away from this war," Jean said.

"This war has changed me," I said. "Paris Mondiale especially. I don't even know if Jacques could even begin to understand that now, we've been apart so long."

"I, for one, am very happy to hear that Paris Mondiale has changed you," Jean said with a genuine smile, and still an undercurrent of flirtation as he locked eyes with me again. He put his fingers up to his lips and, lowering his voice, said, "It is early days, but things are starting to happen now that we have de Gaulle in London."

"Not a moment too soon," I said.

"Indeed. Now, there are a couple of things I have to tell you before we head into dinner." His voice was still low, and he was holding his glass in his hand, looking into it as if reading tea leaves.

"What?" I asked.

"I need another operation," Jean said. "Very soon. They found cancer when I was operated on in Bordeaux."

"Oh, Jean," I said, taking a breath in, and this time, without even thinking, I reached out and touched his arm. "I am so sorry. You look so much better, I thought all was fine."

"Unfortunately, no. I told my doctor I'm going to Paris to have it done. I don't care that it's occupied; the hospitals are still the best. And I can meet with associates, friends I know who will be joining the Resistance fight."

"You'll have to be careful. And by careful I mean in taking time to fully recover from your surgery."

He waved his hand, dismissing the comment.

"Jean, Drue, just the people I was looking for." Someone tapped on my shoulder lightly, and I shifted on my barstool to see Charles Bedaux. It seemed both unexpected and obvious that he would be here.

"Charles Bedaux, you seem to just pop up in the most unusual places," I said. "Like a spy in a Hollywood movie."

"You would know," he said with a smile, flattered, as he kissed me on both cheeks. Jean ordered him a drink. "You look beautiful this evening."

"Why thank you," I said. "Where is your lovely wife?"

"She is in Antibes, with Wallis and Edward—forgive me, *the Duke and Duchess of Windsor*," Charles said, rolling his eyes. "Jean actually invited me to join your dinner with Pierre Laval."

"Oh, this is a surprise," I said.

"Sorry, that was the other thing I had to tell you," Jean said with a sheepish look.

Bedaux reached into his suit coat and pulled out a thick envelope.

"Here is everything you need, including papers for you also," Bedaux said, nodding at me. "And your maid."

Jean opened the envelope to show me. It contained the necessary passes to get us across the line of demarcation into occupied territory, so that we could return to Paris.

"Thank you," Jean said, giving Charles a warm embrace that was out of character. "If you'll excuse me, I'll be right back."

We watched him walk to the staircase, down to the toilet.

"You got the papers because you know he's sick," I said. "That was very good of you; thank you."

"Well, I am an excellent judge of character, and Jean is a very good man," Charles said. "He is brilliant and well connected and admired by powerful people of various political leanings. I'm not sure how much you realize that about him. I believe he has the potential to be one of the most powerful leaders in France someday."

"I understand why you would believe that," I said. I had worked with Jean long enough to understand how smart, politically savvy, and well respected he was.

"Yes," Charles said. "He has enormous potential. I am a business-man first, but, in this world, I need to place bets across the board. I am betting on him to be part of France's future."

"I hope you're right. Because I am betting on him too," I said.

"That future is not the same as Pétain's France; that is why I wanted to come to dinner tonight. I need to know what he wants from Jean. I don't trust any of these Vichy players."

Jean downed his drink when he returned to the bar and summoned the bartender for the bill.

"Well," he said. "Let's enter this den of thieves, shall we?"

Chapter Nineteen

The *maître d'hôtel* of the Chantecler restaurant brought us over to a table near the windows. Several of the tables of guests we walked by took notice of us, a few whispering under their breath, others straining to get a look at who was heading to meet with the second most powerful man in the exiled French government. I kept my eyes focused on the table where Pierre Laval was sitting, alone, at the front of the restaurant near the windows. On either side of the table were men in military uniforms, one focused on the inside of the restaurant, the other never taking his eyes off the street, even as we approached. Pierre Laval, the former prime minister of France, now officially the minister of state under Pétain, was sitting at the table smoking a cigarette and drinking a glass of red wine, the bottle on the table almost empty. He was in his late fifties, with a wide nose and a thick, dark mustache above his fleshy lips. His salt-and-pepper hair was slicked back with pomade.

He stood up to welcome us, a sullen expression on his face, as Jean introduced me as a key member of his staff. Jean and Charles had known him for years, but this was my first glimpse at the former prime minister.

"Pleasure to meet you, Madame Tartière," he said in French, kissing my hand, and he cracked the slightest smile.

"And you also," I said, again relieved that my French-language skills had improved so much. I still spoke French with a distinct American accent, but I could converse easily now, without feeling awkward or embarrassed.

A waiter appeared out of nowhere with another bottle of red wine and proceeded to fill our glasses.

"Forgive my mood," he said, motioning to the men standing on both sides of the table. "I have had to increase my security. Someone in the park tried to take a shot at me today. I felt the bullets from the revolver whiz by my head."

We all murmured our shock and outrage and told him no apologies were necessary. We exchanged a little more polite conversation as we browsed the menu and placed our orders, and Laval got right to the point after our first course arrived.

"I am glad to see you are in better health now," Laval said to Jean.

"Yes, much better," he said. "The first surgery was a success."

"That's good, because I have an exciting opportunity for you," Laval said. "Since Paris Mondiale is no longer, we are in desperate need of a *new* government radio station—'Vichy Radio.' Naturally, we would like you to be the director in charge of it. You'll be given a large budget and can hire all the old personnel from Paris Mondiale, except any of the British staff. It's quite an important and prominent role, and Pétain and I want you in it."

"Ah, I am flattered, thank you," Jean said carefully, taking a sip of his wine. "So please tell me more about what you have in mind for this new station."

"Yes—for instance, would we still be able to broadcast to America?" I asked. Charles's sour expression made it clear he was not pleased that I was already asking this question. And Laval looked at me like I was ridiculous.

"Bah!" he said with a deep laugh. "No, of course not."

"Why not?" I asked.

"What would be the point?" Laval said. "America is only interested in exploiting us economically. They only care about their beloved dollar."

I bit my lip, trying to control my anger. Jean gave me a look of caution, but the comments infuriated me, and I blurted out a reply.

"Excuse me, you might keep your insults against Americans for when I am not at the table," I said. "I am married to a Frenchman, but I am still a proud American citizen."

Pierre Laval sat back in his chair and looked at me, his expression hard to discern, but something like amusement with shadows of annoyance crept across his face.

"*Pardon*, madame," he said, this time smiling widely in a way that gave me chills as he emphasized the *pardon*. "I did not mean to offend; I know women get so emotional about these things. I have nothing against Americans, but since the American war-debt policy of the last war, America has many enemies in France due to her greed."

Charles launched into a coughing fit that I knew was meant to distract, and Jean shot me a warning look, mouthing, *Enough*, when Laval wasn't looking.

"Please, let's get back to discussing Vichy Radio, which is why we are here," Jean said, clapping his hands together and changing the subject. "What type of programming did you have in mind?"

"You must understand, taking on this role, that the objective of the French government now is to bring France into the closest possible accord with Germany," Laval said. His smile had vanished, and he was looking at Jean, as if daring him. "So, the main purpose of Vichy Radio is to convince the French people that a firm alliance with Germany is the way forward. It is the country's only hope."

I had to clench my teeth to keep my jaw from dropping, and I could tell Jean was a little taken aback by the bluntness of the words. Charles was looking at both of us, eyebrows raised in a way that said, *I told you so*. While I knew from Bill Bullitt and others that Laval was pro-Germany, it was still jarring to hear one of the major leaders of the French government confirm it out loud. An alliance with the Nazis the only hope? If that was true, the country was doomed.

I took a huge gulp of wine, and Charles gave me a gentle kick under the table as a warning. I knew I had crossed a line before, and for the rest of the evening I would take Bill's advice and keep my thoughts to myself.

The wine kept flowing, our appetizers arrived, and the tension eased as Charles, showing his business acumen, flattered Laval in subtle ways and also directed the conversation toward lighter topics.

As we were finishing up dessert and getting ready to leave, Laval looked across the table at Jean, sipping his aperitif, and asked, "Now, when do you think you can start taking on the role as director of Vichy Radio?"

"Oh," Jean said, "I . . . ah . . . I'm sorry, Pierre, I cannot take the role right now. I need to go back to Paris for a second medical procedure. My health is better, but I need another operation."

"I'm sorry to hear that," Laval said, thick eyebrows furrowed as if he didn't quite believe what Jean was saying. "Let's meet again after you have recovered and discuss the role then. There is nobody in France who is more perfect for it than you. You must take it."

"Again, thank you for the kind words," Jean said.

We got up to leave, and, as we did, Laval kissed my hand and looked up at me, surveying my face.

"A face too beautiful for radio anyway," he said. "I would not be so eager to get back to radio work, Madame Tartière. Perhaps go back to other pursuits?"

I looked at him, my eyes steady, wondering if this was a thinly veiled warning. Did he know me as Drue Leyton, or was I being paranoid? In any case, his eyes and his words sent a chill through me. I didn't dare look at Jean or Charles.

"Thank you for the compliment," I said, giving him what I hoped was a breezy smile. "And perhaps you are right. I have much more I could be doing right now to help the war efforts—I will most likely focus on that type of work if Jean does not need me."

"That would be wise," he said with a nod, and, with our final good-byes, Jean, Charles, and I walked out into the night air, and I finally exhaled.

～

"We need to talk. I know a bar that is safe; we'll go there," Charles hissed as the three of us walked down the street at a fast clip, getting distance from our dinner conversation. "Do not say a word until we get there; assume every other person you see is a spy or collaborator, because they probably are."

The air had finally cooled, and there was a slight breeze off the river that I was grateful for after the stuffy, smoke-filled restaurant and the words Laval had said to me as I was leaving. We entered a tiny bar on a side street near the inn where I was staying. Its interior was long and narrow, with dark wood paneling, and it smelled of stale wine and cigarettes. The weary-looking bartender nodded at Charles in greeting as we made our way to a table in the back corner, near the basement staircase. Charles went to get us drinks, and I accepted a cigarette from Jean, hoping it would help calm my nerves.

"I am sorry for mentioning broadcasting to America," I said. "I should have known he'd balk at that; that was foolish."

"Yes, it was," Charles said as he came back to the table and set the glasses in front of us, pouring from a carafe of red wine. "Although, reprimanding one of the most powerful men in France was probably worse. And Jean—he thought you used your health as an excuse not to take the role. That dinner was an absolute catastrophe for both of you."

"I think you're being a little overdramatic, Charles," I said. "It wasn't—"

"I am not being dramatic," Charles said, slamming his glass down on the table. A few other patrons looked up from their discussions, and he lowered his voice and leaned toward us. "You must understand something. Now that the enemy is within the gates, everything is much more dangerous, and you are both playing a deadly game."

"I am well aware of that, Charles," Jean said, his voice calm and reassuring. "But I had to find a way to gracefully decline the Vichy Radio position. I will never work for this puppet government in any capacity. The medical issue was a way to deflect him."

"Yes, but now you must leave first thing tomorrow morning," Charles said.

"What—why?" I asked.

"Jean, you were under suspicion before you met with Laval—this is not a guess, I know for a fact that you were. And now I guarantee he is talking with other French officials about your turning down the job, officials who are thoroughly pro-Nazi and didn't like you already. You're not safe here."

Charles sipped his drink and turned to me. "As for you, after what he said to you when we were leaving? Do I need to say more? You're both in danger of getting shot at in the park like Laval was. Go to Paris tomorrow. Jean, get your surgery as soon as you can. Drue, you take care of whatever you need to do in Paris, but you must find a place to rent in the countryside where Jean can recover and you can both lie low. Paris is even less safe than here, crawling with German officers and collaborators. *Both* of you need to let them forget about you for a while."

Jean and I sat there, absorbing his words.

"You know I have plans, as do many others in this country, to follow de Gaulle's lead," Jean said to him in a whisper. "I am not going to cower, hiding away in the countryside; I'm not going to do nothing out of fear of retaliation."

I felt a swell of pride for my friend, so brave and so sure of what he needed to do for his country.

"And I would have stopped broadcasting months ago if I was afraid of their threats against me," I said, although I did not feel as courageous as my words. Laval had gotten under my skin; I still had the goose pimples on my arms to prove it.

Charles groaned, downing his glass of wine and pouring another.

"Don't you two understand? Neither of you is any good to the Resistance if they kill you," Charles said. "And let me tell you, the odds of them doing away with you, just because they *can*? They went up significantly tonight."

Chapter Twenty

The next morning before dawn, I knocked on Nadine's door at the inn and told her why we had to leave. She looked at me, still dazed and sleepy, hair in her eyes, but she nodded that she understood the danger. We quietly packed our bags, with Ondie looking on, and were ready and waiting when Jean pulled up in front of the hotel with the beat-up dark-green Citroën he had been driving, a full tank of gas thanks to his government contacts.

It was a beautiful August morning, and we drove with the windows open, inhaling the fresh summer breeze. We passed by some destroyed buildings and other evidence of fighting, but we enjoyed the drive, and I gave a deep sigh of relief when we drove by a field of sunflowers an hour outside of Vichy, glad to be away from a place with such a darkly sinister atmosphere, though I had no idea what to expect back in Paris.

The German checkpoint into the occupied territory was in Moulin. Upon arrival, I handed our papers to a stocky German soldier with a scowl on his face. I held my breath as he frowned at them with skepticism, finally exhaling when he passed them back to me and waved us through. And once again I was struck by this strange new reality. We were in France . . . but France was not free. It hit me again when we reached the outskirts of Paris that evening, where long lines of cars waited to pass through the German control into the city. The papers of each person in each car were examined thoroughly, and the Germans shouted at scared French people who did not have theirs in the exact right order.

The three of us were speechless as we drove into the desolate streets of the city. Thousands of sandbags rested against buildings, wooden barriers blocking many of the side streets, as the Germans had only kept open the major ones. Garish white arrows with bold black German lettering marked directions for the German trucks and staff cars. The city was completely blacked out, and the only people we saw were German guards directing traffic.

"This is not our Paris," Nadine whispered, looking out the window.

"No," I said, "sadly it is not."

"And I still can't believe we're moving to the country," she said in a grumbling tone, patting Ondie's head on her lap. "It's not our Paris, but it still *is* Paris."

"Yes, but we're not going to be that far away," I said. "It's safer, and it's only temporary."

"We'll see . . . Oh, look!" she said. She pointed at our apartment building. "*Home.*"

We pulled up to our building on Rue Saint-Dominique, and I couldn't help but smile at Nadine's enthusiasm. I had also missed our apartment and our lovely neighborhood. She jumped out of the car, grabbed her satchel and travel bag, and went running up the stairs, the dog chasing after her.

Jean, with my suitcase in hand, started walking into the building after her.

"Jean, you should go home. You need sleep."

"Not yet," he said, looking back at me with a tired smile. "I need to talk to you and Claude about next steps. It can't wait."

I entered the building, and the hallway's usual smells of must and floor cleaner made me nostalgic for when I had first moved into this place as a newlywed, and it enveloped me in the comfort and familiarity of the place, with a sting of homesickness for Jacques. Still, it was good to be back, despite everything.

"*Daughter*, welcome home!" Claude, looking as dapper as ever, enveloped me in a hug as soon as I stepped through my apartment door. "I am so happy you are all safe and sound."

"And you also," I said, laughing as we broke away and he took my things from Jean, giving him a slap on the back.

The kitchen and living area were pristine, as if it had all just been scrubbed from floor to ceiling. And the cream-colored walls looked brand new. There was a bouquet of fresh flowers and candles on the kitchen table, the sound of the Glenn Miller Orchestra coming from the radio.

"Do I smell paint?" I asked.

"I thought it needed a fresh coat, so I did it myself," he said proudly as he walked in and poured me a glass of wine. "It is a thank-you for allowing me to stay here in your absence."

"You didn't have to, but I am touched; thank you," I said.

Nadine got to work, humming to herself, Ondie at her heels. She was clearly content to be back in our apartment, surveying Claude's paint job and moving a few things back to their original places—a crystal vase, an end table—because Claude had dared to move them.

Claude, Jean, and I sat down on the sofas. The air had cooled, the summer breeze blowing through the curtains, which had been drawn closed. This time of night I could usually hear the bustling neighborhood below, laughter from the cafés, sometimes music and people walking through the streets. Tonight, there was nothing outside but a dark quiet.

"Nadine," Jean said. "Come sit with us and have a glass of wine. You should hear everything we discuss."

"Really?" Nadine said, looking up from the kitchen cabinets and over at me.

"Yes," I said, patting the place next to me on the sofa. "You absolutely should, Jean is right. You need to understand everything. You're family."

She sat next to me on the sofa, her cheeks bright pink as Jean clinked glasses with her.

"Now, tell me everything that happened at Paris Mondiale the day we left," Jean asked Claude.

"I knew that would be your first question," Claude said. "And before I tell you, please understand I did everything that I possibly could . . . I burned all of your correspondence and many of the compromising scripts and documents that could be dangerous for us if in their hands, but I didn't finish the job before they arrived."

"I'm sure you did your best," Jean said. "Just tell us what happened."

Claude told us that an hour after we had left the station, a "flock" of Germans arrived. They told him to touch nothing and kept him prisoner in the station for two whole days. He had destroyed part of the station's control board for broadcasting, but they managed to get it up and running again in hours.

"I don't know what else they got their hands on; I wish I'd had more time," he said, adjusting his monocle, frustration in his voice.

"It's not your fault you didn't," I said. "I cannot believe they imprisoned you in the station."

"Yes, well, it could have been much worse," Claude said. "I could be dead in a ditch somewhere."

Nadine shivered and crossed her arms, hugging herself.

"Thank you for all you *did* do," Jean said. "Now, here is what we do next. I am going to schedule my surgery when I meet with the doctors tomorrow. Claude, I need you to be our eyes and ears in the cafés; you are good at that. Listen to conversations, but be discreet; I want to know who some of the biggest collaborators in the city are. Do you think you can do that?"

"Aye, commandant, I will do it," he said in a perfect German accent.

"Do you speak German?" I asked.

"Just enough to be dangerous." Claude winked at me, and I had to laugh.

"All right, all right, moving on," Jean said. "I will start writing a series of anonymous newsletters, from the hospital bed if I must. The first one will also include a copy of de Gaulle's speech from June; not everyone heard or read it, and every citizen should. Drue, if you could type it up and make as many carbon copies as you can—buy the paper in multiple places in small amounts; use the utmost discretion.

"I would like the three of you to distribute them to mailboxes in various parts of the city. I'll give you the names and addresses. I need to inspire several important people to have faith in the Resistance to the Nazis, faith in the renaissance of France."

We all nodded in agreement.

"Yes," Nadine said. "Thank you very much for letting me help. And, Claude, you should stick to eavesdropping at the cafés. Drue and I have bikes; we can do the mail drops."

"Yes, that makes sense." I nodded; there was no need for a sixty-year-old man to be trotting all over the city.

"To me too," Claude said with a grateful smile, patting his generous stomach. "I am excellent at sitting and eating; I will stick with what I do best."

It felt good to be doing something productive, but would it matter? Would there ever be a large enough Resistance within France to make a difference? It was hard to feel hopeful when you looked outside at the City of Light, so dark and desolate. But I shared Claude's attitude. Things could always be worse, and hope was still part of my survival strategy.

"One thing you all should know before I leave," Jean said. "I've learned from a reliable source that our phones here are tapped. And keep an eye out for anyone following you in the streets or watching your building. In fact, I would tip that grumpy concierge of yours extra money so that she does the same."

"*Boche* bastards," Nadine said, spitting out the words.

"I couldn't agree more," Claude said, lighting a cigar.

"Be careful with your words in public too. One false move and any of us could be jailed by the Gestapo," Jean said. "The Germans and their growing number of collaborators don't need much of a reason."

"No home phone, continue to look out for spies. Got it," I said with a sigh. It really was not our Paris anymore.

"You need to lease that place in Barbizon too," Jean said when I walked out with him to get my purse out of his car.

"I will."

"I wish we could stay in Paris, but it's not worth the risk. Charles is right; we're useless if we are captured."

"I know. The villa in Barbizon is owned by a friend of Jacques's family. If it's available, I think it will be perfect."

"Yes, it sounds it," he said with a distracted smile. He paused for a moment, then added, "Germaine finally left me . . . for good this time. Before we left Paris. I should have . . . well, I just haven't wanted to talk about it. She's in the South, staying with her sister in the countryside outside of Nice."

"Oh, Jean, I am so sorry," I said, hand over my mouth. "Are you OK?"

"I am," Jean said. "It was a relief; the marriage was broken beyond repair. Believe it or not, I am happy to be going home to an empty house."

"Wait . . . who is going to take care of you after the surgery?"

"Well, I'll be in the hospital for some time," he said, unconcerned. "From there, I have plenty of friends still in the city that would take me in."

"You can come stay with us," I said as he opened the car door and handed me my purse. "Whether it's here or in Barbizon, Nadine and

I, and Claude, who appears to be sticking with us no matter where we go, we will be happy to look after you while you recover."

"Thank you," he said. "We will see what happens. But thank you for the offer . . . I also . . ."

"What is it?" I asked, frowning.

"Nothing, it can wait," he said. "We have a great deal of work ahead of us. I need to get some sleep. I'll talk to you tomorrow."

I kissed him on both cheeks and gave him a hug. He smelled of cigarettes, sweat, and his lemon-bergamot cologne, and he pulled me in so tight I could feel the rapid beating of his heart as we stood there in each other's arms for a brief moment. Fighting your country's enemy and facing down cancer, alone, after your wife left you, was a great deal to handle for one man, even one as strong as Jean.

"Please take care, and let me know what the doctor says," I said as we pulled apart.

"I will. Thank you," he said, grabbing my hand and squeezing it. He gave me a lingering look of affection before getting in the car. "For your friendship . . . For . . . everything."

Chapter Twenty-One

September 9, 1940

"Excuse me, *pardon*, madame, you are Jean Fraysse's wife?"

I had been sitting in the waiting room of the Hôtel-Dieu Hospital next to Notre-Dame, so engrossed in one of the collaborationist newspapers that I hadn't even heard Dr. Porcher, Jean's doctor, approach me. He was of average build and completely bald, with a white beard and dark-framed glasses.

"Yes? I mean, no, I'm just a friend," I said. "But how is he? Is he OK?"

"He is fine," he said with a kind smile. "The surgery was successful; we removed the cancer. But he will be in recovery here for at least a couple of weeks."

"May I see him?" I said.

"In a moment." He cleared his throat. "I have known Jean for a very long time. He's a good man, one of the best. Before surgery he asked me for a favor, and I agreed."

He reached into the breast pocket of his white doctor's coat and handed me an envelope.

"What is this?" I said, staring at my name in black letters.

The doctor sat down next to me and, changing from French to perfect English, whispered in my ear, "Inside you will find a certificate signed by me. It states you have late-stage cancer of the womb."

"What . . . I don't understand," I said, frowning at the envelope.

"Think of it as insurance. I know you are American; I know you have a husband still fighting with the British," he said, still keeping his voice low. "The Germans are frightened of three things—syphilis, tuberculosis, and cancer. Cancer of the womb is the easiest of these things to fake. If they ever capture you, it might be your ticket out."

"Ah," I said, absorbing the words and tucking the envelope in the bottom of my purse. Part of me felt that it was extreme. But I couldn't refuse such a favor—knowing he was risking his own arrest giving it to me. "I don't know how to thank you."

"No need," he said. "I am happy to do my part in whatever small way I can now. For France."

He left me, and thirty minutes later a young nurse came and brought me to Jean's room, warning me that he was still heavily medicated.

He was hooked up to intravenous fluids. He looked over at me and smiled, his eyes slightly heavy.

"*Très chère amie*, come in, come in," he said with a laugh. "It is so good to see you."

"How are you feeling?" I asked, smiling at him. I squeezed his hand and sat down on the lone chair beside the hospital bed.

"Very well," he said. "These drugs are *very* good."

I laughed at this, and the nurse rolled her eyes and left the room.

"The doctor gave you what I asked him to give you?" Jean asked, his face turning serious.

"He did, and I see that you are not too drugged right now after all."

"Just a little." He held up his thumb and forefinger to illustrate.

"Thank you for asking him to do that," I said.

"When are you going to Barbizon?"

"In the morning, with Nadine," I said. "I am meeting Elise and Kathleen after I leave here; they both send you well wishes."

"And you trust them both?"

"With my life," I said, because that was basically what I was about to do.

"Good. I trust them too." He yawned and put his hand on top of mine on the side of the bed.

I flipped over my hand and squeezed his; he already appeared to be asleep.

"You should rest," I said. He nodded, eyes closed.

I picked my purse up off the floor and put it over my shoulder. I was about to pull my hand away from his when he squeezed it again and opened his eyes, studying my face.

"You know what I have been thinking for some time?"

"I have no idea," I said, smiling at him.

"That it's hard to love a woman as breathtaking as you and not fall *in love* with her." He said this in a whisper, his eyes welling with tears. The words, the raw honesty of them, made my heart quicken, and I started blinking back tears too. I cared deeply about this man, and in another life, I might have fallen in love with him too. But somewhere else in the world was a husband that I still loved dearly.

"I think you will manage," I said, biting my lip in a half smile. I squeezed his hand, stood up, and kissed the top of his head. "Get some sleep, my dear friend."

His eyes were closed again, and I heard a soft snore.

I replayed our words to each other as I left the hospital. The fresh September afternoon air was an elixir after sitting in the hospital's stuffy atmosphere for so many hours. I was touched to hear him say our friendship meant something to him, as he wasn't always one to show his emotions. But his talk of falling in love I decided to blame on the drugs.

It was a short walk from the hospital over the bridge to La Brasserie de l'Île Saint-Louis, where I was meeting my friends for a sunset aperitif on the restaurant's terrace. I passed a German military band playing for a crowd and shuddered slightly, holding my purse, thinking of the envelope at the bottom of it with the fake certificate that I needed to put somewhere safe when I got home. I had adjusted to seeing German soldiers in the streets, sitting and talking loudly in their guttural language in the cafés, but I would never get used to them; I would never not feel a kind of tension between anger and fear whenever I passed by them.

I spotted Elise and Kathleen when I arrived, sitting under the restaurant's red awning at a table across from the Seine, a third rattan chair set aside for me.

I greeted them with kisses, and they both started asking me questions about Jean's health at once.

"He is well," I said, telling them what the doctor had told me.

"Thank goodness," Elise said. "I needed some good news today."

The morning after I had arrived back in Paris two weeks before, I had gone straight to her apartment to see her and offer my condolences for the loss of Philippe. When I opened the door, she had collapsed into my arms, sobbing. We stayed in the doorway like that for a long time, and then I brought her to the sofa and made her a cup of tea. Corinne and Elise's mother had gone for a walk, and she said it was one of the first times she had let her guard down and truly revealed her grief. Since then, I had tried to check in on her at least every couple of days, just to have a cup of coffee and be there for my heartbroken friend, though it was hard at times to witness, because it reminded me how easily the situation could be mine. She was wearing a black dress today, looking impossibly thin, but not quite as bereft as she had been that first day.

"Oh, Drue, this is wonderful news; I am so relieved, and I cannot wait to let Tudor know," Kathleen said, signaling the waiter. Her short hair was slicked back, which always made her pale-blue eyes appear even larger than they were. Next to her chair were a half dozen large shopping bags.

"Did a little shopping this afternoon?" I asked.

"I had to," Kathleen said. "Tudor came home from a meeting on the Champs-Élysées the other day very upset. He had been standing looking out the window of the meeting room with a colleague when a group of young men sped down the street in a yellow roadster, yelling, 'Down with the Jews!'"

"What? Germans?"

"No, that's the most terrible part," Elise said, offering us both cigarettes. "They were some young fascists, Montmartre gutter types."

"Yes, exactly," Kathleen said. "They threw bricks through the beautiful shop windows of Vanina, Annabel, Toutmain, Marie-Louise. All owned by Jews."

"That is horrifying," I said, feeling sick to my stomach.

"Truly," Kathleen said. "So I went and spent a small fortune at the shops that were vandalized. All the stores were packed with people, despite the boarded-up windows. Isidore, the owner of Toutmain, was very emotional about all her new customers; she kept kissing everyone who came through the door."

The waiter finally came over, and Kathleen looked at the wine list and ordered the most expensive bottle of champagne on the menu, a plate of cheeses, and escargot.

"You don't need to do that," I said, gasping at the price of the champagne.

"Oh, Kathleen, you really don't," Elise said, eyes wide.

"Oh, sweethearts, I do," Kathleen said. "We have to celebrate the small victories and enjoy good champagne when we can these days; otherwise it's all too depressing."

"Well, thank you," I said. "It's so good to see you both. Kathleen, I am sorry it's been so long. I was surprised when I heard you and Tudor had stayed in the country, to be honest."

"First, no need to apologize, and second, this is my home; I can't imagine running away from it now," she said. "And I think Tudor and I, with his fortune and my connections, maybe we can do some good.

"Elise, I have to ask, how are you holding up?" Kathleen continued, grabbing her hand. "I mean, truly?"

Elise's dark eyes welled with tears at the question, and I handed her a handkerchief.

"More than anything, I am just so angry. I have moments I am consumed with righteous anger for his death. Pure fury," she said, blotting her eyes and composing herself. "But I have Corinne. For her sake I need to show her that we can go on, we must go on living. And all this anger? I need to put that energy toward doing something—helping Jean, helping whoever else is involved in getting our country back."

I knew they were referring to Jean's work with the Resistance, and the three of us all scanned the streets and the café for any German uniforms. The closest table was four teenage girls giggling, but I still lowered my voice and leaned in to speak.

"That's why I wanted to meet with you both, actually," I said. "I need a favor."

"Anything," Elise said.

"You both know I plan to move to Barbizon, temporarily," I said.

The waiter came over with our champagne at that moment, so I paused as he opened the bottle and poured us each a glass.

"To Barbizon," Kathleen said. "You're not going to end up some sort of farm girl out there in the countryside, are you?"

"Hardly," I laughed. I told them about my dinner in Vichy with Laval and the veiled threat.

"Oh no," Elise said.

"Yes, so that's part of why I need to live quietly in the country for a while."

"So what's the favor?" Kathleen asked; she leaned in this time.

"I need you both to spread the news in various expatriate social circles that Drue Leyton has left the country through Spain," I said. "She's no longer in France; say she went to the States, or England, or . . . hell, say I left and joined the circus, I don't care. I just need people to believe I'm gone. I am Drue Tartière, wife of Jacques, not the American actress from Paris Mondiale."

"*Not* the Drue with a Nazi death warrant against her?" Elise said, her face serious as she sipped her champagne.

"Exactly."

"But . . . so you hide out in Barbizon; what if someone recognizes you when you come back to Paris?" Kathleen asked. We were quiet for a moment as the waiter put down an enormous plate of cheeses, and I realized how ravenous I was.

"I will deal with that if it happens, but the more people that think I'm gone, the better," I said. "It can only help."

They both nodded and agreed to do as I asked, and we all helped ourselves to the food.

"If I hear of anyone suspicious asking about you, I will also let you know," Kathleen said. "The German officers in Paris all want to be friends with Tudor because of his wealth and art collection. It's disgusting, frankly."

"Thank you both for your help," I said. "And there will be more opportunities to help with Jean's work, as soon as he recovers and we get settled in Barbizon. I promise you. And I must believe conversations like this are happening all over the country."

"Let's toast to that," Kathleen said as we clinked our glasses.

Chapter Twenty-Two

Early the next morning, Nadine and I took the train from Paris to Melun, with our bikes in tow, as it was a twelve-kilometer ride to the village of Barbizon from there. There was a woman sitting next to us on the train, blotting her eyes with a handkerchief as she read *Autant en emporte le vent*, the French translation of *Gone with the Wind*.

"Is it a good book?" Nadine whispered to me, nodding at the woman. "I see women all over the city reading it."

"I have heard it's a wonderful book; it's hugely popular in the US. I'm embarrassed to admit I haven't read it. I'll get us copies."

Barbizon was a charming village on the edge of the Forest of Fontainebleau, the so-called hunting ground of kings. As we biked through the countryside, the sunlight and natural beauty were a reminder of why the village had been an artists' haven in the nineteenth century.

"This reminds me too much of home," Nadine grumbled as she pulled up alongside me.

"Wait until you see the village; I think you'll like it," I said, not sure if I could ever convince her to like the countryside now that Paris had cast its spell on her.

We biked onto the cobblestones of Barbizon's picturesque Grand Rue, with its mix of small stone and stucco buildings and walls—a blend of villas and cafés and shops, many with shutters painted in pale blues or greens. The beauty of this village was its timelessness—not much had changed for hundreds of years. I felt wistful and sad as the memories of the weeks I had spent with Jacques and his family here in the summer of '39 came flooding back—the two of us strolling down this street hand in hand in the summer heat, stopping by one of the cafés for something cool to drink, Jacques proudly introducing me to everyone we met as his new wife. It had been perfect for a short time, before the world fell apart.

We passed by a few German soldiers sitting on the terrace of the pub, the Grand Bar Américain, owned by an older expatriate named Alfie Grand, who was married to a Frenchwoman, Giselle. Like the last time I had visited, there was still a huge American flag flying out front. Nadine gave me a sideways glance, amused.

I pulled up to Villa L'Écureuil. Its front curtains were drawn, and an untamed wisteria vine framed the dark-green front door, which was in desperate need of a fresh coat of paint. Instead of a nameplate, there was a wrought iron squirrel in a circle hanging on the stucco exterior on the right-hand side of the door.

"This is it? It looks very small," Nadine said, frowning and skeptical. "And so . . . *old*. How old is this house?"

"It's . . . well, it's three hundred years old, but—" I began.

"That is older than my family's old farm," she said with a groan.

When she looked like she was ready to cry at having to return to the country to a house older than the one she had grown up in, I launched into its selling points:

"But it's been modernized. Both the main house and smaller cottage have central heat, good bathrooms, and electric bath heaters! And see the fence on either side—the main villa goes back farther than you think, and it has a hidden courtyard with a gorgeous vegetable and flower garden, and there's another cottage and artist's studio and a garage that also can't be seen from the street. You'll have your own one-bedroom cottage. Jean can take the studio."

"Hmm . . . ," she said, a little more interested when I mentioned her having her own cottage.

I went up to the door and knocked, waiting a minute before trying again. I told her to wait and went down the narrow lane. The rose and lilac bushes along the property's stone wall were in desperate need of pruning. I knocked on the big wooden double-doored courtyard gate, but nobody answered there either, and on my tiptoes I tried to peek inside, but it was too high to see over.

"It's just been requisitioned by the Germans."

"Marion?" I whirled around to see an elderly woman with a silver bun standing in front of the door across the narrow alley. She was framed by the deep-orange trumpet flowers that grew on a vine on the gate to her villa.

"Oh, Drue! So lovely to see you again," she said with a warm smile, walking stiffly across the street to give me a warm embrace. She smelled of lavender and mint. I had met Marion on my visit to Barbizon with the Tartières and had socialized with her on more than one occasion. She was an American from Boston's Brahmin class, with an aristocratic air. "How is dear Jacques?"

I told her in very few words that Jacques was still away and explained why I was in Barbizon, asking what more she knew about the villa.

"That pompous Mayor Voclain believes in carrying out orders to the letter, even if they are Nazi orders," she said with a shudder. "Nobody has been living there for some time. The garden courtyard is a mess of weeds and overgrown plants. I wish you had come earlier; the mayor agreed to let the Germans have it a few days ago."

My heart sank, and, seeing the disappointment in my face, she added, "It's worth asking him if anything can be done. Just be warned— he is, as they say, very 'correct' when it comes to dealing with the Germans."

I thanked her and went back to tell Nadine we had to see the mayor of Barbizon.

"This is crazy," she said, shaking her head. "We can't just 'take it back' from the Germans."

"It can't hurt to try," I said.

Monsieur Voclain, the mayor of Barbizon, was a retired military officer in his midfifties, tall and gruff, with small, dark eyes and a long face. Nadine and I walked into his office at the city's small town hall, and he didn't even look up from the papers he was signing until I finally cleared my throat.

"*Bonjour*, Monsieur Voclain," I said with a smile. "I am Drue Tartière—perhaps you remember me from when I visited your lovely town with the Tartière family a little over a year ago? My husband is Jacques Tartière."

The mayor looked up at me and then Nadine, no warmth in his demeanor. "I don't remember you," he said. "And I am very busy; what's this about?"

"I noticed that Villa L'Écureuil is currently empty. It is owned by a family friend of the Tartières, who has told us we are welcome to use it anytime."

"I need to see your identification, both of you," he said with a grunt, finally looking us up and down with disapproval. "Why do you want the house?"

"I have a friend who is sick, with cancer. I was going to bring him here to convalesce," I said, handing him our *cartes d'identité*.

"And my husband, Jacques, who has also been ill, may be coming out to stay as well," I added; better if he believed that I knew my husband's whereabouts. He examined them for a minute longer than necessary.

"You're too late; the keys are in the hands of the German commandant, Herr Fieger. Please go," he said, handing me our papers and looking back down at whatever he'd been working on when we arrived.

Nadine, eyes wide, signaled me with her thumb that we head out, and I nodded. But halfway out the door I changed my mind.

"As a Frenchman, you would really prefer the Germans in that house to me and my family?" I said, trying to keep my anger in check at his disloyalty to his own country. I heard Nadine let out a small gasp behind me.

"Madame," he said, raising his voice to a growl, placing both hands on his desk, "I am following the orders of Marshal Pétain. France is now under the military government of the occupying German army. I must be *correct* with them, as they are with me. And I don't like it when an American woman comes into my office like she owns the earth and tells me what I should *prefer!*"

"OK, good day, monsieur, sorry to bother you, have a nice day," I said, smiling. I wasn't going to get anywhere with the petulant mayor. I walked backward out of his office as Nadine grabbed on to my arm and pulled me down the hall.

"He is worse than a Nazi," she said, making a sour face. "Maybe we should just go back to Paris? We are never going to get that villa."

We stood next to our bikes, and I looked down the main street, the sun shining, villagers greeting each other, sharing gossip or news of loved ones at war. And amid the provincial calm was the jarring sight of the green-gray uniforms of German soldiers sitting at the cafés and strolling down the streets.

"No, we don't have time to come up with an alternative plan," I said. "And I'm not going to do nothing and let myself be intimidated by a politically calculating mayor."

I got on my bike and started to ride.

"Where are we going?"

"Down the street to the headquarters of the German commandant."

"We are *not*," Nadine said, stopping her bike in the middle of the road, nearly getting run over by an old man driving a cart and mule. "Have you lost your mind?"

"Nadine . . . ," I said, hands on my head, frustrated and tired. "We desperately need a place to move to outside of the city, and I have no alternative plan. I have to at least try."

She looked at me, leaning on her handlebars, and let out a dramatic sigh. "All right. Fine."

"Thank you . . . Oh, one other thing—do you speak German?"

"No," she said, and burst out laughing. "Do you? No, of course you don't."

"Not one word," I said with a wink.

We had to wait for an hour in the lobby of the hotel that the Germans had taken over as their headquarters in Barbizon to see the commandant. Two soldiers who looked no older than teenagers greeted us politely and, in stilted, broken French, communicated that Herr Fieger would be back from lunch soon. There was a German-French dictionary on the lobby's front desk that they let Nadine and me borrow, and I scanned it to try to become fluent at a toddler level before he arrived.

"Look, over there," Nadine said as she pointed to a board of keys behind the front desk, each one with a label attached. "I see the keys to your villa."

"If *only* it were my villa," I whispered back.

Herr Fieger finally strutted into the lobby, and the two soldiers gave him the Hitler salute, which never ceased to make my stomach turn. He had a barrel chest and his pale hair cut very short, and I guessed he was in his late forties. One of the young soldiers pointed to us and told him we were there waiting for him. He looked at us appraisingly, and the stern look on his face softened into a wide smile, taking in our appearance. The Germans admired Nordic looks—blonde hair, pale skin, looks like mine—and I banked on that working in our favor.

"*Bonjour,*" he said, his expression embarrassed due to his stilted diction. But when he detected my accent, he started speaking English fluently.

"I studied at the London School of Economics," he said with a smile. "And you're American?"

"Yes," I said. "My husband is French, and his family spent many summers here in Barbizon."

"How may I help you?" he asked.

"If you please," I said in my sweetest voice, looking into his eyes. "My dear friend is very sick with cancer and needs a place to stay in the country to convalesce immediately. Villa L'Écureuil is owned by a close family friend of my husband, Jacques Tartière. I noticed it was empty, and, if possible, I would be so grateful for the opportunity to lease it."

Herr Fieger nodded at me, and then Nadine, his hand on his chin, thinking it over.

"At your service, madame," he said. Clicking his heels, he kissed both of our hands. Then he snapped his fingers and signaled one of the young soldiers to bring over the keys to the villa.

Offering us each an arm, he proceeded to escort us down Grand Rue. Nadine had looked at his arm like it might set her on fire, but, knowing we had to play this little game, she had put her hand on his elbow. I smiled flirtatiously at him again, not quite believing he was going to go through with it. Villagers stared at us, confused as to who these two women were walking with the German commandant.

Herr Fieger had to drop my arm to salute many German soldiers along the way, and for the sake of getting the villa, I had to hide my revulsion every time. When we arrived at the courtyard-gate side entrance, I saw Marion peeking out from behind her lace curtains, and she smiled and gave me a thumbs-up. The commandant took out the ring of keys and opened the creaking courtyard gate, escorting us inside with a dramatic flair.

"*Voilà*, mesdames," he said, holding his arms wide and taking a bow.

"*Danke schön*, Herr Fieger," I said as he handed me the keys.

"Thank you very much," Nadine said with a coquettish smile.

We both shook his hand, and he left the courtyard, closing the gate behind him, looking quite pleased with his chivalrous ways.

I stared down at the ancient key ring he handed me on the way out, not quite believing what had just happened.

"I cannot believe that he just . . . he just handed them to you, like *nothing*?" Nadine said, still staring at the courtyard gate.

"*Voilà*?" I said with a shrug, holding up the keys. She looked at them in amazement and then we both started laughing.

"Welcome to Villa L'Écureuil," I said, linking arms with her. "Let me give you a tour; we have a lot of work to do."

Part Two

Chapter Twenty-Three

September 22, 1941

Darling Jacques,

My love, today marks two years since you left to serve with the British, and so much has changed in our lives and in the world, it's both heartbreaking and dizzying to think about. I am writing again, trying to be optimistic that some way, somehow, my friends at the American embassy can get this letter to you. The last letter I received from you was in May, when you were heading to parts unknown. I am sure you have sent more since then, but sadly they have yet to reach me here in Barbizon.

The not knowing where you are weighs on me; my anxiety about your whereabouts keeps me up at night more and more lately. I try to remember that I am not alone in this suffering. And that others in this war are so much worse off than the two of us.

I was thinking today of when Nadine, Jean, and I first arrived in Barbizon and moved into the villa last September. At first, everything in the village reminded me of the blissful weeks we had spent here in the summer of 1939. It was like your presence was everywhere, and being back here without you made me feel lonelier than ever before in this chaotic war.

The thing that helped me overcome that difficult time was the work that had to be done; it was once again my salvation. When we first arrived at Villa L'Écureuil, it was sad and neglected, but how I wish you could see it now!

Nadine and I have created an expansive vegetable garden in the courtyard — parsley and peas, carrots and cabbages. People remark on how beautiful it is when they pass by the courtyard gate and peek inside, which makes us both quite proud.

And to add to our quaint village farm, we have animals — rabbits and chickens and four geese that I have grown quite fond of — who knew geese had such personalities! I have learned so much about farm life, and I often think about how shocked my friends in America would be to see me meticulously tending to the garden or building a new hutch out of canvas for our growing family of rabbits. I have become friendly with several of the local peasants and have learned the art of bartering for everything from manure to wine — much to the shock of Nadine and Jean, who thought that as an American I would be hopeless at what is a very specific skill.

I am happy to report that, after months of recuperating, Jean has completely recovered from his illness and finally seems back to himself again. He is heading to Paris for a doctor's appointment and a meeting with our friend O'Brien at the American embassy and will be bringing this letter with him.

Nadine and I are closer than ever, and I don't know how I would have gotten through these past two years without her friendship, humor, and hardworking nature. We've just started reading Gone with the Wind every night, and to say she has become obsessed with the novel is an understatement. She thinks we are living in our own French version of the story.

Oh, Jacques, I keep rambling on in this letter because I miss you more than I can say. I think the hardest part of this war is not knowing when or how it will all end, not knowing when I will see you again. I try so hard to be strong, and I think to the outside world I am, but sometimes at night I miss you so much it hurts to breathe, and I wonder how I will get up in the morning and do it all again.

I will keep praying and hoping in my heart for our reunion someday in the not too distant future. Please be safe, my darling, please come home to me.

All my love,

Drue

Wiping the tears off my cheeks, I addressed the envelope, tracing the letters of his name after I did. Jacques Tartière. Would I see my husband again? I used to be so certain that I would. But now I knew it wasn't a matter of when; it was a matter of *if*—that was what I didn't say in the letter. I was no longer naive enough to believe our reunion was a foregone conclusion. After all, since the beginning of the war, Elise and so many other wives had not gotten theirs.

The letter seemed to say so much but also somehow not enough. There was so much I couldn't tell him because it would land me in a Gestapo prison if anyone discovered it. So much I couldn't say about a life that had at first felt strange and surreal and lonely and that now felt something like . . . normal, and . . . *mine*.

In the initial weeks after moving into Villa L'Écureuil, Nadine, Jean, and I had settled into a routine and lived in a state of quiet paranoia, vigilant around the Germans in the area. Two hotels in

Barbizon—Stevenson's House and Les Pléiades—were well known in France for the fine cuisine and wine cellars, so Nazi officers, including some of the high command, would visit regularly.

In the first couple of months, I thought for sure that the Nazis had a roster of those they had planned to execute upon occupation, and that any day they would be banging on the villa's front door. Jean had finally convinced me that, from what he had learned, the Germans' methods for tracking were archaic and unsophisticated, despite their boasting, and that was reassuring.

Tending to the farm was important for our survival and constituted a large part of our day. It was far from our sole focus, although I could not reveal that to Jacques in writing.

I longed to share with him the work Jean, Nadine, and I were doing for the Resistance, which was still finding its way, as everyone who was a part of it learned to work in an atmosphere that was an odd blend of terror and acceptance. The French Resistance was growing and organizing, in communication with London via illegal shortwave radios all over France, which had to be moved constantly to avoid detection by the Germans.

I couldn't tell him about the anticollaborationist leaflets that Jean wrote and that Nadine and I, and sometimes Claude, would drop in the mailboxes of Resistance sympathizers all over Paris, sometimes staying overnight at our apartment on Rue Saint-Dominique, where Claude still resided. And I'd never be able to reveal our intelligence activity with friends of Jean's in neighboring Seine-et-Marne, who provided sketches of the German airfield there and kept records of the number of German planes leaving and the number of German soldiers in the area. All this intelligence was typed up by me, sometimes passed on by Jean to the British in Paris, other times left by me or Nadine in a specific drop box at the home or workplace of a Resistance member. It was just over the last couple of months that it felt as if the Resistance was finally starting to coalesce into a formidable, underground fighting front against the Nazis.

"Are you OK?"

I looked up from the tiny wooden desk in my cottage to see Jean standing in the doorway to the courtyard, which I often left open for the breeze and because Ondie and the geese liked to wander in and out. Jean was wearing a white button-down and black pants; he had gained the weight back that he had lost when he was ill and looked tan and healthier than I had seen him in ages. The only evidence of the toll taken on his body was his hair, still brown but now white at the temples.

"Yes," I said, standing up and handing him the letter. "I'm fine, just finished the letter. I don't know what kinds of miracles O'Brien can pull to try to get it to Jacques, but tell him I'm grateful to him for trying."

"I will," he said, giving me a sad smile. "And if he doesn't have any news for you, I'll see if any of my British contacts do. I know it's been too long since you've had word. I can't imagine what that's like."

"Thank you. You would think I'd be used to it by now. But as the war goes on . . . I don't know, I have this feeling of dread lately, more than ever before."

"It's understandable, and I'm sorry," he said.

"Oh, I have the basket. A bounty of vegetables and fresh eggs for Elise and Claude too. Please tell them to come visit soon." I grabbed the basket from the rear entryway.

"Is everything packed in the basket?"

"Yes, it's all there," I said. The basket had a false bottom; the intelligence papers he was taking were hidden there. "Nadine and I are going to go to Alfie's tonight, with Marion; you'll meet us there when you get back?"

"I will," he said. Alf's Grand Bar Américain remained a favorite spot for villagers to convene in the evenings, despite the fact that it had become popular with the Germans as well.

After Jean left and our morning chores were done, Nadine and I took Ondie for a walk in the countryside, as had become part of our routine.

"If the Americans ever come here, I would like to meet my Rhett Butler," Nadine said, smiling. "Do you think there are any Rhett Butlers in the American military?"

"Anything is possible," I said with a laugh. "Although, honestly, Rhett Butler was dashing but such a rogue. We need to expand your romantic-leading-men horizons. I'm going to get us the French and English versions of *Pride and Prejudice* next. You need to meet Mr. Darcy."

"Mr. Darcy? He sounds boring," Nadine said with skepticism, clearly enjoying this conversation.

"Oh, trust me, you're going to love him in the end," I said. "Did you know I met Clark Gable, who plays Rhett Butler in *Gone with the Wind*?"

"Really?" Nadine gasped.

"Really. I've been meaning to tell you that. And he is far more charming and handsome than Rhett."

"I cannot wait to see the movie."

"Me too. I hope it releases here this year."

"Do you miss acting?" Nadine asked, whistling to Ondie, who had run far ahead of us.

"That is a very good question," I said. "Sometimes. There is something about doing it that fills my soul in a way that nothing else can. But I was tired of a lot of things about Hollywood. And when you are a woman over the age of thirty, they're ready to put you out to pasture like those cows over there. When I met Jacques, I was ready for a change. And I loved moving to France."

"I saw you writing a letter to him," Nadine said in a soft voice. "I'm so sorry you haven't heard anything from him. I'm so sorry he's been gone so long."

"Thank you," I said with a deep sigh. "Me too."

We kept walking, and the beauty of our surroundings in the September light cheered me after my morning of tearful letter writing.

"No wonder artists have loved to come here to paint for centuries. It's so breathtaking."

"It is," Nadine said. "And I must confess something to you."

"Oh? What is it?"

"I know I was unhappy about moving here, but it's the perfect place to live during occupation. Safer than Paris, with more food available. I am sorry I complained."

"No need to apologize, I understand," I said, linking arms with her. "I'm glad you don't hate it."

"Quite the opposite," she said. "Though I want to live in Paris when the war is over. I can't imagine ever going back to my sleepy life in Colmar. I dream of maybe someday opening my own *brasserie* with someone . . . wherever *he* is."

"Nadine, you've never told me that before," I said, squeezing her arm. "You're a wonderful cook, and you're so organized, and . . . I have no doubt you could open your own restaurant someday."

"We'll see," she said, beaming, her cheeks turning pink. "Though that is far in the future; I am quite happy working for you now."

"Thank goodness for that," I said.

We came upon an isolated gray stone house with a red tile roof surrounded by farmlands. It was set back from the road, on the edge of some woods. On the right-hand side was a path to a small orchard filled with apple, pear, and cherry trees, and at least a couple acres of cultivated land. The area, the famous "plain of Barbizon," was considered the most fertile in the Seine-et-Marne region of France.

I stopped and leaned over the dilapidated wooden fence that surrounded the property as Ondie ran into the orchard looking for fallen fruit.

"Have you ever seen anyone here?" I asked her.

"I have; there's an old man, a cobbler who works in town, he lives here."

"Hmm . . ."

"What is it?"

"I just—I'm feeling restless. And so many are going hungry in Paris; if we could provide even more food for people there, that would be something. Our courtyard animal farm and garden are bursting at the seams. It would be nice to have more room to grow vegetables and raise the animals."

"Oh no. No. *No*," Nadine said, arms crossed, an amused but annoyed look on her face. "I tell you that I have finally gotten used to living in Barbizon, and you want us to move out of the village and live in isolation out *here?*"

"I was only thinking out loud," I said, laughing. "I'm not making any decisions."

"Good. Let's head back to the village before you get any crazier ideas."

When Nadine, Marion, and I arrived at the bar that night, Alfie Grand met us at the door, looking like the quintessential British bartender in his crisp white shirt, black bow tie, and suspenders. An American veteran of the Great War, Alfie Grand had emigrated from England to America on a tramp steamer when he was nine, so his accent was an odd combination of London cockney and pure New York. He was a short, chubby man in his sixties who had presided over restaurants and hotels all over Europe. His lovely wife, Giselle, was French, tall, and thin, with an aristocratic bearing in sharp contrast to her husband's scrappy, street-fighter appearance. The couple were unabashed de Gaullists—and Alfie was not afraid to openly argue with the German officers that frequented his establishment. And, because they liked him and especially his pub, they were very happy to spend a great deal of money for the privilege.

"There they are! Nadine and my two favorite Yanks," Alfie said, greeting us all with kisses. "I've a table by the fireplace for you; I know it's your favorite, madame."

He nodded to Marion and took the older woman by the hand, leading us inside to a rustic, dark wooden table next to the cozy stone fireplace. Above it hung a massive deer's head that Nadine always scowled at because she thought it was creepy.

I looked around the room; I now recognized most of the villagers in this small town, as well as some of the Germans who had been there at least as long as I had. Mayor Voclain was sitting with some of his cronies in the corner. He caught my eye, raised a glass, and gave me a nod. He had never warmed to me after our first encounter.

I scanned the bar area and spotted a man I had never seen before. He had longish dirty-blond hair and was very tan and was wearing a polo coat and pink shirt that made him stand out in the crowd.

"Alfie, who is the newcomer at the bar?" I asked when he returned to the table with our glasses, Sancerre for me, Burgundy for Nadine and Marion.

"Funny you should ask," he said, keeping his voice low, for there was a table of German officers a few feet away. "Just rented a villa here. Name's Daan Koster; he's a Dutch motion-picture producer. He was just going on about his Hollywood days.

"Don't like the look of him; don't trust him," Alfie said in my ear as he walked away.

Marion and Nadine and I all shot glances at each other, not saying a word for a moment. Outside of Jean, they were the only ones in the village who knew my life as Drue Leyton. It was warm by the fire, but I was covered in goose pimples.

"Should we leave?" Marion asked in a whisper, leaning into the table. "Do you know him?"

"No, I've never seen him before. I think we should stay," I said, though a chill had gone through me when Alfie mentioned the Hollywood connection. "I highly doubt he knew my true identity."

"Leaving right after we sit down would draw more suspicion in this crowd."

"I think we should leave," Nadine said, biting her thumbnail. "He looks like the type that would be friends with the Boche. And you heard Alfie; I don't trust him either."

"No, please, it'll be fine," I said, taking a cigarette case out of my purse and offering Nadine one. I had been smoking more than ever due to my nerves. Next to the bar, a band made up of local teenagers was setting up to play. "We all need this night out. Jean is meeting us here soon too. And there's music tonight, that young girl who sounds like Édith Piaf is singing."

Alfie's wife, Giselle, came over to talk with us, as did a few other villagers we had gotten to know, and as the band started to play, I relaxed and let myself enjoy the music and camaraderie. After an hour, with no sign of Jean, I excused myself and made my way to the bathrooms, located down a tiny staircase next to the bar. As I was on the way back to my table, the Dutchman stepped in front of me.

"*Pardon*," he said in accented French, pointing at my face. "My name is Daan Koster; I am in the movie industry. I saw you sitting at the table with your friends and . . . I was trying to remember where I knew you from when someone mentioned you were an American. And I realized, you are a movie actress! I recognize you from American films."

I was glad I had been forewarned about his background. Instead of looking panicked even for a second, I blinked and pivoted to the words I had rehearsed for months for when a moment like this ultimately arrived.

"Well, I am American, and I did do some film work years ago," I said, keeping my voice steady and calm. "But I only played a few bit parts; I am sure you have mistaken me for someone else. There are a lot of blondes in Hollywood, most more successful than I ever was."

"No, I know your face; it was you . . . What was the film . . . ," the Dutchman said, staring at me, fingers on his lips, undeterred. I could feel Nadine and Marion watching the exchange.

"That is very flattering, but I assure you what little film work I did was not that memorable," I said, pretending to be amused. "I bet you are thinking of the movie actress Carole Lombard; I've been told I look like her . . ."

"No, I . . ." He started to say something else when I spotted Jean walking through the door behind him. He was searching the crowd for us, his expression serious even when Alfie greeted him.

"Excuse me," I said. "My friend just arrived, but it was a pleasure to meet you, Monsieur Koster."

I squeezed by him and headed to the door, where Jean was still scanning the crowd.

"Jean," I said, finally exhaling after getting away from the Dutchman. "You made it; I was getting worried. I think I may leave, though, because that man . . . What . . . what is it?"

He had an anguished look on his face.

"Was it your doctor's appointment? Are you well?"

"I am fine, Drue . . . We should go outside."

"Oh no," I said. My stomach lurched, and I grabbed his arm to steady myself. "This is about Jacques—you know something."

He put his arm around my shoulder and steered me outside, and I started shaking. Neither of us said a word until we were inside the courtyard of our villa, and he helped me sit down on the little bench by the rosebushes and took my hand.

"He's gone, isn't he?" I whispered.

"He's gone," Jean said. "I am so sorry, my dear friend."

"He . . . but I just wrote him a letter . . ."

I let out a gasp and buried my head in my hands as the reality of his words hit me. I ran from the bench, only to collapse in the vegetable garden. Kneeling in the dirt, I sobbed, hugging myself, and Jean came running over and put his hand on my back. The courtyard gate clanged open, and Nadine was there next to me, knowing the news without asking.

I am not sure how long the three of us knelt in the dirt. I sobbed until I was hoarse. After some time, Nadine finally got up and said she was going to make us some tea. And Jean picked me up off the ground and held me up as he led me to a seat in the courtyard.

Chapter Twenty-Four

Nadine, Jean, and I sat at the wrought iron table in the courtyard, the pot of tea on it untouched. There was a sliver of a moon and a dazzling sky full of stars above us, and as I looked up, my first thought was that my husband, the love of my life, Jacques Tartière, was no longer on earth to see it. I would never again wake up to him sleeping next to me, or sit on a blanket with him for a sunset picnic in front of the Eiffel Tower. My worst nightmare had come true. He was gone, and the reality was both shocking and sickening.

"Tell me everything you know," I said to Jean when I finally had no tears left to cry.

"Elise told me first when I went to deliver the food. She had just been to the hairdressing shop and overheard the woman next to her say that her husband had just returned from Algiers. He said that in the Battle of Damascus, between the Vichy troops and the Free French, Jacques Tartière had been killed with the Free French force along with two others."

"She said Jacques's full name?" I asked, still not believing it.

"She did," Jean said.

"But wait—is this confirmed?" I said. "We can't take one woman's word in a hairdressing shop."

Nadine nodded and poured us tea; her face was also stained with tears.

"I know," Jean continued. "I didn't want to tell you unless I knew for sure. That's why I went to Richard O'Brien at the embassy. He . . . he confirmed it. Jacques's father and stepmother had a Mass for him in the States. This . . . this horrible news is true. Again, I am so sorry. And I am sorry to be the one to tell you."

"He was such a lovely man—I cannot believe it is true." Nadine started crying, and this time I gave her a hug, to comfort her and myself. I still didn't want to believe it either. Our married life had just begun; how could it already be over?

"Drue," Jean said, looking in my eyes, "I . . . I'm so sorry, but there are some things we must discuss that can't wait."

"What?" I asked, already knowing in my heart what he was going to say.

"First, he was working for the British, which was bad enough, but he was just killed fighting with Charles de Gaulle and the Free French. I think this might present a new danger for you."

"Why? Are you concerned about the Vichy government finding out?"

"Yes." Jean nodded. "If they don't know already, it will get back to Vichy officials that he was killed fighting with the Free French. The Nazis and their Vichy collaborators might take out their bitterness against such a brazen de Gaullist on his widow."

"Great," I said, putting my head in my hands. "Yet another reason for them to want to kill me. What do you propose I do?"

"You need to get rid of any letters he wrote you in service to the British, especially anywhere he makes it clear he's a de Gaullist."

I looked at Jean, stunned, trying to absorb what he was saying to me.

"I'll . . . I'll burn the letters."

I felt myself welling up again and put my handkerchief in front of my face as I choked on a sob, the pain in my chest almost too much to bear. I would never receive another letter from Jacques, and now I had to burn his last written words to me. That I couldn't keep these precious pieces of our history together, his handwritten words of love for me, was beyond devastating.

Nadine rubbed my back, muttering quiet, consoling words, and after a few minutes I composed myself again.

"I'm sorry," I said, waving my hand in front of my face to try to ward off more tears. "I . . . just . . ."

"No, don't apologize. It truly kills me to be the one to tell you all this," Jean said, a pained look in his eyes as he reached across the table to squeeze my hand.

"Is there any more?" I said. "That you have to tell me?"

He paused and lit another cigarette, his eyes never leaving mine.

"There is one other thing," he said with a sigh. "And it's horrible, but we do have to discuss it; I wish we didn't, but it's too important for your safety," Jean said, his voice filled with anguish.

"Tell me," I said in a whisper.

"I think it's best you keep his death a secret, as incredibly difficult as that may be," Jean said. "Besides us, only Elise and Claude and Richard O'Brien know, and it should stay that way."

"So you're telling me I have to pretend Jacques is still alive?" I said, grabbing his cigarettes off the table.

"If you want to stay in France . . . ," he said.

"I have to stay in France," I said, getting aggravated. "This is my home. And I think Jacques—no, I *know* Jacques would want me to stay, especially now."

"I agree, he would," Nadine said, nodding.

"I'll do anything for the cause now; you know I will. What have I got to lose?" I said this and bit my lip to keep from crying again.

"But don't you see?" Jean said, with the utmost patience. "You are not a French citizen. And with your husband . . . *gone*, it deprives you of an excuse for staying in France."

Nadine looked at me. We both knew he was right. Though it seemed a betrayal to not even acknowledge my husband's death, it was for my own security.

"You're right. It makes sense. I'll keep it a secret. Sorry, I'm just . . ." My voice started to crack.

"It is late, and you've had the most terrible shock. You should try to get some sleep," Jean said, patting my hand. "We can talk more tomorrow."

"I agree," Nadine said. "Try to get some rest."

"I might go lie down," I said. "But it's going to be a long time until I can truly rest again."

∼

I had finally fallen asleep as the sun was coming up. And when I woke the next day, for a few blissful seconds I forgot my husband was dead, before the horror of reality came rushing in. I put the covers over my head, not wanting to get out of bed, afflicted with the kind of fatigue that is only caused by grief. My body physically ached from the loss of Jacques as I tried to conjure all of the details of our last weekend in Paris together. I closed my eyes and summoned the memories of his smile and his laugh, the way he loved me like nobody else ever had, as my tears flowed until my pillowcase was damp with them.

I was not sure how long I had been lying in bed when I heard a knock on my door and Jean's muffled voice.

"Drue? It's noon. I thought you might want to go for a walk and get some fresh air."

I didn't want to go. I didn't want to do anything but dwell in my pain.

"I know how much you are hurting. We don't have to even talk. But getting out in the sun might feel good."

"OK," I said with a croak. "Just let me get dressed; I'll be down shortly."

We took the same route Nadine and I had the day before, and Ondie was overjoyed to join us. For the first half hour we didn't say a word, and I was grateful for the silence. I closed my eyes and turned my face to the sun, wondering how many months, or years, it would take before I didn't feel so broken.

I opened my eyes to the sound of Ondie barking. Several yards ahead of us, he had greeted a person coming from the other direction, and he was jumping up and down with excitement.

"Ondie, down!" Jean yelled, and we both ran over to get him under control.

It took me a second to recognize the Dutchman, and I wished I had told Jean about him before this moment. He was again dressed in more American-style attire, wearing a pale-blue button-down, khakis, and a straw hat.

"We meet again. Such a beautiful day for a walk in the country," Daan Koster said to me.

"Nice to see you again. This is my friend Jean Fraysse," I said, introducing them.

"Oh, I thought this might be your husband," Daan said, and I jerked my head toward him.

"No," I said, blinking, trying to stave off the tears. "He's . . . away. Fighting."

It had been less than twenty-four hours since I had learned of Jacques's death, and I had to pretend to this stranger that he was still alive. I hoped my acting skills were enough not to betray my emotions.

"Fighting," he said with a nod. "Have you heard the latest BBC news today?"

"No, I can't say either of us have," Jean said, now looking at this man as the threat that he was. "We don't have a radio at the villa."

Of course, we *did* have a radio at the villa, but we listened to it in secret on the second floor of the back cottage.

"It seems the Allies are making some progress in the war finally," he said with a smile. At that moment I was grateful for Ondie's energetic nature, as he had run ahead toward the farmhouse orchard that we had stopped by the day before.

"Oh, that's new to us," I said, trying to appear neutral, because I had guessed which side Daan Koster was on. "If you'll excuse us, my foolish dog has run ahead again, and I want to make sure he doesn't disappear into the woods."

"I'll see you in town, I am sure," Daan said with a tip of his straw hat.

I waited until there was enough distance between us, and then I let the tears fall. Jean stopped walking and pulled me into a tight embrace, one I hadn't realized I desperately needed.

"I'm so sorry you have to lie," Jean said after I had composed myself. "Though it's necessary with characters like that in the village. He's got to be a spy, and not a very discreet one."

"I didn't even tell you what happened last night," I said. And I told him about how the Dutchman had been in Hollywood and thought he recognized me from the movies.

"We must be very careful around him, obviously," Jean said.

"Yes," I said. Ondie had run back to us, an apple in his mouth, as we turned around to head back to the village.

We walked for a while in silence, and I appreciated the fact that Jean understood exactly what I needed.

"Did you know that, behind that farm with the orchard, there's a field that used to be used as a landing strip for small planes?"

"I had no idea," I said. "How . . . how did you know that?"

"I've been looking into it," he said. "We need a place where arms and ammunition can be delivered at night from England—by small plane, mostly by parachute. I'm thinking I'm going to offer to buy out the lease from the cobbler that lives there."

"Are you suggesting we move there?"

"I'm suggesting we keep the villa and also have the farm," he said. "Particularly if people like that Dutch filmmaker man are arriving in town, it's nice to have a more isolated option."

"Funny you should say that." I told him about my conversation with Nadine the day before about growing more food for our Parisian friends.

"There you go," he said with a smile. "Another excellent reason to lease the farm."

"And supplies from England, that's really going to happen?"

"Yes, I can finally say that the French Resistance is becoming less of an idea and more of a movement," Jean said. "I've been frustrated, as you have, at our inability to do more. But it's growing into an organization that will give us some power to fight—through sabotage and intelligence operations."

"Thank God. I needed that kind of news today," I said, the grief washing over me again, making me feel like I could buckle under the weight of it, and I crossed my arms, hugging myself. "The only way I can avenge Jacques's death is by doing the things that matter to help get his country back. This work . . . it's all I have now. That's all I have left."

"Oh, Drue," he said, putting his arm over my shoulder. "You have so much more than that. You are not as alone as you're feeling right now. In fact, Elise and Claude should be arriving from the city soon. They wanted to see you, to be there for you in your sadness."

"They are?" I said, blinking fast, moved by this news. "Now you're going to make me cry again, and I just told myself no more tears today."

"They are," he said. "You're loved by many, Drue Tartière. More than you know."

Chapter Twenty-Five

December 7, 1941

In the months after learning of Jacques's death, every moment was shadowed in grief. Sometimes the pain of it would pull me under, and I would feel like I was drowning in my sadness, finding it hard to even get out of bed. After living for two years in a state of constant anxiety about his safety, the devastation of finally learning he would never return to me, to our life together, shattered me. It would hit me in unexpected waves; I would be going about my chores and I would realize, suddenly, that he wasn't just away. He was gone. I would never hear Jacques's voice again or feel his kiss or sleep next to him in bed, and I would dissolve in a puddle of tears. I found myself obsessing over memories, our last weekend together in Paris, our days in this very villa in Barbizon. Some nights I dreamed of him still being alive, of him walking into the villa's courtyard in his uniform, of it all being a horrible mistake. But it wasn't a mistake. And I had to adjust to the new reality of a world without him in it.

I kept my head above water and pushed through it all because I had to, because there was so much work to be done getting our newly rented farmhouse on the plain near the forest cleaned and painted and in move-in condition, for ourselves as well as for my chickens, geese, and rabbits. Jean moved out to the house on the plain full time, while

Nadine much preferred the villa. I decided I would go back and forth between both, with plans to spend more time on the farm in the spring to work on planting a much larger vegetable garden than the one in our courtyard. There were many families going hungry in Paris, and the least I could do was provide some of my friends and their friends with food to supplement their meager rations.

Nadine would say that, along with long hours of hard work that made my hands raw and my body ache, *Gone with the Wind* had helped me during those months too, as we read it together every night until we finished all one thousand thirty-seven pages at the end of November. It was a welcome distraction in the evenings, when my mood was often at its lowest. The kind of story that took you out of your head and put you into another world. And I understood why so many Frenchwomen were reading it, because it was a reminder that human beings had persevered through dark and difficult times in history before and come out the other side, not unscathed but still whole.

It was a Sunday evening, and Elise and Claude had come to stay for the night in the villa to pick up food supplies before heading back to Paris in the morning. We were all enjoying a glass of wine by the woodstove, and Nadine was preparing a late dinner of chicken and potatoes and leeks. The two of them had been coming to visit us once a month. Claude was a reliable courier of messages to Jean from other Resistance members, and Elise enjoyed the break from her family. And they were also keeping tabs on me, both worried about how I was doing since Jacques's death. Their visits had helped me heal. They would help us with chores, and we would have a lively dinner at the villa, where Claude always had stories to tell along with imitations of people, famous and infamous, often making us laugh until we cried.

Claude was regaling us with one of these stories, doing a hilarious impression of my neighbor Madame Vachon wrangling her dogs, when Jean opened the back door.

"We need to go upstairs and turn on the BBC on your shortwave, Drue—you all have to hear what's happening," he said, his voice frantic.

"Oh God, now what? Give us a hint, please," I said, gripping the arm of my chair, unsure if I could handle more grim news.

"Japan attacked America," Jean said, bolting upstairs, and the rest of us jumped up and followed. I took my shortwave out of its hiding place under a loose floorboard and turned it on:

"The latest facts of the situation are these. Messages from Tokyo say that Japan has announced a formal declaration of war against both the United States and Britain. Japan's attacks on the United States naval bases in the Pacific were announced by the White House this evening."

The announcer went on to say that the naval base of Pearl Harbor in Hawaii was under attack, as well as US interests in the Philippines. The number of casualties was unknown, but the death toll was expected to be staggering. Still, the BBC announcer's voice was filled with hope and encouragement that now America would have to come to the aid of the Allies.

"Oh God," I said, sickened for my country. "All those navy personnel dead. Their poor families; it's devastating."

"But think of it; this is the end for the Nazis. They are *kaput!*" Claude said. Clapping his hands together, he grabbed Nadine by the hand and started waltzing her around the room humming "La Vie en Rose."

"I hope you are right, but please, Claude, now it means more American boys killed, along with the French and British," I said, feeling my voice choke with emotion. "That is nothing to celebrate."

"Drue is right," Elise said, looking me in the eyes; we knew what those families would experience, as our own grief was still raw.

"I'm sorry," Claude said, turning more serious, sympathy in his tone. "I am just so relieved that help will be on the way for our own soldiers now."

Jean shushed us so we could continue to listen to the bittersweet news. Finally, after far too long, America would have to come to the aid of the Allies, and it filled me with a roller coaster of emotions—despair for the United States being pulled into this horrible war, but hope that this historic moment might finally bring an end to the suffering of my adopted country.

We listened until it was clear there was nothing else new that would be reported that evening. Jean was quiet and serious after we turned off the news, and as I started downstairs to get ready for a dinner that now felt like a celebration, he touched my elbow and told me to wait.

"What is it?" I said as I was putting the radio back in its hiding place under the floorboard.

"Do you still have that fake medical certificate that my doctor gave you that says you have very serious cancer?"

I paused and looked up at him. America entering the war was good news for France, but not necessarily for me.

"I do . . . Do you . . . do you think they might really *arrest* me? I mean, if they haven't by now, I have been thinking I might not be in their sights after all."

"Yes, but now all Americans in France will be in their sights," Jean said.

"So what should I do?"

"Richard O'Brien will be at the embassy in Paris for a few days. We should go and see him, see what the situation will be for American expatriates now."

～

America declared war on Japan the day after the attack and three days later declared war on Germany. And at the end of the week, Jean and I took our trip into Paris to see Richard O'Brien. The train car was stuffy and overcrowded, and, as soap was becoming scarcer, the mingled odors were overpowering, and I found myself covering my face with my scarf.

"Nadine came back from the bakery this morning upset," I said, whispering in his ear. "The baker's wife actually asked her if I was afraid of being locked up now that America is at war with Germany."

"What did she say to her?" Jean asked. We were in the back of the car and kept our heads together and our voices low, as you never knew who was listening.

"She said, 'I told that gossipy cow that you paid no attention to ridiculous rumors.'"

"That's Nadine," he said with a smile. "She's right; these are all just rumors at this point."

"Alfie Grand is American, but he's a French citizen. The only other American in Barbizon besides him is Marion," I said after I had composed myself. "I went to see her for tea yesterday afternoon. She laughed at the idea of the Nazis arresting her. She's lived here over thirty years."

We arrived in the city, and while I had grown accustomed to this newer, darker version of Paris, with its German signs on street corners and massive Nazi flag flying on the Eiffel Tower, it still filled me with a longing for a free Paris and everything it represented.

"I have been meaning to tell you, because I thought you could use some good news. We are going to start to receive drops of arms and ammunition at the farmhouse from Britain," Jean said. We were walking down a quiet side street near the American embassy, but he still looked around before speaking and kept his voice low. "English and French airmen will be arriving by parachute as well, to help with sabotage work."

"That is excellent news," I said. "Can I help?"

He didn't answer, and just kept walking.

"Jean, can I help?" I couldn't hide the urgency in my voice. I didn't just want to help; I *needed* to after losing my husband.

"Yes, you can," he said. "I considered saying no, it's too risky, they could already be watching you. But then I realized you wouldn't take no for an answer."

"You're right," I said, smiling. "I wouldn't."

Jean put his arm around my shoulder, and I was touched by the gesture and leaned into him, feeling the warmth of his body, the scent of his cologne, lemon and bergamot. I glanced up at him and we locked eyes, and something passed between us that both comforted me and made me uncomfortable, so I pulled away, just holding on to his elbow instead. He put his hand on mine and squeezed it.

"My friend, the thing that's hard for me," he said with a sigh, "is if anything happened to you, I would never forgive myself. You are too dear to me now."

"Thank you," I said in a whisper, squeezing his hand in return. I did not know what else to say. I cared for Jean a great deal, that much was certain. It was something beyond friendship, that I knew, but nothing I wanted to act on. Because my heart still ached; I was still raw with grief for Jacques and the life we would never get to have together.

We were across the street from the Hôtel de Crillon, now the Nazi headquarters in Paris, just as a group of men were exiting the building, two slick black Mercedes awaiting them. Some were in uniform, two were not, and, as I stared, I realized I recognized one of them.

Daan Koster was dressed in a camel-colored cashmere coat and black wool fedora. Our eyes met, and he paused for a moment, giving me a smile and a small wave before climbing into the car.

I cursed under my breath as they drove away.

"Who was that?" Jean asked. "I didn't get a good look."

"Daan Koster, that Dutchman living in Barbizon," I said. "Cozying up to Nazi officers without a hint of shame."

"Not surprising, though," said Jean. "He wasn't exactly subtle on our walk that day."

"Just another reason to stay paranoid," I said. "And there's something about him, in particular—the movie connection, and his guesses at my former identity."

We had arrived at the American embassy and rang the front bell. Nobody answered the door, so we rang a second time, finally hearing footsteps.

"No receptionist, no staff whatsoever, I had to make a run for it to get the door before you left," Richard O'Brien said when he opened the door, out of breath, his round face flushed as he greeted me with kisses on both cheeks. "It's an absolute ghost town here. I'm glad you called, Jean; it's good to see you both, and I'm leaving again for Vichy in the morning.

"And, Drue, my deepest condolences for the loss of your husband. What a shock that must have been. I am so incredibly sorry," Richard said as he led us upstairs. I was taken aback by the mention; I had forgotten that he was one of the only ones who knew.

"Thank you," I said in a soft voice.

He brought us into a conference room on the second floor that I had never been in before.

"There they are," Richard said in a grim voice as I stood by the window. We had a perfect view of the Hôtel de Crillon, including into a meeting room on a floor above us, where several Nazi officers appeared to be sitting around a long table. "Some of the highest-ranking Nazi officers in Paris are meeting right now."

I shivered at the sight of them so close by, and told him about Daan Koster leaving the building and my recent encounters.

"Yes, spies and collaborationists are everywhere," Richard said. "If he's a filmmaker, I bet he's working with Continental Studios; it's a movie-production company set up by Hitler's minister of propaganda."

"I'm sure he is," Jean said, still looking out the window at the enemy just beyond the glass.

"I have no tea or coffee, but, this being France, there's wine from the ambassador's cellar. I know why you're here, so let's have a glass, and I'll tell you what I know."

We got settled around the table as Richard retrieved glasses from a cabinet and poured us all some Bordeaux.

"My first question is, Are the rumors true?" I said.

"What rumors have you heard?" Richard asked.

"Do the Germans intend to imprison Americans?" Jean said. "That's the rumor I'm hearing from my sources."

"We know of no such plans yet," Richard said. "And I promise you I will try to get word to you in advance if we learn of anything like that. But you have a couple of things in your favor—you are married to a Frenchman."

"Yes, and she—*we* have all kept his death a secret, as we discussed last time," Jean said.

"Good. I'm very sorry that it's necessary," Richard said, giving me a sympathetic glance. "But I think it's safer for you if we do. Also, the last passports we issued all Americans in Paris, right before occupation, were without visas—this was on purpose, so it's not so easy for the Nazis to check up on past movements."

"Well, that's helpful," I said. "I had forgotten that."

"Now, what do you have in terms of property in your name?" Richard asked. "They're going to make you give them an inventory, and they can confiscate what they want."

"At Jean's suggestion, when we moved to Barbizon, I put my furniture, the villa lease, everything in Nadine's name. She's—well, she was my maid, but she's more like family now," I said.

"Good," Richard said. "In that case, I don't think you have anything immediate to worry about. Though I would avoid other Americans in the village, keep to yourself somewhat."

"OK. But you . . . you really think I don't have to worry?" I asked.

"Not at the moment, no," Richard said. "Please trust that I would tell you."

"What if the worst-case scenario happens and they do arrest and imprison me?" I said. "Could the embassy get me out? How does that work?"

"We would try our best, of course," Richard said. "And I know you are friends with Tudor and Kathleen Wilkinson; they might be able to help in that regard. Tudor has built some relations with the Germans due to his enormous art collection, but he is very much on the right side of this war. And believe it or not, Charles Bedaux, although he is on no side but his own, has helped many of his Jewish friends stay safe."

"That is all somewhat reassuring," I said.

"And Drue has something else that could help her if she's arrested," Jean said. Lighting up a cigarette, he told Richard about my fake medical certificate from his doctor friend.

"I'm impressed that you thought that far ahead, but then, of course you would, Jean," Richard said, eyebrows raised, looking back and forth between us. "But pretending to have cancer is a pretty extreme measure."

"It is," I said. "But if it got me released from the Gestapo? I think I could do a good enough acting job to convince them."

"I have no doubt," Richard said with a laugh. "But my God, let's hope it never comes to that."

Chapter Twenty-Six

September 22, 1942

After Pearl Harbor, as an American, I had to register every Saturday with the mayor's office in Barbizon, to let them know I was still in residence in the village. Monsieur Voclain himself oversaw this process with a kind of smug satisfaction, each week asking my name, birth date, and address as if he didn't know me at all.

And in the first six months after the Americans joined the Allies, Jean, Nadine, and I had, once again, lived in a state of hypervigilance, expecting the Nazis to arrive at our door at any moment to take me away. Nadine did most of our shopping, and I had even avoided the cafés and restaurants, and particularly Alfie's Grand Bar Américain, because it had become the absolute favorite of the Germans, even after Alfie refused to take down his American flag at their request.

I had also steered clear of Daan Koster, crossing the street whenever I saw him in the village. Between his vague recognition of me from my films and his ties with the Nazis in Paris, I wanted nothing to do with the man. Only once had I been unable to avoid him, on a gray February morning. I had been standing in front of the villa when I heard him call my name and turned to find us face-to-face.

"Madame Tartière," he said, tipping his fedora to me. "I have not seen you out in so long. Have you been well?"

"Very well, thank you," I said. "Just awfully busy; I've moved most of my animals out to the farm on the plain that we leased, and I am planning out a large vegetable garden there, over an acre in size. It's been exhausting work."

"Do you not need money? I have heard it is very difficult for Americans to access their money now."

It had been such a blunt and obtrusive question, one that he had no trouble asking me.

"Oh no, I have friends in Paris who were generous enough to loan me all I require for now," I said, with a tight smile. It was true, as the Wilkinsons had insisted on helping me out in that way.

"Well, I know you said you only did a little acting, but I am working for Continental Studios," he said, just as Richard O'Brien had surmised. He looked me up and down, nodding admiringly. "With your beautiful Aryan looks, I am sure I could cast you in some of my movies."

"That is kind of you," I said, feeling queasy, wondering if he had figured out any more of my past. "But what little acting I did—well, those days are long over for me."

"That is too bad," he said. "What of your husband? I have seen Monsieur *Fraysse* often, but where is Monsieur Tartière?"

He had given me an insinuating smile, and I had wanted to slap him for what he was implying.

"Yes, Monsieur Fraysse has been recovering from his illness on the farm," I said. "The country air is so good for him. And as for . . . Jacques, my husband, why he was just here, a few weeks ago. But had to leave again on business. Now, if you'll excuse me, I have a great deal of work to do today. *Bonjour*, Monsieur Koster."

"*Bonjour*," the Dutchman had said. "Please, the next time your husband is in Barbizon, I would love to meet him. He's a lucky man. We could have a drink at Alfie's."

"Thank you. That would be nice," I had said, with a hint of sarcasm I doubted he could detect.

After the encounter, I had ducked down the alley as fast as I could without being obvious, my hands shaking slightly as I slammed the courtyard gate behind me, hoping I had convinced Koster that Jacques was still alive. Outright lying was not the same as acting, but I had tried my best.

By the early summer, it had felt safe enough for me to engage in more Resistance activities again. The airdrops of arms and ammunition had resumed, and French and Englishmen had also begun parachuting in to assist in sabotage work. Claude or I would often spend time with Jean on the farm, and the two of us would carefully plan our trips to Paris as couriers, bringing documents and false papers back and forth between Paris and delivering them to Jean and other Resistance members from Melun. Claude had insisted on helping with this because "nobody suspects a fat old man," and I had been able to conceal papers in the hidden compartment of my basket, underneath turnips and carrots and whatever else I was bringing on a particular trip.

And Nadine and I had worked tirelessly to get at least some of the acreage plowed and cultivated. At first, our neighboring peasant farmers had treated me like I was a circus oddity, the American woman who read books on farming. But we had hired Remy and Girard, two towheaded brothers, ages nine and eleven, who lived on a neighboring farm. They had assisted in the backbreaking work of planting an acre's worth of vegetables—carrots, peas, cabbages, and squash, with a large field devoted to potatoes, so critical for our diet and as a bartering commodity. By the late summer, we had gained the respect of our neighbors, who praised us for our bountiful harvest.

When September arrived, I was content in the work I was doing for both the farm and the Resistance and had been lulled into a false sense of security, believing that if they hadn't tracked me down yet, then maybe I would be safe for the duration. Although the question of how long the war would last weighed on the minds of everyone in France. The US Navy had halted the Japanese advance in the Pacific at the

Battle of Midway, but that was the only bright spot of war news from the BBC, as the Germans continued their offensive in the Soviet Union and their forces in North Africa penetrated Egypt. With their military dominance, there was no end of the war in sight yet.

The knock on Villa L'Écureuil's front door came on an unusually warm September afternoon. Nadine and I were digging up potatoes in the courtyard garden, trying to get a large produce basket ready for Elise, who was arriving that evening for an overnight stay.

"Nobody ever knocks on the front door," Nadine said, frowning as she stood up to get it, wiping her forehead with the back of her hand. Her black hair was sticking out underneath a kerchief, and, like me, she wore overalls now covered in dirt.

"The grocer is supposed to drop off a couple of magnums of wine," I said. "It's probably his delivery boy; he wouldn't know better."

She walked down the garden path and disappeared into the house while I kept working. Ondie's hysterical barking was the first clue that something was amiss. I stood up to look, but our towering lilac bushes prevented me from seeing into the house. Nadine appeared on the path, her face ghostly as she tried to warn me with her eyes. Behind her was Mayor Voclain, followed by a Nazi officer, over six feet tall, a silver chain with a big medallion around his neck.

"Madame, he is from the Gestapo in Melun," Nadine said, her voice shaky. She pointed to Mayor Voclain and scowled. "*He* says you have to report to the commandant there at once."

"I am serving as this officer's translator," Voclain said to me in French, with an air of self-importance. "You are to go to Melun for an hour's questioning."

"OK," I said, keeping my voice calm as I replied in kind. "I will bike over in a little while. I must finish getting these potatoes up."

"Oh no," Voclain said, shaking his head and holding up his finger, taking great satisfaction in having the upper hand with me. "No, we have a car. And we are to bring you. Now."

I couldn't even look at Nadine, my heart heavy in my chest. This was the moment we had hoped would never come.

"Why? What is wrong?" I asked, frowning at Voclain and the giant Nazi. *Why now* was my question. There were so many possibilities it was almost ridiculous. Was it because of the death warrant from my radio days? Or had they learned of Jacques's death? Or was it simply because I was an American? *Why now?*

"Nothing is very wrong, madame," Voclain said. "But it is urgent."

I needed to play it cool; I needed them to think I didn't have any reason to worry.

"Look at me," I said, pointing to my dirty overalls, my feet filthy because I was wearing sandals. "I can't go to Melun looking like this, can I? At least give me time to have a quick bath and clean up."

"No!" Voclain said, clenching his fists, his tone aggravated. "It's for an hour's questioning, and you must come at once."

I started to pick up potatoes and put them in my gunnysack, mainly to annoy Voclain but also to consider my next move.

"She can do that," Voclain said, pointing at Nadine, who looked like she was ready to punch him.

"*Nein, nein,*" the giant Nazi said, frowning at me and Voclain, pointing to the house.

"The car is parked out front and we must go," Voclain said.

"All right," I said. "But at least come in and have a drink while I gather my papers and handbag."

Voclain translated this to the Nazi. And to my surprise, he looked at me and nodded in agreement. I took the two of them into the front cottage, and they sat in my small salon while I excused myself to get glasses in the kitchen. Nadine was in there getting out the bottle of cognac, still pale. Her hand holding the bottle was shaking.

"Go out the back through the courtyard and hurry as fast as you can to the farm. Tell Jean he must not come back to the villa this afternoon," I whispered in her ear. "And do you remember the Resistance papers, buried in bottles in the garden? After we leave, move those papers and anything else incriminating to the farm. They will probably come back to search the villa."

She looked at me and nodded, tears in her eyes.

"For God's sake, please don't let them see you cry," I said, kissing her on the forehead. "I'm just going for an hour's questioning. I'll be right back."

She nodded and without another word slipped out the back door to the courtyard.

I returned with the glasses of cognac on a tray, including one for myself, because I needed it more than either of them. The Nazi was sitting in one of my chairs, which was almost too small for his frame, looking awkward and unsure how to behave. Meanwhile Mayor Voclain was leaning back on my settee with his leg crossed like he owned the place.

"I'll give you a one-thousand-franc note if you can give me any information on why they want me," I said to him, knowing the German had no idea what I was saying.

"I don't know," he said with a shrug. "I know they are curious about the man who lives here at times. If you do not get back within an hour, I can tell your maid; that must be worth a thousand-franc note."

"Not quite, Mayor Voclain," I said with a scoff. "How much are they paying you?"

"That's no business of yours," he said, glaring at me over his glass.

"Is it worth forsaking your country?" I asked, downing the cognac.

"Be careful, Mrs. Tartière. We all must do what we need to survive," he said, his voice seething.

The Nazi picked up on his anger and said something to him in staccato German.

"It's time to go," Voclain said with satisfaction. "You need to bring your *carte d'identité* and passport."

"I'll go get them," I said as I poured a second round for all of us before running upstairs to get my paperwork and wash my face.

Minutes later, I walked out my front door with Voclain on one side of me and the Nazi giant on the other. A black Mercedes was parked out front.

"This is my first automobile ride in almost a year," I said, attempting to sound relaxed. I got into the back seat; the warm buzz of the cognac was having the effect on my nerves that I had hoped it would.

We drove slowly down the Grand Rue; clearly the Nazi wanted it to be a spectacle and a warning to the villagers. Neighbors and shopkeepers were standing outside their homes, many of them looking stunned, and as I passed, they waved and shouted words of encouragement to me. When we reached Alfie's bar, he was out front, his face red with anger. Giselle was by his side, blotting her eyes, blowing kisses at me.

My window was down, and I called out to them and blew them a kiss back, and Alfie came running over and grabbed my hand.

"Drue, my girl, what in the bloody hell is going on?"

"I don't know, but—"

The Nazi started shouting in German, and Alfie stepped away from the car.

"Be strong, my dear," he yelled, pointing behind him at the flag above his door. "We will be here for you. This flag flies for *you*."

I started to blink fast; something about the kind words almost made the tears start to fall. But at that same moment, Voclain turned to the back seat to glare at me, and my anger at him and the situation came back in a rush.

"When this war is over, there will be a reckoning for people like you," I said. "God help you when it happens."

"I would not concern yourself with my fate right now, Madame Tartière," Voclain said. "*I'm* not the one that's about to be imprisoned by the Nazis."

Chapter Twenty-Seven

Mayor Voclain was bluffing about my imprisonment. He had to be, because the alternative was impossible to comprehend. After he said it, I wanted to protest but thought better of it. It was clear he wanted to continue the conversation in order to torment me, so my best course of action was to ignore him. I rolled my window all the way down and leaned out for the rest of the ride to Melun. The fresh air and warm sun helped clear the cognac fog from my brain as I considered just why they had decided to take me in at this moment. The mayor had mentioned Jean, and so now I had to wonder if *that* was the reason—had they discovered what was happening out on the farm, the Resistance meetings and the drops of guns and money and agents from Britain?

A wave of nausea came over me, and I closed my eyes and took some deep breaths to calm myself. For so long, I had made the decision not to live a life constantly anxious and in fear of *what if—what if they find out Jacques is dead, or that I'm Drue Leyton from the radio.* But that didn't mean the fear didn't creep in at times. And now it seemed the Germans had caught up to me. Sitting in the back of the Mercedes, I was more than afraid. I was terrified. But I couldn't panic, and I some-how needed to summon enough courage to appear like I had nothing to hide.

Twenty minutes later, we arrived at a nondescript three-story stone villa in Melun. The giant Nazi dropped me and Mayor Voclain at the front door, and two guards led us upstairs to the third floor.

"Commandant Fieger will see you shortly," Voclain said as one of the guards opened the door to what was obviously the servants' quarters. The dust in the room was visible in the sunlight coming through a tiny window. There were two black iron cots with dirty, worn mattresses, and I gasped, because sitting on a dingy red settee was Marion Greenough, wearing a pristine black cotton dress, reading a tattered novel. I rushed over to her as the door locked behind me.

"Marion! What in the world are you doing here?"

"Drue," she said, enveloping me in a maternal hug. "Not you too. You're so young and beautiful."

Her words made me shiver because it was as if she were saying an epitaph for me. But I took the fact that they had arrested her too as a good sign. I sat down next to her on the filthy sofa, and she grasped my hand tightly.

"How long have you been here?" I asked, keeping my voice low in case the guard outside was listening.

"Just an hour."

"Do you know what this is about?"

"No," she said, "I don't know what to think. They said I was being brought in for questioning, but I brought an overnight bag; my sense is we are not going to be going home anytime soon."

"Do you really think that? What makes you think that?"

"My dear, I lived through the first war with these Germans," she said with a deep sigh, squeezing my hand. "That's what makes me think it. I was planning on calling on you today because we haven't had tea in so long. Tell me, have you heard any news from Jacques?"

I sat there, looking down at my dirty overalls.

"Jacques was killed, Marion," I said, my voice wavering as I whispered it. "Some time ago, in Syria. I've kept it a secret . . . the Germans must not find out because that deprives me of an excuse for staying in France."

"Oh, Drue," Marion said. She burst into tears and hugged me again, and I let out a sob against her shoulder as all the emotions I had been holding back all day came bubbling to the surface. "He was so wonderful when I met him that summer. And then to have to keep it a secret? How horrible for you. I am so sorry."

We talked with quiet voices, and I was comforted by this fellow American, so kind and sympathetic to all I had been through. At least two hours had passed when the guard came in with a hot-water-and-roasted-grain concoction that was a horrible excuse for coffee.

"No milk or sugar?" Marion asked in a very sweet voice. The guard just scowled at her, not understanding the question.

"How long are we—" I started to ask, but he just turned and slammed the door behind him, and I heard the click of the lock.

Darkness came, and just when it appeared they would forget us for the night, the door opened, and the guard motioned us to follow him downstairs. He brought us to the office of Herr Fieger, the friendly commandant who had allowed me to have the villa in Barbizon.

"Herr Fieger," I said. I was still in my dirty overalls and unwashed, and too aggravated to be charming. "Your people say you are bringing me here for an hour, and we've been here all day, with no food. If I am going to spend the night here, at least send me to my house to get me some clean clothes and sanitary napkins." I lifted my leg to show him the bloodstain on my overalls.

The commandant was mortified, his face crimson.

"*Ma pauvre madame,*" the commandant said. *My poor madame.* I took this as a good sign. And then he handed me a pen and paper. "Please, both of you, have a seat. Write up what you need, and I will send one of my men to Barbizon right away."

I made up a list for Nadine, including the fake medical certificate that I couldn't believe I might have to use.

"Thank you," I said, and finally smiled. "And what about food? Are your Gestapo men ever going to give us anything to eat?"

"Yes," Fieger said. "You will have food brought to your room after this meeting."

"Back to our room?" I said. "And then what? How long are we to be kept here?"

"The Americans have locked up all German-born women without American naturalization papers," Herr Fieger said. "So, we have no alternative but to take similar measures. I do not believe in making war on women and children, but the Americans have forced Germany's hand."

"I don't believe a word of it!" Marion jumped up and slammed her hand on the desk, shocking both me and the commandant. "We would never do that in America. *Never*."

Marion was outraged, but my immediate reaction was relief. Because they were rounding up all Americans, for no reason other than being American. And for me, that was a silver lining to this terrible predicament.

I could see Herr Fieger's expression change from sympathetic to angry, and I took over the conversation.

"The commandant has explained it nicely; it must be so, Marion." I grabbed her hand and pulled her back down to her seat.

"Doesn't it matter that I am married to a Frenchman?" I said.

"Do you still claim American citizenship?" Herr Fieger asked.

"Of course," I said.

"Then that makes no difference," Herr Fieger said.

"Tell me, up to what age are these German women being interned in America?" I asked, looking at Marion, who was sitting there fuming.

"We have exempted all women with children under twelve years old. And all those sixty-five years of age or older," Fieger said.

"I will be sixty-five in two weeks," Marion said.

"You have to let her go," I said. "She is almost at the cutoff age. You must."

"I will put it to the authorities in Paris," Fieger said. "Where is your husband, Madame Tartière?"

"I don't know," I said, looking Herr Fieger in the eye and lying. "I have no idea. Fighting with the Vichy French, last I heard."

"And there has been another man living with you off and on," he said, watching my reaction.

"Yes, that's true," I said.

"Is that the reason why you stayed on in Barbizon?" Herr Fieger asked.

"Yes. It is . . . it is an affair of the heart," I said, knowing deep down that, after all this time, that might be an underlying truth to my friendship with Jean. Nothing had ever happened between us, but I knew deep down that the way we cared for each other went beyond friendship.

"That explains a lot," he remarked, raising his eyebrows at me.

"It usually does," I said, taking a deep breath. "What happens now?"

"Tomorrow morning you will be brought to a temporary holding facility outside of Paris. Then you will be transferred to the internment camp for English and American women in Vittel, in the Vosges Mountains."

I closed my eyes, willing the tears not to fall. Marion let out a small cry next to me.

"This can't be happening," I said, elbows on the desk, pinching the bridge of my nose. "A camp . . . a prison in Vittel? For how long?"

"That depends on your country's behavior."

Chapter Twenty-Eight

My bag with the blue zipper had arrived later that evening with clothing and food from Nadine. I washed up and changed my clothes, and after sharing with Marion the pâté, large chunk of bread, and honey Nadine had sent, we both felt human again. Before going to bed, I searched through the clothes and cosmetics multiple times for the fake medical certificate, but it was nowhere to be found. Given only a dirty cotton blanket and thin mattress, it took me until after midnight to fall into a restless sleep as my mind raced with thoughts—wondering how Nadine was going to manage the farm on her own, whether they had discovered what Jean was involved with, and if the certificate had disappeared or, worse, been confiscated. That had been my insurance policy, a possible ticket out of this madness; what was I to do if I didn't have it?

We were put on a bus to Paris the next day, along with a half dozen other American women that I did not recognize but who, after some brief introductions, felt like loyal friends.

"Where are you taking us in Paris?" I asked Herr Fieger, who was sitting at the front of the bus.

"First, to pick up more Americans," Fieger answered.

"How many more?"

"As many as we can find; it is expected to be over three hundred total."

"And then?"

"Do you always ask so many probing questions, Madame Tartière?" He gave me a small smile, amused.

"When I am being imprisoned for being American? Yes, I do, Herr Fieger."

"I can't say I blame you," he said with a laugh. "Too bad your country is treating our women so poorly."

"Do you really believe that?"

"Of course. Our intelligence says it is true. Why would they lie?"

"Oh, well, I can't imagine why," I said, hand to my chest. He picked up on the sarcasm.

"That's enough. Go back to your seat, madame."

Sylvia Beach, the renowned owner of the iconic Shakespeare and Company bookstore on Rue de l'Odéon, was the first American we picked up that I knew by sight. Neighbors, friends, and local shopkeepers were standing in the street with her, some crying. Knowing we had many mutual friends, I introduced myself, confidentially, as Drue Leyton. A wisp of a woman in her fifties with sharp features, she wore steel-rimmed glasses and a brown velvet jacket over a dark shirt and bow tie, and carried a rucksack almost as large as she was.

"I closed the shop and hid all my inventory after Pearl Harbor. Still, they've been threatening to come for me for months because one of my employees is Jewish. Today, they finally did," Sylvia said with a shrug. "Anyway, it's lovely to meet you, despite the circumstances."

The bus drove through Paris, from house to house, picking up an extraordinary cross section of American women from all walks of Parisian life. There were several artists and French war brides from the first war, as well as dancers and writers, a few milliners, and a lady who lived at the Ritz. Each time the Germans failed to find anyone at a particular residence, all of us cheered loudly.

As the sun was setting, the last American woman was picked up, and we were driven to the Jardin d'Acclimatation, the botanical gardens, in the Bois de Boulogne. We pulled up behind several other buses and were told to get out and enter the gates, which were lined with guards on both sides. A group of American nuns got off the bus in front of us, followed by two women who looked like they had just come from one of the brothels in Montmartre.

"They are imprisoning *nuns*," I said. "Couldn't they have left the nuns out of it?"

"Couldn't they have left the old ladies out of it?" Marion said. She looked exhausted, her face pale and pasty.

"We're going to get you out, Marion," I said, putting my arm around her. "I promise you."

"You realize the botanical gardens are basically a zoo?" Sylvia said as we looked up at the door of the glass-enclosed structure. "They are putting us in a zoo. Like animals."

"It would be funny if it weren't so horrible," I whispered back.

It was raining, and there was a crowd outside the fence, all grief-stricken and worried, trying to catch a glimpse of their loved ones in this temporary prison. I scanned the crowd for Nadine or Jean but did not see them.

A large contingent from the French Red Cross were standing in the rain, and they handed each of us a bag containing chocolate, biscuits, and some English books.

We were herded into the massive all-glass structure and guided to our cavernous makeshift dormitory on the second floor.

"The monkey house," I said, holding my hand over my nose because it still smelled like animal urine and disinfectant. "Of all the places in Paris, they are putting us here."

"Did you ever in your life imagine that you'd be a prisoner in a monkey house? Do you think they'll feed us bananas?" Sylvia said as she started laughing. "At least we're going to be the only monkeys. I'm sorry. But if I don't laugh, I will definitely start to cry."

"I agree," I said. Her laughter was contagious. "My God. It's all so bizarre and ridiculous. Never mind the horrible stink."

There were rows and rows of cots set up on the second floor, with puddles of rain between the beds from where the glass roof leaked. A few people were lying down already. Others were pacing and talking to themselves, wringing their hands at the predicament. A group of women were waving doctor's certificates at the officer in charge, demanding to see the medical officer to get released. I still had no idea what had happened to my certificate, but it seemed like this wouldn't have been the time to use it, as the officer dismissed all of them.

In the back corner, an older woman was sitting on a cot, an ermine wrap around her legs and a box of chocolates on her lap, talking to a few other women. She turned her head, and, recognizing her face, I grabbed Marion's elbow and ducked, heading to the other end of the expansive dorm, gesturing to Sylvia to follow.

"What is it?" Sylvia asked.

"That woman with the fur wrap, feasting on the five-pound box of chocolates, is Fern Bedaux. I don't want her to see me."

"Why?" Marion said.

"She and her husband, Charles, have questionable . . . ties," I said. "Honestly, I'd feel better if it were Charles here and not Fern. He is at least honest about his loyalties, or lack thereof. But she has a big mouth, and I don't trust her."

"I heard her bragging in the bathrooms that she would not be here long," Sylvia said. "The Nazi ambassador is going to get her released."

"That's not a total surprise," I said, glancing back at her; she was handing out chocolates to some women sitting with her. "Good. I just have to avoid her until then."

After we had all claimed a cot and used the ladies' room, under the watchful eye of Nazi guards, we were led downstairs to a dining room, where German women served us soup, potatoes, and black bread. One of the officers did a roll call, which took some time because there were well over three hundred women. It was a reunion of American expatriates, and, despite the grim circumstances, I was cheered by seeing friends and acquaintances I hadn't seen much of since moving out of the city.

As dinner was wrapping up, I found Herr Fieger standing in the corner with some other officers. He rolled his eyes when he saw me, but then smiled, so I took it as teasing.

"Herr Fieger, poor Marion Greenough is not feeling well at all," I said. "She is nearly sixty-five years old. I am begging you; can you please get her out of here?"

"As a matter of fact, I can," Herr Fieger said, looking pleased with himself. "I told the commandant of the depot about her age, and he agreed to release her tonight. We will arrange transport home."

I was elated for Marion but ached that I couldn't join her. *Home.* How I desperately longed to go too.

"Thank you," I said, clasping my hands and giving him a genuine smile. "Thank you so much. May I tell her?"

"Yes, please tell her and go help her get her things. She should meet me at the main entrance in half an hour."

Marion was so relieved, she hugged me and started to cry. When we got her things, she gave me her sewing kit and a bar of lavender soap from her prewar stock. We waited for Herr Fieger at the entrance of the building.

"Drue, is that you?" I froze at the sound of Fern Bedaux's voice. She was walking with two guards, who were carrying her bags as if they were bellhops, treating her with a respect they had not displayed for any other prisoners that day.

"Fern?" I said, keeping my voice steady. "Hello. I'm sorry to see you under these circumstances, but it looks like you're getting out? This is my neighbor, Marion; she's leaving tonight too."

She and Marion exchanged hellos, but Fern of course turned her attention back to me.

"My God, why are you still in this country?" she said.

"Same reason you are, I guess," I said with a shrug. "It's my home."

"I'm being released by the German ambassador," she said. "Poor Charles was also arrested; can you believe it? It's all been a terrible ordeal. I will inquire about you, see if I can help get you out as well."

"That's kind of you," I said. "But I understand if you can't." I didn't trust her enough to want help from her.

"And my dear, I am so very sorry. Is it true what I heard about your husband Jacques being killed?" she asked, putting her hand on my elbow. Herr Fieger was coming down the stairs behind her, and, by his expression, I knew he was listening. This gluttonous woman with her fur and chocolates was going to get me killed.

"Oh no. No, he hasn't," I said. "That I am sure of."

"Oh well, thank God, I am so happy to hear that. There's so much misinformation these days," she said with a wave of her hand as she kissed me on both cheeks. "It's time for me to go. I hope you get out soon too. Nice to meet you, Marion."

She waddled out of the building, the two officers at her side.

"Why would she think your husband is dead?" Herr Fieger asked, trying to read my face. "You said you didn't know where he was. Is it possible that he is dead?"

"No, he's not dead, and Fern Bedaux is a gossip and a fool," I said. "Imagine asking anyone that question based on rumors."

"It was incredibly rude," Marion said.

"Indeed," Herr Fieger said, frowning at me, trying to tell if I was lying or not. And then, in an act of surprising chivalry, he took Marion's bags from her.

"Ready to go, Madame Greenough?" Herr Fieger said.

Marion and I hugged tightly.

"Remember we can't let them see us cry," I whispered in her ear.

"Be safe, my friend," she said. "We will be drinking tea together in Barbizon soon."

I tried to smile as they walked out the door, a door I couldn't walk out of because I was no longer free. And the reality of that, and all the events of the day, felt like a rock pulling me under a wave of despair. I ran up the stairs to the second floor of the monkey house before any of the guards could see my tears.

Chapter Twenty-Nine

The sounds of so many women—some crying, some snoring, some talking in their sleep—echoed off the high ceiling and made sleep almost impossible. And the rain kept pouring in, creating ever bigger puddles between the beds, the dampness in the air amplifying the odor of monkey urine that permeated the building. Every hour, three guards came in with flashlights to count us. After midnight, it became a game among some of us, so when a guard got up into the hundreds, we would start shouting random numbers and get him so confused he would start cursing in German and start all over again, and we would all burst into laughter. It was a small, but satisfying, act of defiance.

We were awakened early the next morning, and word spread quickly that friends and family were paying an admission fee to enter the zoo, so they could talk to their loved ones over a wrought iron fence and row of hedges just outside the monkey house. Joking about the bizarreness of it all, I hurried outside with everyone to see who had paid to view us. The scene was chaos as prisoners and visitors clamored to find one another over the line of bushes.

"I'm sure Adrienne is somewhere out there. I wish I was taller," Sylvia said, referring to her partner of many years, as she stood on her tiptoes to try to find her. "Frankly, I think a look at us in the zoo is worth much more than five francs."

"I completely agree," I said. But I hoped at least one of my friends had paid the fee—I desperately needed someone beyond the hedges waiting for me.

Guards lined the barrier between the zoo inmates and their loved ones as both sides searched for faces and called out names. And as people reunited, the conversations ranged from poignant to comical. A mother admonishing one of her teenage daughters about a boyfriend, a wife calling out to her husband that the medicine she needed was in the top bureau drawer. I walked up and down the row three times and was beginning to lose hope when I heard Elise.

"Drue! Drue, over here!" I spotted her at the end of the row, jumping and waving like crazy; standing with her were Claude and a very haggard-looking Jean. I put my hands over my mouth, overcome at seeing my dear friends.

"*Ma fille*, my beautiful Drue, how are you? Are they feeding you well? They'd better be feeding you well," Claude said. His eyes were watery, and he had a few days of white stubble.

"Yes," I said, and I couldn't help but laugh. "They are feeding us OK. It is so good to see you three, you have no idea."

"I am so sorry," Elise said. "And so angry I could scream. We will get you freed, somehow. I promise you."

"We will," Jean said, his voice hoarse and full of emotion. We locked eyes, and I bit my lip and blew him a kiss, then one to Claude and Elise.

"Jean is allowed a five-minute visit with you inside," Elise said. "We have a large package for you; he will bring it around."

"How did you manage a visit?" I said.

"They're letting a few visitors in," Jean said. "For the right price."

"Of course," I said. "Thank you."

"Kathleen Wilkinson was already sent to Vittel," Elise said.

"You're kidding? I thought she might be safe from this," I said, thinking of her money and connections.

"Didn't we all?" Elise said.

"I will look for her as soon as I arrive," I said. "I'm still stunned this is happening."

"Everyone is. It is a disgrace and shame that it is happening in our country," Claude said, disgust in his voice. "I packed some chocolate and cheese and sweets for you. Enough to share."

"What a treasure. I won't ask how you got them," I said. "Thank you all; you have warmed my heart. Is Nadine here? Is she OK?"

"I have a letter from her to you. She's a mess; she is beyond distraught over this happening to you," Jean said, and then, raising his voice loud enough for the guards around us to hear, he added, "I also have your medical papers, so they know how very sick you are with the *cancer.*"

At this, one of the guards took a few side steps away from me, as if my fake cancer could jump off my body and onto his.

"Thank you," I said, breathing a gigantic sigh of relief. "When are they letting you in?"

"Later this afternoon," he said.

"I cannot wait," I said, blowing kisses again. "I love you all."

The visits were being allowed just next to the entrance of the monkey house, in front of the floor-to-ceiling plate glass windows. The clouds had finally cleared, and the late-day sun streamed through, warming the place like a greenhouse. I spotted Jean getting cleared by the guards, and, without even thinking, I ran to him, and he picked me up. I took comfort in his strong arms around me.

"I am so sorry," Jean said into my hair.

"Me too," I said. We broke apart and he handed me a satchel. We sat at one of the little benches in front of the windows, keeping our heads together, our voices low. His breath smelled of cigarettes and mint. "There's cold cream and lipstick from Elise and food from Claude. Nadine packed a few more of your things, along with a letter. And the certificate she couldn't find the other day."

"Thank God," I said. "Although some other women were trying to get out for medical reasons yesterday and were denied. Do you think it will even work?"

"I don't know, but you must try," Jean said. "I need you . . . your help with all that's happening on the farm. I am having Dr. Porcher send a copy of the certificate directly to the doctor in charge at Vittel. His name is von Weber. He is . . . well, not easy to convince, from what I have heard. A bit of a bastard."

"Fantastic," I said with a sigh.

"Between your acting skills and your charm, I bet you can convince him."

"I'll do my best; I'm just not sure if it will be enough."

"Your best is always enough," Jean said, looking at me, quiet for a moment. "You're an extraordinary woman."

"I am not," I said, shaking my head.

"You are, and I am not talking about your beauty. I've never met anyone like you. You are strong and . . . maybe a little too stubborn. And passionate about what you believe in. If anyone can get out and get back to Barbizon, it's you."

"I don't know, Jean," I said. "The past two days have done me in. Just when I was starting to feel like we were making a difference, when I started to feel alive again, this happened. And it's . . . I'm trying not to wallow, but . . . look around. Look at where I *am*. I am being held captive in a zoo, headed to a prison in the mountains, with no indication that we will be released anytime soon."

"One minute!" the heavyset guard closest to the doors bellowed. "One more minute and all visitors must exit the premises."

"Listen to me," Jean said, grabbing my hands and pulling me off the bench. "I will do what I can on the outside; you do what you can there. I need you, Drue."

I looked up at him, and we stood there, looking into each other's eyes. So many emotions passed between us in that moment. Though I still mourned my husband, I could no longer deny that I cared for this man in ways that were both simple and complicated. He had become my dearest friend in France.

"Time is up," the guard hollered. "Visitors must file out immediately."

Another emotional scene, this one more final, more tragic than earlier in the day, as this would be the last time the inmates—wives and mothers and sisters and aunts—would see loved ones before leaving for Vittel in the morning. My heart ached as Jean gave me the tightest hug goodbye, and once again it was hard to keep my promise of never crying in front of the Germans.

"Goodbye," I whispered.

"*Au revoir*," he said, and, with a small wave and sad smile, he joined the other visitors as they started to file out. I watched him go, and just as he was about to go through the front door he turned and ran back to me.

Grabbing my face in his hands, he put his lips on mine in an intense, passionate kiss. And I didn't think; I just melted into it. It was like a dam had broken between us, and for a few brief seconds the world disappeared.

"Don't let them make you lose your hope and that fire within you," Jean said, with a lopsided smile that was almost shy as we pulled apart. "I know you'll be back with us soon."

"Monsieur! You must leave *now* or face imprisonment yourself." A guard came over and grabbed Jean by the elbow and started dragging him toward the exit.

Jean looked back at me as he was being pulled in the other direction, and as he was shoved through the doors, he blew me a kiss, which I returned in kind. I stood there watching the doors, stunned and smiling to myself; my feelings of despair had been lifted with that small yet momentous act.

"So, maybe *more* than just an affair of the heart, Madame Tartière?" Herr Fieger had come up behind me, a sly grin on his face.

"Do you always ask so many probing questions, Herr Fieger? I didn't take you for a gossip," I said, arms crossed and eyebrows raised. Thankfully he laughed at this.

"You'll have to be careful with your teasing at Vittel, madame," he said. "Some won't take to it as kindly as I have."

Chapter Thirty

October 14, 1942

Vittel, France

Dear Jean and Nadine,

It has been a month since I arrived at Vittel, and I am sorry for not writing sooner; I naively thought this would be a very temporary situation and I would be back home in Barbizon in days. Sadly, that appears not to be the case. I will spare you the details of our harrowing journey here — they crowded us into dirty, third-class cars with no food or water or even a working toilet.

But the conditions here at Vittel itself are far better than I expected. While it is still very much a prison camp, the facilities are decent, it's clean and spacious, and we are treated well overall. That is because apparently this is the Germans' "model" camp, regularly monitored by the Red Cross, photographed often for the German papers; I'm sure you understand my meaning.

Upon arrival, we received a warm, enthusiastic welcome from the British women. Many of them were hanging out of their windows, with lots of cheering and singing; I felt badly, as we were all too exhausted to show our gratitude. Believe it or not, some of the British women have been here for over a year! They have endured far more than we have, so far from home, and that fact has helped many of us new arrivals keep things in perspective.

This camp, known as Interniertenlager Vittel, is one of the German POW camps known as Frontstalag 194. There are several hotels within it and over two thousand total prisoners. I'm rooming at what used to be the Grand Hotel, a five-story resort. This area must have been elegant in peacetime, but now, with women often hanging out the windows talking with one another and undergarments blowing in the breeze on dozens of clothes-lines, it feels more like a neighborhood of tenement buildings. I'm grateful to have Kathleen Wilkinson and Sylvia Beach as my roommates. We have our own beds — with sheets! — and share a private bathroom. We even have a big balcony overlooking the park and the valley of the Vosges. There is a library and a theater, tennis courts, and many places to roam.

We cook our meals in our room most of the time, and, thanks to the weekly care packages from the American Red Cross, we have better food than I imagined. When my first package arrived, it felt like Christmas — real coffee and butter, condensed milk, biscuits, canned meats, puddings, and ciga-rettes. It does not seem right that as prisoners we are eating better than most Parisians right now.

And so, behind the barbed wire, the Vittel internment camp life has its own rhythm of odd normalcy — artists paint, musicians play music, the British women never miss their tea-time. There are even several shops — a seamstress has set up a shop, she remakes clothes beautifully, and an English woman has become very clever at making espadrilles. Another woman has a garden and a small canteen where she sells produce. And it will come as no surprise that the prostitutes that arrived here from Montmartre have managed to find new clients as well.

Still, I stand on the balcony and look out at the sun setting a little earlier each night, and every bird that flies by reminds me that I am in a gilded cage, no longer free to go beyond the barbed wire fencing that is patrolled by guards around the clock. The weather here is foggy and damp most of the time, and hints at a winter that will be here soon. Even among so many women, I have moments of profound loneliness, and I yearn to get out and get back to you and Barbizon. In a little while, I am finally meeting with Dr. Levy, one of the POW doctors at the small hospital here, which is led by the Dr. von Weber that you mentioned, Jean, and run by a group of nuns from the Little Sisters of the Poor convent. I will let you know if they agree to my release for cancer treatments.

I miss you both so much — and Ondie, my poor Ondie! Will he even know who I am when I return? Hugs to Elise and Claude and all our dear friends and neighbors in Barbizon. I hope that I am back soon.

All my love —
Drue

After the kiss, I didn't quite know what to say to Jean in a letter just for him. I didn't regret kissing him, but I couldn't think beyond that right now. My heart had not yet healed from losing Jacques, though I cared for Jean in a way that was much more than simply as a friend. I was desperate to go back to continue my work as a courier and provide whatever other help he needed for the Resistance. And poor Nadine—all that work on the farm and trying to supply so much food to Paris all on her own with just two young boys to help her. Every day in Vittel was a day wasted, a day where I could have been working and fighting against the enemy instead of being imprisoned by them.

Kathleen came back to our room just as I was leaving for my appointment.

"We were invited to teatime by a friend I knew back in London—can you join us?" Kathleen asked. Her normally short, slicked-back blonde hair had started to grow out, and she was wearing culottes instead of her usual men's suits, both of which made her look a little softer and older.

"I have an appointment with Dr. Levy," I said. "Otherwise, I would love to. I am beginning to appreciate English tea."

"Good luck with your appointment," Kathleen said. "I do hope he can help you—if not get you released, at least give you the medical treatment you need."

"Me too," I said. "Though the best would be to go for X-ray treatments in Paris; I don't think they can do much for me here."

"Then they've got to let you out to get them," Kathleen said. "You need to get better, you poor thing. Are you in much pain?"

"Not much, truly," I said, feeling a pang of guilt as I put on my sweater and grabbed my purse.

I hated being dishonest with my friends. But I had made the decision not to tell Kathleen or Sylvia or anyone else at camp that the medical certificate stating I had cancer of the womb was false. I needed to maintain the ruse. They both knew me in my former life as Drue Leyton; that was enough of a secret for them to keep.

"I'll see you and Sylvia back here for dinner?" I asked.

"Yes, it's my turn to cook, so God help us all," Kathleen said with a laugh. "I meant to ask you—some of the ladies are putting together a talent show; they know my former life as a Ziegfeld girl and asked if I wanted to be in it. I figured, why not? It's something else to pass the time until Tudor gets me out of here. Do you want to do it with me? If you're feeling up to it, that is?"

"I'd love to, but I think I'd better not," I said, though it did sound fun. Which was something I had not had in a while. "Don't want to risk it at this point."

"You're probably right. But then . . . it's just a talent show. And you've gone this long—in the camp, even before that—and they haven't made the connection to your past identity at all. I have to think your secret is safe. Don't you?"

"I won't feel safe until this war is over."

"I just think we all could use some lightheartedness around here. Some of the Brits have formed a singing group, a couple of ladies are tap-dancing, that sculptor that lives in Le Marais brought her piccolo, apparently?"

"*You* aren't going to tap-dance? The famous Rose Dolores from the Ziegfeld Follies?" I teased, bringing up her stage name.

"Oh, darling," Kathleen laughed. "My knees would never forgive me. No, I've decided to organize a group to perform 'There's No Cure Like Travel/Bon Voyage' from the musical *Anything Goes*. A little bit cheeky, because we can't travel anywhere, can we?"

"Oh, I saw that play on Broadway when it opened; I adored it," I said.

"You could join with our group or do anything you want. Promise me you will think about it?"

"All right, I'll think about it," I said as I left the room.

Kathleen was right: I needed some lightness, at the very least a distraction. I dropped the letter home at the improvised post office on the first floor of the hotel and made my way to the hospital. I was anxious to see Dr. Levy, one of only two gynecologists for hundreds of women.

Within the barbed wire enclosures marking off Vittel's hotels and parks, we were allowed to go where we pleased. I waved to a couple of groups of internees that were sprawled on the lawn, sitting on blankets gossiping or writing letters, the most popular pastime at the camp. A few British women had set up a croquet course and were doubled over with laughter.

"Good afternoon, Mother Chad," I said to the English nun at the hospital's front desk. Mother Chad was the de facto administrator of the hospital, the nuns from her convent serving as the hospital's nurses. She was in her forties, with a round face and serene smile that, according to those who had gotten to know her, belied a steely strength and intelligence.

"Good day—Drue, isn't it?" she said.

"Yes, Drue Tartière," I said. "I've been trying to get in to see Dr. Levy. I have an appointment today."

"I remember you, those blonde curls," she said, getting up from her desk. "Come along, I'll show you to his office. I must warn you, though, it might be a bit of a wait."

She took me to Dr. Levy's office on the second floor, the scent of disinfectant so strong it stung my nose. Along the wall outside his door, there was a long line of women sitting in chairs. A freckle-faced nun who had to be no older than twenty was assisting him and attending to each appointment, which was unfortunate, as I needed to talk to him alone. I sat down at the very end of the line. An hour passed, and it was finally my turn.

"Sister," Dr. Levy said to the nun as the door to his office opened. "Will you please escort this patient to my coworker downstairs? I'd like him to give me his opinion."

And so, by lucky chance, Dr. Levy and I were alone in his office, for a few short minutes until the nun returned. He was shorter and a little older than me, wearing dark-rimmed glasses with thick lenses; he reminded me of an owl. As a prisoner of war serving as a doctor for the hospital, I had learned he was universally adored by the women at Vittel.

"Thank you for seeing me, Dr. Levy," I said, clearing my throat, trying to control my nerves. I had been anticipating this appointment since arriving at camp, and so much depended on this man helping me. "I'm Drue Tartière. My doctor, Dr. Porcher in Paris, wrote up this certificate about my late-stage cancer of the womb. He also sent a copy to Dr. von Weber."

Dr. Levy sat and read the certificate, not saying a word for several moments, further contributing to my nervousness. He shook his head and looked up at me, his dark eyes expressing both sadness and sympathy.

"Tell me, Madame Tartière," he said, leaning back in his chair, clasping his fingers together. "Are you suffering as bad as this certificate says, or are you asking me to help you with a false certificate?"

I looked at him, my face red, not wanting to ask but knowing I had to.

"I must get out of this camp. I am finally doing valuable work against the Nazis at my home in Barbizon. I don't want to try to escape and be hunted, because that would put my friends there in danger and jeopardize our work. The best thing is to get out on medical grounds."

"Did you know the last doctor who worked here is now at a forced-labor camp in Germany, because he created a fake medical certificate for an Englishwoman so she would be released? They arrested him because she was overheard bragging at a Paris café that there was not a thing wrong with her."

"No," I said, feeling foolish. "I had no idea."

"I wish I could help you. But my situation here is fraught," he said, and I could hear the anguish in his voice. "My *seventy-two*-year-old father is in a prison camp for Jews because he was arrested on the metro for not wearing the Star of David on his overcoat, though he was wearing one on his shirt. My mother, wife, and daughter are in hiding.

Do you understand the position they have me in here, with my old father locked up?"

"I . . . I am so sorry," I said, my heart aching for him. "I didn't know about the other doctor, and I certainly did not know your story. I . . . I don't even know how you get through every day with all of that weighing on you."

"We all do what we have to in this war, don't we?" he said, shaking his head as he looked out the window at the mountains.

"That we do," I said. We both looked out at the mountains for a moment, but I was compelled to say more before the nurse returned.

"Dr. Levy, I can't begin to imagine the stress you are under. But you are quite literally my only hope. All I would need . . . all I would need is for you to tell Dr. von Weber that I am as ill as my certificate says I am. I am sorry to have to ask, but I have lost my husband in this war, and I need to do something to honor, to avenge, his death. I need it for my sanity. I can't be trapped here for however long this war goes on. I just can't."

I held my hands together tightly, almost in prayer, mentally willing him to help me. He looked at me, and I knew he understood my desperation; I was sure he had seen it with dozens of other women before me. He put his elbows on his desk, hands over his mouth, and started reading through the certificate again, thinking. I was considering getting on my knees and begging when he finally spoke in a very soft voice.

"I'm sorry about your husband. How did he die?"

"He was killed in Syria." I whispered it, worried that the walls had ears. "Fighting with de Gaulle's Free French. I . . . I am still not sure what happened. But I must pretend he's still alive, so that they won't decide to punish me for his being a de Gaullist. I trust you can keep my secret."

"You have my word," Dr. Levy said, giving me a solemn look. He seemed to wrestle with what to do. "Tell me, are you hemorrhaging?"

"No," I said. "But in the envelope with the certificate, there were pills. For that purpose."

I took the little bottle out of my purse to show him.

"It would help your cause," he said. "But then of course at some point you'd have to take some medicine to stop the hemorrhaging, so you don't lose too much blood."

"Do you have that?" I asked.

"Of course."

At that moment there was a knock on the door and the nun poked her head inside to tell Dr. Levy he had more patients waiting.

"Madame Tartière, I need to consider your case before I make up my mind," he said as we both stood up. "I promise I will follow up with you soon to let you know either way."

"Thank you, Dr. Levy, I appreciate anything you can do," I said. "And I am so incredibly sorry for what your family is going through."

"I'll be in touch."

Chapter Thirty-One

October 23, 1942

After my appointment with Dr. Levy, I decided to take matters into my own hands and began taking the pills that would make me hemorrhage the morning after I met with him. The doctor had said it would help my cause, and if he decided to help me, I wanted to be already down the path in terms of symptoms, so no time was wasted. The only problem was, the pills worked almost too well, causing incredibly heavy menstrual bleeding. And they often made me nauseous to the point that my appetite was nonexistent. It had been over a week, I had already lost weight, and I still hadn't heard anything from the doctor.

When I had gone to his office to schedule a follow-up appointment, the line of patients waiting outside his door was down the corridor. Mother Chad said he had been incredibly busy and was booked for the next month. I had left a message with her, to tell him that I had started taking the medicine he had recommended and that it was urgent that I see him sooner because I was having terrible symptoms. But he still had yet to contact me.

It was the evening of the talent show, and Sylvia, Kathleen, and I were sitting at our wobbly wooden table near the windows of our hotel room, eating a soup Sylvia had prepared, but that I could hardly stomach because of my nausea. Of the three of us, Sylvia was the best cook, though that was not saying much.

"I realize we are going to turn into potatoes soon, we have been eating so many of them, but this is something I can actually make that is decent," Sylvia said. "Adrienne does the cooking at home."

"Have you heard any more from her?" I asked.

"Yes, she hopes to visit again this weekend," Sylvia said. "So I can give her some of my Red Cross goods. The food situation in Paris continues to deteriorate. All those poor mothers trying to keep their children fed."

"I got a note from Tudor today," Kathleen said. "His hair is on fire trying to get me out, and both of you as well."

"I also sent a letter to Richard O'Brien," I said. "Though I have no idea if the American embassy is even functioning in Vichy right now."

"Drue, I have to tell you, Kathleen and I are worried about you," Sylvia said to me, looking at my untouched soup. "You're pale, you're not eating, you seem to have gotten worse since going to Dr. Levy. Is this doctor truly going to do anything to help?"

"Thank you for your concern," I said, again hating that I had to deceive them, and trying to take another spoonful of the dinner she had cooked. "He was supposed to get back to me by now. I left another message with Mother Chad yesterday."

"If he doesn't see you in the next couple of days, I am going to march over there myself and demand he does," Kathleen said.

"I'll go with you," added Sylvia. "There's got to be something he can do, you poor thing. I see how many trips to the bathroom you're taking."

"Thank you, ladies," I said. "It has been hard, but the talent show will be a nice distraction."

"It should be exactly that," Sylvia said. "I've even convinced a few friends to do a skit based on our experience at the zoo. It's called *Boches and Bananas* and we're going to dress like monkeys. It's going to be hilarious."

"Sylvia! You are not," I gasped, shocked at her boldness.

Kathleen put a hand over her mouth, nearly spitting out her soup.

"You're right. I'm not," she said, laughing. "But . . . honestly, don't you wish I would? Just to see the officers' shocked faces?"

∼

The first and, God willing, only Vittel Internment Camp Annual Talent Show got off to a rocky start, as the opening act of the evening was the piccolo-playing sculptress who lived in Le Marais. She had a wild mane of golden hair and wore a blouse and long skirt that the French peasants favored, though I knew she came from a wealthy family from Boston. She floated across the stage playing her piccolo in what seemed an odd trance. It was clear her family had not spent much money on her lessons, because, despite her boasting, she was not much of a musician. Most of the audience remained quiet, politely listening, but some of the younger guards in the back of the theater could not control their laughter and had to be shushed multiple times.

After that, things started to improve. A young, pretty brunette came out onstage and sang "La Vie en Rose," a cappella, in a clear, beautiful soprano that moved the entire audience so much, they jumped to their feet in a spontaneous standing ovation. Even the group of guards to the right of the stage was whistling and cheering wildly. One of them, a tall, lanky, fair-haired young man, caught my eye and gave me a small wave as if he knew me, so I just nodded and waved in return.

The show continued, and the audience enthusiastically applauded each number—there were tap-dancers and jugglers, and two choirs of nuns—the Sisters of the Holy Spirit and Little Sisters of the Poor, the first one being decidedly better than the second. As the second group of nuns exited the stage, I felt someone tap me on the shoulder. It was Dr. Levy's assistant, the young one with the freckles.

"Mrs. Tartière, I have been looking for you," she said in a whisper, crouching down next to my chair, "to remind you of your dentist's appointment tomorrow morning at Dr. Rolland's."

"Dentist's appointment?" I said. "Don't you work for Dr. Levy?"

"I do; I'm his assistant. My name's Sister Nancy," she said. She lowered her voice and gave me a pointed look. "And that is why I am reminding you of your appointment with *Dr. Rolland*. His dental office is in suite ten on the first floor of the Hôtel des Sources. It is very private, with not so many patients and nuns coming and going. Please be there by seven o'clock tomorrow morning."

"Oh . . . OK," I said, understanding. "I will be there."

She nodded and hurried away just as Kathleen and her *Anything Goes* ensemble took the stage.

Though I had declined to join the performance, I had offered to assist in stage direction for Kathleen because it was a large, inexperienced, but extremely lively group. We hadn't had time for many rehearsals, but it had been a joy to work with these women on something that had nothing to do with our circumstances, and it also distracted me from my self-induced medical issues. Practices were filled with lots of laughter, and Kathleen choreographed a simple routine for the group, more arm movements and swaying from side to side than actual dancing.

We had raided the costume closet and managed to find enough outfits—wigs and white dresses and straw hats, and a couple of generic nautical uniforms—that the ensemble resembled an actual theater company when they took the stage. On my cue, one of the British nuns started to play the first notes of "There's No Cure Like Travel/Bon Voyage" from *Anything Goes* on the piano, and the number began. The audience was delighted, and in on the joke, since none of us would be traveling anytime soon.

Kathleen was dressed in a navy-blue men's suit that she had found in the costume closet and carried the group of happy amateurs with her professional-level singing and dancing. Her stage presence was luminous; nobody could take their eyes off her, and it was clear why she had been one of the most famous Ziegfeld Follies dancers of all time.

The performance concluded, and once again the audience leaped to their feet; most of the Germans were even clapping and smiling at the end. After it was over, Kathleen had organized a cast "party" for all of us in the theater lobby, with champagne that she had somehow managed to procure through the camp's thriving black market.

"I was really hoping I could convince you to do a soliloquy," Sylvia said, handing me a glass of champagne. "Maybe something from *Macbeth* or *Hamlet*."

"I know, and I would have loved to," I said, gratefully accepting it. "But I couldn't take the risk."

"Do you miss it?"

"Performing? You know, Nadine asked me that a while ago, and I do—at least, being onstage; films not so much."

"If ever there's a time we need books and art and theater, it's during war," Sylvia said. "I know some people thought this talent show was a frivolous idea, but look at the joy in this lobby. We all needed a dose of joy."

"I agree," I said, smiling at all our fellow inmates enjoying themselves.

"Excuse me."

I turned, and the young guard who had waved at me was standing there.

"Yes?" I said.

"I'm so sorry to interrupt, but I had a question. My name is Frederich Damasky," he said, and he seemed nervous.

"Herr Damasky, how do you speak English so well?"

"I worked in a sugar factory in Yonkers before the war started," he said. "Do you know Yonkers?"

"Everyone knows Yonkers," Sylvia said.

"Did you like it?" I asked.

"Very much, I loved it," he said, nodding several times. "I am going back after this war is over."

"What is your question, Herr Damasky?" I asked.

"You look so familiar, and I couldn't place you, but then I remembered, you're the film actress. From the *Charlie Chan* films? I loved those movies. It was you, wasn't it? I'm sorry I can't remember your name."

The lobby was warm, but I froze, my arms breaking out in goose pimples. I had been losing so much blood lately, I knew I was more susceptible to fainting, and a few black dots in my vision were a telltale sign that I might. Sylvia sensed this and grabbed me by the elbow.

"Do you know, you're the *third* person who has asked her that since we've been here," Sylvia said, and it was enough to snap me out of my panic. "She gets that all the time, don't you?"

"I really do. I am not that actress, though I suppose I should be flattered," I said, smiling and rolling my eyes, trying to play it off. But he had seen my fear.

"You're the spitting image," Damasky said, tilting his head and frowning. "Are you related or something?"

"No, no," I said. "Just another American blonde. What can I say?"

"If you'll excuse us, we have to go help clean up backstage," Sylvia said, still gripping my elbow as if to catch me if I fell. "We promised our friend; it's a mess back there."

"Nice to meet you, Herr Damasky," I said.

"You too," he said.

We walked as fast as we could without seeming obvious.

"Sylvia . . . ," I said in a soft voice, feeling sick, and not just from the medicine I was taking.

"I don't think he's going to say anything," she said in a whisper.

"I think he knows we were lying."

"Oh, my dear, he *definitely* knows we were both lying. Let's just pray he loves America and your films enough to keep his mouth shut."

Chapter Thirty-Two

The morning after the talent show, Saturday, I got up extra early, tip-toeing around my room as I got dressed so as not to wake Sylvia and Kathleen. The late-October air was cold and damp, and a thick fog blanketed the camp as I made my way to the Hôtel des Sources. The Germans had constructed a raised wooden walkway around the perimeter of the camp so the guards could monitor everything from above, a constant reminder that we were captive.

I entered the hotel. There was no one at the desk, as it was so early, so I wandered down one of the marble-floored hallways off the hotel's lobby and finally found suite ten. When I knocked, I heard a muffled voice tell me to enter, and was greeted by a man with a cleft chin and sandy-brown hair, a white doctor's coat over his beige pants and black button-down shirt.

"Madame Tartière, I presume?" He gave me a warm smile and held out his hand.

"Yes," I said. "Dr. Rolland, thank you for seeing me."

"I'm sure you have questions about this clandestine dentist's appointment."

"I do," I said.

"Come into the exam room, and I will explain."

I sat in the dental chair to keep up appearances in case any Germans came knocking. Dr. Rolland explained that he was not a prisoner of the camp but lived nearby and was serving as the camp dentist at the "request" of the Germans. He had an aunt in Barbizon who knew that I had been sent here, so she had reached out to Jean and Nadine, thinking that Dr. Rolland might help me in some way.

"I have letters for you from both of them," he said. He opened one of the cabinets and pulled out two envelopes.

"Thank you," I said, an ache in my chest at seeing their handwriting—Jean's dark, jagged scribbles contrasting with Nadine's delicate swirls. I had not realized just how much I needed to hear from them, to see on paper their words that were just for me. "Thank you very much. I . . . I needed this. I am terribly homesick."

I clutched the letters and got out of the chair to leave.

"Oh, madame . . ."

"Call me Drue, please," I said. "And thank you for doing this."

"That is not all; please sit," he said. "You see, I've arranged for Dr. Levy to meet you here shortly."

"I was hoping that was the case," I said as I breathed a sigh of relief. I had been too cautious to ask Sister Nancy the night before.

"He's been trying to find a way to see you again privately. Here he's not surrounded by sisters, and there's no chance of Dr. von Weber barging in. Have you met Dr. von Weber yet?"

"I have not," I said, feeling better than I had in days. Dr. Levy and this kind man wanted to help me. It was something.

"He is as awful as you've heard," Dr. Rolland said, with a sour expression. "The way he treats Dr. Levy and the other Jews in this camp is vile. But you need his sign-off, to get you out of here. So you may have to put your disgust aside when you meet him."

"I'll keep that in mind," I said just as there was a knock on the outside door of the suite. Dr. Rolland put a bib on me and returned a few seconds later with Dr. Levy.

"Thank you so much for seeing me again," I said to him. "I know how much of a risk you are taking."

"I am going to be out in the waiting area standing guard," Dr. Rolland said. "I will cough loudly if anyone comes in, and that's your cue to go in the storage closet, Dr. Levy. And I'll come back and examine your teeth, Drue."

"Thank you for arranging this, Dr. Rolland," I said as he shut the door to the exam room.

Dr. Levy just nodded; he was still looking me over, concern in his eyes, which were magnified behind his thick lenses.

"You started taking the hemorrhaging medicine; I can tell just by your complexion," he said.

"We didn't discuss whether I should take the medicine or not when we met, so I decided to start," I said. "I need to get out, and this medical certificate is all I've got."

"I don't need to warn you about what a dangerous game we are playing," Dr. Levy said as he took my vital signs. "I told Dr. von Weber about your case, and he asked to see you on his next visit."

"Oh God," I said. "When?"

"At my office, at the end of the week," Dr. Levy said.

"Is he . . . is he going to examine me?" I said, the thought of it making me feel woozy.

"Not if I can help it," Dr. Levy said. "He's a complete brute—and he knows very little about a woman's insides. He has asked for my diagnosis, but I have not committed to giving it to him until I know he *cannot* examine you. If he does examine you and even slightly suspects the certificate is false, then . . . For my family's sake, I cannot appear that I am conspiring with you in any way."

"I understand. But how . . . what do I need to do?" I said. Thinking about a Nazi doctor examining me was making my skin crawl, and I crossed my arms in front of my chest, shivering at the thought of it.

"Keep taking the medicine, because if you're bleeding too much, there is no way he will want to examine you himself," Dr. Levy said.

"OK," I said with a nod. This was good news. And if an appointment with Dr. von Weber meant getting out of Vittel, I would do it. I would do anything.

"But I am giving you pills to *stop* the hemorrhaging immediately after you see him," he said, taking a vial of pills out of his coat pocket. "If you've already been taking it for over a week, I'm very concerned about you losing too much blood."

"Me too," I said.

"I will see you Friday morning at ten with Dr. von Weber."

"Thank you again," I said as I got up from the dental chair and reached out to shake his hand.

"I think this can work if we are careful," Dr. Levy said, taking my hand in both of his.

"Words of gratitude are not enough." I reached out to give him a hug.

"Don't thank me until we get you out of here."

~

"I gave Adrienne some of my Red Cross provisions when she visited yesterday," Sylvia said as we sat at our hotel table Friday morning having breakfast. "But I didn't give her any of the coffee. Is that wrong of me? I probably should have. But I thought, if I must be a prisoner of the Nazis, at least let me have real coffee."

"It's not bad," I said, smiling. "If any of my friends come to visit, I will happily give them the Red Cross chocolate or cigarettes, but I don't think I'll even tell them about the coffee."

"OK, that makes me feel better," she said, pouring herself some more from the ancient little pot we had procured from the hotel kitchen. "Are your friends coming to visit anytime soon?"

"I don't know," I said as a pang of homesickness for my life in Barbizon hit me. "They didn't mention anything in their most recent letters. It's difficult to get visitation papers. Plus, the logistics of traveling here are not easy."

"True," Sylvia said. "Maybe you will be released soon anyway. What time is your appointment with the notorious Dr. von Weber?"

"In about an hour," I said, sipping from my cup. "I can't wait to get it over with; I've barely slept all week thinking about it."

"Are you feeling any better at all?" Sylvia asked, a worried expression on her face.

"Not really. Still very heavy bleeding, trying to eat more, despite my lack of appetite."

The bleeding was a good thing today, given what Dr. Levy had said.

"After my work at the post office, I'm going to attempt to make you gingerbread this afternoon. One of the British ladies gave me a recipe, and we have everything we need thanks to the Red Cross. I bet you'll have an appetite for that."

"You are too kind," I said, thinking of how fortunate I was to end up with Kathleen and Sylvia in this grim situation. "I'm going to head out soon, get some fresh air."

"Do you want me to go with you to the appointment? Or Kathleen? She's just down at the theater."

"No, it's honestly OK," I said. "Thank you, though. I will let you know how it goes."

"May you get the best news about your prognosis," Sylvia said as we cleaned up our breakfast things. "And permission to get the heck out of here."

We said our goodbyes, and I took a brisk walk around the perimeter of the camp; the air was crisp and smelled like moldy leaves and mud. I doubled back and arrived at the hospital at a little before ten o'clock. Mother Chad was not at the reception desk but came hurrying down the hall a minute after I arrived.

"Oh good, you're here," Mother Chad said, gesturing me to follow her down the hall. "Sister Nancy is out sick because she is terrified of

Dr. von Weber. So I am assisting Dr. Levy and managing the front desk. One of the other sisters will be arriving soon to help."

"Is he that horrible?" I said, getting nervous again.

"Dr. von Weber? He's a real devil," Mother Chad said, chuckling to herself. "His bark scares everyone to death. But you mustn't be frightened of him. Or if you are, don't show it. That's the best way to deal with a man like him."

"Thank you," I said. There wasn't anyone waiting in the corridor as she led me into Dr. Levy's office.

"Is he still coming?" I asked, not wanting to have to reschedule; the anticipation had been stressful enough already.

"He will be shortly," Dr. Levy said. "Are you still hemorrhaging?"

I looked at Mother Chad and back at Dr. Levy.

"She knows," Dr. Levy said. "I would trust Mother Chad with my life."

"Your secret is safe with me, dear," she said.

"I am still, worse than ever," I said.

"Good," Dr. Levy said with a nod as he checked my vitals. "For today that's good. But I don't want it to continue much longer at all. You're very pale, and your heart rate is faster than I'd like. Are you feeling dizzy or lightheaded?"

"Only once in a while," I said, although it had been more like a few times a day.

We heard someone shouting in the hallway, a man's voice berating someone.

"Here he comes . . . ," Mother Chad said, rolling her eyes. "I'll bring him in."

Dr. Levy stood up from his desk and grabbed a notebook and pen; his right hand was shaking.

Mother Chad opened the door and stepped back into the room, and Dr. von Weber entered behind her, changing the atmosphere in the room like a darkening storm. He was well over six feet tall, with silver hair and an aristocratic face, and he glanced at Dr. Levy with such revulsion it was all I could do to control my temper. I'd use my anger to get me through this appointment. I would not be bullied by this man who lived to bully others. He shook my hand and motioned me to sit down across from him at the desk as Dr. Levy and Mother Chad stood to the side.

He looked through my records and asked Dr. Levy if he had examined me, and he confirmed he had.

"Is she hemorrhaging?" Dr. von Weber asked in heavily accented English.

"A great deal, Herr Doctor," Dr. Levy said.

"Very bad," Dr. von Weber said, looking at my medical certificate. "This is very bad cancer. You must have an operation."

"I don't want an operation," I said, careful to keep my emotions in check, to not sound as desperate as I felt. "I want to go for X-ray treatments. In Paris. My doctor, Dr. Porcher, in Paris, is an expert in X-ray treatments, and he said that would be best."

"X-ray treatments are old-fashioned. Why don't you want an operation? Because you don't want a Jew to do it?" Dr. von Weber said, pointing at Dr. Levy.

"No, I don't want to scar my body like that," I said, again taking a deep breath to control my temper with this awful man. "I'm still a relatively young woman."

Dr. von Weber looked at me across the desk and went through my papers again. My heart sank; he wasn't going to let me go. I couldn't even look at Dr. Levy or Mother Chad.

"You are also a very pretty woman, with lovely Scandinavian features."

"Thank you," I said. I was repelled by the comment but managed to bat my eyelashes at him and smile anyway. If flirting with this terrible man helped my cause, then that was what I would do.

"You look like you could be a fashion model or an actress," he said, and I shuddered at this, thinking of the guard at the talent show, my former life, my husband, these secrets that shadowed my every waking hour at Vittel.

"You are too kind, Herr Doctor, thank you, but I have no talent for either profession," I said, putting my hand to my chest.

"You are going to get very fatigued if you keep bleeding; you could go into shock if it gets too bad," Dr. von Weber said. "I am giving you some medicine to help stop it. Dr. Levy will monitor your condition, and you will come back to see me a week from today. If you'll excuse me, I have other patients to attend to."

"Thank you," I said.

He shook my hand, got up from the desk, and left, slamming the door behind him.

"Isn't he a delight?" Mother Chad said, after we knew he was well out of earshot.

"Oh yes, a real charmer," I said. Looking at Dr. Levy, I added, "And I wanted to smack him for the way he treated you."

"I'm used to his treatment by now," Dr. Levy said after Mother Chad left to attend to the front desk. "It's the power he has over my life that makes my hands shake."

"What do you think he'll do?" I asked him.

"I think there's still a chance he'll let you go to Paris," Dr. Levy said. "You should take the medicine to stop hemorrhaging tonight. He didn't examine you today, and he's not keen to do it because, as I said, he has no idea what he's doing when it comes to women."

"But . . . if I take the other medicine and stop losing blood, there's a chance he will examine me? Or that he'll think my condition is not as bad as we're trying to make it seem?"

"Yes, but you are losing too much blood *now*. It's too much of a risk to your health, and I can't condone it."

"It's only for one more week. I can do anything for seven days."

"*No,*" Dr. Levy said, his voice urgent as he took my hand. "Listen to me: Dr. von Weber was right when he mentioned shock. And other dangerous complications. You must take the medicine to stop the bleeding starting today."

"OK," I said with a nod. "I will. Thank you. For everything."

He gave me a look as if he wasn't sure he believed me but said no more.

I left the office, both bottles of pills in my purse, touched by Dr. Levy's concern, but I was desperate for Dr. von Weber to believe me and set me free. I'd take the pills to stop the bleeding as Dr. Levy had urged. Just not quite yet.

Chapter Thirty-Three

November 1, 1942

A couple days later, I received a note from Dr. Rolland's secretary, telling me to come for my emergency cavity filling at four that afternoon. It was a Sunday, and I had no such appointment, but I hurried over at four, hoping he had more letters or news from home.

"Drue, come in," Dr. Rolland said with a smile as he opened the door to his office. His smile faded when he saw me. "You do not look well. How are you feeling? You aren't still taking the hemorrhaging medicine, are you?"

"I am," I said. "Just until I see Dr. von Weber this Friday."

"Did Dr. Levy tell you to do that?" Dr. Rolland asked, frowning.

"He . . . um . . . well, no, actually he told me to stop, but . . . ," I said, explaining to him what Dr. Levy wanted and why I decided not to.

"What you are doing is foolish and dangerous," Dr. Rolland said, shaking his head at me.

"But it will be worth it if it gets me out of here," I said. "It's only a few more days." Hoping I could change the subject, I asked, "Why did you ask me to come today?"

"Good news. Jean Fraysse is arriving in Vittel tonight," he said, his smile returning.

"He is?" I said. "Really?"

"Yes. You will be able to see him tomorrow during visiting hours at the censor's office, at the end of the park. A guard will escort you. And I have arranged the transportation and special permit he needs to be allowed to visit with you here."

"This is exactly what I needed to cheer me up," I said, reaching out to give him a hug, overcome with happiness that I would get to see my friend. "Thank you for your help arranging it. I cannot wait—I've missed him; I've missed *home*. Thank you."

"It's no problem," he said, smiling. "You may have to talk in the presence of a guard, so if there are private things you want to tell him, I would suggest writing a note you can secretly pass to him. If you do get time alone, I would be careful what you say, and check the room for bugs. I don't know why I'm telling you; Jean already knows all this."

"Thank you again," I said. "I'm going to go back to my room and put some things together for him from my Red Cross packages."

"Drue . . . before you go, I know you changed the subject, but I'm begging you: stop the medication. I know you are desperate to get out of here, like most women, but it's not worth risking your life in this way."

"Doctor, by virtue of being in here, my life is already in danger. Taking the medicine will be worth it if it gets me released."

∾

"I am thrilled for you, but also slightly jealous," Kathleen said, giving me an exaggerated pout. We were having coffee as I got ready for my visit with Jean.

"Is Tudor visiting again soon?"

"Possibly. I'd prefer he'd focus on getting me home instead of visiting," Kathleen said. "In the meantime, the talent show was such an enormous success I've decided to form the Vittel Dramatic Society, something to pass the time."

"That's an excellent idea," I said.

"I'm not even going to ask you to be a part of it, because I expect you to be released long before our first play, at Christmas. I hope you are, Drue; I hate to see you suffering this way."

"Thank you—me too," I said. I was looking in the mirror of our room, applying red lipstick. I had put on some pancake makeup, heavier than I normally would, to cover up the purplish circles under my eyes. And I had taken care to wash my hair the night before and pressed my outfit—one of my tartan skirts and a white blouse. The skirt was loose around my waist, further evidence of the weight I had lost.

"This is the best I can do given the way I'm feeling," I said, blotting my lipstick and looking at my face with a critical eye. I knew I looked sick. I was sick. The dizzy spells were coming more frequently, and just standing up too fast made me want to faint. Just a few more days until my follow-up with Dr. von Weber, and I could stop this charade.

"You look beautiful, my friend," Kathleen said.

"Liar," I said with a laugh.

"I'm not," she said. "Just a little . . . *paler* than normal, but it's not your fault you aren't well."

"True," I said, with a sigh, because it was completely my fault.

"Jean will be so thrilled to see you it won't matter."

"I must admit, I am nervous to see him, after . . . after the way we said goodbye at the monkey house."

I had told her and Sylvia about our goodbye kiss at the zoo.

"I bet he's feeling the same," Kathleen said.

"I don't know . . . ," I said. "I tell myself I can't even think about the feelings I have for him right now, and then I find that I can't not think about them. About *him*. And yet I still have dreams about Jacques; I miss him every day. I'm a mess."

"Sweetheart, aren't we all?" Kathleen said with a laugh.

At that moment the loudspeaker in the hallway announced a visitor for Madame Tartière, and I had butterflies in my stomach like I was a schoolgirl going to meet her first crush.

"Just enjoy the visit, that's all," Kathleen said, giving me a kiss on both cheeks as she handed me my purse.

I went downstairs to meet the guard who was to bring me to the visitors' area in the censor's office across the park. The lobby was bustling with people, and I scanned the crowd, trying to determine which guard was for me.

"Madame Tartière, we meet again."

I looked up to see Herr Damasky, the lanky, fair-haired guard from the night of the talent show.

"I am to escort you to the visitors' area across the way. It's a pleasure to see you again."

"And you as well," I said with a silent groan. Of all the guards in Vittel, I got the one from Yonkers who loved the *Charlie Chan* films.

"I've been wanting to apologize about thinking you were that actress from the *Chan* films; I still can't remember what her name was," he said, a sheepish look on his face. "Anyway, that's why I volunteered for this, so I could tell you. Your friend had said it happens all the time; it must be annoying."

"Oh, please, no need to apologize. It's flattering," I said, breathing easier at his apology. "That actress is an attractive woman."

"Attractive? She's gorgeous," Damasky said. His accent was an odd blend of German and New Yorker.

"Oh, I don't know about that," I said. "She was just another Hollywood starlet."

"Oh no, *she* was something special."

I chuckled, thinking Kathleen and Sylvia would love this conversation. We walked across the park, and he talked the entire way, particularly about how much he missed New York, and a girl he met there who had emigrated from Ireland.

"She works as a seamstress," he said, a look in his eyes as if he were gazing across the ocean into the window of a Yonkers bridal shop. "It's been a long time since I've been gone now. I wish I had never left. I want to marry her. I don't know if she'll really wait for me. She said she would."

"I hope she does," I said. He held the door for me as we entered the administration building, which was just outside the barbed wire fence. Three other inmates were sitting in a sparsely furnished reception area, also waiting to see visitors. The guard at the desk went through my bag—I had two packs of English cigarettes, chocolates, and a bar of soap for Jean. In case we were monitored, I also had a note I had written for him tucked in the top of my skirt, per Dr. Rolland's suggestion.

I sat waiting with Damasky for half an hour, and finally my name was called, and we both got up.

"Are you going with me?" I said.

"Yes, ma'am, madame," he said.

We entered a small square room with just a table and three chairs, and a window with a view of the park. I sat down; Herr Damasky stayed by the door. As we waited, I started to worry that I might not get my visit after all. Finally, the door opened, and Jean walked in, escorted by two guards who remained outside the door. There was a look of shock on his face at the sight of me, and we ran to each other and embraced. He smelled of sweat and cologne, and the visceral memory of the kiss came rushing back. He looked thinner and paler too, but I knew I was the worse of the two of us. When we pulled apart, he put his hands on my face, and tears were running down his.

"What have you all *done* to this woman?" Jean said, growling at Damasky.

"Jean, they have done nothing; it's just the cancer," I said, grabbing his hands, looking in his eyes, trying to make him understand. "The *medicine* I'm taking is not helping. Yet."

"You're sick?" Herr Damasky said, eyes wide with alarm, looking back and forth at me and Jean. "Nobody told me you were ill."

I explained my fake condition, and the young German looked at me with a genuine sympathy and kindness.

"Is this your sweetheart?" he said, pointing at Jean.

"Ah . . . yes," I said, my cheeks burning. I couldn't look Jean in the face. It wasn't true, but it wasn't false.

"Love is hard in war," the guard said, scratching his cheek as he seemed to be mulling something over.

"Indeed. I know you understand," I said.

"Look, I am not supposed to do this, but I will give you twenty minutes. Alone." He pointed to my bag and looked at Jean. "She has things for you. You should hide them in your pockets; it's not allowed, but we often look the other way."

"I don't know how to thank you," I said to Herr Damasky.

"Twenty minutes," he said with a small smile before closing the door.

Jean was wiping tears off his face again as he took me in his arms, and we stood by the window like that.

"Please don't cry," I said. "I never cry in front of them. I don't want to give them the satisfaction."

"Ha," Jean said, stroking my hair. "Then you are stronger than me."

"I am not," I said. "Just more stubborn."

"Well, that is definitely true," he said, tilting my chin up with his hand so we were nose to nose, then giving me a long, lingering kiss that felt as natural as breathing, and my worry about any awkwardness between us melted away.

"Nadine sends her love. She is managing the farm wonderfully, with her helpers Remy and Girard," Jean said in a voice louder than necessary. He walked to the table and looked under the chairs and anywhere else in the room that might be bugged with Dictaphones. "Elise and Claude and so many of the neighbors have asked for you. They all miss you terribly."

He pulled two chairs next to the window and we sat side by side.

"We don't have a lot of time, so you need to listen carefully," he whispered. "I have been trying very hard to get you out. I have reached out to all my friends in Vichy and Paris with Gestapo connections."

"I've been doing what I can too," I said, also keeping my voice low. "That's why I've been taking the medicine; that's why I have lost weight and look so terrible."

"You're still as beautiful as ever. But, Drue, I talked to Dr. Rolland. He and Dr. Levy are very worried about your condition and how much blood you're losing. You've *got* to stop taking that medicine immediately."

"I was going to wait until after I see Dr. von Weber again this Friday," I said.

"No, no!" he said. "I came here, without the right papers, at great risk, because I have a plan, one that I came up with, with these two incredible doctors who are helping you. And if it doesn't work, I have an alternative plan. But mark my words, we *will* get you out of here, without you risking your life by possibly bleeding to death."

I didn't like that they had concocted a plan without me, but then, they didn't have any other choice. And I knew he was right.

"I am so tired," I said, blinking back angry tears. "Of this ruse, and of how I am feeling not just physically but mentally and emotionally . . . keeping so many secrets that I can barely keep them straight myself. It's completely and utterly exhausting! I just desperately want to get back to Barbizon."

"I know; I want the same. Things have been going very well with our deliveries, but I need you back," Jean said, referring to the supply drops. He kissed my hair. "So, this is what you need to do. You need to fake a health crisis, an incident in your hotel room, and get yourself into the hospital right away."

"OK. When?"

"Tonight," he said. "Dr. Levy will be there tonight to check in with you."

I took a deep breath and put my head in my hands. It would be a relief to stop bleeding, no more feeling weak and dizzy and nauseous all the time.

"What if Dr. von Weber still won't let me leave?" I said, sitting back up. "Or insists on surgery?"

"Dr. Levy will try to convince him otherwise," Jean said. "And if he can't, and you're still not released, there is the backup plan."

"Which is what?"

"That head nun at the hospital—what's her name again? She says she will disguise you as a nun, and you will escape that way."

"What? Mother Chad?" I said with a laugh, raising my eyebrows. "You can't be serious."

"I am completely serious," he said.

"Dressing up as a nun? This sounds like a crazy caper from the movies."

"They've done it before apparently. Dr. Rolland will keep you informed of the details if that is what we must do. One way or another, we are getting you out."

I looked at his face, putting my hand on his cheek.

"I am in awe of the selfless bravery of people like her and Dr. Levy," I said. "And, of course, you."

"I am in awe of you," Jean said, kissing me again, more passionately this time as he pulled me into his arms, and for a brief moment, I forgot the rest of the world and all our problems in it.

But after a few minutes, the spell was broken, and he pulled away from me with a groan of frustration and looked at his watch. "I know our time is running out, and there is one more thing. I must go on a trip out of the country in a few days. If you need anything, you should send word to Claude or Elise."

"Where are you going?" I said, an ache in my chest at the thought of him leaving, of him not being in Barbizon if I did finally get out.

"It's best if you don't know," he said. "I wouldn't go unless I absolutely had to. It's Resistance work that can't wait."

"The last time someone I loved left, they never came back." I took both his hands in mine, wishing we could just walk out of this building and disappear together.

Jean gripped my hands tightly when I said this, the look on his face telling me what I already knew.

"You—" he started to say when there was a knock on the door.

"Time's up," Herr Damasky said as he stepped inside. He looked at Jean and asked, "Can I see your papers?"

"I don't have the correct papers to travel here," Jean said. "And I've been fortunate, as you're the first person to ask for them."

Damasky frowned at both of us, deciding.

"Do you know how serious this could have been? If you had a guard who was less understanding?" Damasky asked.

"I do," Jean said, and then, looking at me, he added, "But it was a risk I was willing to take."

"You're lucky that I'm practically an American."

Jean and I said we understood and thanked him profusely, shaking his hand as we exited the room.

"You cannot leave together," Damasky said to me, and then, in an apologetic tone, added, "The guards outside the door will escort you back through the gate to the camp."

I willed myself not to break down as we embraced for the last time.

"I love you, Drue," he whispered in my ear. "I have from the moment we met."

"I love you," I whispered back, my voice wavering. "And that's why you must promise me you'll be safe. Come back to me."

"I promise you. We will be together in Barbizon."

I bit my lip, too emotional to say any more, and, as I followed the guards out, I blew him a kiss. I felt my knees buckle a little as I walked out of the building and back through the barbed wire gate, turning to wave goodbye until he was out of my line of sight. The guards left me on my own as soon as we entered, so I found a secluded pine tree in the park, leaned up against it, and sobbed.

Chapter Thirty-Four

It is possible to hold two people in your heart at the same time; that was what I knew for certain leaning against the pine tree in the park. I would always love Jacques, and I would miss him until the day I died, but my feelings for Jean had been growing for a long time, and my arrest and imprisonment made it impossible to deny them anymore.

After I composed myself, I went back to my room and took a nap, relieved that both of my roommates were out. The fatigue from the blood loss was getting worse every day, and my emotional state after saying goodbye to Jean made me feel even more drained.

I decided my pretend medical crisis would happen after dinner that night, when some of the women who lived on our floor were coming to our room to play bridge and drink bottles of red wine that Kathleen had once again managed to procure through the black market.

After everyone arrived, Sylvia and I sat by the window and smoked cigarettes, as neither of us were big bridge players. We were both wearing wool sweaters, and Sylvia had a blanket wrapped around her legs. It was early November, but the nights were already near freezing, and it had rained every day for a week.

"I cannot believe there's not enough fuel available to heat this hotel," she said. "And that they're going to keep us all here through the winter. It's going to be dreadful; I hate the cold."

"Me too," I said, imagining how grim it would be if we were still here in January. "That's the one thing I miss about California, the weather."

She offered me another cigarette, and I accepted. The English cigarettes from the Red Cross were heavenly compared to the ones I had been smoking in Barbizon.

"Should you be smoking, given your condition right now?" Sylvia said, lighting my cigarette. "Not that I'm going to stop you."

"Probably not," I said, with a shrug. "But it helps me relax."

"Me too. And we deserve some of life's little luxuries right now."

"I agree," I said with a smile. "Please . . . now tell me about when you first met Ernest Hemingway," I said. Kathleen and I loved to encourage Sylvia to share stories about the vast circle of literary friends that she had met through her bookshop.

"It was in 1921," she said as I passed her the tin ashtray. "He just walked into the shop one day, and we sat and had a long chat. He was tall and dark, with a little mustache and this deep, booming voice. He came in limping, and he showed me his dreadful scars from fighting in Italy. Did you know he spent two years in a military hospital getting back the use of his leg?"

"I had no idea," I said.

"Yes, it was quite a recovery. So, after that first day, he kept coming back to the shop. He would browse and buy books and then sit by the fire and talk to me and Adrienne or whoever was there. He called himself my best customer, and he was. We were great friends from that day on. Like found family."

"Found family," I said. "I understand that so well."

The bridge players started roaring with laughter over some misunderstanding, and I crushed my cigarette in the ashtray and decided it was now or never. I got up to go to the bathroom and swayed a little, putting a hand on my forehead.

"Are you all right?" Sylvia asked, standing up and putting her arm on my back.

"I'm . . . I'm OK," I said. "Just need to use the bathroom to change my sanitary pads. Again."

"You poor thing," she said, concern on her face. I was looking forward to no longer having to deceive my friends, as the guilt was getting to me.

Shutting the bathroom door, I rehearsed what I was going to do one last time. I would be as loud as possible and make it look like I had fallen on the floor and fainted, knocking over the water glass on the sink along with the lipstick and hairbrush in an attempt to hold on to the counter.

There was more laughter outside the door, and I planned to some-day apologize to these lovely women for the deception and for ruining a rare, perfectly fun night in the prison camp. The laughter died down, and I knew I had to do it when they would hear me. I took a deep breath and started the charade before I could second-guess myself.

"Kathleen," I yelled, sounding as distressed as possible. "Could you come here . . . I feel . . ."

Then I knocked the items off the counter and fell to the floor. I didn't anticipate the water glass smashing, and when I fell, I cut the palm of my hand on a large shard. I cursed myself as I closed my eyes and pretended to be out cold, despite the stinging pain in my hand, just as the door opened.

"Oh no, oh no, Drue! Drue, can you hear me, sweetheart?" Kathleen was next to me, kneeling in the glass and holding my hand. "She's bleeding! Sylvia!"

She was checking my pulse, and I heard a neighbor say she would run and get one of the nuns.

"I'm calling the doctor!" I heard Sylvia yell from the other room as I tried to remain perfectly still, not even moving my eyeballs under my eyelids to avoid giving any indication I was still awake.

Five minutes later, none other than Sister Nancy was waving an ampoule of smelling salts under my nose, and I was finally able to pretend to regain consciousness.

"There you are," she said when I opened my eyes, giving me a serene smile.

"Oh, thank God, you're awake," Kathleen said, bandaging my hand. "I was terrified when I saw you sprawled on the floor in here."

"How long was I out?" I said, making my voice hoarse. "I don't even remember coming into the bathroom."

"Long enough to get yourself a trip to the hospital," Sister Nancy said. "Dr. Levy is working tonight; I am sure he'll want to see you right away."

Sylvia packed my bag with my nightgown, toothbrush, and other personal items, and I left our hotel room with Kathleen and Sister Nancy walking on either side of me, both holding on to an elbow all the way to the hospital, where I was put in an antique wheelchair and brought up to a private room on the second floor with my very own bathroom. Sister Nancy checked my vitals, and Kathleen accompanied me into the bathroom as I changed into my nightgown, making sure I didn't pass out again.

"Oh, well, this is lovely and heated, and during the day you'll have a nice view of the park," said Kathleen after I had settled into bed. She sat on the end of it and patted my foot. "How are you feeling? Sister is going to bring you up something to eat."

"Better, I think," I said. "Anxious to see Dr. Levy."

"I'll let you get some rest before he arrives," she said. "I'll be back tomorrow. Sylvia and I will visit in the afternoon, bring you some books and goodies. And just maybe Tudor or Jean will get us out of here soon, somehow."

"Maybe," I said.

She still looked so worried about me, I longed to tell her the truth, and, in that moment, I almost did. But I thought of the doctors here that were risking everything to help me, so I held my tongue.

"I hope you're feeling better by tomorrow," she said, kissing me on the forehead.

"Me too," I said. "Thank you, friend."

I fell asleep after Kathleen left, and when I woke up, Dr. Levy was standing over me in the dim light of the room.

"Hello," I said. "What time is it?"

"Time to try to get you out of Vittel," he whispered, his hand on my wrist as he checked my pulse.

"How is your family?" I asked.

"The same, nothing new; no bad news, at least," he said. "When was the last time you took your hemorrhaging medicine?"

"This morning," I said. "I am so sorry I disobeyed you, but . . ."

"I know," he said with an exasperated sigh, taking a vial of pills out of his pocket and picking up the glass of water by my bed. "I know why you did it. But you need to stop those pills now. I have the medicine that will stop the hemorrhaging here with me, and you must start it tonight. It's far past time, Drue. You cannot go on losing blood a minute longer. You could go into shock, your organs could fail, you could *die*. You will be no good to Jean Fraysse if that happens. You must take this."

"But what about von Weber?"

"He's in Berlin, and he will see you Friday as planned. I will tell him your condition has worsened and that you should go to Paris for treatment."

"But if he examines me?"

"I think we can make sure he doesn't. I've discussed it with Mother Chad. Now, please, take the new medicine."

He handed me the glass of water and placed a pill in the palm of my hand. He was right: I had gone far enough, risked enough with this medical deception; it was method acting in the extreme. I was weary of feeling so terrible all the time. I put it in my mouth and swallowed it.

"You're not hiding it under your tongue, are you?" he asked, so I opened my mouth to show him.

"I'm sorry for being stubborn; I'm just desperate to get out of here. Thank you again for everything."

"I understand, and you're welcome. Von Weber likes you. I think you will be able to convince him to let you go. Shed a few tears—he's a tyrant, but, believe it or not, he hates to see his patients crying. That surprised me."

"OK; tears, drama, I can do that pretty well when I make the effort," I said.

"That *doesn't* surprise me," he said with a quiet chuckle, and, patting my foot, he added, "Goodnight. Get some rest."

"Dr. Levy?" I called to him just as he was closing the door.

"Yes?"

"If I do . . . if this works, please let me know if there's anything that I can do for your family. Anything at all."

"Thank you," he said with a nod, and I blew him a kiss goodnight as he shut the door behind him.

Chapter Thirty-Five

November 4, 1942

I didn't know if it was the new medicine or the emotional relief that my health was going to improve, but I slept almost the entire day on Saturday, only to wake up in the late afternoon and have a little cabbage soup and brown bread for dinner with Kathleen and Sylvia and then go back to bed. On Wednesday morning, I awoke to Sister Nancy shaking me.

"Drue, you have a visitor. A young guard, Herr Damasky. Would it be all right if he came in to see you?"

"Yes, just give me a moment to freshen up," I said.

"Let me help you to the bathroom and get your robe on," Sister Nancy said. I was already feeling a little better, not quite as weak, as well as calmer and more rested than I had felt in days.

Herr Damasky was standing in my room fifteen minutes later, looking shy and nervous and holding a small box wrapped in silver paper.

"How nice of you to visit me," I said, giving him a warm smile. "And thank you again for the other day with my friend."

"You're quite welcome, madame," he said.

"You may call me Drue," I said.

"And you may call me Frederich."

"Pull up a chair, Frederich," I said.

He talked to me about America, his love of baseball, and his plans for after the war. Of course he brought up his sweetheart, Bridget, again. As he was describing their first date, Dr. Levy came flying into the room, startling both of us.

"He's here, he's downstairs, he'll be up here in minutes, Sister Nancy is coming up with the—" Dr. Levy stopped speaking as he registered that Damasky was in the room listening.

"Von Weber? Now?" I said. "Oh my God."

"I've got the rags, Doctor!" Sister Nancy came running in holding up a bag full of blood-soaked rags. She stopped short and gasped.

"What the . . . ?" Damasky looked at the three of us, bewildered.

"Drue . . . ," Dr. Levy said, but I held up my hand and looked in his eyes. I would handle it.

"Sister Nancy, you may put those in my bed. Frederich, I am going to need your help. I am trusting you this time with my actual life," I said quietly. "Please tell me I can do that."

"You can," he said, putting his cap back on. "Tell me what I need to do."

"I'm going to get on the floor, and I want you kneeling next to me, along with Sister Nancy, as if you both found me like that, passed out cold. Maybe you could even lift me up into the bed in front of the doctor for full effect. Do you think you can do that?"

"I . . . I . . . yes, I can," he said. "I'll do it."

"Thank you. Dr. Levy," I said. "You can go find him; we'll be ready."

"OK—remember tears will help too," Dr. Levy said as he exited.

As Sister Nancy arranged the rags under my blanket, I climbed out of bed and Damasky held on to my elbow as I sat and then sprawled on the floor, faceup, my pale-pink nightgown and robe strategically placed so I wouldn't appear indecent. We soon heard Dr. von Weber screaming at Dr. Levy out in the hallway, and I closed my eyes and took a few deep breaths as Sister Nancy, shaking with fear, and Herr Damasky, looking almost as scared, knelt beside me.

"What on earth is going on here?" Dr. von Weber yelled when he opened the door to our scene.

"We found her like this," Sister Nancy said, her sweet voice shaking. "I don't know what happened; I had just left to get her visitor and—"

"Get her off the floor!" von Weber said to Damasky. "Dr. Levy, get me the smelling salts."

Damasky picked me up with genuine care and placed me in the bed. I heard von Weber gasp at the blood all over the sheets.

"What is all of *this*? She can't stay like this. Has the medicine not been helping?" he asked. And it took every ounce of discipline to be still and keep my eyes closed while being placed on a bed covered with blood that wasn't mine.

"Not much, Herr Doctor," I heard Dr. Levy say. "She is in very bad shape."

The whiff of smelling salts under my nose meant I could finally open my eyes, and the towering doctor was standing over me. The look of compassion on his face caught me off guard.

"*Ma fille*, how are you? I hear that things do not go well," Dr. von Weber said. *Ma fille*, my daughter, like Claude always called me. And that was all it took for me to conjure tears, because I thought of Claude, ruddy cheeks and expansive belly, and of Jean and Nadine and Elise, and I was overcome with a melancholy homesickness.

"Not at all well, Herr Doctor," I said, letting the tears roll down my cheeks. "I am getting no better."

"I should examine you," he said. "Sister, get me rubber gloves and some Vaseline."

I thought I might pass out for real, this time from the horrible specter of this man giving me an internal gynecological exam.

"Please, I am in a great deal of pain. Dr. Levy examined me earlier. I can't take it right now," I said, crying real tears now and choking back a sob.

"It's true; I examined her. There is no improvement, even with the medicine you gave her," Dr. Levy said. "It's all in her records. She is a very sick woman, and she needs more than we can provide."

Sister Nancy brought him the Vaseline and gloves, and I swallowed the bile in my throat.

He looked at them and waved her away, and I took a deep breath in.

"I think you should go to Nancy for surgery and X-ray treatments," Dr. von Weber said. "It's not too far; one of the ambulances could take you."

"Oh no. There's been bombing there every single night. Please, you can't send me there, I'm begging you," I said, and the tears kept flowing, no acting required. I was frustrated and distraught to the point of being almost hysterical. Making myself sick for days, lying to my friends, terrifying Jean—all of it would be for nothing if he didn't set me free. I grasped his hand, enormous and warm against my freezing-cold one.

He grabbed my file from Dr. Levy and started looking through it as I kept crying.

Finally, he let out an exasperated sigh, and I held my breath, waiting for the verdict.

"All right. I will send word to Berlin that you should be sent back to Paris," von Weber said, putting a hand on my forehead and patting it. "The order for your release should come through within a few weeks. In the meantime, I will give you some stronger medicine for the pain, and I know the sisters will take very good care of you."

I tried to smile, but I couldn't stop crying. I was relieved beyond words and so grateful to those who had helped me.

"Aren't you happy?" von Weber said.

"I am," I said, "I truly am; I am just overcome with so many emotions right now. Thank you, Herr Doctor. Thank you for your kindness."

And to put a final touch on our orchestrated performance for the German doctor, I held his hand in both of mine and kissed it.

Chapter Thirty-Six

December 10, 1942

With the possibility of leaving Vittel on the horizon and the Americans invading North Africa, the weeks after Dr. von Weber's decision were a time of indescribable relief and recovery. Dr. Levy thought it best that I stay in the hospital, to keep up appearances with von Weber and also to regain some of my strength before leaving. And there was a flu outbreak at the camp, so von Weber had become incredibly busy, which was an unexpected blessing for me. After he had made the decision to release me for treatment, he never mentioned examining me again and left my care primarily to Dr. Levy.

My cozy, heated room at the hospital became a gathering place for my friends living in the unheated buildings. Visiting hours were from two until four in the afternoon, and every day I was inundated with people bringing presents and sympathy. Sylvia and Kathleen came daily and brought me treats from their Red Cross packages and books from the library, and several of the British women on our hallway stopped by as well. Some of the *Anything Goes* talent-show girls even came by with a dry but otherwise edible lemon cake made from rations and Red Cross provisions. The nuns at the hospital were so lovely, and Sister Nancy would often sneak in to have a cup of tea with me when Mother Chad wasn't around.

It was the tenth of December, and I was still waiting to hear about my paperwork from Berlin and starting to get anxious about whether it would ever arrive—or if they had put it on hold because they had discovered I was Drue Leyton, or that Jacques had been fighting for de Gaulle, or both. Late at night, I would lie awake, trying to distract myself from the possible nightmare of being sent to Germany for execution instead of home to Barbizon.

There was a full moon, and it was a clear but freezing-cold night in the Vosges Mountains, so Sylvia and Kathleen were planning on sneaking into my room for a glass of wine, an excuse to keep warm until they absolutely had to go to sleep in our frigid hotel room. My door opened, and I thought it was them, but it was Sister Nancy, with a curious look on her face.

"That guard's here to see you again, the odd one who's German but basically American. He has a present and couldn't give it to you that night . . . you know, the night . . ."

"I know," I said; she was referring to the night of our dramatic act for Dr. von Weber.

"I can tell him to leave," she said.

"It's OK; he's not bad. Please send him in," I said.

A minute later he was standing at the end of my bed, looking awkward, slouching as if trying to minimize his height and unsure of what to do, so I told him to pull up a chair. He did, and he handed me the box, still wrapped in silver paper.

"I want to thank you for helping me that night," I said. "And also, for your kindness when I visited with Jean. I feel like I should be giving *you* a present."

"I felt terrible when I learned how sick you were," he said, removing his cap, which always made the guards look so much younger. "Now I realize . . . are you sick? Never mind—don't answer that. In any case, it's just a little something; my older sister had one like it, and I saw it at that trinket shop in the lobby and thought you might like it. For luck."

"I can definitely use some of that," I said with a smile as I opened the gift.

Inside was a little silver bracelet with a ladybug charm.

"Oh, how darling," I said, touched by such a sweet gesture. "Will you help me put it on?"

"Of course," he said, his cheeks a bright red. "Ladybugs are called Marian beetles. In Germany they're considered lucky, especially ones with seven black spots, like this one. They protect young and old and heal the sick."

"I'm so touched," I said, admiring it on my wrist. "Thank you, Frederich."

"It's for luck," he whispered, "because I want you to get out of here safe. And I know you have had to keep the secret about who you are."

"I figured I wasn't fooling you," I whispered back with a smile.

"Yes. And I would never tell a soul."

"Thank you. Do you know why I must keep that a secret?"

"I guessed it was because of the radio work at the beginning of the war," he said.

"They put out a death warrant for me."

"No surprise. They've put out death warrants for far less."

"I am just shocked that it hasn't been discovered yet. Even now, I'm holding my breath that they'll discover who I really am before my release papers go through."

"The thing I've realized, being on this side of things," he said, "and I hate being on this side, if you haven't noticed—but what I have seen is, the Nazis, the Gestapo, they are not as organized as they seem; they can be very careless."

"I'm counting on that," I said.

"I have to go," he said. "I really shouldn't be here after hours, and I don't want you to get any questions. But I wanted to give you that and say that meeting you was a pleasure and an honor."

"Thank you for being my friend when I really needed one here," I said. "I will look you up when I am back in America."

"Yes, you and your sweetheart Jean," he said. "You can both meet my wife."

"That would be lovely; I look forward to it," I said, an ache in my heart. These were the plans we made in war that helped get us through. But neither of us knew what was going to happen tomorrow, much less years from now.

"Goodnight, Madame Tartière," he said, and he took my hand and kissed it, then slipped out of my hospital room.

~

"We bribed Sister Nancy with some Red Cross chocolate," Kathleen said, barging into my room a little while later. "I think she took pity on us because the Grand Hôtel feels even colder inside than it is outside tonight."

"Selfishly, I am glad you are still here, in this comfortably warm hospital room," Sylvia said as she sat down in the chair Damasky had pulled over and offered me a cigarette while Kathleen opened the bottle of Burgundy she had brought. "But have you had any news?"

"Dr. Levy told me yesterday that there's still nothing," I said with a shrug.

"You must be anxious about starting treatments," Kathleen said. "Although I have to say, you seem better than you were."

"I agree," Sylvia said. "It's as if the news of getting released has already improved your health."

"I think there's something to that," I said. "I am doing a little better, still very weak. And so tired all the time."

"So, my news is, Tudor says he thinks he might be able to get me and Sylvia out before the new year," Kathleen said as she poured us another glass of Burgundy. "Some of the high command, particularly Hermann Göring, have become obsessed with our art collection, so he's trying to use that to our advantage, even if it means selling him one of his portraits by the artist Holbein."

"He wouldn't do that, would he?" I said. "Sell a masterpiece to the Nazis?"

"If it meant getting us out, because it also throws them off the trail, so to speak," Kathleen said, referring to Tudor's Resistance work.

"If all else fails, maybe one of you can just put me in your suitcase; I'm pretty small," Sylvia joked, just as the wineglass on my little nightstand started to vibrate and the sound of a dull roar grew outside, followed by the voices of women upstairs hollering.

"What on earth . . . ," I said as I jumped out of bed, forgetting to feign illness out of pure excitement and happiness at what I guessed was causing the sound. We pulled back the room-darkening curtains and opened the doors to the tiny balcony.

All through the camp, there were curtains being opened and lights coming on, with many women banging pots and pans. I looked up to see waves of British Royal Air Force bombers flying low across the full moon, clear and beautiful in the night sky. And as more and more women throughout the camp realized what was happening, all Vittel erupted in unadulterated joy and chaos, with raucous cheering and screaming from every balcony. Two balconies over, there were doctors and nuns hugging each other and laughing. At one point, one of the RAF planes flickered its red and green wing lights at us, and the entire camp lost its collective mind.

Hundreds of voices started to sing "It's a Long Way to Tipperary," followed by "God Save the King," at the top of their lungs. Women from the Grand Hôtel were shouting, "Are we downhearted?" in unison, and women on the balconies of the hotel next door shouted back, "A thousand times no!" Mother Chad stood on one of the balconies in her white robe, her hands together in prayer as she looked up at the sky, smiling as tears streamed down her cheeks.

The German guards were apoplectic, but they had no control from the start. Frantically they tried to quell the unbridled enthusiasm by whistling or firing their guns in the air, but it was a hopeless cause. Forty-five minutes in, they finally cut the power for the entire camp, but at that point things were calming down, as the last of the planes had flown past.

Celebrations continued in the dark hallways of the hospital, with nuns and patients and doctors having an impromptu party. Sister Nancy was doing a Highland Fling with one of the young doctors, and someone was passing out bottles of beer. Sylvia, Kathleen, and I had brought our wineglasses out in the hall and were enjoying the scene, laughing, and hugging and dancing. I had never seen Dr. Levy happier, but when he spotted me, he pointed and ordered me straight back to my bed. I gave him my best sulk but turned around.

"You must stay in bed, or you'll ruin everything," he said in a whisper, coming into my room behind me, but he was still smiling.

"I'm sorry, I got caught up in the excitement; I promise I won't do it again," I said.

"I can't say I blame you," he said. "This is the best I have felt in months."

"Me too," I said.

"Also, I came in because I have news," Dr. Levy said, sitting on the edge of my bed once I was settled. "I was going to wait until tomorrow because I thought you were sleeping. But I see you've been having visitors instead." He raised his eyebrows and nodded at the ashtray full of cigarette butts and the bottle of wine.

"What? Tell me, is it good or bad?" I said, gripping my sheets, preparing myself.

"Your papers came through; they have approved you for release and treatment in Paris."

"Are you serious?" I said, putting my hands over my mouth. "Really?"

"Of course I am serious."

"Do I get to leave before Christmas?"

At this he chuckled. "Drue, you get to leave *tomorrow*."

I stared at him, and he just nodded and smiled at me while I absorbed this monumental news and burst into tears.

Chapter Thirty-Seven

The next twenty-four hours were an emotional blur as I packed up my things while still trying to appear like I was struggling and weak. And I remained extremely paranoid that something would happen and my release would be canceled somehow at the last minute. It wasn't until Dr. von Weber handed me my certificate just before I left the hospital that it felt like it was really happening.

"*Freigelassen am 11. Dezember 1942*," which translated to "released on December 11, 1942."

"You will have to report to the Gestapo headquarters at eighty-four Avenue Foch upon your arrival in Paris," Dr. von Weber said. "The chief there will review your file and issue you a pass to travel from Barbizon into Paris for treatment."

"I thought my file was already reviewed?" I said with a groan, as it seemed impossible to believe I'd get through another file review without anything being found.

"It's just a formality," he said, waving his hand in the air. "Do not worry."

"Thank you very much for your help and your interest in my case," I said, hoping he was right, looking at the word "freed" on the certificate.

"Please, you must consider an operation in addition to X-ray treatments to have the best chance of survival," he said, and I was surprised to see him visibly moved.

"I will," I said, looking up at him, thinking about how even terrible people had a tiny dose of humanity lurking inside them. "I will consult with my doctor in Paris about it."

"I hope that you will tell the Americans someday that your stay in this camp was not too painful," he said. "It is an unfortunate thing that we are at war with your country."

Having heard stories of some of the horrific conditions at other internment camps from the nuns, I knew how lucky I had been to be in the relative luxury of this place.

"It is an unfortunate thing," I said. With a final goodbye, he walked out of my hospital room, and I lay down on my bed and exhaled.

A little while later, Kathleen and Sylvia helped me with my two bags, one with my clothes, another with food for the trip, including some of their Red Cross rations. I felt sad and angry they couldn't come with me, and I could tell by how unusually quiet they were that they both felt the same. We went downstairs, where an ambulance was waiting to take me to the train station. A French Red Cross worker would meet me at the station and accompany me all the way to Paris to make sure I made the trip without fainting or collapsing. I gasped when I walked outside and saw many of the doctors, sisters, and fellow inmates lined up in front of the ambulance to say goodbye.

I went down the line, kissing and embracing Dr. Rolland, Mother Chad, Sister Nancy, and so many others, and there were tears and laughter as well as lingering guilt on my part for letting many of these dear people believe I was gravely ill. I showed the ladybug bracelet on my wrist to Frederich and thanked him again for his kindness. Dr. Levy was my last goodbye, holding the door of the ambulance open for me to climb in.

"And I will be grateful to you for the rest of my life. I hope your father is released and your family stays safe," I said, kissing him on both cheeks.

"Thank you. And you're welcome, my dear," Dr. Levy said, and behind his thick glasses his eyes were watering. He then whispered in my ear, "Go home, get well; you need to rest and recover. Only after that, when you are strong enough, fight on. If you can, you should."

"I will. I can promise you that."

~

"Hello, my darling Drue, are you awake? We have a visitor." Elise was sitting at the end of her daughter Corinne's twin bed, the one I had collapsed into when I had finally arrived at her apartment.

The journey back to Paris had not been easy, and it made me realize how much strength and stamina I had lost in a matter of weeks. After leaving Vittel, we had to change trains in Nancy in the pitch dark, and just as we were boarding, the air-raid sirens started blaring, so we were stuck in the station's Red Cross canteen for hours. The next train we were on was filthy and cramped and packed with German soldiers, and it was impossible to get comfortable on the long ride back. We had finally arrived at Gare de l'Est in the early-morning hours, and since I did not have keys and wasn't sure if Claude was at my apartment, I had a Red Cross station wagon take us to Elise's building, where her concierge had greeted us with alarm. I vaguely remembered our tearful reunion in the hallway before being helped up the stairs and collapsing into bed.

"How long have I slept?" I said.

"Well, let's see, you arrived at five o'clock this morning and it is now four in the afternoon, so a little while. I have some coffee, thanks to you. Come see who just arrived."

"Is it Jean?" I said, sitting up, smoothing out my curls, my heart beating out of my chest.

"No, my friend, I wish I could say it was," she said. Her voice sounded as worried as I felt. "I'm afraid there's still no word from him since he left for his trip."

"I am going to believe that no news is good news and he'll show up in Barbizon soon," I said, swinging my legs over the side of the bed.

"Me too. Do you need help getting up or changing out of your nightgown?" She was looking me up and down, arms crossed. "You are very pale, and you've lost weight."

"I know, but I am OK, Elise. I shouldn't have taken that medicine for as long as I did, but I am improving every day now."

"I am glad to hear that; I almost had a heart attack when I saw you downstairs," she said. "You look like death warmed up."

"I've missed your honesty," I said, giving her a wink. "I will be fine. How are *you*? How are Corinne and your mama?"

"We are managing," she said. "I've been working, not with the Nazi filmmakers, but with some of the theater companies. The Germans love the theater, and the shows are sold out most nights. Dear Nadine has been sending eggs and potatoes to us when she can. She cannot wait to see you."

"And I cannot wait to go home to the villa," I said. "I've got to get my pass from the Gestapo first, so I can come back weekly for my so-called treatments with Dr. Porcher. I'm heading there tomorrow."

"To their headquarters?"

"Yes," I said, and Elise visibly shivered.

"Do you need me to go with you? No, don't even answer, because I know you'll say no. I'll go with you. I insist."

She shut the door of Corinne's closet-size room, and I changed into my worn black culottes and the one camel-colored wool sweater I had brought with me to Vittel. I was still fatigued from the journey, but I stood and looked out the bedroom window at their street, Quai d'Anjou on Île Saint-Louis, beautiful even in December. All at once the exhilaration of what had just happened washed over me. I was a free woman again; I had made it back from behind the barbed wire of Vittel.

I walked into the living room, and Claude rushed over to hug me.

"*Ma fille!* It is you, you are really back," he said as he practically lifted me off the floor. "You are so thin; what did they *do* to you? My poor girl," he said, putting a hand on my cheek before enveloping me in a hug again.

I was overcome with emotion once again, to be among these friends that I loved as much as my family back home. I had been imagining this reunion for weeks. The only thing that made it bittersweet was Jean's absence.

"I have missed you all so much," I said as Elise's mother, Yvonne, grabbed me by the arm and insisted I sit down on the sofa, and little Corinne, adorable in thick, dark braids, brought me a cup of coffee. The Red Cross biscuits were on a plate on the table, and I handed Corinne a chocolate bar I had in my pocket just for her.

"It's not as good as French chocolate," I said, "but any chocolate right now is pretty good, isn't it?"

"What a treat this is. Thank you, thank you so very much," she said, delighted. She glanced at her mother for approval before she ripped it open and headed into her room to enjoy it without interruption. Elise's mother, ever quiet, kissed me on both cheeks before retreating to her bedroom for her afternoon nap.

"Tell me, how is my apartment here? How are things in Barbizon?" I asked Claude.

"Your apartment is in good condition; I got it ready for you, if you'd like to stay in Paris," he said. "Barbizon is . . . I just returned from there. Good and bad. It is teeming with Gestapo and collaborators, and you will have to be more careful than ever. There is a clear divide now between people who are pro-Allies and those who are pro-Nazi. The pro-Nazis are becoming more vindictive against foreigners. That Daan Koster, he's responsible for getting several of Jean's Resistance contacts in Melun arrested."

"That is not a surprise," I said. "But what of the Resistance work? Besides the arrests, what's been happening?"

Now that I was finally out, I was itching to do something to help, anything to contribute to the cause.

"That is the good news. The Resistance is much better organized, in Barbizon and all over the country," Claude said. "I have been working with some of Jean's contacts there and here in the city. There are more guns and money coming in, more acts of sabotage. But I think we need to stop airdrops on the farm for a time, for your safety. You do not want to end up back in Vittel or worse."

"He is right," Elise added. "The Germans are making more and more arrests in and around Paris; these are terrible times."

"I agree, after what I've been through," I said with a groan, sitting back on the sofa, feeling fatigue wash over me again. "But it is going to be hard waiting in the wings until I can do more."

"There are many hungry families in Paris that you can help feed," Elise said. "I can help you transport the food from there to here."

"I am happy to do that," I said. "But it's not enough."

"I know it's not," Elise said. "Remember, they murdered my husband too. You'll be able to do more soon, I promise you."

"You will," Claude said, putting his arm around my shoulder. "But you just got released, so at first the Gestapo will be watching your every move. And you still have secrets for them to discover."

"As if I need reminding," I said, rubbing my hands over my face, fighting fatigue again. "It will be interesting to see what they know when I meet with them tomorrow morning."

"Tomorrow morning?" Claude said with alarm. "Ah, *ma fille*, be so very careful with what you say and do there. You are entering the dragon's lair."

Chapter Thirty-Eight

Elise was more nervous than I was as we arrived at eighty-four Avenue Foch for my appointment with the chief of the Gestapo in Paris. After being imprisoned by Nazis and dealing with them up close every day for weeks, they were not as formidable to me anymore, not as intimidating. Still, I wore the ladybug charm bracelet Damasky had given me, for luck, just in case.

The head of the Gestapo office in Paris was a soft-spoken, polite Austrian man named Hutterman. He led Elise and me into his office and told us to have a seat while he sent his assistant out for my dossier.

"You look very frail, madame," he said in heavily accented French. "Is that why your friend is with you?"

"Yes, she came with me, as I have had fainting spells," I said.

"*Bonjour*," Elise said, introducing herself. "She stayed with me last night and is not well at all."

I proceeded to tell him the details of my illness and reasons for release.

"I am sorry to hear this," he said. "I hope you are well taken care of now that you are back in Paris."

"Yes, I have an excellent doctor here, Dr. Porcher," I said. "I have an appointment with him next week."

The young assistant came back with a file that was several inches thick, and I swallowed hard. Hutterman opened it up and started going through it, and Elise gave me a wild-eyed look, as if to say, *What is all of that?*

"My goodness," I said. "I didn't think I was important enough to require so many documents. May I see them?"

Elise kicked me under the desk for asking, and Hutterman looked up at me, surprised.

"Absolutely not," he said, smiling. "So, madame, there's one thing in your dossier that almost prevented you from getting released."

"I can't imagine what it would be," I said, gripping the seat of my chair because I could imagine a dozen things it could be at this point.

"Your father-in-law's friendship with a man who is now prominent in the British government. He was among his houseguests at a party in the summer of thirty-six."

"But I didn't marry into the Tartière family until thirty-eight," I said.

"Other than that, the people in Barbizon speak very highly of you, including Commandant Fieger. Though Mayor Voclain is not as enamored with you."

"That would be accurate," I said.

"It is said you are in poor health, you don't share political views, and you mind your own business."

"That is all true," I said.

"Very well," Hutterman said, and he started filling out some paperwork. Elise had her fingers crossed, and I strained my neck to see what he was writing.

"Here is your *laissez-passer*, giving you complete freedom to go back and forth to Paris as often as you need," he said. "Do you know when you will be done with treatments?"

"I do not," I said. "I know it's going to be a long time."

"Then there will be no expiration date for the pass," he said as he handed it to me. "Good luck to you, Madame Tartière. I hope you get well."

We said our goodbyes to the shockingly mild-mannered Gestapo officer. Elise and I did not speak until we felt it was safe.

"I cannot believe how easy that was. How odd that the only thing he brought up was your father-in-law," she said.

"Very bizarre," I said. "Of all the things. I met a guard from America at the camp, and he was telling me the Germans can be very careless. I am finally beginning to believe he was right."

"We can only hope that's true," she said, and paused for a second before adding, "An open pass to travel in and out of Paris anytime. That might be quite helpful for other reasons."

"I was thinking the same thing, my friend," I said. "And not just to bring food into the city."

She hooked arms with me as we made our way to the train station, our heads down because it was cold and drizzling. I had my bags with me and was heading straight back to Barbizon that afternoon.

"Are you sure I can't convince you to stay? Not with me, at your own apartment—just until you get your strength up. Claude and I would be happy to help you recover here."

"I know you would, but I am dying to sleep in my own bed in Villa L'Écureuil, to reunite with Nadine and my animals and see what shape the farm is in. I will be back next week."

"And you're really well enough to travel on your own?"

"Of course," I said. "It's not even that far; I'll be fine."

∼

I arrived at the station in Melun in the pouring rain, weak and light-headed again, and distraught to find that the bus to Barbizon was not running. There were two Belgian women standing nearby whom I vaguely recognized from the village.

"Excuse me," I said, coming up behind them, "but would you like to share a taxi to Barbizon? I was going to ask the station attendant for a number to call."

They turned to look at me, and, upon recognizing me, they both stepped back in revulsion.

"How is it you are even free?" the taller of the two women said, scowling and getting in my face.

"You dirty Americans have caused us enough misery," the other one added, spitting on the ground in front of me. "Why would we go with *you* in a taxi?"

I was shocked into speechlessness; even in prison nobody had ever spoken to me this way. I turned and walked away, and, not knowing what to do, called Alfie from a pay phone because I knew he had a truck, and I was soaked and desperate. The warmth in his voice reassured me that not everyone in Barbizon had turned this ugly.

He pulled up twenty minutes later, and, alarmed at my skinny, drenched appearance, he whisked me into the front seat of his antique red pickup truck, placing a wool blanket on my lap. Just as we were pulling away, the two Belgians came running out of a nearby café and hurried toward the truck.

"Oh no, Alfie, I will pay you five thousand francs not to take those women."

"My dear, I have no choice. And you mustn't make a scene. Those two are very dangerous."

They climbed into the back of the truck, and I was grateful we were separated by a heavy windshield. Alfie drove slowly, quietly explaining that both women were powerful Nazi collaborators, and the taller one worked with the Gestapo in Barbizon.

"It is not the same village that you left. You must be on guard. But," he said, patting my shoulder, "I am so very happy you are back."

By the time we dropped off the two Belgians, I was half-asleep, my head against the truck's cold window. But the sight of Villa L'Écureuil filled me with such emotion that I almost jumped out the door before Alfie pulled completely to a stop. He insisted on helping me get out of the truck to make sure I was OK. I thanked him and promised to come by the bar soon, stumbling to knock on the villa's front door.

The sound of Ondie's barks brought happy tears to my eyes. How many times I had imagined this moment over the past couple months.

"Nadine!" I yelled as she opened the door. "I am home!"

She whooped with joy, and we fell into each other's arms, crying happy tears as Ondie barked and jumped on us.

"*Très chère amie*, you are home! You are home! Thank God, you are *home*."

Chapter Thirty-Nine

December 19, 1942

I spent the first week at the villa not leaving my bedroom, catching up on desperately needed sleep, as Nadine brought me soup and bread or eggs seemingly every hour.

"You are stuffing me with too much food," I said, sitting up in bed Saturday morning, finally feeling somewhat rested.

"And you are far too thin. You need to eat and gain your strength back," Nadine said, just as there was a knock on the door.

"It's the front door," Nadine whispered. "Like last time. None of our friends knock on the front door."

"You'd better go get it," I said, my appetite gone. "They can't be arresting me again; I just got out, for God's sake."

She hurried downstairs to get it, and I grabbed my robe and a cane I had found in the back cottage, slowly making my way downstairs behind her. I was holding on to the railing, feeling weak again. When I reached the bottom of the stairs, Nadine, her face gone pale, was standing next to Mayor Voclain, who was looking as pompous as ever.

"Hello, Monsieur Voclain," I said, with a tight smile, as Nadine pulled out a chair for me for fear I would keel over. "So nice to see you again."

"It's Saturday, madame. You were supposed to come to the mayor's office to register as one of the only Americans in the village."

"As you can see from my appearance, I am not well," I said. "I've been recovering from my journey from Vittel. I have cancer; that is why I am home. I'll be going to weekly appointments in Paris for treatment."

"I am sorry you are sick. But if you don't comply with the rules the Germans imposed, you may end up back in Vittel," he said.

"Would you like that, Mayor Voclain?" I said, glaring at him. "Is that why you are here?"

Nadine put her hand on my shoulder, to warn me to control my anger.

"It doesn't matter what I would like. As an American citizen you must do what is required of you under the laws here now," he said. "We must all follow the rules to the letter or face consequences."

He turned on his heel and marched out, slamming the door behind him.

"You shouldn't have said that," Nadine said. "He would probably like nothing more than to send you back."

"That man is drunk on what little power they have given him," I said, furious.

"Still, Alfie was right: things have become more dangerous here," she said. "Be more careful. And just register every week so he has no reason to report you."

"I will, I'm sorry," I said. "Speaking of, do you think it's safe enough to go to Alfie's? Just to say a quick hello and thank him for picking me up the other night. I am ready to get some air and see some old friends."

Nadine looked at me, considering.

"Is it really not safe enough to go for a glass of wine? I thought it might be good if people see me as the invalid that I am right now."

"That's actually a perfect reason to go," she said. "Bring the cane, put on a show for the Germans and collaborators in town. Maybe you can convince them not to bother with us."

~

Alfie and Giselle gave us both a rousing welcome when we arrived at the bar and whisked us over to our favorite table by the fire, coming back minutes later with mugs of hot, spicy mulled wine. There were two tables of German officers, but a few familiar faces from the village, including some of the shopkeepers, came over to the table to welcome me back with kisses and kind words.

I spotted Daan Koster at the bar, and he locked eyes with me and gave me a wave and a smile that made my skin crawl. I gave him a small wave back.

"That Dutch filmmaker is here," I whispered to Nadine. I could still feel his eyes on me.

"Yes, unfortunately," Nadine whispered back. "And he's coming over."

"Madame Tartière, it is good to see you back," Koster said. I had to stop myself from recoiling when he leaned down to kiss me on both cheeks, far too familiar for this odd acquaintance. "How are you feeling?"

"A little better now that I am home, thank you," I said. "And I'll be seeing my doctor for cancer treatments."

The more people who believed I had cancer the better, particularly collaborators like him.

"I'm sorry you are sick," he said. "Is there anything I can do for you? How will you both manage with the man of the house gone?"

"We'll be just fine, I'm sure," I said with a fake smile.

"When will Jean Fraysse be returning?" he asked.

"Any day now," I said. "Right, Nadine? That's what he told you."

"Yes, any day," Nadine said with a smile.

"And what of your husband?" he asked, and I hated him for it.

"He will also be returning soon," I said, and he looked me in the eye and smirked; he knew I was lying.

"Well, in the meantime, please let me know if I can help you both at all."

We thanked him, and I didn't realize how tense I had been while talking to him until he walked away and my entire body relaxed.

"There are German cars in front of his villa almost every single night," she said. "Do you remember the Spanish couple who live two doors down from him?"

"Only vaguely . . . ," I said. "Is she pregnant?"

"She is, and he had worked as a diplomat in Paris and Berlin. Right before you came home, the Germans arrested both of them; the wife is nine months along. They searched their apartment for French Resistance documents—digging up their courtyard and slashing their mattresses and upholstered furniture."

"And what the hell happened to them?" I said, feeling a chill go through me as I caught Koster staring again.

"They are in La Santé Prison," Nadine said. "It was horrible; they dragged her out by her hair. Everyone said Koster was responsible."

"That is sickening," I said.

"It is," Nadine said.

"My dear Drue," Giselle said, coming over to sit with us for a minute. "How are you? Tell me about your experience."

It was the first time I'd spoken about my time at Vittel, and I shared stories of the wonderful people I had befriended, as well as the medical ordeal, not in too much detail.

"Before I get up to leave, I have a message for you," Giselle said, her voice low though she was smiling like we were talking about something lighthearted.

"Tell me it's not from that lecherous Dutchman who keeps looking over here."

"No, but he bears watching," Giselle said, offering me a homemade cigarette as skinny as she was.

"So Nadine warned me," I said.

"Everyone must be wary of him, but you in particular," Giselle said. "Alfie has overheard him talking about you at the bar. About your Scandinavian beauty, how he knows he's seen you in American films before; he's a bit obsessed."

"Oh, lovely," I said with sarcasm. "But given that he's been looking over here all night, I guess I am not surprised. What is your message?"

"Dominic, Jean's friend, you remember him. He is going to meet you in your courtyard to discuss some things. He said he will be there in an hour, after dark."

"Do you know what it's about?" I asked. Dominic was one of Jean's Resistance contacts in Melun.

"My friend," she said, laughing, "I know never to ask a man like *him* that question."

An hour later, Nadine and I returned to the villa, and I spotted the glow of a cigarette in my courtyard, among the chattering geese.

"He shouldn't be here," Nadine said, her arms crossed, shaking her head as we both looked out the kitchen window at his silhouette. "He has a nerve to show up. You just got back; you are not yet recovered. The mayor is threatening you. His presence alone could get you arrested."

"I agree with all of that," I said. "But maybe he has some news about Jean's whereabouts, or . . . I need to at least talk to him. I'll keep it brief."

I walked outside, leaning on my cane, and one of the geese who had become more like a domestic cat than waterfowl came waddling over to him, chattering.

"I see you have made a friend," I said.

"Do you remember me, madame?" Dominic said in a deep but quiet voice. He was short and muscular, with a thick, dark beard and prominent nose.

"I do," I said. I had only met him once, on the farm during a drop. "I am hoping you have some word about Jean?"

"I am sorry," he said. "I do not know anything more other than that he should still be in North Africa."

"Nadine is very worried about you being here," I said. "You know I just got out of prison."

"I do," he said. "And I am sorry to trouble you; from your condition you have clearly endured a great deal."

"Yes, so why are you here exactly?"

"Two reasons. One is I suggest you move out to the farmhouse on the plain," he said. "Jean would agree with me if he was here. This village is too small, and you have reason to be paranoid; people are being arrested all the time. As an American you will continue to be under constant suspicion."

"I am starting to realize that myself," I said with a sigh. "Plus, this courtyard's getting too small for all these animals."

I saw a smile cross his face in the shadowy darkness. "Indeed," he said.

"What is the other reason?"

"We need places for our drops from the British. We stopped using the house when Jean left, but I'd like to start up again—for drops of guns and ammunition—and storage, in the barn or the house."

I was feeling tired, and I sat on the bench, torn between my yearning to help and my need to avoid arrest.

"I want to say yes to your request," I said, leaning on my cane. "I desperately want to help in any way I can. But you just told me yourself how dangerous things are. And you must understand, I just nearly killed myself to get out of prison. I can't risk it yet."

He stood, smoking his cigarette, not saying anything; then he finally nodded.

"I understand," he said, a tone of frustration in his voice.

"We will move to the farm. Let me get my strength back and just live quietly for a while, so they believe the lie that I am very ill and not going to cause trouble. Give me a little bit of time, and I promise you, I will do anything I can to help you."

"All right," he said. "And I am sorry; these are desperate times. But I understand; what you say makes sense."

"And I bet Jean will be back soon too," I said.

"He . . ." He started to speak but stopped.

"You really don't know anything about his whereabouts or when he'll return?"

"I don't," he said. "You know, he shared little information with me because it was not my network. That is how it works; the less we know of each other's activities the better."

"Visit me on the farm in a couple months," I said. "I should be in a better position to help you then."

"I will do that. Thank you, madame. Be well," he said, tipping his cap to me, and he stepped back into the shadows and was gone.

Chapter Forty

February 24, 1943

After Dominic's urging, Nadine and I had packed up some of our belongings and all of our animals and spent the winter on the farm. The first couple of months there, with just the two of us and all our chickens and ducks and geese, had been good for my recovery; the air was so clean, and in time I started to gain my strength and began to feel like myself again. We had taken care to make the farmhouse a more cozy and comfortable dwelling. It had a good-sized salon and kitchen downstairs, as well as Jean's office and a small room off the kitchen where I locked the geese at night so they wouldn't be stolen. Nadine and I each had our own bedroom upstairs, and mine had a breathtaking view of the expansive Forest of Fontainebleau.

But this quiet period of recovery after being freed from prison was shattered on a freezing-cold morning in February, when, out of the blue, Claude pulled down the driveway in Alfie's pickup truck.

"Drue, it's Claude," Nadine called to me as I was putting away dishes in the kitchen. "In Alfie's truck. I thought he wasn't coming until Sunday."

"He wasn't," I said, frowning as I opened the front door and let Ondie run outside to be the first to greet him.

Nadine and I followed, always happy to have our dear friend visit, whatever the circumstances. But the look on Claude's face as soon as he stepped out of the truck made my stomach drop.

He was unshaven, and there was anguish in his bloodshot eyes. In his hand was an envelope addressed to me. I immediately recognized the handwriting as Jean's.

"Claude," I said, shaking my head, pointing at the envelope. "What . . . why are you here? What is that?"

Nadine gripped my elbow, as we both braced ourselves for the words I had hoped I'd never hear.

"My—my Jean," Claude said, his breath forming misty white clouds. "He is . . . he is *gone* . . . oh, my dears, I am devastated to be the one to tell you this horrible news."

"No, no, no!" I said as tears started streaming down Claude's face. "You are . . . No, Claude. You cannot do this to me. He . . . he cannot be gone. It's *not* true!"

"I am so very sorry, but it is true," Claude said, his voice cracking. "I feel like I . . . like I have lost a son."

Nadine cried out, and I sank down on the freezing porch step, my head in my hands, shaking and sobbing uncontrollably. Ondie ran over to me, barking, trying to comfort me and lick my tears.

After several minutes of raw emotion, Nadine, the first to calm herself, ushered Claude into the kitchen, came back out, and took my arm.

"Please, you must come inside," Nadine said, her voice wavering. "I put on some tea. You don't want to get frostbite. You've barely recovered from prison."

I nodded, feeling numb as she led me inside, my body still shaking as I sat down at the kitchen table.

Claude grabbed the wool blanket off the settee and threw it around my shoulders, as my teeth were chattering from both the cold and the terrible shock. I stared at the envelope on the table.

"How?" I whispered to Claude as he blotted his eyes with his handkerchief. Nadine poured us all tea and sat down next to me. "What happened to him?"

"After visiting you at Vittel, he came home for a week and then left for Marseille," Claude said. "He didn't even tell me where he was going; this I have just learned. From there he went to North Africa with a group of Resistance members. He carried no identification papers."

Claude took a deep breath and a sip of tea before continuing.

"A ship from Marseille to North Africa sank around the time of his departure. It is . . . it is now believed he was on board."

I started crying again as Nadine sniffled beside me. Claude came over and wrapped his arms around me, and I sobbed into his coat.

"But these reports . . . What if he wasn't on board?" I said, looking up at Claude, pleading with him to give me some hope. "They could be wrong. Please, God, let them be wrong."

"Oh, my darling, I wish that they were wrong. And I waited to tell you; I waited to be sure that this horrible news was true," he said as I put my head in my hands, still trying to absorb this devastating news. My stomach churned, and I felt gutted as I remembered our last kiss at Vittel, when we finally admitted our love for each other.

"This is not what we planned. He *promised* me! He promised me he would come back to me. That we would be together after I was released. This can't be happening. How could I lose him too? *How?*"

Claude just shook his head, his eyes sorrowful, as Nadine wiped the tears from her face and handed me a fresh handkerchief.

"He was so very much in love with you, *ma fille*," Claude said to me. "He . . . he asked me to give you this letter if anything happened to him."

"Thank you," I said, letting out a heavy sigh as the tears flowed down my cheeks. I traced my name on the front of it. "I am not ready to open it. Not yet."

≈

December 1, 1942

My dearest Drue,

I am sitting here writing this letter in my drafty office in what I've come to think of as our farmhouse on the plain. If you are receiving this letter, that means things have not gone well for me on this trip to North Africa. Claude has promised me he will make sure you receive it if I don't return.

Seeing you at Vittel in the shape that you were in devastated me, but I know your release is imminent, and that gives me peace as I get ready to go abroad. Please, above all else, take care of your health and recover.

I hate to leave you for this trip just before you come home, to leave this farm and village that I have come to love, but the cause is too important for me not to go. I must go, because the Americans and British are helping us now in real ways, with guns and supplies and agents. I know the risks of this journey, but there are more dangers in not doing enough right now in the face of such a brutal enemy. My love for my country is stronger than my fear of what might happen to me.

I have dreamed of a life with you after the war, walking the plain around Barbizon together, drinking Sancerre in the villa's courtyard. I imagine you perhaps returning to the theater and me helping a Free French government rebuild our broken nation. I envision a future, together. But if you are reading this letter, that isn't meant to be. I am not arrogant enough to believe that your feelings for me are the same as for your Jacques, but now I know that you love me. As I said in Vittel, I have loved you from the

*moment I saw you at our first meeting at Paris Mondiale,
and I am grateful I got the chance to tell you that.*

*Do not let your losses in this war turn you bitter
and disenchanted and make you lose that beautiful light
and strength that defines you. Get yourself well and keep
fighting, and remember to always choose love over fear,
though I know that feels impossible at times in this war.
We will never be defeated if we continue to maintain our
humanity and fight against these dark forces.*

*I love you, my darling. I know you have so much to
give, and so much ahead of you in life. Be brave and keep
me in your heart.*

Yours,

Jean

I had read the letter so many times there were tearstains that had made
the ink at the bottom of the page run, and now Jean's name looked
like it was bleeding off the page. It had been three months since I had
received it, but I still couldn't quite believe he was never coming back.
His office on the farm, with books and ashtrays scattered everywhere,
made it seem as if any minute he would stroll in from a walk on the
plain. I had told Nadine I was not ready for her to clean it out. Not yet.

The weeks following the news of Jean's death had gone by in a haze
of grief and sadness, as I couldn't quite believe that I had lost him now
too. Being imprisoned in Vittel had not broken me, but Jean's death,
after everything else, nearly did. I sank into a depression and slept the
days away for the first couple of weeks, losing my appetite and my
motivation to do anything at all, thinking I would never feel joy again.

Nadine had finally dragged me out of bed, placing a cup of Red
Cross coffee in my hand one morning and ordering me to get dressed.

"I know how much you loved each other," she said as we sat at the kitchen table. "I think I knew you loved him before you did."

"That might be true," I said, tracing the chipped rim of my coffee cup.

"He would not want you to go on like this," Nadine said. "It's like I can hear him telling me to get you up, to stop you from sinking into your sadness."

"I know, it's just . . . I thought we had so much more time," I said. "I thought whatever we did in this war, we would do together. And after it ends . . ."

"I know, and my heart breaks for you, for all of us. I cannot believe that he is not going to walk into the house at any moment. But what you're doing right now . . . this isn't living, *chère amie.*"

I had looked up at her and nodded, wiping my face, so sick of the tears that kept falling without warning. She reached across the table and squeezed my hand.

"I insist you get dressed, start moving again. Let's take a walk into the village; we need a few gardening tools at the villa. And then it's time to get to work. We are not going to have the beautiful vegetable garden we imagine if we don't get started. If we are to feed not only ourselves but many others, we are going to need every scrap of food we can grow."

And so we had worked the land and tended to our growing barnyard of animals, hiring Girard and Remy again to help. We plowed the fields and spread more wheelbarrows of manure than I ever imagined. We planted potatoes and leeks, sugar beets, tomatoes, and carrots. Cigarettes were scarcer than ever, but I had tracked down a gardener in Barbizon who sold me tobacco plants. Though they were illegal to grow, I planted them anyway, hiding them among sunflowers and sweet corn. It was backbreaking farm labor, and at the end of each day I collapsed into my bed, relieved to sleep without dreaming. Once again it was hard work that helped me stay distracted and push through my grief.

Though some nights, I would wake up after midnight with tears on my pillow and get up and look out my bedroom window at the treetops with a sense of restless, lonely sadness that I carried on my shoulders like a heavy blanket. Mourning my past and my future, and not one but two men whom I cared for more than words could possibly say. What would I do with my life now that would be enough to make sense of their loss? How could I honor them? I was healthy and strong again, and my desire for some sort of vengeance was even stronger; planting seeds was not enough.

On an early morning in late June, after one of these nights, I was up with the sun, wearing a floppy straw hat and dirt-stained overalls, doing some weeding among the tomato plants. The temperature was warm and mild; the skies were the kind of blue that the artists knew only existed in this place. I was pondering the questions of the night before when I heard Ondie barking and saw a man on an old bicycle riding up the road among the fruit trees. I stood up, and as he got closer, I recognized the stocky frame of Dominic, who had only paid me that one visit when I had first returned from Vittel.

I called out to him, waving him to come over.

"Madame," he said, removing his cap. "My sincere condolences for your loss. Jean Fraysse was a brilliant man and a loyal friend. And he cared for you a great deal."

"Thank you," I said, with a sad smile. "I miss him very much."

"Me as well," he said, looking around the garden, not admiring it so much as surveilling the area to see if anyone could be watching us.

"Would you like to come inside for a cup of tea?" I asked, taking my hat off and squinting at him.

"Yes, inside is better," he said. "There are things we need to discuss."

"I agree."

A short time later we were sitting at the kitchen table over cups of tea. He politely asked me about the farm, though I knew that wasn't the purpose of his visit.

"Is anyone else here now?" he asked.

"No, Nadine is at the villa, getting some of the sewing supplies she left there. We are making summer dresses out of those rose-colored curtains behind you, like they did in *Gone with the Wind*."

"Gone with what?"

"Never mind," I said with a smile.

"Are you glad that you moved out here? I think it is much safer than in town for you."

"It is," I said. "I feel a little more free, not constantly paranoid like when I am in the village. Though it can be lonely with just the two of us and the animals."

"Do you have a gun here?" he said.

"Well, yes, Jean's gun is still hidden here, though I don't know how to use it. Why are you asking?"

"I will show you how," he said. "I should have asked you when you first moved here. You should have a gun just in case."

"OK . . . ," I said. "But what is the real purpose of this visit? Other than telling me to get a gun? And is it just in case, or am I in some immediate danger?"

"Not immediate," he said. "But things are heating up here. Do you still have the shortwave?"

"We do," I said. "I hide it under a floorboard beneath my bed. We listen to the BBC every night."

"Then you know that things are improving for the Allies, and for the Resistance," he said.

"Yes. Though I thought the Allies would be here in France by now," I said.

"You are not the only one," he said, giving me a grim look. I remember Jean saying he was a quiet man, more of action than words, and that was proving to be true as he sat sipping his tea. Finally, he spoke.

"Now that some time has passed since your internment, I wanted to—"

"Dominic, are you here to ask to use the farm for airdrops again?" I interrupted him, wanting to get to the point.

"I am. We still need somewhere for parachute drops, and storage for arms and ammunition," he said. "I know it is a dangerous risk to you, but . . ."

"Yes, yes, I have heard that before," I said, waving my hand. "And I agree, the Nazis are not paying as much attention to me anymore. I am happy for you to use the farm again," I said.

"Thank you," he said, breathing a sigh of relief. "There is more . . . Now, some of these planes are carrying explosives and other delicate materials. They need somewhere to land."

"And you're thinking this should be your new French Resistance airport?"

"I do," he said, with a smile. "Not an airport, just a landing strip. The planes are Lysanders, compact and light enough to land on small fields like the one behind this house. And you are far enough outside the village that they won't be heard. This is the perfect place, and we have a critical need," he said, and he stood to look out the window at the fields behind the house. "Jean and I had talked about this eventuality. You have the land; I work for a construction company that works for the Germans, so I have use of a truck, and I would bring out a surveyor to make sure it is level enough. Will you let us do this?"

"I think as long as you don't land planes on my vegetables, I am happy to let you use it," I said.

"Thank you. This will be an enormous help to the cause. And we will not harm your tomatoes."

"Good," I said with a small laugh. "When does the first drop happen?"

"In two nights," he said. "When the moon is full. We will survey the land tonight."

"That's fine." I paused and sipped my tea, thrilled to be involved, yearning to find passion and purpose in this war again beyond just supplying food. "I have been thinking of you, about contacting you. You see, my health is much better now, and I have been restless here. Is there more I can do to help? Anything at all? Remember, I have a pass that lets me travel back and forth to Paris for my doctor's appointments without question."

He lit a cigarette and paced the room, looking out the windows, thinking. "Yes, there most definitely is. I will let you know soon," he said.

"Good," I said. "When will that be?"

"Patience, Madame Tartière," he said, blowing out his cigarette smoke. "We will only win this war with patience."

Chapter Forty-One

June 18, 1943

I did not sleep the next two nights, thinking about the parachutes falling and planes landing right outside my window by the light of the full moon. The night of the drop, Nadine and I stayed up, sipping wine by candlelight and listening to the sounds of the British planes as they approached. The plan was for Dominic and his men to hide everything in the barn underneath the hay and retrieve it the next morning, and he had specifically told us to stay inside.

"I hope all these guns and ammunition mean the invasion is happening soon."

"You always think the invasion is happening soon," Nadine said. "You've been saying it for *two years*."

"I know, but at some point, it *has* to happen," I said. "It's quiet now; do you think that it's done?"

"Probably," she said, yawning. "We should go to bed."

Just as I was turning down my covers, the geese, who were better watchdogs than Ondie, started chattering excitedly in their little room downstairs off the kitchen. Ondie followed with hysterical barking, and Nadine and I rushed downstairs.

I grabbed the scythe, which Remy had taught me to use that week. "What are you going to do with *that*?" Nadine said, horrified.

"Use it as a weapon if I have to," I said with a shrug. "Something is out there. Maybe it's just an animal."

"Could it be Dominic?"

"No, he would have told me. I'll be right back."

"Good God, be careful. Do you want me to come with you?"

"No, stay here—it could be someone who wants to steal our animals. I'll holler if I need you. Come, Ondie, let's go."

I was stiff and sore from learning how to use the scythe, and I held it awkwardly as Ondie led me through the orchard. He sensed something, and I shivered as we got farther away from the house. We got to one of my illegal rabbit traps, and as I walked over to check it, Ondie started barking at a man lying against a nearby tree.

"Don't move or I'll kill you," I said, holding the scythe over my head, trying to keep my voice steady.

"I won't move," the man said in heavily accented French.

"Oh. Are you English?" I asked.

"If you want me to be," he said, amusement in his voice. "Would Canadian do?"

He got up from the ground, and we both started to laugh as I realized how ridiculous I must look in my pajamas holding a scythe.

"I don't know who you are," he said, "but I think I've found a friend."

"I think you have," I said. "Come to the house with me."

It was close to midnight, and Nadine and I and this stranger sat in the living room, in the dark, smoking cigarettes. I didn't know what to do with him. He wouldn't tell us his name or where he came from. Dominic had told me nothing of men landing tonight, only supplies, which made me wonder who this man was and what he was really doing here.

"I'm a foreigner in these parts, and I'm on a mission, so I have to get moving soon," he said, pacing the room. The geese and the dog started going crazy again, and we sat still in the dark and listened.

"Ondie, it is just me," Dominic said as he tapped on the front door. "Sorry, I hoped to get here sooner. One of the drops was bad, and there were cases scattered on the plain that we had to track down."

"I was also scattered," the Canadian said.

"Are there others?" Dominic asked, sizing him up.

"Two others somewhere out there," he said.

"Let's go find them," Dominic said as the Canadian put on his backpack and grabbed his musette.

"Do you want me to feed them before they go?" I asked Dominic as the Canadian thanked us and headed back out into the night. "Nadine and I can prepare a meal here, or in Barbizon."

"There's not enough time, unfortunately," Dominic said. "Things went well tonight, despite the bad drop. Thank you."

"You didn't tell me they'd be dropping agents here too," I said.

"You know how it is." He shrugged. "The less you know the better. I'll be in touch soon."

Nadine said in a quiet voice after he left, "You were just in prison not so long ago. Is all this worth the risk?"

"Absolutely."

~

"There was a redhead in our apple tree," Girard said, standing in my front door a few days later, hands on his little hips, wearing a summer outfit that had definitely been bedsheets in another life.

"I'm sorry, I don't understand." Nadine and I couldn't help but smile at his earnest expression.

"Madame! Madame!" Remy came sprinting up the path, scolding Girard for not waiting for him.

"How can we help you both?"

"Mesdames," Remy said, catching his breath. "There was a *garçon*, a young man, who fell into our apple tree. An American. We have been hiding him at our house."

Nadine gasped, and the two of us looked at each other.

"Why did you come to us?"

"Because you are an American." The older boy frowned at me as if it were a stupid question. "And Dominic is a good friend of our parents; he said to send for you."

"Give me ten minutes, and I will get my bike and ride back with you," I told them. "Go see the animals." I pointed to the barn and the yard, where the geese were cavorting. "The geese miss you. Nadine, will you help me pack a bag with some of Jean's clothes and shoes?"

"What are you going to do with this American, exactly?" she asked, her voice exasperated as we went upstairs and opened the trunk in the corner of my bedroom that contained Jean's clothes.

My breath caught for a second at the sight of his belongings, remembering him in the white linen shirt that lay on top. I lifted it out of the trunk, hugging it like a blanket.

"I don't know. I'm guessing I will find out," I said. "But he needs our help. I'm going to pack some clothes for myself too. Will you meet me at the villa? I'll bring him there first but will probably have to take the train to Paris tonight."

"No," Nadine said through her teeth, standing with her arms crossed as I searched my closet for a bag to pack.

"What?" I said, frowning at her. Her cheeks were flushed, and her flyaway black hair was now long and wild, pinned up in a haphazard bun, stray pieces falling out.

"I said no, Drue. I won't meet you at the villa. I don't want any of this," she said, shaking her head in anger, tears in her eyes. "Don't misunderstand—I want to fight back as much as you do. But I . . . I lost Jean and Jacques too, you know. And it broke my heart, and I mourn them every day. I cannot lose someone else. I especially cannot lose *you*."

"Nadine, I . . . I'll be careful," I said.

"You have no idea what it was like for me and Jean when you were in prison," she said, raising her voice. "I was devastated; we were both so worried they were going to kill you. Every night I went to bed too anxious to sleep. Why would you take the risk to do these things now? You agreed, without asking me, to have planes landing on our farm— now you're bringing fallen pilots in our house? It's too dangerous. If they catch you, they will *kill* you this time, I am sure of it! And I cannot see you die. You are like family to me . . . I don't want to . . . I don't want to lose my sister."

She sat on the bed, crying, and I sat next to her, putting my arm around her shaking shoulders. It hadn't occurred to me to ask her, because it hadn't occurred to me that she wouldn't want to do this. But the losses of Jacques and Jean had taken their toll on my strong-willed friend too.

"I'm so sorry," I said softly. "So very sorry. You're right, I had no idea what that was like, but I would have felt the same way had it been you or Jean. And I should have told you about the planes and the drops; I should have discussed it with you and not just agreed. You are like a sister to me too. I could not have survived this war without you."

"I understand why you want to resist; I do too, but I fear this time your luck will run out," Nadine said, wiping her face.

"Nadine, I . . . I just can't live through the rest of this war doing nothing but growing vegetables. I lost two people I love. And I don't want their deaths to have been in vain. I have no recourse, no other way to honor them than to do whatever I can until it's over."

"I know," she said, throwing up her hands, standing up and walking to the window. "I feel much of what you are feeling. I am so angry! I hate the Germans, I hate this war, and I want to support the cause too. But you've already been imprisoned once; if they ever find out about your past, about Jacques, they will execute you on sight. The thought of that terrifies me."

"Believe me, I have nightmares of exactly that," I said. "But . . . you understand . . . I still must do this. Be a part of the Resistance. Or I will go crazy. If I live to be an old woman, when people ask me about this time, I want to say I did something that mattered, not that I did nothing because I was *afraid*."

She didn't say anything for a minute, just looked out the window at the forest treetops, thinking. I could hear the boys in the barnyard, giggling with the geese.

"I understand," she whispered with a nod. "I do. OK. But it is not just you doing this. *We* are. From now on, you must tell me everything, so we can discuss plans. And you will let me help, and you will take all precautions. No stupid risks, promise me?"

"I will," I said, giving her a hug. "I promise."

"You'd better promise," she said as we began to pack the bag. "Now go get that American. Maybe he looks like Rhett Butler."

I followed Girard and Remy to their home on the plain, a few miles away from ours, stopping only once for water on the side of the road.

The boys' mother opened the door, visibly relieved they were back safe with me. She was short, her face heavily lined from a life of working in the fields, and she greeted me warmly.

"You've come to collect our new friend Todd," she said, smiling and taking my hand. "He is so handsome and is no longer limping."

She brought me into their small living room, and there was the American flier, looking like the epitome of a fish out of water in his French-peasant surroundings.

"Hello, Todd," I said, holding out my hand. "I'm Drue Tartière."

"Oh boy, to speak English again!" he said, pulling me in for a hug as if I were an old friend. "It's so great to meet an American here."

Todd Spellman, the redhead from Jefferson, Indiana, did not look remotely like Rhett Butler. He did, however, have a story of survival that sounded like something straight out of a Hollywood movie. A week earlier, he had jumped from his burning plane under heavy anti-aircraft fire from the Germans. Remy and Girard had been watching from their bedroom windows, thinking nobody could have possibly survived. But knowing where Todd had most likely gone down, they went for a walk and found him stuck in an apple tree, his parachute tangled. Todd had been shot in the hip and had flak in his lower leg and ten holes in his parachute. The boys and their father had helped Todd down and managed to bury the parachute, along with his logbook and watch, in a ditch on the side of the road. Remy's parents had made sure that Todd got medical attention from a local doctor and had kept him on their little farm in the middle of the plain ever since.

"As you know, whenever a plane goes down, the Gestapo search homes for fliers," the boys' mother told me. "We hid him in the chicken house the day that they did. We would love for him to stay, but it is not safe. I'm sure they'll come back again to search."

"Have you ever been to Paris?" I asked Todd.

"No, ma'am," he said.

"We are going to go there by train this afternoon," I said. "I have an apartment there where you can hide until we find a way to get you out of the country."

The family insisted we have a champagne toast to their newfound flier friend before we left. And after an emotional goodbye and some parting gifts of food for the young American, I left my bike with them, and Todd and I set off to Melun to take the train into Paris. He was wearing a new cotton shirt and brand-new bright-yellow shoes the family had given him, and a pair of Jean's pants, as well as a black beret to cover his hair, which was an unusual color for a Frenchman. I bought him a copy of *Rustica*, a farm journal, and told him to pretend to read it or sleep when we were on the train. I knew we were taking a huge risk, as he had no false papers, but the Germans had settled into a level of complacency since the early days of the occupation. And I was betting our safe journey to Paris on that.

We got into a compartment with an elderly French couple and some German soldiers. I held my breath, but Todd did what he was told, and I made my best effort to appear relaxed and attempted to read my copy of Jane Austen's *Emma*. At one point, I looked over at him when he was napping, and he looked even younger than nineteen in sleep. A sudden fierce protectiveness of this American boy came over me as I thought of his family in Indiana, terrified that *missing in action* meant *dead*. And in my heart at that moment, I knew I would do whatever it took to get him out of the country safely.

Chapter Forty-Two

July 7, 1943

Two weeks later, I was back in Paris, toting a large bag of food and clothing to my apartment on Rue Saint-Dominique. As I suspected would happen, Claude and Todd had already formed a fast friendship in my absence, sharing black-market cigarettes and wine and playing poker and gin rummy and the French game *belote*.

They both jumped up to help me with the basket when I came in the door sideways because it was so wide. We unloaded the food in the kitchen, and Todd gratefully accepted the additional clothing.

"What a relief. You have no idea how hard it was to get this thing from Villa L'Écureuil," I said, my arms aching from the journey.

The Picasso print, which had been in Nadine's room, where Todd was staying, was leaning against the wall in the living room.

"Why is the Picasso print out here?" I said.

"He's afraid of it," Claude said, rolling his eyes to the ceiling, totally amused.

"It gives me the creeps," Todd said. "I just don't want to sleep under it."

"You fall ten thousand feet in a parachute but you're afraid of a . . . Picasso?" I said, laughing.

"Aw, come on, don't tease me; look at the thing, it's downright creepy," he said, but he was laughing too. "Do you have any news for me?"

"I will soon; that's why I am here," I said. "Dr. Porcher called. I am meeting him at an apartment in Le Marais, where I guess he is going to tell me what to do with you next."

"Good," Claude said and, calling Todd by his nickname, added, "*Le rouquin* here is getting bored. The other day I caught him whistling at pretty girls on the street below."

"Todd, you can't do anything like that," I said, scolding him like the teenager he was.

"I'm sorry, I just figured they would think it was you," he said, and Claude laughed at this.

"I'm far too old to whistle at pretty young girls," Claude said. "Even if I wanted to."

I left them to another card game, packing some produce and eggs to bring to my rendezvous with Dr. Porcher.

"This is a change from the office," I said as he greeted me at an apartment building down a narrow street in Le Marais.

"Yes, well, given the circumstances of your visitor, I wanted to show you something. And I'll also explain what you'll need to do next."

"Show me something in this apartment building?" I said, giving him a skeptical look. "Now I am curious. What does this have to do with . . ."

"No more questions," he said, holding a finger up to his lips as we greeted the concierge and walked up to the third floor. "It's a surprise."

He softly knocked three times, paused, and then knocked another two. A matronly woman opened the door, and when she saw me standing next to Dr. Porcher, she gave him a nervous look.

"She's an American," he said in French. "Drue Tartière."

The woman's face lit up, and she grabbed my cheeks and kissed me.

"There's one in the kitchen," she whispered as we stepped in the door.

"One what?" I whispered back.

"American," she said, eyes wide with surprise that I had no idea. "Go surprise him."

A boy was sitting with his back to me, and I tiptoed in and tapped him on the shoulder.

"Guess who?" I said.

He jumped up from the table and whirled around.

"Christ, are you an American?" he said. He looked younger than Todd, with a light-brown crew cut and dimples.

"I am just as American as you are," I said, and, not being able to help myself, I gave him a hug, and he started to cry into my shoulder, and my heart ached for yet another boy stranded in a foreign land all alone. I looked over and the woman who had answered the door was crying too.

After we all composed ourselves, we sat down at the table and had tea.

"What's your name, sweetheart?" I said.

"Bob. Bob Carter," he said, practically bouncing out of his seat. "I can't believe you're here. Gee, if I knew you were coming, I would have shaved. These French blades will tear your hide off, so I don't shave more than I have to."

"Well, it's a pleasure to meet you, Bob Carter, even unshaven," I said with a laugh.

"Hey, can you ask Madame to bring my buddy to see you too?" Bob asked. "He's downstairs. I can't speak French, but he'd love to see you. We were shot down south of Paris together. You can surprise him like you did to me."

"I can do that," I said, delighted at how happy he was.

Moments later, Bob's buddy, Carrol, a short, olive-skinned boy from Chicago, was standing in the living room.

"I would like to introduce you to a friend of mine," Bob said very formally.

"*Bonjour* . . . ," Carrol said in pained French.

"Hello, darling, it's lovely to meet you," I said, giving him a hug.

"What's this, are you kidding?" Carrol said, his face turning bright red.

"No, she's an American!" Bob said. "Can you believe it?"

"It's just too much," Carrol said, blinking. "This has been so . . . *hard.*"

He covered his face with his hands and started to sob, and this time even Dr. Porcher got emotional.

We stayed for an hour. I helped translate between them and their caretakers, and that thrilled all of them, especially the boys, who could finally express their gratitude in words. After Dr. Porcher had examined their injuries and I had given them all the provisions in my basket, promising to come visit again, the two of us went to have coffee on a terrace at a nearby café before I took the train back to Barbizon.

"That was a lovely afternoon," Dr. Porcher said after the waiter took our order.

"Truly," I said, smiling as bright as the sun. "It was . . . it was good for my soul."

"I'm glad. I am sure it has been unimaginably hard losing Jacques . . . and then Jean," Dr. Porcher said.

"It has," I said, touched by his words. "But the work helps. At least I feel like I'm doing something worthwhile."

"I agree."

"What happens to them now? And what do I do with Todd?"

"In the next few weeks, you will receive a call from a woman named Genevieve about where and when she will meet you for a rendezvous. You will take Todd to meet her—providing him with enough food for three days, and adequate clothing. And from there, Genevieve will guide him on the first leg of his journey out of France through her network."

"OK, I will wait to hear from her. Doctor . . . how did you get involved in this?"

"You might be surprised to learn that there are British and American boys hidden in homes all over the city. I'm part of a group of doctors that have been helping them find shelter and gathering donations of food and clothing. Would you be interested in helping too?"

"Of course," I said. Helping Todd, translating for the two boys today, had brightened my spirits in a way nothing else had since Jean died.

"It will be dangerous for you."

"Please; do you know how many times that has been said to me since this war started?" I said with a grim smile. "It hasn't stopped me yet."

"All right," Dr. Porcher said, with a soft chuckle. "Let's order another coffee, and I'll tell you what I need you to do."

Chapter Forty-Three

July 18, 1943

The call from the mysterious Genevieve finally came on a Sunday, just when I thought poor Todd was going to lose his mind from boredom hiding out in my apartment.

"*Bonjour,*" I said, answering the phone at Villa L'Écureuil.

"Is this Madame Tartière?" a woman, speaking French in a low voice, asked.

"It is; who is calling?"

"This is Genevieve. You are to meet me at the carousel in the Tuileries tomorrow at four o'clock. Bring yourself and your package and nothing else. Do you understand?"

"I do. Tomorrow at four o'clock," I said.

"I will be standing about twenty feet away from it, wearing a green blouse and a navy-blue skirt. I will take the package from there. You and I will not speak. Any questions?"

"No, no questions," I said. And with a quick goodbye she hung up the phone.

So, early the next morning, I made my pilgrimage into Paris, with my two large market baskets filled to the brim with food and clothing for the hidden aviators around the city, including freshly baked bread from Nadine and socks and hats knitted by Marion Greenough. Todd was packed and ready to go when I arrived, with a better pair of shoes for walking than the bright-yellow ones he had first been given, and a raincoat Claude had managed to find him for the journey.

Both men were somber as I packed Todd's food box with *pâté*, hard-boiled eggs, and gingerbread.

"You two are unusually quiet. Aren't you excited?" I asked Todd. "You'll be one step closer to home after today."

"I can't wait, but I'm a little nervous, not knowing how the heck we're getting out," Todd said, going through the contents of his backpack one last time.

I knew it was a difficult physical trek, and some fliers suffered accidents navigating the canyons or mountains they had to cross or ended up captured along the way. But I didn't have to tell him of these inevitable risks; deep down I knew that he knew.

"The people who are in charge of this underground network have been doing it for a while," I said in a tone I hoped was reassuring. "They know what they're doing. Just do what they say, and you'll be fine."

"May I come back and visit you both?" Todd said. "After the war?"

"You absolutely must," Claude said, slapping him on the back and smiling, though I saw his lip wavering as he tried to maintain his composure. "Come back when we can really show you our beautiful city."

But when they hugged goodbye and Todd started getting emotional, Claude could not keep the tears from falling.

"Goodbye, my sweet boy," Claude said, his voice cracking on the word *boy*. "Until next time."

Walking the streets to the Tuileries Garden, we passed several Luftwaffe officers with women on their arms, and Todd pulled his cap tighter over his red hair. I had been unable to convince him to dye it brown, but he had at least agreed to have it cut very short.

We entered the gardens on the north side by way of the Castiglione entrance and reached the carousel just before four. As it was a beautiful July afternoon, the area was crowded, with children and young mothers socializing and waiting their turn on the whimsical carousel that reminded me of a life-size jewel box. I guessed the crowds and the choice of the carousel were by design, as there were not any German officers nearby to monitor an innocent group of children playing on a summer day.

It was easy to spot the six other French hostesses, each one standing with an American aviator dressed in French clothing and shoes, carrying their rucksacks or backpacks.

At exactly four, Genevieve, a heavyset blonde woman I guessed to be in her early twenties, arrived wearing a green blouse and navy skirt, standing at the distance as she had said she would.

"That's her. It's time to go."

"How can I ever repay you?" Todd said. His face was white, the reality of the perilous journey ahead sinking in.

"By getting out of this country safely and living a great life. That's how," I said, smiling, as I smoothed down his shirt and double-checked his bags like he was a boy going off to summer camp.

"You bet I will," he said, giving me a final tight hug, and then he followed the group, turning one more time to wave and smile at me as they walked away.

I was once again stunned by how young the fliers all were as they ambled off together, trusting that this young woman, not much older than they were, would lead them to safety.

I stood in front of the carousel with the other hostesses; the worry and emotion in their faces mirrored my own as we watched the group leave.

"It seems quite risky, all of them walking away together like that?" I whispered in French to the hostess closest to me. She was blotting her eyes with a handkerchief.

"I thought that too the first time," she replied with a nod. "But I have been doing this awhile, and now I trust she knows what she's doing. She gets them into hiding and out of the city quickly."

I wanted to ask for more details, for reassurance that Todd would be safe, but she was already walking away, and I knew it was best if I did the same.

So all of the hostesses, some quietly crying, left one by one, and I was sure I wasn't alone in praying that these American sons would make it home alive.

~

That evening, I had a much-needed dinner with Kathleen and Elise behind the blackout curtains at the Wilkinsons' mansion. Tudor had finally been able to secure Kathleen's and Sylvia Beach's release from Vittel two months after I had been freed. And though I had reunited with Kathleen since our time at Vittel, Kathleen, Elise, and I had not gotten together socially in this way in months. I had asked Kathleen to arrange it because I had decided that, with so much need among these downed fliers and their host families, I could use reinforcements.

After a dinner of roast chicken and vegetables courtesy of my farm, we brought our glasses of wine into their sitting room. The same one that I had sat in with Dorothy Thompson what now felt like a lifetime ago.

"How is Dorothy Thompson?" I asked Kathleen. "Have you heard anything about her lately? I feel like we are so cut off from the news of the rest of the world these days."

"Last I heard, she was back in the States, but working for CBS, broadcasting anti-Nazi propaganda into Germany by shortwave radio," Kathleen said.

"Well, that is no surprise," I said with a smile.

"Not at all," Kathleen said. "Now, you must tell us what you need to speak with us about," she added as she offered us each a cigarette.

"Yes, I am dying of curiosity," Elise said.

"Thank you. I am here because I need your help; Tudor's too," I said, looking at Kathleen. "And I'm sorry Sylvia couldn't make it tonight; I'm going to talk to her about it next time I'm in the city."

And I explained to them everything about the Allied fliers being hosted all over the city, starting with Todd's story and Dr. Porcher's revelations about the underground network.

"My American flier Todd left today with a small group," I said, explaining what he'd needed before he left and how the rendezvous worked.

"How in the world are they getting out?" Kathleen said.

"All I know is that it is an incredible trek. Probably not all of them will survive."

"God bless them," Elise said. "Their poor mothers."

"So, Dr. Porcher said I could reveal this all to you because, frankly, we need all the help we can get," I said. "We need more food and clothing for them, more places to hide them. I've started bringing whatever food I can from Barbizon. But the demand is much more than Nadine and I can provide."

"I'm in," Kathleen said. "And you know Tudor will be. Though unfortunately we can't house them here, because Tudor is now storing a massive amount of guns, ammunition, and radios for the Resistance in the walls."

"Seriously?" I said, surprised she'd share that so openly.

"Yes," Kathleen said, and then, biting her thumb, added, "I just realized I probably shouldn't have revealed that, but it's too dangerous to have any fliers here when Tudor's smuggling weapons. However, we will help provide food and clothing, and anything else you need."

"And I can host one of them," Elise said. "In Corinne's room."

"Are you sure, Elise?" I said. "That would be wonderful."

"Of course," Elise said. "And I speak English too, which I know they will appreciate."

"Oh, you have no idea how much this will help," I said, taking a deep breath, relieved and happy to have their support in this. "Thank you both. The more of them we can get out of the country in one piece, the better I will feel."

"Now I know why you had a look about you tonight," Elise said, tilting her head and examining my face. "Not just healthier, but . . . *better* in other ways."

"I agree," Kathleen said. "It's good to see. You were a shadow of yourself for a while, after Vittel . . . after everything."

"After losing Jacques and then Jean, you mean?" I said.

"Yes," Kathleen said. "So much loss in such a short time. Too much."

They were right. I hadn't realized how much I had sunk into a fog of depression until now, when it was finally starting to lift. Since learning of Jean's passing, in many ways I had been just going through the motions. Aiding the fliers was the type of work I hadn't realized I needed.

"It has been a very hard time. Thank you for being there for me," I said, toasting them. "And I must tell you, it feels good to be coming back to life again."

Chapter Forty-Four

May 15, 1944

Throughout the fall and winter, my role with the underground network for Allied fliers continued to expand, and I worked tirelessly to house and feed dozens of British, Canadian, and American aviators in apartments all over Paris, getting them started on their journeys to freedom. I had developed relationships with many of the women hosting these fliers, some of whom had very little to spare in terms of food or money but who did it out of a patriotic duty and gratitude for the Allies. They would leave cryptic notes for me at my Paris apartment whenever they needed something—more food, or a certain size pair of shoes, and always more cigarettes.

My success in this role was due in large part to the discreet generosity of friends, neighbors, and strangers who donated whatever they could spare. At least once or twice a week I would bring my large market baskets of food into the city, and thanks to the kindness of a woman who worked as the ladies' room attendant in the Gare de Lyon station, I was able to avoid the inspectors searching bags.

It was quite difficult for these young men to be cooped up in small, dark rooms day and night without much to entertain them, so Sylvia Beach paid visits to the boys, delighting them with stories of life in Paris in the twenties with "lost generation" writers like Hemingway and James Joyce. She and her partner, Adrienne, rounded up all the English-French dictionaries they could find and started a small lending library of books for them as well.

Elise, her mother, and Corinne loved having these young fliers as guests, often disguising them to take them to the movies or to the park to get fresh air. And every time they had to say goodbye to one, Corinne would be inconsolable for days.

Kathleen also visited the boys and donated money and food, as well as clothing she gathered from wealthy friends in her neighborhood. She would help me by taking them out for brief excursions to the barbershop, where she would talk to the barber the entire time, and he quickly understood not to ask the boys questions.

In Barbizon, Nadine worked from dawn until dusk on the farm and in the kitchen to help provide food, bartering with the farms in the area and gathering donations from Marion and Alfie and other friends. And Dominic was able to provide us with batches of false identity cards for the fliers through his Resistance contacts in Melun.

Now in the spring of 1944, a fatigued and anxious French nation waited and prayed, desperate for an Allied invasion that had still not come. If the increase in Allied air raids was an indication of the impending invasion, it had to be on the horizon soon. For the network, more air raids meant more downed aviators, and providing them all with hiding places, food, and clothing had become an all-consuming mission.

It was a crisp May evening, and, having just returned from Paris, I stopped by Villa L'Écureuil to pick up some bed linens. I was unnerved once more when I ran into Daan Koster on the walk to the farm.

"Madame Tartière," Daan Koster called to me from his bike, and I cringed at the thought of having to speak with him. He had disappeared for most of the winter, and I was not happy to see him in the streets when he returned in the spring. Anytime I ran into him, I kept it polite and short, as his reputation as a loyal Nazi collaborator had been solidified in the region.

"You are looking very well," he said, climbing off of his bike on the dirt road in front of me, dressed in one of his dapper pastel linen shirts and black trousers, his fedora replaced by a straw hat.

"Thank you," I said. I was wearing a pale-blue cotton sundress, one that Nadine had made for me from the villa's bedroom curtains.

"And strong too. I see you carrying those large baskets to Paris once a week; are those for your doctor?"

"What? Oh yes, for my doctor, and for my friend who leases my Paris apartment."

"How do the cancer treatments go?"

"They are going well enough," I said, uneasy with all these questions.

"Since you are improving, perhaps I could take you to dinner at Les Pléiades sometime," he said. The restaurant had become a favorite among the Nazis and German military that visited Barbizon. What did this man want from me?

"Oh, I am sorry, I don't think so," I said. "You see, I may not look it, but I am still quite sick."

"Ah, well, maybe when you are completely recovered, then," he said, but his tone had gone from warm and flirtatious to flat. He wasn't used to being refused. "It must be lonely out there on the farm, without your husband or your *friend* Jean Fraysse."

"Nadine is great company; we are fine," I said. "And if you'll excuse me, she is expecting me before sundown. *Bonsoir.*"

"*Bonsoir,*" he said, tipping his hat to me and getting back on his bike. And it was probably my perpetual paranoia, but I swore I heard him call, "Be careful, Madame Tartière," as he biked away.

～

That night at the farm, Nadine and I were upstairs listening to the BBC on our shortwave when Dominic arrived to pick up some of the latest drops of arms and ammunition. As I shut off the radio and put it away, I told him what the Dutchman had said to me on the road.

"Asking *you* to dinner with *him*?" Nadine said, spitting out the words with disgust. "Ha!"

"I know I have been letting my guard down," I said. "I'm going to have Dr. Porcher send a note to Gestapo headquarters saying my cancer is back. And I clearly need to be more cautious; he commented about how 'strong' I look."

"That would be wise, but what bothers me is he seems particularly obsessed with you," he said, lighting a cigarette, leaning against a haystack in what had become known as the geese's room.

"Yes, he is," Nadine said. "I have never liked the way he leers at you."

"And it's no surprise that the Germans and their sympathizers are getting increasingly paranoid and reckless, because they know the invasion is coming."

"The invasion," Nadine groaned. "I'm so tired of hearing of this invasion that never happens."

"The whole country is tired of waiting," Dominic said. "Do you have the rifle hidden somewhere you can get to easily if you need to?"

"I do," I said. "Although I am not sure what good it will do if two dozen Germans storm my home."

"Things are changing all the time now," he said. "It's going to get worse, as the Germans feel the Allies closing in. I'm glad I taught you how to use it."

"I feel *I* know how to use it now," Nadine said, and then, teasing me, added, "Her, not so much."

"Thanks," I said, giving her a smirk.

Dominic had given Nadine and me a few shooting lessons that fall. The weapon felt awkward and unnatural in my arms, and I proved to be a terrible shot. Nadine was a natural from the start; she had some experience because she had grown up in the country.

"The other thing to remember is that when the invasion does come, and it *will*"—he looked at Nadine—"these underground networks for the aviators will be shut down. It will be too dangerous to get any of them out."

"Yes, I've been discussing that with Dr. Porcher and the others," I said with a sigh. "We will just have to figure out a way to keep them all safe if that happens."

We helped Dominic load his truck. He said he would be back in two days, for the next full moon, as he was expecting another drop.

Before I went to bed, I looked out at my beautiful view of the Forest of Fontainebleau, but my solace in the quiet calmness was lessened by the constant unease of knowing that German anti-aircraft gunners were lurking somewhere deep in the trees.

I was so tired I didn't remember falling asleep, but I did remember dreaming of being in a tunnel, a tremendous roaring all around me, and all the animals in the area were barking and squawking. I sat up in bed. It was well past midnight, but by now I recognized the sounds of Allied planes coming back from a night mission.

Wave upon wave of Allied Flying Fortresses passed over our house, their dark shadows visible in the clear star-filled sky. I ran out the front door in my nightgown into a scene of eerie noise and chaos. A foggy mist blanketed the fields, and hundreds of silver coils of aluminum fell to the ground like a weather system from a children's fairy tale, dropped by the American planes to disrupt German radar.

"Americans," Nadine said, breathless as she joined me with Ondie at her heels, and I just nodded.

"Maybe British too."

Suddenly one of the planes was hit by German anti-aircraft fire. It burst into flames and started spiraling toward the ground, bits of flame breaking off from it as it fell somewhere between Barbizon and Melun. Ondie started to cry from the thunderous noise, and I knelt, hugging him tightly to comfort him as much as me, feeling sick with worry about the boys in the sky.

Nadine launched into a string of curse words aimed at the Germans. Then another plane was hit, falling to earth after a massive explosion that made the night sky glow so brightly it lit up the plains.

"God help them all," I whispered.

"Do you think there are any survivors?"

"I don't know," I said, looking at the smoke as the last plane passed over the area, as the sounds of German motorcycles in the distance grew louder. They would be combing the area for the downed airmen. "If they are, I hope they find a good place to hide. We'll see what we can find in the morning."

Chapter Forty-Five

Nadine and I were both up at sunrise a few hours later, having barely slept. I was putting on coffee when I heard someone at the door. It was Remy, breathless from running, his face red.

"Another redhead in the apple tree?" I said, letting him in.

"No—our neighbors found one, though," he said.

"Where? And is he hurt?" I said, encouraged to hear that at least one had survived.

Remy explained that his seven-year-old neighbor had been out cutting grass for her rabbits and found one of the downed fliers hiding in a haystack in the field.

"We did not move him yet, because he is in plain sight of Mayor Voclain's house," Remy said, "You know what he'll do if *he* spots him."

"I do," I said. I scribbled a note for the American and put it in a sack with some hard-boiled eggs and hard cheese, along with wine Alfie had given me.

"Give him this," I said. "We will come for him after dark."

Two hours after Remy left, another visitor was at the door. This time it was a middle-aged farmer I recognized from Achères-la-Forêt. He had made the twelve-kilometer trek on his bicycle, and he stood in my doorway drenched in sweat and covered in dirt from working in the fields.

"I was told you could help me," he said, looking at Nadine and me in anguish. "There are two boys in the forest near my house, in terrible condition, burned and covered in blood. One of them begged me to stitch his lip, but I didn't know how. The Boches are searching all over my neighborhood, so I didn't dare move them. Can you come back with me to see them?"

"Yes, let's go now," I said as Nadine handed him some water. "Give me a minute to pack some things."

As I packed some men's shirts and pants, bandages, cotton, my sewing kit, and some food, I told Nadine to hurry to Villa L'Écureuil to call Dr. Porcher, telling him it was an emergency and that he needed to come from Paris to see me right away, and to try to get a message to Dominic in Melun that we might need him and his truck that evening.

"I'll meet you at the villa when I get back," I said to her as I hopped on my bike.

The farmer and I biked the twelve kilometers as fast as we could, passing no fewer than six German patrols on the way, and I held my breath every time, sweating from the journey and the fear that we would be stopped. When we got to the place in the forest, we were met by one of the farmer's neighbors, an elderly man, missing most of his teeth, who motioned us to follow him to his home nearby.

"After my house was searched a second time, a few of us moved them; they are now hiding in my house," the man explained to me in French, shaking his head, before adding, "They are children, *children!*"

When we got inside, the elderly man's tiny, hunched wife took my hand and brought me upstairs to a small, dark back bedroom where the fliers were hiding out. She told me she had done some volunteer nursing in the last war and would boil water to clean their wounds.

I had met several downed Allied fliers over the past few months, but this was the first time I had met two immediately after they had fallen from the sky, and it was hard for me to maintain my composure at the sight of them. They *were* children. They lay with their heads on opposite ends of a narrow twin bed, their Army Air Forces flight suits caked with dried blood, their beat-up leather jackets serving as inadequate blankets. The shorter of the two had dirty-blond hair, some of which had burned off; his eyes were closed, and his left leg was propped on a pillow, burned, and clearly broken. The tall one, whose legs hung off the end of the bed, had thick black hair and a tan complexion. There was a gash on the side of his head, his lip was hanging down in need of stitches, and there was an angry burn on his arm.

"Hello, sweetheart, I'm here to help," I said to him in a quiet voice so as not to wake the other.

He was holding a silver strand of rosary beads and looked at me in surprise as I kissed him and his crew member both on the forehead.

"Did you just speak English?" he whispered, though his lip made it difficult for him to talk.

"My name's Drue; I'm an American living nearby," I said. "And I'll try to stitch that lip if you'll let me."

"Oh yes, please, ma'am," he said, a tear sliding down his dirty cheek. "I'm Captain Danny O'Connor; I'm from Boston. This fella is Second Lieutenant Tommy Frame from Newark. We both have first aid kits that are well stocked."

Danny pointed to their bags on the floor, and I sorted through and found both kits, breathing a little easier when I saw all their supplies.

"Who is this?" Tommy squinted at me.

"Our American angel," Danny said, smiling through tears.

"Not an angel, just an American. I'm Drue," I said, touching Tommy's cheek. "We're going to do what we can to fix you up now, and then my plan is to come back and get you tonight so we can have a real doctor look at you."

"You sound kind of like an angel to me," Tommy said. "Nice to meet ya, Drue."

The kits contained alcohol, morphine, hypodermics, and an oilskin of disinfectant powder to ward off infections in cuts, as well as salves for burns. The old woman and I cleaned their cuts and burns with alcohol, and Danny almost fainted twice when I stitched his lip, but neither of them complained. By the time we were finished it was starting to get dark. We had done the best we could with their injuries, and after discussion, we realized the safest place for them to hide for now was back in the forest.

"They may search the house again," I explained to the boys as the farmer and the elderly couple came upstairs to help move them. "And there's a reward of ten thousand francs for anyone who turns in downed aviators. I will come back for you as soon as I can."

"We understand, ma'am," Tommy said. "Please tell these kind people how grateful we are."

"Yes," Danny said, looking at the three peasants. "We will never be able to repay them."

I translated, and both the old woman and man kissed them on their cheeks, and the farmer shook their hands.

We left them in the forest with quilts, water in their canteens, eggs, and bread. It pained me to say goodbye and leave them that way, and I pedaled back to Barbizon as fast as I could, as it was after curfew, and it was sheer luck that I didn't run into any patrols. I didn't get to the villa until eleven thirty. My legs ached and my head hurt from exhaustion, but there was still work to do.

"We've got to go back out," I said. "To get the boy hiding in the haystack."

"Finish your dinner first," Nadine said as if she were my mother, pointing to the omelet and salad on my plate. "You need your strength for this long night. Dr. Porcher had multiple emergencies, but he will be here tomorrow. I still haven't heard from Dominic yet. I thought we could ask Alfie."

I didn't want to involve anyone else, but it had started to rain, and I couldn't stop thinking about Danny and Tommy in the forest.

"Let's get the boy, and if Dominic doesn't show up, I think we have to ask Alfie," I said, grabbing a trench coat and hat. "If we run into any patrols on the way, just start stumbling and giggling, act drunk."

"Perfect idea," said Nadine.

On the way, we checked the farm to see if there was any sign of Dominic, but he wasn't there. We arrived at the two-bedroom house on the plain where the boy had been found, opening the gate lightly so the bell wouldn't clang. I tapped on the front door, announcing who I was.

A light went on inside, and the woman of the house opened the door in her nightgown.

"We are here for the boy in the haystack," I said.

"I brought him inside," she said. "I couldn't stand him being out there in the rain."

She let us inside, but there was no sign of him, and I looked at her, curious as to where she could hide someone in such a small house.

"We put him in bed with my mama," the woman said with a shrug, leading us to the back room of the house.

A wizened and toothless old woman with a red kerchief was propped up in her feather bed with pillows; she was beaming at us as she pointed to the lump next to her and lifted the covers. There was a young man in an oversize nightshirt, fast asleep. It took a minute to shake him awake.

"Who are you? I don't understand," he said, rubbing his face. He had chestnut hair cut very short and dark-blue eyes and a roman nose.

"I'm Drue; this is Nadine," I said to him.

"I'm First Lieutenant Lorne Murphy; nice to meet you both," he said with a dazzling smile and a Southern accent.

"Come with us," I said. "We're going to bring you somewhere to hide out for a while."

"Do I have time to get dressed?" he asked, looking down at his borrowed nightshirt. The old woman in the bed seemed sad that he was leaving.

"Of course," I said, and he smiled at me and then Nadine, and when the two of them locked eyes, Nadine's cheeks turned bright red, and she giggled a little like she really *was* tipsy.

A few minutes later he came out of the bedroom with his AAF flight suit and leather jacket still covered in hay. I put the overcoat on him and gave him the instructions about acting drunk as I linked arms with him on one side and instructed Nadine to do the same. When she did, Lorne was the one who blushed.

"Where are you from, Lorne?" I asked when we were safely in the back cottage, putting sheets on one of the twin beds. We had already decided Nadine was going to move into my room for the time being.

"From just outside Memphis, Tennessee, ma'am," he said, looking at me and then Nadine, who had not stopped blushing. "And where are you from? Both of you?"

"I'm from Los Angeles," I said.

"Colmar, a few hours east," Nadine said.

"Where'd you learn how to speak English so well?" he asked her.

"Drue has been teaching me," she said with a smile, nodding at me.

We got him settled in and said our goodnights. Before we even shut out the light he was passed out on the bed, fast asleep again.

"I'm going to ask Alfie first thing tomorrow if he'll take me back for those other boys," I said.

"I think he's more a Mr. Darcy than a Rhett Butler," Nadine said. She was gazing back at the cottage, a dreamy look in her eyes that was very uncharacteristic of her. "What do you think?"

"Nadine Cadieux! I think that we both need to go to bed before you say one more word," I said, laughing, as I put my arm over her shoulder.

~

"You know I would love to do it, but I cannot," Alfie said to me. The sun was already warm, so we were sitting in the shade at one of the tables on the bar's terrace. "The Germans only allow me to keep my truck because they want to make sure I keep my bar well stocked with alcohol."

"Alfie, I wouldn't ask if I weren't desperate," I said. "If I do it with a cart and horse, it will take me and Nadine eight hours and put us at much more risk."

A half dozen little boys ran by us laughing, a few of them carrying the radar-disrupting silver coils the Americans were dropping regularly now.

"Just yesterday I was stopped three times by patrols," he said, though I could tell he was torn. "They inspected the inside of the truck and looked under the tarp in the back. I just don't think I can take the chance, mostly because Giselle would kill me if I ended up in prison."

"Ah, good morning, Madame Tartière and Monsieur Grand," Mayor Voclain called out to us, and came over to the terrace with a woman on his arm.

"Such a vile man," I whispered, and quietly groaned.

Alfie kicked me under the table. "Be nice, because he could put you back in prison," he said through his teeth as he grimaced and waved.

"*Bonjour* on this beautiful morning," Alfie said when the couple reached the table. "Madame Voclain, I don't believe you have met Drue Tartière."

"Pleasure to meet you," Madame Voclain said. She had dark, curly hair streaked with gray that was pulled back in a severe bun and a nervous energy about her.

"And you as well," I said, forcing myself to be friendly.

"You are looking *very* well, Madame Tartière," the mayor said. "I saw you out biking yesterday. Your health seems to be much better?"

"It is, though I still have cancer, and I continue my treatments in Paris," I said.

"I'm so very sorry you've been unwell," Madame Voclain said, holding her hand to her chest, true compassion in her eyes. It appeared she knew nothing about who I was. "I wish you a full recovery."

"Thank you," I said.

"We are heading to breakfast with Herr Fieger and some of his comrades in town from Paris," the mayor said.

"Please tell him hello from me," I said, wondering if he picked up on the sarcasm as I gave him a wide smile.

"I will do that," Voclain said with a nod, tipping his hat. "Be careful with all that biking. You don't want to overdo it, given your health."

Alfie and I watched them walk away, and I cursed him under my breath.

"That idiot is still keeping an eye on you," Alfie said when they were out of earshot.

"That's no surprise," I said, lighting up a cigarette. "I would expect no less at this point."

"And you still do these things, take these chances with helping the aviators?"

"I have to," I said. "It has helped so much with my grief I can't begin to explain it to you. It's like each life I help save helps me recover a little more from the loss."

Alfie put his hands together and leaned on the table, looking me in the eyes.

"Well, my dear, how can I not help you when you put it that way?"

"Oh, thank you," I said, jumping up and giving him a hug. "You have no idea what this means to me."

"Let's go at noon, when the traffic is light. Giselle will forgive me if I explain my reasons. And if we get it, at least we get it together!"

"We get it together," I said with a laugh. "See you soon."

A few hours later, Alfie pulled into the alleyway in his yellow Renault and helped me load my trunk in the back of the truck, where we would have to hide Danny, as the cuts and burns on his face would give him away immediately. Coming upon a German convoy en route, we braced ourselves, but they waved us by without hesitation. We arrived at the home of the farmer at quarter to one, and he jumped into the back with me as we drove as close to the location of the boys in the forest as we could.

"The one with the broken leg needs a doctor right away. He has a high fever, his leg is swollen, and I think there's an infection," the farmer said as we walked into the forest where they were hiding. The old man was there, waiting with Danny and Tommy like a doting grandfather, having refilled the boys' water and put together a care package of apples and brown bread.

"You two ready?" I said. "I am so sorry, you're going to have to hide in the trunk, Danny. The ride's not too long though."

"That's fine, as long as we get this fella to a doctor very soon," he said, pointing at poor Tommy, who was drenched in sweat, his face contorted in misery.

I placed their uniforms in the trunk first, and then we helped Danny climb into it as the farmer gently lifted Tommy into the front seat.

"Sit tight. We're going to get you some help, darling," I said, tucking the trench coat around him so his bandages couldn't be seen.

I sat in the back on top of the trunk, grateful I was just wearing a blouse and shorts, as the summer sun was beating down on us.

As we pulled out of the forest and waved goodbye, the old man started to cry, and both he and the farmer blew kisses after us.

At a crossroads on the way back, there was a German patrol randomly checking cars that passed through. I could see Alfie in the front drenched in sweat, and I said a prayer that our luck would hold.

A German soldier stood in front of our vehicle, holding up his hand for us to stop, and my stomach lurched as Alfie slowed down and showed him his papers. The soldier just glanced at Tommy before coming around the back and pointing at the trunk.

"*Was ist?*" he said, frowning at me.

"Oh hello, we are moving to a new villa," I said in French, beaming at him. I got off the trunk and reached for the lid, holding my sweaty hand on the latch tightly to keep it from shaking. "Would you like to see the contents?"

"*Nein, alles gut,*" he said, grinning, admiring my legs, as he signaled to Alfie to pass through. I sat back down, trembling uncontrollably. When we got to the villa, Alfie pulled into the alleyway and once again maneuvered the truck so that it backed into the courtyard. Nadine and Dr. Porcher greeted us there, and I told Nadine to be our lookout as we got the boys inside the back cottage as quickly as we possibly could.

Alfie nearly hit the stone wall, he pulled out of the alleyway so fast, and as soon as he left, I took a deep breath and exhaled.

As Nadine went to prepare dinner, in the cottage there was an emotional reunion of the three young men; Lorne was part of the same Flying Fortress squadron.

"It's so good to see you guys," Lorne said, hugging them both. "You look like hell, but I'm so happy you're alive."

"Barely," Tommy gasped.

"How'd you end up without a scratch, pretty boy?" Danny asked him.

Dr. Porcher redressed Tommy's leg and gave him penicillin for the infection; then he put medication on his burns so they would heal on their own. He treated the cuts and burns on Danny as well and restitched his lip so perfectly he promised it would only show a tiny scar after it healed.

"Your leg is broken, but an X-ray is impossible," Dr. Porcher said as he finished up. "The best we can do right now is heal it, but it may need to be broken and reset after liberation."

"Don't worry, doc, that's going to be happening soon," Lorne said with a smile as brilliant as Cary Grant's. No wonder Nadine was starry-eyed. "The English Channel is filled with barges as far as the eye can see. And all leave has been canceled."

"We have been waiting so long, we have almost given up," Nadine said to him, returning with a pitcher of water, and I just nodded in agreement. The waiting had made us both skeptical of any good news regarding the invasion.

"Oh no, I promise you both," Lorne said. "If you saw what I did, you'd believe me. Help is finally on the way for France."

Chapter Forty-Six

June 5, 1944

"*Courage, madame, cela ne devrait plus être très long.*"

"Courage, madame. It won't be long now."

I found the note scrawled on an issue of *Le Courier de l'Air*, the newspaper the Allies dropped—the red-white-and-blue paper had become an invaluable comfort to all of us, and I grinned at the note of encouragement just for me. One of my neighbors had left a copy in my mailbox, and I planned to read it to our houseguests later.

The Allied bombings of German installations continued to intensify all around us. Every railroad junction in the area was hit—in Orléans, Chartres, Villeneuve-Saint-Georges, among others. And though it made life and travel more difficult and more dangerous, we were encouraged by these actions, and I started to believe these were for the arrival of the Allied troops by land, as Lorne had promised. This coincided with the Maquis, the rural bands of guerrilla fighters in the French Resistance, gaining strength thanks to the Allies supplying guns, ammunition, and agents.

Of course, with these developments, the Germans became increasingly paranoid and sadistic. In one of their many horrific acts against humanity, the Nazis burned down the village of Oradour-sur-Glane and massacred the villagers, in retaliation for Maquis activities in the area.

Everything happening was a grim reminder that while the end might be approaching, life was still volatile and extremely dangerous, particularly if you were involved in the ways that Nadine and I were. I had to be more cautious than ever, exhausting as it was at times.

In the weeks after their arrival, Nadine, "our boys," and I settled into a clandestine routine. It had been a pleasure getting to know them. Tommy was the youngest, a fun-loving jokester who played a mean game of bridge thanks to his grandmother. Danny was the leader of the three, more serious and thoughtful, listening to the BBC on short-wave with notebook in hand. Handsome, rakish Lorne was a flirt and a charmer, but very helpful with the chores, particularly when they were Nadine's, and I was trying not to be concerned about the obvious spark between the two of them.

Finding food—for both those hidden in Paris and now the three young men with big appetites in my own home—continued to be a daily challenge. Nadine or I would have to go to one of the neighboring farms for mutton, lamb, and milk every couple of days. We also had to tend to our own gardens in the courtyard and on the farm as well as keep up with the care of our animals. And laundry was a never-ending task. The boys helped however they could, weeding the courtyard garden at night, preparing vegetables, doing dishes after meals, and keeping the back cottage picked up and tidy.

This day, like most mornings, they had slept late, something I encouraged because the quieter they were during the day the better. At ten, Lorne stumbled into the kitchen first, for a breakfast of barley coffee and milk and whole wheat muffins made with goose grease.

Nadine was at the stove pouring them coffees, and Lorne snuck up behind her and she started laughing, their hands touching when she handed him a cup.

"Good morning, fellow squirrels," Tommy said. He had dubbed us this after learning the translation of Villa L'Écureuil. He came through the door in the courtyard, holding himself up on my cane, looking at the two straw baskets filled with eggs, milk, and garden vegetables.

"You going into the city today?" he asked, as Danny, his lip and face looking much improved, came in the door behind him.

"I am," I said. "Nadine's going out to the farm. I'm going to deliver these to homes where some of your Allied buddies are hiding out."

"How many?" Danny asked. Nadine and Lorne were making eyes at each other across the kitchen table.

"Right now? It's hard to say," I said. "At least a couple dozen that I know of."

"And how many have gotten out?" Tommy asked, looking at the goose muffin with skepticism.

"I've helped find shelter, food, and clothing for well over a hundred," I said. "And I've helped about forty escape."

Lorne whistled, and the three of them looked at me in surprise. "You've helped that many get out?"

"Out of Paris, yes," I said, feeling my cheeks grow warm. I was proud of the work, and I had been keeping track on a notepad; no details, just a check mark each time another one left with Genevieve.

"Do you think we'll get a chance to leave with Genevieve?" Tommy asked, and the hopeful look in his eyes made my heart ache because I knew the answer.

"No," Danny said. "I think nobody's getting out until after the Allied invasion. That's my guess."

Lorne and Tommy looked at me for confirmation, and I nodded.

"I think that is probably true, yes," I said. "You might be stuck with us for a while. And we can't get lazy about our safety."

"I don't mind staying for a while," Lorne said, sipping his coffee and looking at Nadine, who was back at the stove. She didn't say a word, but her face was crimson. Danny looked at me and rolled his eyes. I was going to have to address the flirtation at some point soon.

"Marion will be here later to play bridge, and she has some more books for you boys," I said. We had decided to let Marion in on the secret, and she was thrilled to be a part of it. "I'm not sure what the train situation is like, so I might be a little late. Please, just follow the plan if you hear a knock at the front door."

The five of us had done practice drills in case the Gestapo or the mayor or anyone showed up to search the house, and within seconds the boys could get the cottage cleared out like nobody but Nadine lived there. They could hide in the woodshed in the garage; or, if it was after dark, there was a ladder at the back wall of the courtyard, and they could get over it and run for the woods.

"You got it, Mama," Tommy said, winking at me.

We said our goodbyes, and Nadine walked with me to the bus, carrying one of my baskets.

"I wish you didn't have to go," she said. "It might take you hours with the railways being what they are. Not to mention the possibility of being accidently blown up."

"Thanks for that reminder," I said sarcastically, elbowing her. "I wish I didn't too. We have so much work here. But Elise said that she is entirely out of food, and she has two at her house. Claude is in the same situation. And I could use some more clothes for the boys."

"Which means more laundry. Lorne will just have to help me more often."

"I noticed he's your favorite," I said in a quiet voice, as there were German soldiers in the vicinity.

"Oh, not really," she said, waving her hand like my comment was nonsense, but her smile gave her away.

"Uh-huh," I said, giving her a doubtful look.

"Maybe a little."

"You are a grown woman, but . . . just be careful there?" I said. "He's a flirt and a charmer. One who will be leaving."

"Drue Tartière, you should know me well enough to know I can handle myself with a charmer," she said, still smiling, as the bus pulled up to take me to the station.

~

I arrived in Paris with over fifty pounds of food and came home on the late-afternoon train with more shirts and pants for the boys, as well as a pair of men's alligator-skin shoes, all from Tudor Wilkinson's vast wardrobe. The train slowed to a near stop as we passed through the Villeneuve-Saint-Georges train station, which had been obliterated by the Allies, debris strewn everywhere and locomotives demolished into twisted piles of metal. Despite the Germans on the train, many of the French passengers looked out at the destruction and didn't hide their delight at these attacks by the Allies.

I got off the bus in Barbizon after eight, anxious to get back to the villa before curfew, especially with the men's clothing in my baskets. The streets were quiet, and these days only Germans and collaborators went to Alfie's bar after dark, which kept him in business but incensed him at the same time.

I had almost reached my door when I heard someone clear their throat behind me, and I turned to see Daan Koster, smoking a cigarette, as he lifted his hand in a wave. Just the sight of him gave me a chill, even in the humid night air.

"Good evening, Drue," he said. "May I help you with your bags?"

"Oh, no, I am almost at the door, that's not necessary," I said, forcing a smile.

"How about dropping them off to come have a drink with me at Alfie's?" he asked, and again that appraising look in his eyes made my skin crawl.

"Oh, thank you for the invitation, but I am quite tired," I said. "I had a doctor's appointment in town and dropped off some food to a sick friend while I was there. I also picked up some clothes for Nadine and myself from my friend Kathleen. It has been a long day."

I was saying too much, and I knew it. I was coming across as guilty of something.

"Ah, well," he said. "One of these times you will say yes."

He said it like an order.

"Yes," I said, nodding, relieved I had reached the alleyway to the courtyard gate. "Now, if you'll excuse me, have a good night."

I turned and walked down to the side entrance and tried not to hurry.

"The *Charlie Chan* films," he called out, and I whipped around, glad that it was just dark enough he couldn't see my shocked expression.

"I'm sorry, what?"

"I remembered, you're the blonde in the *Charlie Chan* films. Though as Drue Leyton, not Tartière."

"Oh no, I was never in any big films like that," I said, using my standard excuse, attempting to laugh. "I *wish* I was, but I told you, I was never that successful."

"I have a good memory for faces," he said. "And you share the same first name. Now, the question is . . . why would you deny it?"

"I told you, a lot of us blondes look the same. I'm flattered, but that wasn't me. Goodnight."

I turned, and this time I couldn't help myself: I hurried to the gate and rattled it open, slamming it behind me.

Ondie came running up to me barking, and Nadine came out behind him, carrying glasses.

"You were gone so long I worried . . . What's the matter? You're shaking."

I told her about my exchange with Koster.

"He's a collaborator," I said. "He could look up Drue Leyton, find out that the Germans had a death warrant out for me."

"It will never happen," Nadine said, as if saying it out loud would make it true. "The Gestapo in Paris didn't even know it."

"I swear, if this war ever ends, I am not sure if I'll ever stop looking over my shoulder for the rest of my life," I said.

"Let's find out if it will—we're in the cottage listening to the BBC on shortwave," she said. "Dominic is here."

"He is?" I said, thinking it was foolishly risky of him. "How did he get in? Was he seen?"

"You know him; he came over the back wall, with a sack of champagne no less. He would never let himself be seen."

I received a warm greeting when we walked through the door. All the curtains were closed, and we huddled around the shortwave on the coffee table as Nadine poured champagne.

"Sorry for the unexpected visit," Dominic said. "I needed to hear this broadcast, and you were the closest house."

Part of the BBC nightly broadcasts from London included coded messages for the French Resistance.

"And he brought the bubbly," Tommy said, examining his glass, "which has always seemed kind of fancy, but I'm beginning to like it."

"How are you going to get out? There are patrols with submachine guns," I asked him.

"I'll be fine," Dominic said. "I've faced worse than those."

Lorne and Nadine were sitting knee to knee on the settee, and Danny was fiddling with the shortwave to get the clearest broadcast.

"Is anyone going to tell her?" Danny asked, looking around at all of them with a grim expression.

"Tell me what?" I asked.

"We had a close call today," Danny said, and I gratefully took a glass of champagne from Nadine and braced myself. "That mayor and some Gestapo came to the front to search the house."

I swore under my breath.

"But it worked out fine," Danny continued. "We hid in the wood-shed in the garage as planned. We stayed there for almost two hours, though, in case they circled back around, because it's possible they saw . . . well, they didn't come back."

"Saw what?" I said.

"It was my fault," Nadine said, biting her lip.

"What was?" I said, not sure my frayed nerves could take much more.

"I was mending Lorne's flight suit," she said. "The . . . the mayor might have seen it. He went up to our room. I . . . I had shoved it under my bed, but part of it was visible. I didn't realize."

"Oh, good God, Nadine, do you think he saw it or not?" I said, putting my hand over my mouth.

"Well, they didn't come back, and he didn't say anything, so I don't think he did," she said, getting defensive.

"You know better! That was careless; I can't believe you did that," I said, knowing exactly why she'd slipped. Because her head was in the clouds over the owner of the flight suit.

"Hey, it's OK," Lorne said, holding up his hand. "No harm done; they didn't come back."

"Not *yet*," I said. "We should have Marion hide the uniforms, that way—"

Aggravated, tired, and on edge, I was about to get into an argument about it when Dominic shushed us as the BBC French-language broad-cast started, interspersed with coded messages to the French Resistance, his face stoic as he listened to the nonsensical phrases until he heard the very last one.

"*Blessent mon coeur d'une langueur monotone*," the announcer said—in a calm voice, but the shock on Dominic's face was obvious.

"What did it say?" Danny asked.

"Wound my heart with monotonous languor," Nadine said, and we all looked around, afraid to say what we all prayed it might mean.

"I have to go," Dominic said, shooting out of his chair like someone had just set it on fire. "I need to get back to Paris tonight."

He walked out the door, leaving us all stunned, and I followed him to the courtyard wall.

"It's happening, isn't it?" I whispered. "It's finally here?"

"Maybe," he said. "Maybe not."

"Be safe," I said.

"You too. Now more than ever. If things happen the way I think they will, consider moving to the farm," he whispered. "It might be safer for all of you."

"But how will I move them?"

"Knowing you? I have faith that you'll find a way," he said as he slipped over the back wall into the forest.

～

The next morning, Nadine woke me up at six thirty, shaking me so hard I thought something terrible must have happened.

"It is here! It is here! The invasion!" she said, falling into my arms, laughing and whooping. "Alfie came running outside to tell me he heard it on his shortwave. They landed this morning!"

We hurried downstairs to tell the boys, getting out our own radio to listen to the BBC, not daring to start cheering yet. The radio broadcast warned about areas to avoid and instructions for the French forces.

I went to the bakery midmorning; you could feel the tension in the air as we all held our collective breath, and villagers I barely knew came up and shook my hand.

"The Americans are magnificent," an old woman said to me, tears streaming down her face. "They are here! They are *here!*"

The five of us barely left the radio all day, and by nightfall we could hear the movement of German men and vehicles as they brought up their reinforcements.

"I am jumping out of my skin," Lorne said, pacing back and forth in the cottage.

"Man, I wish we could join them," Tommy said. "Stupid bum leg."

"We have to be patient," Danny said. "We have no other option right now."

"We could make a run for it," Lorne said, and Nadine looked up at him, agonized, and he touched her cheek, not even caring that we were all in the room.

"And leave me?" Tommy said, alarmed at the thought.

"We are *not* making a run for it," Danny said, shutting down the conversation.

Beginning that night, the German patrols started making regular rounds every two hours, people were ordered to keep off the roads after sundown, and it was announced that anybody on the streets after ten thirty would be shot.

As I suspected, the underground network stopped running after the invasion. And so, all fliers in hiding, including ours, would have to remain so until the Allies liberated France. At least we had adequate food supplies on hand. I was more concerned with all the fliers still hidden away in Paris, because things continued to deteriorate there. The city's electricity had been cut, and gas was only supplied for an hour a day. With the constant threat of bombings and air-raid drills and low-flying planes overhead, every trip to Paris delivering food had grown more arduous and would consume my entire day. But every time I came home from these journeys with my back and legs aching, I would think of the suffering Parisian hosts and the fliers, sitting in their tiny apartments in the heat and the dark, with barely any food or news from the outside. That was what pushed me to keep up the deliveries no matter what.

Weeks passed, and for all of us who had waited for so long, the Allied advance seemed achingly slow. And the boys had grown restless, wanting to do something in the fight rather than play cards and listen to the radio and wait. Long formations of Allied planes flew over Barbizon, sometimes taking almost a half hour to pass by. Tommy, Danny, and Lorne would run to the windows, and soon I could tell a Flying Fortress from a Lancaster or a Black Widow. They had never walked down the Grand Rue but would watch behind the shutters and felt like they knew many of the villagers by sight based on our descriptions of them. They adored Marion Greenough and were teaching her how to play poker, since they had grown tired of bridge.

After my trip into Paris on Bastille Day, I came home and fell asleep after dinner, only to wake in the middle of the night to find Nadine missing from her bed. Looking out into the courtyard, by the light of the moon, I saw her and Lorne, sitting under the cherry tree, locked in a passionate embrace, while just over the courtyard wall behind them lingered German patrols, walking back and forth in the alleyway in their heavy boots.

An hour later, I heard Nadine tiptoe into the bedroom. I sat up, and she jumped.

"What are you doing? Did you not notice the German soldiers with machine guns a few feet from you? Didn't you hear them?"

"I . . . no, not at first, but then we noticed them and came in . . ."

"Nadine, I will not have any of us killed so close to the Americans arriving," I said. "You can't be so careless. I know you are fond of him, and you're both young and . . . please don't do that again . . ."

"I know," she said, getting ready for bed. "You're right, I'm so sorry."

She lay down in her bed, facing away from me, and I tried to go back to sleep.

"I love him," she whispered, and I sat up in bed again.

"You barely *know* him," I said, my voice more compassionate now. "You've only known him a few weeks."

"I know, but as we say in French, it was *le coup de foudre*, like a thunderbolt; it was love at first sight," she said.

"Have you ever been in love before?" I asked, with an ache in my chest, as it was the way Jacques had described our love, what seemed like a lifetime ago.

A pause and then: "No."

"Then how do you know?"

"*That's* how I know." Her voice choked with emotion. "I've never felt this way before. I didn't know you could feel like this about some-one. The stories that we've read together—*Pride and Prejudice*, *Gone with the Wind*—I understand them so much better now. I love him and he loves me, he's told me so. And we are going to get married after the war."

"Does he know this?"

"Not yet, but he will," she said.

Chapter Forty-Seven

August 3, 1944

Every single time we heard a car coming down the Grand Rue, we rushed to the window, thinking this time it would finally be an American car, and we were always disappointed. The Germans remained in Barbizon, more arriving than ever before, with trucks and vehicles camouflaged in the forest beyond the village. Allied planes flew over constantly, and the troops on the ground were advancing, but not fast enough. We listened to the BBC like the lifeline that it was, and we remained on edge and irritable, partly from the summer heat but mostly from the oppressive anxiety of hiding and waiting.

On a particularly stifling late afternoon in early August, Danny, Lorne, and Tommy were sitting outside at the wrought iron table in the corner of our hidden courtyard, playing cards and smoking cigarettes in the shade. When there was a series of loud knocks on the villa's front door, we all looked at each other and nodded as they scooped up the cards and cigarette butts and ashtray and, walking as lightly as they could, disappeared into the woodshed in the garage. Nadine was out doing errands with Ondie, so I answered the door alone, closing my eyes and taking a deep breath to calm myself before opening it.

"Herr Fieger, Mayor Voclain, good afternoon. How may I help you?" I said, forcing myself to smile.

"Good afternoon, madame," Herr Fieger said.

"Herr Fieger would like to know how many beds are on this property," Mayor Voclain asked, holding a notebook and pencil.

With more Germans arriving, they needed more beds. That was the only reason they would be asking the question. They wanted Villa L'Écureuil for their own.

"It's quite small," I said. "There's one bedroom in the main house and one very small one in the back cottage."

"And how many people live here?" the mayor asked, studying me with his dark eyes.

"Just two of us," I said. "One in each bed."

I didn't mention what I still referred to as Jean's studio, or the fact that there were four actual beds total, and room for five if you added the studio. As soon as I lied, I realized the mayor knew all about the property, and I bit my lip, waiting for him to contradict me, thinking it might be a trap. But instead, he only kept glaring at me.

"Very well," he said, writing in his notebook, and I was stunned that he didn't bring it up. "German officers are arriving and need more bedrooms in the village. You have the farm, yes? You will be required to be out of the house by Sunday."

"OK," I said, trying not to panic. So close to the Allies' arrival, and now *this*? "We will move there in the next couple of days, then."

"Thank you, madame," Fieger said.

Both men tipped their caps to me, and I cursed them under my breath as they walked away.

Nadine returned just as they were leaving, and I told her what happened.

"So we should move them today, obviously," she said.

"Yes, before nightfall."

"Have you thought about how to do this?" Nadine asked, already unloading cabinets of food to bring with us.

"No," I said, my arms crossed as I nearly wore a hole in the floor walking back and forth, thinking. "OK, how's this for an idea?"

I explained what I was thinking, and she started to laugh.

"Um . . . that is pretty crazy," Nadine said, amused.

"I know, but do you have a better one?"

"No."

"I'll bike out to Remy and Girard's family's house and borrow a horse and wagon, some bales of hay, and a couple chicken cages for cover. Tell the boys to pack up and clear out the cottage of any signs of them. And get Marion to be the lookout for when we go. The sooner we leave the better."

Remy and Girard's family were more than happy to lend me the things we needed. My blouse drenched with sweat, I arrived back at the villa with an old speckled gray horse and an even older wood wagon filled with hay, as well as two cages with a couple of my better-behaved chickens.

I had just tied up the horse in the courtyard, and was about to call Nadine to come help me bring the wagon down the alley to the courtyard as well, when Daan Koster came walking by, which I knew by now could not be coincidence; he was keeping a constant eye on me and anyone else deemed suspicious in the village. I took comfort in the fact that if he were a mercenary and knew about the fliers, he would have collected his thousands of francs by now.

"What is this?" he said. "Where are you going, Madame Tartière? Or should I say Leyton?"

"It's Tartière; my husband is Jacques Tartière. Again, monsieur, you flatter me, but I was not much of an actress, and I have *no* idea who you're talking about. My housekeeper and I are moving back to the farm temporarily," I said, short with him, anxious to get on the road but knowing I had to play along. I leaned against the wagon as if I were feeling weak. "The Germans are requisitioning the villa."

"Ah," he said with a nod. "So far I have been spared that trouble."

"Of course you have," I said with heavy sarcasm. He picked up on it, raising his eyebrows and tilting his head at me. I was hot and irritable, and the secrets and lies and suspicion—it was all getting to me.

"You must remember, the Allies are still not here."

"Yes, and I am surprised that *you* are. Isn't your work for the Germans done yet?"

"Oh, I still have a few jobs left to do for them," he said, giving me a wink and a steely look that made the hair on my arms stand up.

"Be careful at the farm; lots of bombing in the countryside," he said, tipping his hat. "Good day, madame."

"Good day, monsieur."

I turned to see that Nadine had been listening to the whole exchange from the front door.

"I shouldn't have been so flip with him; I let my emotions and the heat get the best of me," I said.

"It's understandable."

"Should we be worried about him, do you think?"

"No, I really don't," Nadine said. "He would have done something by now. I think he's just infatuated with you."

"Maybe," I said, but that uneasiness I got every time I saw him hadn't left me.

She helped me drag the wagon down the alleyway, to the side entrance of the courtyard, and inside.

After being cooped up for so long, Tommy and Lorne seemed excited about the prospect of an adventure, even if it meant being squished together, hiding under bales of hay and smelly chicken cages. Danny was more skeptical.

"How long is it to the farm?" he asked as Tommy and Lorne piled in and Nadine helped bury them under the hay, stealing a kiss from Lorne while doing so now that their romance was no longer a secret.

"As long as the horse cooperates, we should be there in a half hour or so," I said.

"You said there are anti-aircraft in the woods near the farm," Danny said. "And I'm sure it's crawling with German vehicles now too."

"I know, so we'll have to be incredibly careful, but we can't stay here," I said, wiping the sweat dripping down the side of my face.

"I just don't feel good about changing our routine that's kept us all safe all this time," Danny said, but he was already climbing under the hay.

"I know, I don't either," I said. "But it's the only option."

"You all OK in there?" I asked when they were properly buried.

"Can you breathe?" Nadine added.

"Barely," coughed Tommy.

"We're fine," Lorne said, his voice muffled. "Let's get this show on the road."

Marion, watching us from the villa, gave us a wave and a thumbs-up that it was safe. Nadine and I dragged the wagon down the alley, hitched it up to the horse, and took our seats, with Ondie between us. Horses and wagons were more common than cars since the war started, so none of the villagers thought much of it as we drove down the Grand Rue, greeting people as we went, until we were out of the village and on the open road.

The two of us were too nervous to speak, and I held on to the reins with white knuckles as we passed by a few people on bicycles and one German truck full of anxious-looking soldiers who paid us no attention. Turning the corner onto the path through the orchard, I finally relaxed, and, though nobody was in sight, we brought the wagon into the barn.

The three young men emerged from the hay and picked it off their clothes as Nadine freed the chickens.

"We'll bring you out some lunch. You should stay here until it's dark; then we can sneak you into the house," I said.

"It's kind of nice having a change of scene," Tommy said, looking around the old barn.

"What would we do without you two?" Lorne added, coming up behind Nadine and wrapping her in a hug.

"Again, I don't like having to change up our routine," Danny said. "But thank you."

"You're welcome. Let's just do our best to stay alive until liberation."

Chapter Forty-Eight

August 11, 1944

The Germans' heavy bombardment and shelling continued in Barbizon and the surrounding area for the next week, nearly blowing out the windows of the house on the farm a few nights later.

"If we get killed now, after all we've been through? I am going to be furious," I said as the five of us retreated to the basement of the farmhouse.

"With all due respect, Mama," Tommy said, "you'll be dead, so it won't matter how angry you are."

This made me laugh, and I loved that he called me *Mama*. We had settled into farm life well, Nadine and I tending to our animals and garden with our local helpers while our fliers stayed inside and pitched in with laundry and cleaning and whatever else they could do. We were sure to keep the curtains drawn during the day and only let the boys take brief breaks outside at night in the shadows of the orchard.

It wasn't the first evening we had ended up in the basement for safety, so this time we brought some provisions—wine, hard cheese, and green olives. Nadine and Lorne were leaning against each other, holding hands, and Tommy and I smoked cigarettes, sitting against the opposite wall as Danny fiddled with the shortwave radio.

"Hey, Drue, did the Krauts really put you in the zoo?" Lorne asked.

"Indeed they did," I said with a wry smile.

"No way," Tommy said, eyes wide, incredulous. "I thought Nadine was pulling our leg when she told us."

"It's true. They arrested all the American women they could find in Paris and nearby villages and put us in the zoo's monkey house. Our friends paid five francs' admission to see us."

The boys were shocked by this revelation, launching into exclamations of disbelief and questions. So I shared some of the stories of my internment, which helped pass the time in the dark, musty basement.

"Hey, it's Bing Crosby," Tommy said when Danny got a faint music station on the shortwave. He reached for my hand. "Come on, Mama, dance with me. Nobody can hear us down here."

"Oh, I don't know," I said, "I can't remember the last time I danced."

"And that's why you have to tonight," Tommy said, pulling me off the floor. "You've got to get back into practice, for after the war."

So Tommy and I and Nadine and Lorne danced to the sounds of Bing Crosby and the Andrews Sisters and Dinah Shore, and I finally got Danny to jitterbug with me when "In the Mood," his favorite Glenn Miller song, came on.

After a couple hours had passed, we decided it was safe to go up. The boys and Nadine, all tired and a little tipsy from the wine, went to bed right away, but I was feeling restless, so I stayed up, putting away dishes and cleaning the kitchen.

"Drue?" Danny said, knocking on the kitchen door.

"Yes? Is everything OK, hon?"

"It is," he said. He was holding his silver rosary beads in his hand and noticed me looking. "Saying the rosary, it helps me get to sleep at night."

"That's nice," I said, giving him a smile.

"I just wanted to tell you: Lorne is a solid young man."

"They barely know each other," I said. "They are so young."

"That's how it happens sometimes, though, right? He is crazy in love with her. You must see that too. I promise you, he'll do right by her."

Something about this statement made my heart swell, and my eyes welled up.

"I do see it, but I'm just very protective of her," I said, wiping my eyes with the back of my hand.

"Oh no, I didn't mean to upset you." He took out a handkerchief and handed it to me.

"You didn't; I don't know what got into me," I said, waving a hand in front of my face, smiling.

"Nadine told us some other things," Danny said in a soft voice, leaning against the doorframe. "About your husband and your . . . friend Jean. I am so sorry for all you've lost."

"Thank you," I said.

"You've been through a lot the past couple of years."

"Oh, sweetheart, haven't we all, though? You parachuted out of a burning plane. You've lost way too many friends," I said.

"That is all true," he said in a quiet voice, looking down at his rosary.

"We should get to bed; it's late."

He nodded and said goodnight, but just before he headed up the stairs he turned back. "Drue?"

"Yes?"

"I would have paid at least twenty francs," he said, beaming at me.

"Goodnight, Danny," I said with a laugh.

∽

I woke up in the middle of the night to a house that was quiet and still, and yet something felt wrong. And then I heard it. The sound of Ondie, instead of sleeping at the end of my bed, barking from somewhere outside, and the geese chattering the way they did when someone was nearby.

"Nadine, do you . . . ," I whispered, only to glance over to see she wasn't in her bed.

Looking out the window from behind the curtains, I saw the silhouettes of Nadine and Lorne in the orchard. Their voices were raised in alarm, talking to someone, and I was gripped with sheer terror for their safety.

Cursing, I ran downstairs and grabbed the rifle and decided to go out the back door of the house so I could approach the orchard from the side. Closing the back door quietly behind me so it wouldn't slam, I tiptoed in my bare feet as fast as I could without making a sound. Ondie's barking was still muffled, coming from inside the barn.

"Monsieur, just take me, you'll get at least ten thousand francs for me," Lorne said, his voice calm and measured. "Let her go. I'm begging you."

Nadine and Lorne were now kneeling in the grass under an apple tree, hands on their heads as a man stood above them, his gun on them. I had to bite my lip to keep from screaming as I raised the rifle and tried to remember what Dominic had taught me.

"Oh no, all of you are coming with me. The commandant and his officers will be quite happy to take their anger out on an American flier and those foolish enough to hide them," Daan Koster said.

"Drop the gun!" I yelled, rage coursing through me.

"You're not even holding it right, Drue Leyton," Koster said, with a sinister sneer. "Here, I'll show you how it's done."

He aimed at me, cocking his pistol, and a bang went off as I pulled the trigger at the exact same time, missing him, and I was knocked off my feet as if someone had whacked me with a baseball bat, my arm burning with an intensity that made me let out a wail.

When I hit the ground, the sound of another gunshot rang out from somewhere in the apple trees, and this one hit the Dutchman in the back of the head, and he crumpled to the ground.

Danny and Tommy burst out of the house, their pistols drawn, and Nadine screamed and came running to me, and I was terrified that the unknown assassin in the trees was going to kill us all.

"Lower your weapons," I heard a distinctly familiar voice say. "I'm not here to kill anyone else tonight."

"Mayor Voclain," Nadine whispered as he emerged from the darkness; then, looking down at me, she said, "Oh my God, Drue, you are bleeding. There's a lot of blood. Come help! Let's get her into the house."

"Who? Don't trust him," I said, my voice hoarse, feeling faint as I tried to sit up. "Don't . . ."

And then the world went black.

~

I woke up on the settee in the farmhouse living room. The sun was just rising, and the smell of real coffee was coming from the kitchen. My head ached, and there was a bandage wrapped around my forearm, which was throbbing with pain.

"What happened?" I said. "Is everyone OK?"

"Everyone is fine," Nadine said with a smile as she stretched her arms. She was still in her nightgown and robe, curled up in the armchair next to the settee, and it was clear she had been sitting there all night.

"Drue, thank God," Lorne said, coming down the stairs. "You had us all a little worried."

"She's awake," Danny said with a smile, coming in from the kitchen to sit across from me. "How are you feeling?"

"Not too bad. Better than I thought," I said. "Thank you to whoever bandaged my arm. How bad is it?"

"You got lucky," Danny said. "The bullet only grazed you, which burns like hell, but it will heal pretty quickly."

I tried to sit up and winced at the pain in both my head and my arm.

"Settle down there, soldier," Danny said. "No need to get up just yet."

"Do I smell real coffee?" I said.

"Yes," Tommy said, bringing me a cup from the kitchen. I closed my eyes and inhaled the smell. We had run out of Red Cross coffee weeks ago.

"Where did you get it?"

"I brought it." Mayor Voclain walked out of the kitchen behind Tommy. "Glad you're feeling well, madame."

I squinted at him. "What happened? I thought you were . . . You saved our lives," I said, trying to make sense of this person I had thought was the enemy.

"Damn right he did," said Lorne, leaning against Nadine's chair, holding her hand.

"I have some things I need to talk to you about," Mayor Voclain said, and, looking around the room, he added, "in private. Are you strong enough to sit out on the front porch?"

"I am," I said.

Danny and Lorne supported me on either side, getting me settled in one of the rattan chairs with a cotton blanket before going back inside.

"We've hidden the body in the barn," Mayor Voclain said. "I think you know of men who can get rid of it."

"I do," I said. I would have to tell Dominic to have his men take care of it.

"You knew we were hiding them?" I said, nodding to the door of the house.

"I did," he said.

"How did you know?"

"I saw the uniform under the bed upstairs."

He had seen it after all. But he hadn't told.

"When did Daan Koster find out about them? Who was he?"

"The Dutchman was a collaborator and a mercenary. He works as a filmmaker, but he's also made a great deal of money tracking down hidden fliers, Resistance members too. And he was quite taken with you, if you hadn't noticed. He was not pleased you refused his invitations."

"I could tell," I said. "And he's been spying on me."

"He has, more than you know," he said. "He knew something was amiss, but you had gained sympathy with the Gestapo in Paris due to your 'illness.' Although you weren't a priority to them, you remained one to him. He figured it out when you moved out here. He witnessed those young lovers sneaking out to the barn at night. And then on another occasion he saw the other two aviators smoking in the orchard. I can't tell you how much it enraged him that you were hiding three Americans right under his nose."

"And he told you he was coming here tonight?" I said.

"Yes. He trusted me, because he's seen me cooperate fully with the Germans in town from the start. And so I followed him here, because, with the Allies so close, I suspected he might not be interested in keeping you alive. I didn't plan on killing him, mind you, but when I saw him pointing at those two young people in the orchard and then shooting at you . . . well, I didn't have a choice." He sighed and pulled out his pack of cigarettes.

I watched him, this man who a few hours ago would have repulsed me if I saw him on the street.

"I'm sorry—I just don't understand. All this time, I thought you were a collaborator."

"Ah, well, not a collaborator, more of a cooperator," he said. "Getting along with the Germans for my own survival, but mostly to keep my loved ones safe."

"Your wife?"

"She is Jewish. She has fake papers, but she is Jewish."

"Oh," I said, thinking of how nervous his wife had seemed when I met her. No wonder.

"However, her mother and sister do not have fake papers," he said. "They have been hiding in our house on the plain for the past three years."

He exhaled, shaking his head, as if he couldn't believe it had been that long.

"What?" I gasped, looking at this man, realizing I didn't know him at all.

"This war, for most, comes down to protecting those you love. Can I keep them safe from harm? That is *all* that has mattered to me. I have had to make choices to save my wife and her family. And I am not proud of the way I have acted some of the time, definitely not. But before you judge me, ask yourself: If you were in my shoes, what would you do?"

"I think I might do the same," I said. "You played the role you had to play."

"As have you," he said, pointing back at the house. "You are a patriot. They'll be calling you a hero, you know."

"Oh, I highly doubt that," I said, waving him off. "And thank you. You saved all of us, and you didn't have to. I'm still in shock, to be honest. And I . . . I don't know how to repay you."

"That's the reason I wanted to talk with you alone. Because I know of a way that you might," he said.

I looked at him, surprised.

And he told me exactly what I would need to do.

Chapter Forty-Nine

August 18, 1944

After the shooting, Mayor Voclain informed me that the Germans had not requisitioned Villa L'Écureuil after all, and, with news that the Americans would arrive in the area within the week, we threw the boys in the wagon under more hay and moved back to the villa. And a few days later, I awoke at five o'clock to the sounds of jackboots and looked out the window in disbelief at the sight of the mighty German army retreating from Barbizon. As the late-summer sun rose, they left in chaotic bedlam, a steady stream of wounded men in carts, automobiles with tires missing, and trucks piled high with looted furniture.

I made the boys get up so they could peek at this incredible scene from behind the upstairs window shutters, and Tommy had to bite his fist to keep from whooping. Nadine and I stood outside the villa, as did most of the people in the village, and we all looked at each other, peeking out of shops and standing in front of our homes with smiles of utter satisfaction. And many women wept with joy as children cheered, waving fists of the silver streamers that had been dropped by the Allies.

"Now, what are you both crying about?" Lorne asked us as we walked into the courtyard after most of them had passed.

"That was the most beautiful thing I've witnessed since the war started," I said, and he put one arm around Nadine, wiping a tear off her cheek.

Every day, we watched as more Germans paraded down the Grand Rue in full retreat. And when word reached us that the Americans were now just six kilometers away, near the Château de Fortoiseau, Nadine fetched the boys' flight suits and leather jackets from Marion Greenough and we both worked to sew any last rips in the suits, pressing the khaki outfits so they looked decent. I also brought over Barbizon's only hairdresser, and she was delighted to cut the hair of our three secret houseguests as they teased and joked with her.

On the morning of August 23, we heard that some Americans would be arriving in the village that day, and the boys shaved and put on their flight suits for the first time since they had arrived under our roof.

"Mama, why are you crying again?" Tommy asked as I admired him in his leather jacket and patted him on the cheek.

"I wasn't sure I would live to see this day," I said, blotting my eyes with the back of my hand. "It feels like a small miracle."

"Not so small," Danny said, beaming at me, the cut on his lip healing well.

"It's all right, sweetheart," Lorne said to Nadine as they held on to each other, knowing everything was about to change. He kissed the top of her head. "No matter what happens, we'll be all right."

At a little after ten there was the sound of a car beeping and children hollering, and, for the first time ever, the five of us walked out the front door together, and I couldn't help but laugh at the stunned expressions of my neighbors. An American Jeep was slowly driving down the Grand Rue, with just about every child in town running alongside it, clapping and cheering. I ran out of the villa and stood in the street, waving them over, and the Jeep pulled up in front of my house.

The American officer in the passenger seat jumped out at the sight of our boys.

"What the hell is going on here?" he said. "Nobody told me there were airmen in the neighborhood."

I briefly explained the story as villagers began hugging and kissing the newly arrived American soldiers and our boys. The soldier introduced himself as Captain Whipple and his tall baby-faced driver as First Lieutenant Close.

The army officers greeted Tommy, Danny, and Lorne like old friends, slapping them on the back, and the boys basked in the attention of the villagers.

"Come back tonight for a party in the courtyard," I announced to the crowd.

Just as we were going to retreat inside with the army officers, Madame Voclain came running down the street toward us, crying hysterically, and I immediately knew the reason why.

"Madame, you have to save my husband, they are going to execute him, in Dammarie-lès-Lys," she said, her eyes wild with grief as she gripped my good arm. "You can save him! These Americans can save him!"

"But he saved your family, was that not enough for them?" I asked, trying to calm her.

"No, no," she said, shaking her head. "They still say he's a guilty Boche collaborator. He was afraid of this. That is why he sent for you; he risked his life to save all of you. Please help him, I beg you."

"Madame, I will do whatever I can," I said. "I promise you."

I told Madame Voclain to go home and that I would go to Dammarie. After she left, I explained the situation to the army officers.

"This vigilante justice is happening everywhere," Whipple said. "We're under strict orders to permit the French to manage their affairs on their own."

"Dammarie is not far; could you please take me? The man saved me, Nadine, and these three American fliers. That surely must count for something. I just need you to be there; I'll do the talking."

"I'll go with her," Danny said. "As someone else who was also there that night."

Whipple and Close exchanged glances.

"OK," Whipple sighed. "Get in the Jeep; we'll take you there."

"We'll be back for the party; can you get ready without me?" I said to Nadine, Lorne, and Tommy.

"Are you kidding?" Tommy said. "I've been waiting my whole life for a party like this."

~

We arrived in Dammarie to a scene that resembled a medieval war tribunal. There were thousands of people in the town's square. In one area they were shaving the heads of Frenchwomen who were accused of having affairs or collaborating with Germans, and people yelled "Dirty whores!" and other horrible curses as they spit on them.

As I walked through the crowd in my green plaid skirt and white blouse flanked by three military officers, the people started jeering at me as well, but when I quickly told a few of them that we were Americans, the mood around us changed entirely, and they started chanting, "*Vive les Américains!*"

There was a long table of six self-appointed judges on a raised stage in the middle of the square. I looked at Danny and the two other officers.

"Stay here for now," I said, and I walked onto the raised stage.

"Where is Mayor Voclain?" I asked, and the judge at the end of the table looked at me, frowning.

"He is in the town prison," the judge said.

"Bring him out; I have a story to tell you about him."

The judge called someone over to go fetch Voclain.

The mayor looked like he had aged ten years overnight, with deep, dark circles under his eyes, his hair greasy, and his clothes covered in grime.

"This man is a collaborator with the Gestapo," the judge said to me. "His abetting led to the deaths of Frenchmen. He is to be executed."

"Do you have evidence of these deaths?"

"A man denounced him for this," the judge said.

"One man? Where is this man?" I asked.

"I don't know . . . ," the judge said with a shrug, waving his arm in the air. "Somewhere in the crowd."

"This man saved Jews," I said.

"There is no proof of this besides his *wife's* testimony," the judge said, looking down his nose at me.

"This man saved my life, the life of my French friend, and those of three American military officers." I looked into the audience and raised my voice, speaking in French, pointing to Voclain.

This made the judge pause, and the other judges were now listening.

"It's true," Danny said, coming up behind me onstage, looking at the judges, and then raising his voice to the crowd. "I'm Captain Daniel O'Connor in the United States Army Air Forces. A Gestapo collaborator tried to kill me and two other American airmen. Monsieur Voclain saved us. We owe him our lives."

I translated what Danny had said to the crowd for those who didn't speak English.

"These two American army officers," I continued, pointing to Whipple and Close down below, "believe this man should be released, as a result of these heroic actions." Not understanding French, Whipple and Close just looked solemn and nodded along.

"Hurrah for Voclain!" someone in the crowd yelled, and more people started clapping and repeating it.

"*Vive les Américains!*" The chant started again.

"I am taking this man with me back to Barbizon," I said, glaring at each of the judges at the table, daring them to question me.

The judges looked at each other and shrugged.

"All right," the one on the end said to me, and I shoved Voclain toward the two army officers.

"Please, go, hurry," I said in a whisper. "We need to get him to the Jeep before the mob changes its mind."

"Thank you, thank you all so much. I thought . . . I was a dead man." Voclain covered his face with his hands and wept as we hightailed it out of the town.

"Now that was something," Whipple said, clapping his hands together. "That whole scene was better than the movies."

Chapter Fifty

"In homage to Madame Tartière and Madame Cadieux, from all of Barbizon."

A little boy in the neighborhood had painted this message of gratitude to Nadine and me on a canvas sign, decorating it with fancy wreaths and American and French flags, and his father had hung it on the courtyard gate of Villa L'Écureuil. It was the first thing I saw as I arrived back for the party, and led to the first of many more happy tears I would shed that evening.

And Tommy was right: it was the party of a lifetime. A delegation of villagers had transformed the courtyard in a matter of hours, with red, white, and blue ribbons tacked up and lanterns hanging everywhere and little glass vases of patriotic floral bouquets on every surface.

As the guests started to arrive, the five of us made an informal receiving line at the side gate to greet them. Tommy, Lorne, and Danny shook hands with everyone as they arrived and received many hugs and kisses, and nearly every guest brought a gift of wine, brandy, or flowers.

People began filling up the courtyard. We had put out all the wineglasses, coffee cups, and water glasses we had, and Alfie and Giselle took over as bartenders behind a table we had set up for them.

A cheer went up when Officers Whipple and Close came back with a Colonel Hudson, a silver-haired gentleman who oversaw civil affairs for the military. The Americans delighted the party guests with gifts of cigarettes, chocolate bars, and soap. All the officers—both our boys and the new arrivals—were visibly moved as some of the elderly men and women in the village became speechless with emotion and kissed their cheeks or hugged them, breaking down in tears.

I stood in a corner, taking it all in, moved beyond words that, after so much loss and sorrow, I could still feel such an overwhelming sense of joy.

"You're the little lady who kept these boys alive." The colonel came up to me and shook my hand.

"Nadine and I, yes. And so many others."

I told him the story of how they had ended up in the villa, and the work I had done with hidden American and British fliers hiding all over Paris as well.

"Yes, I've already met some of the boys who were hidden in the city."

"I hope to celebrate with my friends there someday soon too. I haven't made it back to the city since it was liberated," I said, thinking of Elise and Claude and the Wilkinsons and Sylvia. "Before they leave, do you think I could take the boys on a trip to Paris? Just so they could see it and meet some of my dear friends there?"

"I'm afraid that's not possible, ma'am," he said. "It's still very dangerous there—fighting in the streets, shelling from above. And, well . . . the boys must be sent home as soon as possible."

"Oh no, how soon?" I said, and my stomach dropped.

"They've got to report to headquarters in Fontainebleau the day after tomorrow," he said. "They'll be sent to London, then home from there."

"So soon?" I said, looking over at Nadine sitting on Lorne's lap, blissfully happy as she sang "La Marseillaise" with the crowd, and at Danny and Tommy, arm in arm, toasting with the old man and the farmer from Achères-la-Forêt who had rescued them in the woods.

"I'm afraid so," he said, giving me a sad smile. "You've done good, Mrs. Tartière. You're an American hero."

~

Two days later, I awoke at dawn to the sound of a regiment of black American soldiers singing church hymns as they marched down the Grand Rue.

Sing a song full of faith that the dark past has taught us
sing a song full of the hope that the present has brought us . . .

Listening from my bedroom window, I was struck by the beauty of the singing and found some solace in the words. Saying goodbye to our boys today would be difficult, but it had been hard fought too. And I couldn't be sad when these young men were going home to their families. I would grieve for Jacques and Jean for the rest of my life, but it was becoming easier to remind myself that it was an incredible gift to have loved not one but two remarkably good men in my lifetime. Many were not given half that privilege. And today, it was time to say goodbye to our dear friends and celebrate the fact that the five of us had survived and that France was, finally, free.

We had stayed up late the night before and consumed multiple bottles of champagne and had a dinner cooked and served by Alfie and Giselle under the lanterns in the courtyard. But ultimately, before bed, Nadine and I both broke down in tears. And I didn't think any of us had slept through the night.

As Officers Whipple and Close pulled up in the Jeep to take the boys to Fontainebleau, their first stop on their long journey back to the States, Nadine started sobbing into Lorne's shoulder.

"What is this? I feel like I've arrived at a funeral," Whipple said, as even Danny and Tommy had tears in their eyes.

"Listen," I said, linking arms with the two of them. "This is just goodbye for now. It has been one of the joys of my life to get to know the three of you."

"You saved us, Mama," Tommy said, giving me a hug. "I know my own mother would love to meet you."

"You and Nadine, you are our angels," Danny said, lifting me off my feet as he gave me a hug. "Thank you for saving our lives."

"The thing is, you boys saved mine too. More than you know," I said, waving my hand in front of my face. "I told myself I had shed enough tears."

"Thank you, Drue," Lorne said, and when he hugged me, he spoke into my ear. "Take good care of my girl while I'm gone. I'll be back for her."

"You'd better be," I teased, patting his cheek.

Tommy and Danny climbed into the Jeep with their gear as Lorne and Nadine shared one last passionate kiss goodbye that went on long enough for Whipple to clear his throat.

I put my arms around Nadine as the Jeep pulled away and children in the village started running after it. The three of them turned and leaned out of the back so they could wave and blow kisses to us.

"*Je t'aime*, Nadine! I love you!" Lorne yelled. "I'm going to marry you. Take care of her, Drue. Take care of my future wife!"

"*Je t'aime*, Lorne!" Nadine hollered back. "I love you!"

"Goodbye! *Au revoir, mes Américains!*" I yelled until my voice was hoarse.

And Nadine and I hugged and laughed through our tears, waving goodbye until the Jeep was out of sight.

Author's Note

I first learned of the actress Drue Leyton Tartière's life in France when I was researching my novel *The Secret Stealers*. The story of her imprisonment in the zoo outside Paris and then at the Vittel internment camp with several hundred other Americans was discussed in the nonfiction book *Americans in Paris* by Charles Glass. I came across her story a second time during that research and knew I had to dig deeper. Who was this movie star who left Hollywood behind for love and ended up becoming a key figure in one of the underground networks that helped downed airmen escape France? The more I learned, the more fascinated I became, and I knew I had to tell her story.

Much of this novel is based directly on the facts of Drue Leyton's life in France, from her days working at Paris Mondiale to her experience being arrested and interned by the Germans and to her ultimately becoming part of the clandestine organization to help Allied fliers escape occupied territory. But it is a work of historical fiction, *inspired* by her life, as I had to incorporate many fictional characters and events to shape the overall narrative. In some instances, I had to slightly alter dates, such as when referring to the dates she performed on Broadway and in London's West End, as well as the date of her performance in Molière's play at the Comédie-Française. Of course, I tried to adhere to the facts of her life as closely as I possibly could, but this is just one writer's interpretation of who Drue Leyton Tartière was as a person, and an imagined account of her life and experiences in France during the war.

I obtained Drue's slim, out-of-print autobiography, *The House Near Paris: An American Woman's Story of Traffic in Patriots*, written with MR Werner, through a British seller on eBay. It was an invaluable road map of her life in wartime France and a glimpse at Drue's voice and personality, as were her letters home to her and Jacques's family in America, which I obtained through the US Holocaust Memorial Museum. Some of the conversations and letters in the novel are based directly on actual dialogue and conversations relayed in both her autobiography and her correspondence.

The transcripts of Drue's Paris Mondiale broadcasts to America no longer exist, according to more than one obscure reference I found on the history of transcontinental radio during the war. So this part of Drue's life in France, as essentially the first Voice of America in Europe, is a bit of a black box, and I had to take some fictional leaps as a result. I knew there had to be a reason the Nazis had issued a death warrant for her as a result of her radio broadcasts. So my personal theory that drove the novel's narrative is that, as the war went on, Drue got increasingly bolder in her on-air criticism of Germany and the Nazis. It is quite possible she followed the lead of international journalists like the iconic Dorothy Thompson, who appeared on Drue's program at least once and was sounding the alarm on the Nazis from the early 1930s. The interview and conversations between Dorothy and Drue are very much based on Thompson's own writings and speeches as she tried to convince America that involvement in the war was both critical and inevitable. *American Cassandra: The Life of Dorothy Thompson*, by Peter Kurth, was a particularly helpful resource in this regard. The excerpt from her radio broadcast regarding the heartbreaking scene of French troops leaving a Paris railway station is taken from Thompson's nationally syndicated On the Record column from May 1940, titled "On a Paris Railway Station."

Drue also interviewed the iconic entertainer and American expatriate Josephine Baker—though, again, there are no recordings. The interview in the novel is based on several of Baker's media interviews and actual words about life as an African American who fled the United States for freedom and acceptance, and adulation, in France.

The details about Drue's husband Jacques Tartière—their love, his war experiences—are all based in fact, though the exact dates of their marriage and time living in Paris are slightly altered. In real life, Drue saw Jacques more than once while he was stationed in Brittany, so the visit in the story is representative of more than one reunion.

In some instances, I created composite characters based on several people who were similar or played a similar role in her life. For instance, Elise, Drue's agent in Europe, is a fictionalized version of her agent in Paris, and she also represents many of Drue's friends and neighbors who were trying to survive in Paris during the war and also help the Resistance in ways large and small. Dominic, the Resistance member, is a composite of several members of the Resistance that Drue and Jean were in contact with over the course of the war. Also, Sister Nancy and Mother Chad were composite characters based on the many kind and generous nuns at Vittel.

The real Jean Fraysse was head of Paris Mondiale, as well as Drue's dear friend and possible lover. It is clear in her autobiography that they cared deeply for one another, although in real life he remained married to Germaine, despite living in Barbizon with Drue. I believe they may have fallen in love in Barbizon, though she only hinted at this in her autobiography.

Drue's housekeeper, Nadine, became her closest friend in France. The character of Nadine and her life with Drue are very much based on true stories, including their shared love of *Gone with the Wind*. Of the five fliers that stayed at their villa at the end of the war, the real Nadine talked of having a favorite. It was unclear if it was a romantic connection or not.

Ambassador Bullitt is based on the real ambassador William Bullitt. He was also a friend of Drue's. All scenes with Bullitt are fictional. Bullitt's right-hand man Richard O'Brien is also fictional.

Charles and Fern Bedaux are based on the real couple. Fern was also interned at the zoo outside Paris, but immediately released due to Charles's Nazi connections.

Drue's doctors at Vittel—Levy, von Weber, and Rolland, as well as Dr. Porcher in Paris—are all based directly on Drue's doctors in her real life during that time. Her experiences at the Vittel internment camp are all based on the accounts of Drue and some of the other American and British women who were interned there at the time.

Though not her roommate, Sylvia Beach, the iconic owner of Shakespeare and Company, was interned with Drue at Vittel, and the two became friends. Beach also helped entertain the hidden fliers by visiting them, telling stories, and supplying them with books.

Kathleen and Tudor Wilkinson were real people and dear friends of Drue's. They did hide weapons for the Resistance in their home in

Paris. Kathleen was also interned at Vittel, but Drue does not mention her being there at the same time, so they were not actually roommates.

Frederich Damasky is based on a real German soldier from Yonkers that Drue met at the prison, though the events with my Damasky are entirely fictional.

There was a Dutch film producer in Barbizon who was a highly suspicious collaborator—the real Dutchman was the inspiration for the fictional Daan Koster.

Some of the people Drue introduces in her autobiography are so interesting that I included them, but I had to use my imagination to fill in the details of who they were. This includes her coworker Claude Molet and Alfie and Giselle Grand in Barbizon.

Marion Greenough is based directly on Drue's American neighbor in Barbizon, who was arrested by the Germans on the same day as Drue—but was ultimately released due to her age.

Mayor Voclain is fictional, but inspired by many of the French people who had to make impossible choices during the war, for their survival and the survival of their loved ones. The scene where Drue prevents him from being executed is based directly on a true story in which Drue and some American military officers helped save a neighbor from a similar fate at the very end of the war.

In the novel, the harrowing stories of the Allied aviators landing, hiding, and escaping enemy territory are based on several true stories. The three American pilots at the villa at the end of the novel are composites of the many American fliers Drue helped rescue and escape. In real life, there were three British and two Canadian pilots that she and Nadine were hiding in the villa at the end of the war. The details of the party at the end of the novel are based on the party they had when the American military arrived in Barbizon and the fliers could finally come out of hiding.

By the end of the war, Drue Leyton Tartière had overseen the escape of at least forty-two American, British, and Canadian aviators, and assisted in helping over one hundred other Allied fliers escape France via the French Resistance's underground network.

These are minor details, but I would be remiss if I didn't mention that the dates of the full moon in December 1942 and May 1944 are slightly altered to fit the narrative.

Finally, Nadine and Drue really did have a beloved black poodle named Ondie.

To learn more about the history behind this novel, including what happened to Drue Leyton Tartière after the war, please visit my website at janehealey.com and subscribe to my mailing list.

Acknowledgments

The fact that I am writing acknowledgments for my fourth novel feels very surreal to me. I wish I could go back in time and tell my unpublished self to keep going, despite the rejections and the detours, because someday her literary dreams are going to come true in ways she can't begin to imagine. Though writing this novel was, as always, a very solitary experience, publishing and getting it out into the world takes the effort of so many people. I may be a bit biased, but I think I work with some of the most talented professionals in the book business.

To my managing editor, Alicia Clancy—how incredibly lucky I was to work on another book with you. Thank you so much for everything—from your amazing editorial instincts to your seamless management of the entire process from beginning to end—here's to many more projects! You're the absolute best at what you do.

To my developmental editor, Faith Black Ross—what an absolute gift it has been to work with you on all four books. I can't even begin to thank you for your brilliant and meticulous notes and for always pushing me to write the best possible book I can. I am so grateful to have you in my corner.

To my French editor, Christine Gemenne—thank you for your thorough and thoughtful edits regarding language and culture.

I am so thankful to the entire team at Lake Union Publishing, particularly editorial director Danielle Marshall, who plucked *The Saturday*

Evening Girls Club manuscript from obscurity years ago—so thankful you're still at the helm! Thank you to the fabulous Gabriella Dumpit and the entire marketing and sales staff, and the amazing team of copy-editors and proofreaders who always make the book better in every way.

To Drue Leyton Tartière's grandchildren—David Kimball Anderson and Tracy Connolly—thank you for supporting my writing of this fictionalized tale inspired by your grandmother's life. Discovering her story was a gift, and I'm so grateful.

An enormous thank-you to my agent, Carly Watters, at P.S. Literary—it's a joy to have you on my team, and I'm looking forward to many more literary adventures with you!

Thank you to the wonderful Ann-Marie Nieves of Get Red PR—you are the best there is in the book-publicity business, and I'm so very grateful for your hard work and your friendship.

To Dick Haley of Haley Booksellers—thank you for traveling all over New England with me to sell my books, and more importantly for your friendship.

To the author community—I am constantly blown away by the generosity and kindness of my fellow fiction authors. I'm so grateful to write for a living, but the publishing industry can be very difficult to navigate at times, and it means so much to be able to look to so many of you for support and advice. It would take a couple pages to name all of you—please know how thankful I am and how much I hope to see more of you in person this year!

To the fantastic book influencers Andrea Peskind Katz of Great Thoughts' Great Readers and Suzy Weinstein Leopold of Suzy Approved Book Reviews—you've both been so amazingly supportive of me since book one. I am so grateful to have your continued support and friendship.

To all of my readers, many of whom have become friends—I would not be able to do any of this without your incredible support over the past seven years. A million thanks for reading my stories, for telling your friends and book clubs about my books, for writing reviews and sharing on social media, and for showing up to my events.

Female friendship is a theme in my stories, and I'm often asked if the friendships in my novels are inspired by my own. As we celebrate a milestone birthday this year, I'm incredibly grateful for this group of lifelong friends—Paula Albertazzi, Erika Cohen-Derr, Catie Corbin, Heather DiFruscio, Kathy Doody, Julie Driscoll, and Beth Mittelman—love all of you A-town girls (you will always be "girls" to me)!

To my parents, Tom and Beth Healey, quite simply the best parents in the world. Thank you for the carpooling and the dog-sitting and for everything else—love you!

To my daughters, Ellie and Madeleine—being your mom is my most favorite job of all, and I love you more than words.

To Charlie, who long ago believed that I could write novels before I believed it myself. Thank you for being my best friend and, at times, my marketing department, therapist, French translator, and tech support. You are the love of my life, and that's why this book is dedicated to you.

About the Author

Photo © 2018 Sharona Jacobs

Jane Healey is the author of *The Secret Stealers* and *The Beantown Girls*, a *Washington Post* and Amazon Charts bestseller. A graduate of the University of New Hampshire and Northeastern University, Jane shares a home north of Boston with her husband, two daughters, two cats, and a dog. When she's not writing, she enjoys spending time with her family, traveling, running, cooking, and going to the beach. For more information on the author and upcoming events, or to schedule a virtual book club visit, please visit her website at www.janehealey.com.